Alternative
Histories

GARLAND REFERENCE LIBRARY
OF THE HUMANITIES
(Vol. 623)

Alternative Histories

*Eleven stories of the world
as it might have been*

Edited by
CHARLES G. WAUGH
and MARTIN H. GREENBERG

with an afterword by GORDON B. CHAMBERLAIN
and a bibliography by BARTON C. HACKER
and GORDON B. CHAMBERLAIN

GARLAND PUBLISHING, INC.
NEW YORK & LONDON
1986

ACKNOWLEDGMENTS

Cover: © M.C. Escher Heirs c/o Cordon Art, Baarn, Holland.

"Delenda Est" by Poul Anderson: copyright 1955; renewed © 1983 by Poul Anderson. Reprinted by permission of the author and his agents, the Scott Meredith Literary Agency, Inc., 845 Third Avenue, New York, NY 10022.

"The Wheels of If," by L. Sprague de Camp: copyright 1940 by Street & Smith Publications, Inc.; renewed © 1968 by L. Sprague de Camp. Reprinted by permission of the author.

"In the Circle of Nowhere" by Irving E. Cox, Jr.: copyright 1954 for *Universe Science Fiction;* Holding Agent Forrest J Ackerman, 2495 Glendower Ave., Hollywood, CA 90027, has a check for the author, his heirs, or assigns.

"The Lady Margaret" by Keith Roberts: copyright © 1966 by Keith Roberts. Reprinted by permission of the author and the Carnell Literary Agency.

"He Walked Around the Horses" by H. Beam Piper: copyright © 1959 by King-Size Publications, Inc. Reprinted by permission of the agents for the author's estate, the Scott Meredith Literary Agency, Inc., 845 Third Avenue, New York, NY 10022.

"Custer's Last Jump" by Steven Utley and Howard Waldrop: copyright ©1976 by Terry Carr. Reprinted by permission of the authors.

"The Curfew Tolls" by Steven Vincent Benét: from *Selected Works of Stephen Vincent Benét.* Copyright 1935 by Stephen Vincent Benét; renewed ©1963 by Thomas C. Benét, Stephanie B. Mahin and Rachel Benét Lewis. Reprinted by permission of Brandt & Brandt Literary Agents, Inc.

"Hush My Mouth" by Suzette Haden Elgin: copyright © 1986 by Suzette Haden Elgin. An original story. Used with permission.

"Interurban Queen" by R.A. Lafferty: copyright © 1970, 1978 by R.A. Lafferty. Reprinted by permission of the author and the author's agent, Virginia Kidd.

"The Lucky Strike" by Kim Stanley Robinson: copyright © 1984 by Terry Carr. Reprinted by permission of John Schaffner Associates, Inc.

"Afterword: Allohistory in Science Fiction" by Gordon B. Chamberlain: copyright © 1986 by Gordon B. Chamberlain.

"Pasts That Might Have Been, II: A Revised Bibliography of Alternative History" by Barton C. Hacker and Gordon B. Chamberlain: copyright © 1986 by Barton C. Hacker and Gordon B. Chamberlain.

Library of Congress Cataloging-in-Publication Data

Alternative histories.

(Garland reference library of the humanities ; v. 623)
Bibliography: p.
Contents: Hands off/Edward Everett Hale—Delenda Est/Poul Anderson—The wheels of if/L. Sprague de Camp—[etc.]
1. Fantastic fiction, American. 2. History—Fiction. I. Waugh, Charles. II. Greenberg, Martin Harry. III. Series
PS648.F3A47 1986   813'.0876'08   85-45130   ISBN 0-8240-8659-7

Design by Jonathan Billing

Printed on acid-free paper

Manufactured in the United States of America

Contents

Contents

Hands Off

Edward Everett Hale

I was in another stage of existence. I was free from the limits of Time, and in new relations to Space.

Such is the poverty of the English language that I am obliged to use past tenses in my descriptions. We might have a verb which should have many forms indifferent to time, but we have not. The Pyramid Indians have.

It happened to me to watch, in this condition, the motions of several thousand solar systems all together. It is fascinating to see all parts of all with equal distinctness—all the more when one has been bothered as much as I have been, in my day, with eyepieces and object-glasses, with refraction, with prismatic colors and achromatic contrivances. The luxury of having practically no distance, of dispensing with these cumbrous telescopes, and at the same time of having nothing too small for observation, and dispensing with microscopes, fussy if not cumbrous, can hardly be described in a language as physical or material as ours.

At the moment I describe, I had intentionally limited my observation to some twenty or thirty thousand solar systems, selecting those which had been nearest to me when I was in my schooling on Earth. Nothing can be prettier than to see the movement, in perfectly harmonic relations, of planets around their centers, of satellites around planets, of suns, with their planets and satellites, around their centers, and of these in turn around theirs. And to persons who have loved Earth as much as I have, and who, while at school there, have studied other worlds and stars, then

1

distant, as carefully as I have, nothing, as I say, can be more charming than to see at once all this play and interplay; to see comets passing from system to system, warming themselves now at one white sun, and then at a parti-colored double; to see the people on them changing customs and costumes as they change their light, and to hear their quaint discussions as they justify the new and ridicule the old.

It cost me a little effort to adjust myself to the old points of view. But I had a Mentor so loving and so patient, whose range—oh! it is infinitely before mine; and he knew how well I loved Earth, and if need had been, he would have spent and been spent till he had adjusted me to the dear old point of vision. No need of large effort, though! There it was, just as he told me. I was in the old plane of the old ecliptic. And again I saw my dear old Orion, and the Dipper, and the Pleiades, and Corona, and all the rest of them, just as if I had never seen other figures made from just the same stars when I had other points of view.

But what I am to tell you of is but one thing.

This guardian of mine and I—not bothered by time—were watching the little systems as the dear little worlds flew around so regularly and so prettily. Well, it was as in old days I have taken a little water on the end of a needle, and have placed it in the field of my compound microscope. I suppose, as I said, that just then there were several thousand solar systems in my ken at once—only the words "then," "there," and "once," have but a modified meaning when one is in these relations. I had only to choose the "epoch" which I would see. And of one world and another I had vision equally distinct—nay, of the blush on a girl's cheek in the planet Neptune, when she sat alone in her bower, I had as distinct vision as of the rush of a comet which cut through a dozen systems, and loitered to flirt with a dozen suns.

In the experience which I describe, I had my choice of epochs as of places. I think scholars, or men of scholarly tastes, will not wonder when I say that in looking at our dear old Earth, after amusing myself for an instant with the history of northern America for ten or twenty thousand of its years, I turned to that queer little land, that neck between Asia and Africa and that mysterious corner of Syria which is north of it. Holy Land, men call it, and no wonder. And I think, also, that nobody will be surprised that I chose to take that instant of time when a great caravan of traders was crossing the isthmus—they were already well on the Egyptian side—who had with them a handsome young fellow whom they had bought just above, a day or two before, and were carrying down south to the slave market at On, in Egypt.

This handsome youngster was Yussuf Ben Yacoub, or, as we say, Joseph, son of Jacob. He was handsome in the very noblest type of Hebrew beauty. He seemed eighteen or nineteen years old: I am not well enough read to know if he were. The time was early morning. I remember even the freshness of the morning atmosphere, and that exquisite pearliness of the sky. I saw every detail, and my heart was in my mouth as I looked on. It had been a hot night, and the sides of the tents were clewed up. This handsome fellow lay, his wrists tied together by a cord of camel's hair which bound him to the arm of a great Arab, who looked as I remember Keokuk of the Sacs and Foxes. Joseph sat up, on the ground, with his hands so close to the other that the cord did not move with his motion. Then with a queer trick, which I did not follow, and a wrench which must have been agony to him, he twisted and changed the form of the knot in the rope. Then, by a dexterous grip between his front teeth, he loosened the hold of the knot. He bit again, again, and again. Hurrah! It is loose, and the boy is free from that snoring hulk by his side. An instant more, and he is out from the tent; he threads his way daintily down the avenue between the tent ropes: he has come to the wady that stretches dry along the west flank of the encampment. Five hundred yards more will take him to the other side of the Cheril-el-bar (the wall of rock which runs down toward the west from the mountains), and he will be free. At this moment two nasty little dogs from the outlying tent of the caravan—what is known among the Arabs as the tent of the warden of the route—sprang after him, snarling and yelling.

The brave boy turned, and, as if he had David's own blood in his veins, and with it the precision of David's eye, he threw a heavy stone back on the headmost cur so skillfully that it struck his spine, and silenced him forever, as a bullet might have done. The other cur, frightened, stood still and barked worse than ever.

I could not bear it. I had only to crush that yelping cur, and the boy Joseph would be free, and in eight-and-forty hours would be in his father's arms. His brothers would be saved from remorse, and the world—

And the world—?

I stretched out my finger unseen over the dog, when my Guardian, who watched all this as carefully as I did, said: "No. They are all conscious and all free. They are His children just as we are. You and I must not interfere unless we know what we are doing. Come here, and I can show you."

He turned me quite around into the region which the astronomers call the starless region, and there showed me another series—oh! an immense and utterly unaccountable series of systems, which at the moment seemed just like what we had been watching. "But they are not the same," said my Guardian, hastily. "You will see they are not the same. Indeed, I do not know myself what these are for," he said, "unless—I think sometimes they are for you and me to learn from. He is so kind. And I never asked. I do not know."

All this time he was looking around among the systems for something, and at last he found it. He pointed it out, and I saw a system just like our dear old system, and a world just like our dear old world. The same ear-shaped South America, the same leg-of-mutton-shaped Africa, the same fiddle-shaped Mediterranean Sea, the same boot for Italy and the same football for Sicily. They were all there. "Now," he said, "here you may try experiments. This is quite a fresh one; no one has touched it. Only these here are not His children—these are only creatures, you know. These are not conscious, though they seem so. You will not hurt them whatever you do; nay, they are not free. Try your dead dog here and see what will happen."

Sure enough there was the gray of the beautiful morning; there was the old hulk of an Arab snoring in his tent; there was the handsome boy in the dry valley, or wady; there was the dead dog—all just as it happened— and there was the other dog snarling and yelping. I just brushed him down, as I have often wiped a green louse off a rosebush; all was silent again, and the boy Joseph turned and ran. The old hulk of an Arab never waked. The master of the caravan did not so much as turn in his bed. The boy passed the corner of the Cheril-el-bar carefully, just looked behind to be sure he was not followed, and then, with the speed of an antelope, ran, and ran, and ran. He need not have run. It was two hours before any one moved in the Midianite camp. Then there was a little alarm. The dead dogs were found, and there was a general ejaculation, which showed that the Midianites of those days were as great fatalists as the Arabs of this. But nobody thought of stopping a minute for one slave more or less. The lazy snorer who had let him go was well lashed for his laziness. And the caravan moved on.

And Joseph? After an hour's running, he came to water, and bathed. Now he dared open his bag and eat a bit of black bread. He kept his eyes all around him, he ran no more, but walked, with that firm, assured step of a frontiersman or skillful hunter. That night he slept between two rocks under a terebinth tree, where even a hawk would not have seen him. The next day he treaded the paths along the hillside, as if he had the eyes of a lynx and the feet of a goat. Toward night he approached a camp,

4

evidently of a sheik of distinction. None of the squalidness here of those trading wanderers, the Midianite children of the desert! Everything here showed Eastern luxury even, and a certain permanency. But one could hear lamentation, and on drawing near one could see whence it came. A long procession of women were beating their arms, striking the most mournful chords, and singing—or, if you please, screaming—in strains of the most heartrending agony. Leah, Bilhah, and Zilpah led the train three times around old Jacob's tent. There, as before, the curtains were drawn aside, and I could see the old man crouched upon the ground, and the splendid cloak or shawl, where even great black stains of blood did not hide the gorgeousness of the parti-colored knitting, hung before him on the tent pole as if he could not bear to have it put away.

Joseph sprang lightly into the tent. "My father, I am here!"

Oh, what a scream of delight! What ejaculations! What praise to God! What questions and what answers! The weird procession of women heard the cry, and Leah, Bilhah, and Zilpah came rushing into the greeting. A moment more, and Judah from his tent, and Reuben from his, headed the line of the false brethren. Joseph turned and clasped Judah's hand. I heard him whisper: "Not a word. The old man knows nothing. Nor need he."

The old man sent out and killed a fatted calf. They ate and drank, and were merry; and for once I felt as if I had not lived in vain.

And this feeling lasted—yes, for some years of their life. True, as I said, they were years which passed in no time. I looked on, and enjoyed them with just that luxury with which you linger over the charming last page of a novel, where everything is spring, and sunshine, and honey, and happiness. And there was the comfortable feeling that this was my work. How clever of me to have mashed that dog! And he was an ugly brute, too! Nobody could have loved him. Yes; though all this passed in no time, still I had one good comfortable thrill of self-satisfaction. But then things began to darken, and one began to wonder.

Jacob was growing very old. I could see that, from the way he kept in the tents while the others went about their affairs. And then, summer after summer, I saw the wheat blight, and a sort of blast come over the olives; there seemed to be a kind of murrain among the cattle, and no end of trouble among the sheep and goats. I could see the anxious looks of the twelve brothers, and their talk was gloomy enough, too. Great herds of camels dying down to one or two mangy, good-for-nothing skeletons; shepherds coming back from the lake country driving three or four wretched sheep, and reporting that these were all that were left from three or four thousand! Things began to grow doubtful, even in the home camp. The women were crying, and the brothers at last held a great council of the head shepherds, and camel drivers, and masters of horse, to know what should be done for forage for the beasts, and even for food at home.

I had succeeded so well with the dog that I was tempted to cry out, in my best Chaldee: "Egypt! Why don't you go down to Egypt? There is plenty of corn there." But first I looked at Egypt, and found things were worse there than they were around Jacob's tents. The inundation had failed there for year after year. They had tried some wretched irrigation, but it was like feeding the hordes of Egypt on peppergrass and radishes to rely on these little watered gardens. "But the granaries," I said, "where are the granaries?" Granaries? There were no granaries. That was but a dull set who were in the Egyptian government then. They had had good crops year in and year out, for a great many years, too. But they had run for luck, as I have known other nations to do. Why, I could see where they had fairly burned the corn of one year to make room for the fresher harvest of the next. There had been no Yussuf Ben Yacoub in the ministry to direct the storing of the harvest in those years of plenty. The man they had at the head was a dreamy dilettante, who was engaged in restoring some old carvings of some two-hundred-and-fifty years before.

And, in short, the fellaheen and the people of higher caste in Egypt were all starving to death. That was, as I began to think, a little uncomfortably, what I had brought about when I put my finger on that ugly, howling yellow dog of the sleepy Midianite sentinel.

Well, it is a long story, and not a pleasant one; though, as I have said, as I and my companion watched it, it all went by in no time—I might even say in less than no time. All the glory and comfort of the encampments of Jacob's sons vanished. All became a mere hand-to-hand fight with famine. Instead of a set of cheerful, rich, prosperous chiefs of the pasture country, with thousands of retainers, and no end of camels, horses, cattle, and sheep, here were a few gaunt, half-starved wanderers, living on such game as they could kill on a lucky hunt, or sometimes reduced to locusts, or to the honey from the trees. What grieved me more was to see the good fellows snapped up, one after another, by the beastly garrisons of the Canaanite cities.

Heaven knows where these devils came from, or how they roughed it through the famine. But here they were, in their fortresses, living, as I say, like devils, with the origins of customs so beastly that I will not stain this paper with them. Here they were, and here they got ahead. I remember how disgusted I was when I saw them go down in ships into the Nile country, and clean out, root and branch, the Egyptians who were left after the famine—just as I have seen a swarm of rosebugs settle on a rose garden and clean it out in an hour or two. There was the end of Egypt. Then I watched, with an interest not cheerful now, Dido's colony as she sailed with an immense crew of these Moloch-worshipping Canaanites, and their beastly rites and customs, and planted Carthage. It was interesting to see poor Aeneas dodging about on the Mediterranean, while Dido and her set were faring so well—or well they thought it—on the African shore.

I will own I was rather anxious now. Not but what there was something—and a great gaudy city it was—on the slopes of Mount Moriah and Zion. But it made me sick to see its worship, and I stopped my ears with my fingers rather than hear the songs. O God! the yells of those poor little children as they burned them to death in Hinnom, a hundred at a time, their own mothers dancing and howling by the fires! I cannot speak of it to this day. I dared not look there long. But it was no better anywhere else. I tried Greece; but I could make nothing of Greece. When I looked for the arrival of Danaus with his Egyptian arts and learning—Toonh, I think they called him in Egypt—why there was no Toonh and no Egyptian arts, because these Canaanite brutes had cleared out Egypt. The Pelasgians were in Greece, and in Greece they stayed. They built great walls—I did not see for what—but they lived in cabins at which a respectable Apache would turn up his nose; and century after century they built the same huts, and lived in them. As for manners, they had none, and their customs were very filthy. When it came time for Cadmus, there was no chance for Cadmus. Perhaps he came, perhaps he did not. All I know is that the Molochite invasion of Egypt had swept all alphabet and letters out of being, and that, if Cadmus came, he was rather more low-lived than the Pelasgians among whom he landed. Really, all Greece was such a mess that I hated to follow along its crass stupidity, and the savage raids which the inhabitants of one valley made upon another. This was what I had done for them when I mashed that little yellow dog so easily.

Aeneas and his set seemed to prosper better at first. I could see his ships, with the green leaves still growing on the top-masts, hurry out from the port of Dido. I saw poor Palinurus tumble over. Yes, indeed, queer enough it was to have the old half-forgotten lines of Dryden—whom I know a great deal better than Virgil, more shame to me—come

7

back as poor Nisus pleaded for his friend, as poor Camilla bled to death, and as Turnus did his best for nothing. Yes, I watched Romulus and the rest of them, just as it was in Harry and Lucy's little inch-square history. I took great comfort in Brutus; I shut my eyes when the noble lady Lucretia stabbed herself; and the quick-moving stereoscope—for I really began to feel that it was one—became more and more fascinating, till we got to the Second Punic War.

Then it seemed to me as if that cursed yellow dog came to the front again. Not that I saw him, of course. Not him! His bones and skin had been gnawed by jackals a thousand years before. But the evil that dogs do lives after them; and when I saw the anxiety on Scipio's face—they did not call him Africanus—when I looked in on little private conferences of manly Roman gentlemen, and heard them count up their waning resources, and match them against the overwhelming force of Carthage, I tell you I felt badly. You see, Carthage was simply an outpost of all that Molochite crew of the East. In the history I am used to, the Levant of that time was divided between Egypt and Greece, and what there was left of Alexander's empire. But in this yellow-dog system, for which I was responsible, it was all one brutal race of Molochism, except that Pelasgian business I told you of in Greece, which was no more to be counted in the balance of power than the Digger Indians are counted in the balance today. This was what made poor Scipio and the rest of them so downhearted. And well it might. I, who saw the whole, as you may say, together, only, as I have explained, it did not mix itself up—I could see Hannibal and his following of all the Mediterranean powers except Italy, come down on the Romans and crush them as easily as I crushed the cur. No, not as easily as that, for they fought like fury. Men fought and women fought, boys and girls fought. They dashed into the harbor of Carthage once with fire ships, and burned the fleet. But it was no good: army after army was beaten; fleet after fleet was sunk by the great Carthaginian triremes. Ah me! I remember one had the cordage of the admiral's ship made from the hair of the Roman matrons. But it was all one. If it had been Manila hemp or wire rope, the ship would not have stood when that brutal Sidonian admiral rammed at her with his hundred oarsmen. That battle was the end of Rome. The brutes burned it first. They tumbled down the very walls of the temples. What they could plough, they ploughed. They dragged the boys and girls into slavery, and that was the end. All the rest were dead on the field of battle, or were sunk in the sea.

And so Molochism reigned century after century. Just that, one century after another century: two centuries in all. What a reign it was!

Lust, brutality, terror, cruelty, carnage, famine, agony, horror. If I do not say death, it is because death was a blessing in contrast to such lives. For now that there was nobody to fight who had an idea above the Earth and dead things, these swords that were so sharp had to turn against each other. No Israel to crush, no Egypt, no Iran, no Greece, no Rome. Moloch and Canaan turned on themselves and fought Canaan and Moloch. Do not ask me to tell the story! Where beast meets beast, there is no story to tell worth your hearing or my telling. Brute rage gives you nothing to describe. They poisoned, they starved, they burned; they scourged and flayed and crucified; they invented forms of horror for which our imagination, thank God, has no picture, and our languages no name. And, all this time, lust, and every form of pestilence and disease which depends on lust, raged as fire rages when it has broken bounds. It was seldom and more seldom that children were born; nay, when they were born, they seemed only half alive. And those who grew to manhood and womanhood—only it is desecration to use those names—transmitted such untamed beastliness to those who came after!

One hundred years, as I said. Fewer and fewer of these wretches were left in the world. I could see fields grow up to jungles and to forests. A fire wasted Carthage, and another swept away On, and another finished Sidon, and there was neither heart nor art to rebuild them. Then another hundred years dragged by, with worse horrors, if it were possible, and more. The stream of the world's life began to run in drops, now big drops, with a noisy gurgle; black drops, too, or bloody red. Fewer men, and still fewer women, and all mad with beastly rage. Every man's hand was against his brother, as if this were a world of Cains. All this had come to them because they did not like to retain God in their knowledge.

No, I will not describe it. You do not ask me to. And if you asked, I would say "No." Let me come to the end.

The two centuries had gone. There was but a handful of these furies left. Then the last generation came—and for thirty years more of murder and fight it ground along. At the last, how strange it seemed to me, all that are left, in two unequal parties, each of which had its banner still for fight, and a sort of uniform as if they were armies, but only four on one side and nine on the other, met, as if the world were not wide enough for both, and met in that very Syria where I had helped Joseph, son of Jacob, to fling his arms round his father's neck again.

Nor, indeed, was it very far from that spot. It was close to the wreck and ruin of the Jebusite city which had been one of the strongholds last destroyed of one of these clans. That city was burned, but I saw that the ruins were smoking. Just outside there was an open space. I wonder if it had a weird, deadly look, or whether the horror of the day made me think so? I remember a great rock like a man's skull that peered out from the gray, dry ground. Around that rock these wretches fought, four to nine, hiding behind it, on one side or the other, on that April day, under that black sky.

One is down! Two of the other party are kneeling on him, to take the last breath of life from him. With a yell of rage three or four of his party, dashing their shields on the heads of the two, spring upon them; and I can see one wave his battle-axe above his head, when—

Did the metal attract the spark? A crash! a blaze which dazzled my eyes, and when I opened them the last of these human brutes lay stark dead on the one side and on the other of the grim rock of Calvary!

Not a man or a woman, nor a boy or a girl, not a single soul left in that world!

"Do not be disturbed," said my Mentor. "You yourself have done nothing."

"Nothing!" I groaned. "I have ruined a world in my rashness."

"Nothing," he repeated. "Remember what I told you: these are— what shall I say?—shadows, shadowy forms. They are not His children. They are only forms which act as if they were—that you and I may see and learn, perhaps begin to understand—only it passes knowledge."

As he spoke, I remember that I moaned and struggled with him like a crying child. I was all overwhelmed by the sight of the mischief I had done. I would not be comforted.

"Listen to me," he said again. "You have only done, or wanted to do, what we all try for at first. You wanted to save your poor Joseph. What wonder?"

"Of course I did," sobbed I. "Could I have thought? Should you have thought?"

"No," said he, with that royal smile of his—"no. Once I should not have thought it—I could not have thought it—till I, too, tried my experiments." And he paused.

Perhaps he was thinking what his experiments also were.

Then he began again, and the royal smile had hardly faded away: "Let me show you. Or let me try. You wanted to save your poor Joseph—all sole alone."

"Yes," I said. "Why should I not want to?"

"Because he was not alone; could not be alone. None of them was alone; none of them could be alone. Why, you know yourself that not a raindrop in that shower yonder but balances against a dust-grain on the other side of creation. How could Joseph live or die alone? How could that brute he was chained to live or die alone? None of them is alone. None of us is alone. He is not alone. Even He is in us, and we are in Him. But the way with men—and it is not so long, dear friend, since you were a man—the way with men is to try what you tried. I never yet knew a man—and how many have I known, thank God!—I never yet knew a man but he wanted to single out some one Joseph to help—as if the rest were nothing, or as if our Father had no plans."

"I shall never try that again!" sobbed I, after a long pause.

"Never," said he, "is a long word. You will learn not to say 'never.' But I'll tell you what you will do. When you get a glimpse of the life in common, when you find out what is the drift—shall I say of the game, or shall I say of the law?—in which they all and we all, He in us and we in Him, are living, then, oh, it is such fun to strike in and live for all!"

He paused a minute, and then he went on, hesitating at first, as if he feared to pain me even more, but resolutely afterward, as if this must be said.

"Another thing I notice in most men, though not in all, is this: they do not seem at first to understand that the Idea is the whole. Abraham had left Ur rather than have any part with those smoke-and-dust men— Nature-worshippers I think they call them. How was it that you did not see that Joseph was going down to Egypt with the Idea? He could take what they did not have there. And as you saw, in the other place, without it, why, your world died."

Then he turned around and left that horrid world of phantoms, to go back to our own dear real world. And this time I looked on today. How bright it seemed, and how comforting to me to think that I had never touched the yellow dog, and that he came to his death in his own way!

I saw some things I liked, and some I disliked. It happened that I was looking at Zululand, when poor Prince Lulu's foot slipped at the saddle-flap. I saw the assegai that stabbed him. Had I been a trooper at his side, by his side I would have died too. But no, I was not at his side. And I remembered Joseph, and I said, "From what I call evil, He educes good."

Delenda Est

Poul Anderson

The hunting is good in Europe 40,000 years ago, and the winter sports are unexcelled anywhere. So the Time Patrol, always solicitous for its highly trained personnel, maintains a lodge in the Pleistocene Pyrenees.

Agent Unattached Manse Everard (American, mid-Twentieth A.D.) stood on the glassed-in veranda and looked across ice-blue distances, toward the northern slopes where the mountains fell off into woodland, marsh and tundra. He was a big man, fairly young, with heavy homely features that had once encountered a German rifle butt and never quite straightened out again, gray eyes, and a brown crew cut. He wore loose green trousers and tunic of Twenty-Third-Century insulsynth, boots handmade by a Nineteenth-Century French-Canadian, and smoked a foul old briar of indeterminate origin. There was a vague restlessness about him, and he ignored the noise from within, where half a dozen agents were drinking and talking and playing the piano.

A Cro-Magnon guide went by across the snow-covered yard, a tall handsome fellow dressed rather like an Eskimo (why had romance never credited paleolithic man with enough sense to wear jacket, pants, and footgear in a glacial period?), his face painted, one of the steel knives which had hired him at his belt. The Patrol could act quite freely, this far back in time; there was no danger of upsetting the past, for the metal would rust away and the strangers be forgotten in a few centuries. The main nuisance was that female agents from the more libertine periods were always having affairs with the native hunters.

13

Piet van Sarawak (Dutch-Indonesian-Venusian, early Twenty-Fourth A.D.), a slim, dark young man with good looks and a smooth technique that gave the guides some stiff competition, joined Everard, and they stood for a moment in companionable silence. He was also Unattached, on call to help out in any milieu, and had worked with the American before. They had taken their vacation together.

He spoke first, in Temporal, the synthetic language of the Patrol. "I hear they've spotted a few mammoth near Toulouse." The city would not be built for a long time, but habit was powerful.

"I've got one," said Everard impatiently. "I've also been skiing and mountain climbing and watched the native dances."

Van Sarawak nodded, took out a cigarette, and puffed it into lighting. The bones stood out in his lean brown face as he sucked in the smoke. "A pleasant interlude," he agreed, "but after a time the outdoor life begins to pall."

There were still two weeks of their furlough left. In theory, since he could return almost to the moment of departure, an agent could take indefinite vacations; but actually he was supposed to devote a certain percentage of his probable lifetime to the job. (They never told you when you were scheduled to die—it wouldn't have been certain anyhow, time being mutable. One perquisite of an agent's office was the longevity treatment of the Daneelians, ca. one million A.D., the supermen who were the shadowy chiefs of the Patrol.)

"What I would enjoy," continued van Sarawak, "is some bright lights, music, girls who've never heard of time travel—"

"Done!" said Everard.

"Augustan Rome?" asked the other eagerly. "I've never been there. I could get a hypno on language and customs here."

Everard shook his head. "It's overrated. Unless we want to go 'way upstairs, the most glorious decadence available is right in my own milieu, say New York. If you know the right phone numbers, and I do."

Van Sarawak chuckled, "I know a few places in my own sector," he replied, "but by and large, a pioneer society has little use for the finer arts of amusement. Very good, let's be off to New York, in—when?"

"1955. My public *persona* is established there already."

They grinned at each other and went off to pack. Everard had foresightedly brought along some mid-Twentieth garments in his friend's size.

Throwing clothes and razor into a small handbag, the American wondered if he could keep up with van Sarawak. He had never been a high-powered roisterer, and would hardly have known how to buckle a swash anywhere in space-time. A good book, a bull session, a case of beer, that was about his speed. But even the soberest of men must kick over the traces occasionally.

Briefly, he reflected on all he had seen and done. Sometimes it left him with a dreamlike feeling—that it should have happened to *him,* plain Manse Everard, engineer and ex-soldier; that his ostensible few months' work for the Engineering Studies Company should only have been a blind for a total of years' wandering through time.

Travel into the past involves an infinite discontinuity; it was the discovery of such a principle which made the travel possible in 19352 A.D. But that same discontinuity in the conservation-of-energy law permitted altering history. Not very easily; there were too many factors, the plenum tended to "return" to its "original" shape. But it could be done, and the man who changed the past which had produced him, though unaffected himself, wiped out the entire future. It had never even *been;* something else existed, another train of events. To protect themselves, the Daneelians had recruited the Patrol from all ages, a giant secret organization to police the time lanes. It gave assistance to legitimate traders, scientists, and tourists—that was its main function in practice; but always there was the watching for signs which meant that some mad or ambitious or careless traveler was tampering with a key event in space-time.

If it ever happened, if anyone ever got away with it. . . . The room was comfortably heated, but Everard shivered. He and all his world would vanish, would not have existed at all. Language and logic broke down in the face of the paradox.

He dismissed the thought and went to join Piet van Sarawak.

Their little two-place scooter was waiting in the garage. It looked vaguely like a motorcycle mounted on skids, and an antigravity unit made it capable of flight. But the controls could be set for any place on Earth and any moment of time.

> *"Auprès de ma blonde*
> *Qu'il fait bon, fait bon, fait bon,*
> *Auprès de ma blonde*
> *Qu'il fait bon dormir!"*

Van Sarawak sang it aloud, his breath steaming from him in the frosty air, as he hopped onto the rear saddle. Everard laughed. "Down, boy!"

"Oh, come now," warbled the younger man. "It is a beautiful continuum, a gay and gorgeous cosmos. Hurry up this machine."

Everard was not so sure; he had seen enough human misery in all the ages. You got case-hardened after a while, but down underneath, when a peasant stared at you with sick brutalized eyes, or a soldier screamed with a pike through him, or a city went up in radioactive flame, something wept. He could understand the fanatics who had tried to write a new history. It was only that their work was so unlikely to make anything better . . .

He set the controls for the Engineering Studies warehouse, a good confidential place to emerge. Thereafter they'd go to his apartment, and then the fun could start.

"I trust you've said goodby to all your lady friends here," he murmured.

"Oh, most gallantly, I assure you," answered van Sarawak. "Come along there. You're as slow as molasses on Pluto. For your information, this vehicle does not have to be rowed home."

Everard shrugged and threw the main switch. The garage blinked out of sight. But the warehouse did not appear around them.

For a moment, pure shock held them unstirring.

The scene registered in bits and pieces. They had materialized a few inches above ground level—only later did Everard think what would have happened if they'd come out in a solid object—and hit the pavement with a teeth-rattling bump. They were in some kind of square, a fountain jetting nearby. Around it, streets led off between buildings six to ten stories high, concrete, wildly painted and ornamented. There were automobiles, big clumsy-looking things of no recognizable type, and a crowd of people.

"Ye *gods!*" Everard glared at the meters. The scooter had landed them in lower Manhattan, 23 October 1955, at 11:30 A.M. There was a blustery wind carrying dust and grime, the smell of chimneys, and—

Van Sarawak's sonic stunner jumped into his fist. The crowd was milling away from them, shouting in some babble they couldn't understand. It was a mixed lot: tall fair roundheads, with a great deal of red hair; a number of Amerinds; half-breeds in all combinations. The men wore loose colorful blouses, tartan kilts, a sort of Scotch bonnet, shoes, and high stockings. Their hair was long and many favored drooping mustaches. The women had full ankle-length skirts and hair coiled under hooded cloaks. Both sexes went in for jewelry, massive bracelets and necklaces.

16

"What happened?" whispered the Venusian. "Where are we?"

Everard sat rigid. His mind clicked over, whirling through all the eras he had known or read about. Industrial culture—those looked like steam cars, but why the sharp prows and figureheads?—coal-burning—post-nuclear Reconstruction? No, they hadn't worn kilts then, and they still spoke English—

It didn't fit. There was no such milieu recorded!

"We're getting out of here!"

His hands were on the controls when the big man jumped him. They went over on the pavement in a rage of fists and feet. Van Sarawak fired and sent someone else down unconscious; then he was seized from behind. The mob piled on top of them both, and things became hazy.

Everard had a confused impression of men in shining coppery breast-plates and helmets, who shoved a billy-swinging way through the riot. He was fished out and supported while handcuffs were snapped on his wrists. Then he and van Sarawak were searched and hustled off to a big vehicle. The Black Maria is much the same in all times.

He didn't come out of it till they were in a damp and chilly cell with an iron-barred door.

"Name of a flame!" The Venusian slumped on a wooden cot and put his face in his hands.

Everard stood at the door, looking out. All he could see was a narrow concrete hall and the cell across it. The map of Ireland stared cheerfully through those bars and called something unintelligible.

"What's happened?" Van Sarawak's slim body shuddered.

"I don't know," said Everard very slowly. "I just don't know. That machine was supposed to be foolproof, but maybe we're bigger fools than they allowed for."

"There's no such place as this," said van Sarawak desperately. "A dream?" He pinched himself and lifted a rueful smile. His lip was cut and swelling, and he had the start of a gorgeous shiner. "Logically, my friend, a pinch is no test of reality, but it has a certain reassuring effect."

"I wish it didn't," said Everard.

He grabbed the rails, and the chain between his wrists rattled thinly. "Could the controls have been off, in spite of everything? Is there any city, anywhen on Earth—because I'm damned sure this is Earth, at least—any city, however obscure, which was ever like this?"

"Not to my knowledge," whispered van Sarawak.

Everard hung onto his sanity and rallied all the mental training the Patrol had ever given him. That included total recall . . . and he had

17

studied history, even the history of ages he had never seen, with a thoroughness that should have earned him several Ph.D.'s.

"No," he said at last. "Kilted brachycephalic whites, mixed up with Indians and using steam-driven automobiles, haven't happened."

"Coordinator Stantel V," said van Sarawak faintly. "Thirty-eighth century. The Great Experimenter—colonies reproducing past societies—"

"Not any like this," said Everard.

The truth was growing in him like a cancer, and he would have traded his soul to know otherwise. It took all the will and strength he had to keep from screaming and bashing his brains out against the wall.

"We'll have to see," he said in a flat tone.

A policeman—Everard supposed they were in the hands of the law—brought them a meal and tried to talk to them. Van Sarawak said the language sounded Celtic, but he couldn't make out more than a few words. The meal wasn't bad.

Toward evening, they were led off to a washroom and got cleaned up under official guns. Everard studied the weapons: eight-shot revolvers and long-barreled rifles. The facilities and the firearms, as well as the smell, suggested a technology roughly equivalent to the Nineteenth Century. There were gas lights, and Everard noticed that the brackets were cast in an elaborate intertwined pattern of vines and snakes.

On the way back, he spied a couple of signs on the walls. The script was obviously Semitic, but though van Sarawak had some knowledge of Hebrew through dealing with the Jewish colonies on Venus, he couldn't read it.

Locked in again, they saw the other prisoners led off to do their own washing—a surprisingly merry crowd of bums, toughs, and drunks. "Seems we get special treatment," remarked van Sarawak.

"Hardly astonishing," said Everard. "What would you do with total strangers who appeared out of nowhere and used unheard-of weapons?"

Van Sarawak's face turned to him with an unaccustomed grimness. "Are you thinking what I am thinking?" he asked.

"Probably."

The Venusian's mouth twisted, and horror rode his voice: "Another time line. Somebody *has* managed to change history."

Everard nodded. There was nothing else to do.

They spent an unhappy night. It would have been a boon to sleep, but the other cells were too noisy. Discipline seemed to be lax here. Also, there were bedbugs.

After a bleary breakfast, Everard and van Sarawak were allowed to wash again and shave. Then a ten-man guard marched them into an office and planted itself around the walls. They sat down before a desk and waited. It was some time till the big wheels showed up. There were two: a white-haired, ruddy-cheeked man in cuirass and green tunic, presumably the chief of police; and a lean, hard-faced half-breed, gray-haired but black-mustached, wearing a blue tunic, a tam o'shanter, and insignia of rank—a golden bull's head. He would have had a certain hawklike dignity had it not been for the skinny hairy legs beneath his kilt. He was followed by younger men, armed and uniformed, who took up their places behind him as he sat down.

Everard leaned over and whispered: "The military, I'll bet. We seem to be of interest."

Van Sarawak nodded sickly.

The police chief cleared his throat with conscious importance and said something to the—general? The latter turned impatiently and addressed himself to the prisoners. He barked his words out with a clarity that helped Everard get the phonemes, but with a manner that was not exactly reassuring.

Somewhere along the line, communication would have to be established. Everard pointed to himself. "Manse Everard," he said. Van Sarawak followed the lead and introduced himself similarly.

The general started and went into a huddle with the chief. Turning back, he snapped: "*Yrn Cimberland?*"

"No spikka da Inglees," said Everard.

"*Gothland? Svea? Nairoin Teutonach?*"

"Those names—if they are names—they sound a little Germanic, don't they?" muttered van Sarawak.

"So do our names, come to think of it," answered Everard tautly. "Maybe they think we're Germans." To the general: "*Sprechen Sie Deutsch?*" Blankness rewarded him. "*Taler ni svensk? Niederlands? Dönsk tunga? Parlez-vous français?* Goddammit, ¿habla usted español?"

The police chief cleared his throat again and pointed to himself. "Cadwallader Mac Barca," he said. The general hight Cynyth ap Ceorn.

"Celtic, all right," said Everard. Sweat prickled under his arms. "But just to make sure—" He pointed inquiringly at a few other men, being rewarded with monickers like Hamilcar ap Angus, Asshur yr Cathlann, and Finn O'Carthia. "No . . . there's a distinct Semitic element here too. That fits in with their alphabet—"

Van Sarawak's mouth was dry. "Try Classical languages," he urged harshly. "Maybe we can find out where this time went awry."

"*Loquerisne latine?*" That drew a blank. "*Ελλενίξεις?*"

General ap Ceorn started, blew out his mustache, and narrowed his eyes. "*Hellenach?*" he snapped. "*Yrn Parthia?*"

Everard shook his head. "They've at least heard of Greek," he said slowly. He tried a few more words, but no one knew the tongue.

Ap Ceorn growled something and spoke to one of his men, who bowed and went out. There was a long silence.

Everard found himself losing personal fear. He was in a bad spot, yes, and might not live very long; but anything that happened to him was ridiculously insignificant compared to what had been done to the entire world.

God in Heaven! To the universe!

He couldn't grasp it. Sharp in his mind rose the land he knew, broad plains and tall mountains and prideful cities. There was the grave image of his father, and yet he remembered being a small child and lifted up skyward while his father laughed beneath him. And his mother—they had a good life together, those two.

There had been a girl he knew in college, the sweetest little wench a man could ever have been privileged to walk in the rain with; and there was Bernie Aaronson, the long nights of beer and smoke and talk; Phil Brackney, who had picked him out of the mud in France when machine guns were raking a ruined field; Charlie and Mary Whitcomb, high tea and a low little fire in Victoria's London; a dog he had once had; the austere cantos of Dante and the ringing thunder of Shakespeare; the glory which was York Minster and the Golden Gate Bridge—Christ, a man's life, and the lives of who knew how many billions of human creatures, toiling and suffering and laughing and going down into dust to leave their sons behind them—*It had never been!*

He shook his head, dazed with grief, and sat devoid of real understanding.

The soldier came back with a map and spread it out on the desk. Ap Ceorn gestured curtly, and Everard and van Sarawak bent over it.

Yes . . . Earth, a Mercator projection, though eidetic memory showed that the mapping was rather crude. The continents and islands were there in bright colors, but the nations were something else.

"Can you read those names, Van?"

"I can make a guess, on the basis of the Hebraic alphabet," said the Venusian. He read out the alien words, filling in the gaps of his knowledge with what sounded logical.

North America down to about Colombia was Ynys yr Afallon, seemingly one country divided into states. South America was a big realm, Huy Braseal, with some smaller countries whose names looked Indian. Australasia, Indonesia, Borneo, Burma, eastern India, and a good deal of the Pacific belonged to Hinduraj. Afghanistan and the rest of India were Punjab. Han included China, Korea, Japan, and eastern Siberia. Littorn owned the rest of Russia and reached well into Europe. The British Isles were Brittys, France and the Low Countries Gallis, the Iberian peninsula Celtan. Central Europe and the Balkans were divided into many small states, some of which had Hunnish-looking names. Switzerland and Austria made up Helveti; Italy was Cimberland; the Scandinavian peninsula was split down the middle, Svea in the north and Gothland in the south. North Africa looked like a confederacy, reaching from Senegal to Suez and nearly to the equator under the name of Carthagalann; the southern continent was partitioned among small countries, many of which had purely African titles. The Near East held Parthia and Arabia.

Van Sarawak looked up. There were tears in his eyes.

Ap Ceorn snarled a question and waved his finger about. He wanted to know where they were from.

Everard shrugged and pointed skyward. The one thing he could not admit was the truth. He and van Sarawak had agreed to claim they were from some other planet, since this world hardly had space travel.

Ap Ceorn spoke to the chief, who nodded and replied. The prisoners were returned to their cell.

"And now what?" Van Sarawak slumped on his cot and stared at the floor.

"We play along," said Everard grayly. "We do anything to get at our scooter and escape. Once we're free, we can take stock."

"But what happened?"

"I don't know, I tell you! Offhand it looks as if something upset the Roman Empire and the Celts took over, but I couldn't say what it was." Everard prowled the room. There was a bitter determination growing in him.

"Remember your basic theory," he said. "Events are the result of a complex. That's why it's so hard to change history. If I went back to, say, the Middle Ages, and shot one of FDR's Dutch forebears, he'd still be born in the Twentieth Century—because he and his genes resulted from the entire world of his ancestors, and there'd have been compensation. The first case I ever worked on was an attempt to alter things in the Fifth

21

Century; we spotted evidence of it in the Twentieth, and went back and stopped the scheme.

"But every so often, there must be a really key event. Only with hindsight can we tell what it was, but some one happening was a nexus of so many world lines that its outcome was decisive for the whole future.

"Somehow, for some reason, somebody has ripped up one of those events back in the past."

"No more Hesperus City," whispered van Sarawak. "No more sitting by the canals in the blue twilight, no more Aphrodite vintages, no more—did you know I had a sister on Venus?"

"Shut up!" Everard almost shouted it. "I know. What counts is what to do.

"Look," he went on after a moment, "the Patrol and the Daneelians are wiped out. But such of the Patrol offices and resorts as antedate the switchpoint haven't been affected. There must be a few hundred agents we can rally."

"*If* we can get out of here."

"We can find that key event and stop whatever interference there was with it. We've got to!"

"A pleasant thought," mumbled van Sarawak, "but—"

Feet tramped outside, and a key clicked in the lock. The prisoners backed away. Then, all at once, van Sarawak was bowing and beaming and spilling gallantries. Even Everard had to gape.

The girl who entered in front of three soldiers was a knockout. She was tall, with a sweep of rusty-red hair past her shoulders to the slim waist; her eyes were green and alight, her face came from all the Irish colleens who had ever lived, the long white dress was snug around a figure meant to stand on the walls of Troy. Everard noticed vaguely that this time-line used cosmetics, but she had small need of them. He paid no attention to the gold and amber of her jewelry, or to the guns behind her.

She smiled, a little timidly, and spoke: "Can you understand me? It was thought you might know Greek—"

The language was classical rather than modern. Everard, who had once had a job in Alexandrine times, could follow it through her accent if he paid close heed—which was inevitable anyway.

"Indeed I do," he replied, his words stumbling over each other.

"What are you snakkering?" demanded van Sarawak.

"Ancient Greek," said Everard.

"It would be," mourned van Sarawak. His despair seemed to have vanished, and his eyes bugged.

Everard introduced himself and his companion. The girl said her name was Deirdre Mac Morn. "Oh, no," groaned van Sarawak. "This is too much. Manse, you've got to teach me Greek, and fast."

"Shut up," said Everard. "This is serious business."

"Well, but why should you have all the pleasure—"

Everard ignored him and invited the girl to sit down. He joined her on a cot, while the other Patrolman hovered unhappily close. The guards kept their weapons ready.

"Is Greek still a living language?" asked Everard.

"Only in Parthia, and there it is most corrupt," said Deirdre. "I am a Classical scholar, among other things. *Saorann* ap Ceorn is my uncle, so he asked me to see if I could talk with you. There are not many in Afallon who know the Attic tongue."

"Well . . ." Everard suppressed a silly grin. "I am most grateful to your uncle."

Her eyes rested gravely on him. "Where are you from? And how does it happen that you speak only Greek, of all known languages?"

"I speak Latin too."

"Latin?" She frowned briefly. "Oh, yes. The Roman speech, was it not? I'm afraid you'll find no one who knows much about it."

"Greek will do," said Everard.

"But you have not told me whence you came," she insisted.

Everard shrugged. "We've not been treated very courteously," he hinted.

"Oh . . . I'm sorry." It seemed genuine. "But our people are so excitable—especially now, with the international situation what it is. And when you two appeared out of thin air—"

Everard nodded grimly. The international situation? That had a familiar ring. "What do you mean?" he inquired.

"Oh, surely . . . of course you know. With Huy Braseal and Hinduraj about to go to war, and all of us wondering what will happen— It is not easy to be a small power."

"A small power? But I saw a map, and Afallon looked big enough to me."

"We wore ourselves out two hundred years ago, in the great war with Littorn. Now none of our confederated states can agree on a single policy." Deirdre looked directly into his eyes. "What is this ignorance of yours?"

Everard swallowed and said: "We're from another world."

"What?"

23

"Yes. A . . . planet of Sirius."

"But Sirius is a star!"

"Of course."

"How can a star have planets?"

"How— But it does! A star is a sun like—"

Deirdre shrank back and made a sign with her finger. "The Great Baal aid us," she whispered. "Either you are mad, or— The stars are mounted in a crystal sphere."

Oh, no! Everard asked slowly: "What of the planets you can see— Mars and Venus and—"

"I know not those names. If you mean Moloch, Ashtoreth, and the rest, of course they are worlds like ours. One holds the spirits of the dead, one is the home of witches, one—"

All this and steam cars too. Everard smiled shakily. "If you'll not believe me, then what do you think?"

Deirdre regarded him with large eyes. "I think you must be sorcerers," she said.

There was no answer to that. Everard asked a few weak questions, but learned little more than that this city was Catuvellaunan, a trading and manufacturing center; Deirdre estimated its population at two million, and that of all Afallon at fifty millions, but it was only a guess—they didn't take censuses in this world.

The prisoners' fate was also indeterminate. Their machine and other possessions had been sequestrated by the military, but nobody dared to monkey with them, and treatment of the owners was being hotly debated. Everard got the impression that all government, including the leadership of the armed forces, was a sloppy process of individualistic wrangling. Afallon itself was the loosest of confederacies, built out of former nations—Brittic colonies and Indians who had adopted white culture—all jealous of their rights. The old Mayan Empire, destroyed in a war with Texas (Tehannach) and annexed, had not forgotten its time of glory, and sent the most rambunctious delegates of all to the Council of Suffetes.

The Mayans wanted an alliance with Huy Braseal, perhaps out of friendship for fellow Indians. The West Coast states, fearful of Hinduraj, were toadies of the Southeast Asian empire. The Middle West—of course—was isolationist, and the Eastern states were torn every which way but inclined to follow the lead of Brittys.

24

When he gathered that slavery existed here, though not on racial lines, Everard wondered briefly if the guilty time travelers might not have been Dixiecrats.

Enough! He had his own and Van's necks to think about. "We are from Sirius," he declared loftily. "Your ideas about the stars are mistaken. We came as peaceful explorers, and if we are molested there will be others of our kind to take vengeance."

Deirdre looked so unhappy that he felt conscience-stricken. "Will you spare the children?" she whispered. "They had nothing to do with it." Everard could imagine the frightful vision in her head, helpless captives led off in chains to the slave markets of a world of witches.

"There need be no trouble at all if we are released and our property returned," he said.

"I shall speak to my uncle," she promised, "but even if I can sway him, he is only one on the Council. The thought of what your weapons could mean if we had them has driven men mad."

She rose. Everard clasped her hands, they lay warm and soft in his, and smiled crookedly at her. "Buck up, kid," he said in English. She shivered and made the hex sign again.

"Well," said van Sarawak when they were alone, "what did you find out?" After being told, he stroked his chin and murmured thoughtfully: "That was one sweet little collection of sinusoids. There could be worse worlds than this."

"Or better," said Everard bleakly. "They don't have atomic bombs, but neither do they have penicillin. It's not our job to play God."

"No . . . no, I suppose not." The Venusian sighed.

They spent a restless day. Night had fallen when lanterns glimmered in the corridor and a military guard unlocked the cell. The prisoners' handcuffs were removed, and they were led silently to a rear exit. A car waited, with another for escort, and the whole troop drove wordlessly off.

Catuvellaunan did not have outdoor lighting, and there wasn't much night traffic. Somehow, that made the sprawling city unreal in the dark. Everard leaned back and concentrated on the mechanics of his vehicle. Steam-powered, as he had guessed, burning powdered coal; rubber-tired wheels; a sleek body with a sharp nose and a serpent figurehead; the whole simple to operate but not too well designed. Apparently this world had gradually developed a rule-of-thumb mechanics, but no systematic science worth mentioning.

They crossed a clumsy iron bridge to Long Island, here as at home a residential section for the well-to-do. Their speed was high despite the dimness of their oil-lamp headlights, and twice they came near having an accident—no traffic signals, and seemingly no drivers who did not hold caution in contempt.

Government and traffic . . . hm. It all looked French, somehow, and even in Everard's own Twentieth Century France was largely Celtic. He was no respecter of windy theories about inborn racial traits, but there was something to be said for traditional attitudes so ancient that they were unconsciously accepted. A Western world in which the Celts had become dominant, the Germanic peoples reduced to two small outposts . . . Yes, look at the Ireland of home; or recall how tribal politics had queered Vercingetorix's revolt. . . . But what about Littorn? Wait a minute! In *his* early Middle Ages, Lithuania had been a powerful state; it had held off Germans, Poles, and Russians alike for a long time, and hadn't even taken Christianity till the Fifteenth Century. Without German competition, Lithuania might very well have advanced eastward—

In spite of the Celtic political instability, this was a world of large states, fewer separate nations than Everard's. That argued an older society. If his own Western civilization had developed out of the decaying Roman Empire about, say, 600 A.D., the Celts in this world must have taken over earlier than that.

Everard was beginning to realize what had happened to Rome . . .

The cars drew up before an ornamental gate set in a long stone wall. There was an interchange with two armed guards wearing the livery of a private estate and the thin steel collars of slaves. The gate was opened, and the cars went along a graveled driveway between trees and lawns and hedgerows. At the far end, almost on the beach, stood a house. Everard and van Sarawak were gestured out and led toward it.

It was a rambling wooden structure. Gas lamps on the porch showed it painted in gaudy stripes; the gables and beam-ends were carved into dragon heads. Behind it murmured the sea, and there was enough starlight for Everard to make out a ship standing in close—presumably a freighter, with a tall smokestack and a figurehead.

Light glowed through the windows. A slave butler admitted the party. The interior was paneled in dark wood, also carved, the floors thickly carpeted. At the end of the hall there was a living room with overstuffed furniture, several paintings in a stiff conventionalized style, and a merry blaze in a great stone fireplace.

Saorann Cynyth ap Ceorn sat in one chair, Deirdre in another. She laid aside a book as they entered and rose, smiling. The officer puffed a cigar and glowered. There were some words swapped, and the guards disappeared. The butler fetched in wine on a tray, and Deirdre invited the Patrolmen to sit down.

Everard sipped from his glass—the wine was an excellent Burgundy type—and asked bluntly: "Why are we here?"

Deirdre smiled, dazzlingly this time, and chuckled. "Surely you find it more pleasant than the jail."

"Oh, yes. But I still want to know. Are we being released?"

"You are. . . ." She hunted for a diplomatic answer, but there seemed to be too much frankness in her. "You are welcome here, but may not leave the estate. We had hopes you could be persuaded to help us. There would be rich reward."

"Help? How?"

"By showing our artisans and wizards the spells to make more machines and weapons like your own."

Everard sighed. It was no use trying to explain. They didn't have the tools to make the tools to make what was needed, but how could he get that across to a folk who believed in witchcraft?

"Is this your uncle's home?" he asked.

"No," said Deirdre. "It is my own. I am the only child of my parents, who were wealthy nobles and died last year."

Ap Ceorn snapped something, and Deirdre translated with a worried frown: "The tale of your magical advent is known to all Catuvellaunan by now; and that includes the foreign spies. We hope you can remain hidden from them here."

Everard, remembering the pranks Axis and Allies had played in little neutral nations like Portugal, shivered. Men made desperate by approaching war would not likely be as courteous as the Afallonians.

"What is this conflict going to be about?" he inquired.

"The control of the Icenian Ocean, of course. Particularly, certain rich islands we call Yyns yr Lyonnach—" Deirdre got up in a single flowing movement and pointed out Hawaii on a globe. "You see," she went on earnestly, "as I told you, the western countries like Brittys, Gallis, and ourselves, fighting Littorn, have worn each other out. Our domains have shrunken, and the newer states like Huy Braseal and Hinduraj are now expanding and quarreling. They will draw in the lesser nations, for it is not only a clash of ambitions but of systems—the

27

monarchy of Hinduraj and the sun-worshipping theocracy of Huy Braseal."

"What is your religion?" asked Everard.

Deirdre blinked. The question seemed almost meaningless to her. "The more educated people think that there is a Great Baal who made all the lesser gods," she answered at last, slowly. "But naturally, we pay our respects to the foreign gods too, Littorn's Perkunas and Czernebog, the Sun of the southerners, Wotan Ammon of Cimberland, and so on. They are very powerful."

"I see . . ."

Ap Ceorn offered cigars and matches. Van Sarawak inhaled and said querulously: "Damn it, this would have to be a time line where they don't speak any language I know." He brightened. "But I'm pretty quick to learn, even without hypnos. I'll get Deirdre to teach me."

"You and me both," said Everard hastily. "But listen, Van—" He reported what had been said.

"Hm." The younger man rubbed his chin. "Not so good, eh? Of course, if they'd just let us at our scooter, we could take off at once. Why not play along with them?"

"They're not such fools," answered Everard. "They may believe in magic, but not in undiluted altruism."

"Funny . . . that they should be so backward intellectually, and still have combustion engines."

"No. It's quite understandable. That's why I asked about their religion. It's always been purely pagan; even Judaism seems to have disappeared. As Whitehead pointed out, the medieval idea of one almighty God was important to science, by inculcating the notion of lawfulness in nature. And Mumford added that the early monasteries were probably responsible for the mechanical clock—a very basic invention—because of having regular hours for prayer. Clocks seem to have come late in this world." Everard smiled wryly, but there was a twisting sadness in him. "Odd to talk that way. Whitehead and Mumford never lived. If Jesus did, his message has been lost."

"Still—"

"Just a minute." Everard turned to Deirdre. "When was Afallon discovered?"

"By white men? In the year 4827."

"Um . . . when does your reckoning start from?"

Deirdre seemed immune to further startlement. "The creation of the world—at least, the date some philosophers have given. That is 5959 years ago."

28

4004 B.C. . . . Yes, definitely a Semitic element in this culture. The Jews had presumably gotten their traditional date from Babylon; but Everard doubted that the Jews were the Semites in question here.

"And when was steam (*pneuma*) first used to drive engines?"

"About a thousand years ago. The great Druid Boroihme O'Fiona—"

"Never mind." Everard smoked his cigar and mulled his thoughts for a while. Then he turned back to van Sarawak.

"I'm beginning to get the picture," he said. "The Gauls were anything but the barbarians most people think. They'd learned a lot from Phoenician traders and Greek colonists, as well as from the Etruscans in Cisalpine Gaul. A very energetic and enterprising race. The Romans, on the other hand, were a stolid lot, with few intellectual interests. There was very little technological progress in our world till the Dark Ages, when the Empire had been swept out of the way.

"In *this* history, the Romans vanished early and the Gauls got the power. They started exploring, building better ships, discovering America in the Ninth Century. But they weren't so far ahead of the Indians that those couldn't catch up . . . even be stimulated to build empires of their own, like Huy Braseal today. In the Eleventh Century, the Celts began tinkering with steam engines. They seem to have got gunpowder too, maybe from China, and to have made several other inventions; but it's all been cut-and-dry, with no basis of real science."

Van Sarawak nodded. "I suppose you're right. But what did happen to Rome?"

"I'm not sure . . . yet . . . but our key point is back there somewhere."

Everard returned to Deirdre. "This may surprise you," he said smoothly. "Our people visited this world about 2500 years ago. That's why I speak Greek but don't know what has occurred since. I would like to find out from you— I take it you're quite a scholar."

She flushed and lowered long dark lashes. "I will be glad to help as much as I can." With a sudden appeal that cut at his heart: "But will you help us in return?"

"I don't know," said Everard heavily. "I'd like to, but I don't know if we can."

Because after all, my job is to condemn you and your entire world to death.

When Everard was shown to his room, he discovered that local hospitality was more than generous. He was too tired and depressed to take advantage of it . . . but at least, he thought on the edge of sleep, Van's slave girl wouldn't be disappointed.

29

They got up early here. From his upstairs window, Everard saw guards pacing the beach, but they didn't detract from the morning's freshness. He came down with van Sarawak to breakfast, where bacon and eggs, toast and coffee added the last incongruous note of dream. Ap Ceorn was gone back to town to confer, said Deirdre; she herself had put wistfulness aside and chattered gaily of trivia. Everard learned that she belonged to a dramatic group which sometimes gave plays in the original Greek—hence her fluency; she liked to ride, hunt, sail, swim— "And shall we?" she asked.

"Huh?"

"Swim, of course!" Deirdre sprang from her chair on the lawn, where they had been sitting under flame-colored leaves in the wan autumn sunlight, and whirled innocently out of her clothes. Everard thought he heard a dull clunk as van Sarawak's jaw hit the ground.

"Come!" she laughed. "Last one in is a Sassenach!"

She was already tumbling in the cold gray waves when Everard and van Sarawak shuddered their way down to the beach. The Venusian groaned. "I come from a warm planet," he objected. "My ancestors were Indonesians—tropical birds."

"There were some Dutchmen too, weren't there?" grinned Everard.

"They had the sense to go to Indonesia."

"All right, stay ashore."

"Hell! If she can do it, I can!" Van Sarawak put a toe in the water and groaned again.

Everard summoned up all the psychosomatic control he had ever learned and ran in. Deirdre threw water at him. He plunged, got hold of a slender leg, and pulled her under. They tumbled about for several minutes before running back to the house. Van Sarawak followed.

"Speak about Tantalus," he mumbled. "The most beautiful girl in the whole continuum, and I can't talk to her and she's half polar bear."

Everard stood quiet before the living-room fire, while slaves toweled him dry and dressed him in the local garb. "What pattern is this?" he asked, pointing to the tartan of his kilt.

Deirdre lifted her ruddy head. "My own clan's," she answered. "A house guest is always taken as a clan member during his stay, even if there is a blood feud going on." She smiled shyly. "And there is none between us, Manslach."

It cast him back into bleakness. He remembered what his purpose was.

"I'd like to ask you about history," he said. "It is a special interest of mine."

She nodded, adjusted a gold fillet on her hair, and got a book from a crowded shelf. "This is the best world history, I think. I can look up details you might wish to know."

And tell me what I must do to destroy you. Seldom had Everard felt himself so much a skunk.

He sat down with her on a couch. The butler wheeled in lunch, and he ate moodily.

To follow up his notion— "Did Rome and Carthage ever fight a war?"

"Yes. Two, in fact. They were allied at first, against Epirus. Then they fell out. Rome won the first war and tried to restrict Carthaginian enterprise." Her clean profile bent over the pages, like a studious child. "The second war broke out twenty-three years later, and lasted . . . hm . . . eleven years all told, though the last three were only mopping up after Hannibal had taken and burned Rome."

Ah-hah! Somehow, Everard did not feel happy about it.

The Second Punic War, or rather some key incident thereof, was the turning point. But—partly out of curiosity, partly because he feared to tip his hand—Everard did not ask for particulars. He'd first have to get straight in his mind what had actually happened, anyway. (No . . . what had not happened. The reality was here, warm and breathing beside him, and he was the ghost.)

"So what came next?" he inquired tonelessly.

"There was a Carthaginian Empire, including Spain, southern Gaul, and the toe of Italy," she said. "The rest of Italy was impotent and chaotic, after the Roman confederacy had been broken up. But the Carthaginian government was too venal to endure; Hannibal himself was assassinated by men who thought him too honest. Meanwhile, Syria and Parthia fought for the eastern Mediterranean, with Parthia winning.

"About a hundred years after the Punic Wars, some Germanic tribes invaded and conquered Italy." (Yes . . . that would be the Cimbri, with their allies the Teutones and Ambrones, whom Marius had stopped in Everard's world.) "Their destructive path through Gaul set the Celts moving too, into Spain and North Africa as Carthage declined; and from Carthage the Gauls learned much.

"There followed a long period of wars, during which Parthia waned and the Celtic states grew. The Huns broke the Germans in middle Europe, but were in turn scattered by Parthia, so the Gauls moved in and the only Germans left were in Italy and Hyperborea." (That must be the Scandinavian peninsula.) "As ships improved, there was trade around Africa with India and China. The Celtanians discovered Afallon, which they thought was an island—hence the 'Ynys'—but were thrown out by the Mayans. The Brittic colonies further north had better luck, and eventually won their independence.

"Meanwhile Littorn was growing vastly. It swallowed up central Europe and Hyperborea for a while, and those countries only regained their freedom as part of the peace settlement after the Hundred Years' War you know of. The Asian countries have shaken off their European masters and modernized themselves, while the Western nations have declined in their turn." Deirdre looked up. "But this is only the barest outline. Shall I go on?"

Everard shook his head. "No, thanks." After a moment: "You are very honest about the situation of your own country."

Deirdre shrugged. "Most of us won't admit it, but I think it best to look truth in the eyes."

With a surge of eagerness: "But tell me of your own world. This is a marvel past belief."

Everard sighed, turned off his conscience, and began lying.

The raid took place that afternoon.

Van Sarawak had recovered himself and was busily learning the Afallonian language from Deirdre. They walked through the garden hand in hand, stopping to name objects and act out verbs. Everard followed, wondering vaguely if he was a third wheel or not, most of him bent to the problem of how to get at the scooter.

Bright sunlight spilled from a pale cloudless sky. A maple stood like a shout of scarlet, and a drift of yellow leaves scudded across sere grass. An elderly slave was raking the yard in a leisurely fashion, a young-looking guard of Indian race lounged with his rifle slung on one shoulder, a pair of wolfhounds dozed with dignity under a hedge. It was a peaceful scene—hard to believe that men schemed murder beyond these walls.

But man was man, in any history. This culture might not have the ruthless will and sophisticated cruelty of Western civilization; in some ways it looked strangely innocent. Still, that wasn't for lack of trying; and in this world, a genuine science might never emerge, man might endlessly repeat the weary cycle of war, empire, collapse, and war. In Everard's future, the race had finally broken out of it.

For what? He could not honestly say that this new continuum was worse or better than his own. It was different, that was all; and didn't these people have as much right to their existence as—as his own, who were damned to nullity if he failed to act?

He shook his head and felt fists knot at his side. It was too big. No man should have to decide something like this.

In the showdown, he knew, it would be no abstract sense of duty which compelled him, but the little things and the little folk he remembered.

They rounded the house and Deirdre pointed to the sea. *"Awarlann,"* she said. Her loose hair was flame in the wind.

"Now does that mean 'ocean' or 'Atlantic' or 'water'?" asked van Sarawak, laughing. "Let's go see." He led her toward the beach.

Everard trailed. A kind of steam launch, long and fast, was skipping over the waves, a mile or so offshore. Gulls flew up in a shrieking snowstorm of wings. He thought that if he'd been in charge, there would have been a Navy ship on picket out there.

Did he even have to decide anything? There were other Patrolmen in the pre-Roman past. They'd return to their respective eras and—

Everard stiffened. A chill ran down his back and into his belly.

They'd return, and see what had happened, and try to correct the trouble. If any of them succeeded, this world would blink out of space-time, and he would go with it.

Deirdre paused. Everard, standing in a cold sweat, hardly noticed what she was staring at, till she cried out and pointed. Then he joined her and squinted across the sea.

The launch was coming in close, its high stack fuming smoke and sparks, the gilt snake figurehead agleam. He could see the dwarfed forms of men aboard, and something white, with wings. It rose from the poopdeck and trailed at the end of a rope, mounting. A glider! Celtic aeronautics had gotten that far, at least—

"Pretty thing," said van Sarawak. "I suppose they have balloons too."

The glider cast its tow and swooped inward. One of the guards on the beach shouted. The rest came running from behind the house, sunlight flashed off their guns. The launch sped for the shore and the glider landed, plowing a furrow in the beach.

An officer yelled, waving the Patrolmen back. Everard had a glimpse of Deirdre's face, white and uncomprehending. Then a turret on the glider swiveled—a detached part of his mind assumed it was manually operated—and a cannon spoke.

Everard hit the dirt. Van Sarawak followed, dragging the girl with him. Grapeshot plowed hideously through the Afallonian soldiers.

There came a spiteful crack of guns. Men were emerging from the aircraft, dark-faced men in turbans and sarongs. *Hinduraj!* thought Everard. They traded shots with the surviving guards, who rallied about their captain.

That man roared and led a charge. Everard looked up to see him almost at the glider and its crew. Van Sarawak leaped up and ran to join the fight. Everard rolled over, caught his leg, and pulled him down. "Let me *go*!" The Venusian writhed. There was a sobbing in his throat. The racket of battle seemed to fill the sky.

"No, you bloody fool! It's us they're after, and that wild Irishman did the worst thing he could have—" Everard slapped his friend's face and looked up.

The launch, shallow-draught and screw-propelled, had run up to the beach and was retching armed men. The Afallonians realized too late that they had discharged their weapons and were being attacked from the rear.

"Come on!" Everard yanked Deirdre and van Sarawak to their feet. "We've got to get out of here—get to the neighbors—"

A detachment of the boat crew saw him and veered. He felt rather than heard the flat smack of a bullet into turf. Slaves were screaming around the house. The two wolfhounds charged and were gunned down.

Everard whirled to flee. Crouched, zigzag, that was the way, over the wall and out onto the road! He might have made it, but Deirdre stumbled and fell. Van Sarawak halted and stood over her with a snarl. Everard plunged to a stop, and by that time it was too late. They were covered.

The leader of the dark men snapped something at the girl. She sat up, giving him a defiant answer. He laughed shortly and jerked his thumb at the launch.

"What do they want?" asked Everard in Greek.

"You." She looked at him with horror. "You two—" The officer spoke. "And me to translate—No!"

She twisted in the arms that held her and clawed at a man's face. Everard's fist traveled in a short arc that ended in a lovely squashing of nose. It was too good to last: a clubbed rifle descended on his head, and he was only dimly aware of being carried off to the launch.

The crew left the glider behind, shoved their boat into deeper water, and revved it up. They left all the guardsmen slain, but took their own casualties along.

Everard sat on a bench on the plunging deck and stared with slowly clearing eyes as the shoreline dwindled. Deirdre wept on van Sarawak's shoulder, and the Venusian tried to console her. A chill noisy wind blew across indifferent waves, spindrift stung their faces.

It was when the two white men emerged from a cabin that Everard's mind was jarred back into motion. Not Asians after all—these were Europeans. And the rest of the crew had Caucasian features . . . grease paint!

He regarded his new owners warily. One was a portly, middle-aged man of average height, in a red silk blouse and baggy white trousers and a sort of astrakhan hat; he was clean-shaven and his dark hair was twisted into a queue. The other was somewhat younger, a shaggy blond giant in a tunic sewn with copper links, legginged breeches, a leather cloak, and a horned helmet. Both wore revolvers at their belts and were treated deferentially.

"What the devil—" Everard looked around. They were already out of sight of land and bending north. The engine made the hull quiver, spray sheeted when the bows bit into a wave.

The older man spoke first in Afallonian. Everard shrugged. Then the bearded Nordic tried, first in a completely unrecognizable dialect but afterward: "Taelan thu Cimbric?"

Everard, who knew German, Swedish, and Anglo-Saxon, took a chance, while van Sarawak pricked up his Dutch ears. Deirdre huddled back wide-eyed, too bewildered to move.

"Ja," said Everard, "ein wenig." When Goldilocks looked uncertain, he amended it: "A little."

"Ah, aen litt. Gode!" The big man rubbed hairy hands. "Ik hait Boierick Wulfilasson ok main gefreond heer erran Boleslav Arkonsky."

It was not any language Everard had ever heard of—it couldn't even be the original Cimbrian, after all these centuries—but the Patrolman could follow it tolerably well. The trouble would be in speaking; he couldn't predict how it had evolved.

"What the hell erran thu maching, anyway?" he blustered. "Ik bin aen man auf Sirius—the stern Sirius, mit planeten ok all. Set uns gebach or willen be der Teufel to pay!"

Boierik Wulfilasson looked pained and suggested that the discussion be continued inside, with the young lady for interpreter. He led the way back into the cabin, which turned out to be small but comfortably furnished. The door remained open, with an armed guard looking in and more on call.

Boleslav Arkonsky said something in Afallonian to Deirdre. She nodded, and he gave her a glass of wine. It seemed to steady her, but she spoke to Everard in a thin voice.

"We've been taken, Manslach. Their spies found out where you were kept. Another group is supposed to capture your machine—they know where that is, too."

"So I imagined," replied Everard. "But who in Baal's name are they?"

Boierik guffawed at the question and expounded lengthily on his own cleverness. The idea was to make the Suffetes of Afallon think that Hinduraj was responsible. Actually, the secret alliance of Littorn and Cimberland had built up quite an effective spy service of its own. They were now bound for the Littornian Embassy's summer retreat on Ynys Llangollen (Nantucket), where the wizards would be induced to explain their spells and the great powers get a surprise.

"And if we don't . . .?"

Deirdre translated Arkonsky's answer word for word: "I regret the consequences to you. We are civilized men, and will pay well in gold and honor for your free cooperation; but the existence of our countries is at stake."

Everard looked at them. Boierik seemed embarrassed and unhappy, the boastful glee evaporated from him. Boleslav Arkonsky drummed on the table, his lips compressed but a certain mute appeal in his eyes. *Don't make us do this. We have to live with ourselves.*

They were probably husbands and fathers, they must enjoy a mug of beer and a friendly game of dice as well as the next man, maybe Boierik bred horses in Italy and Arkonsky was a rose fancier on the Baltic shores. But none of it would do their captives a bit of good, not when the almighty Nation locked horns with its kin.

Everard paused briefly to admire the sheer artistry of this operation and began wondering what to do. The launch was fast, but would need something like twenty hours to reach Nantucket if he remembered the trip. There was that much time at least.

"We are weary," he said in English. "May we not rest a while?"

"*Ja, deedly,*" said Boierik with a clumsy graciousness. "*Ok wir skallen gode gefreonds bin, ni?*"

Sunset smoldered redly to the west. Deirdre and van Sarawak stood at the rail, looking across a gray waste of waters. Three crewmen, their brown paint and Asian garments removed, poised alert and weaponed on the poop; a man steered by compass; Boierik and Everard paced the quarterdeck, talking. All wore heavy cloaks against a stiff, stinging wind.

Everard was getting some proficiency in the Cimbrian language; his tongue still limped, but he could make himself understood. Mostly, though, he let Boierik do the talking.

"So you are from the stars? These matters I do not understand. I am a simple man. Had I my way, I would manage my Tuscan estate in peace and let the world rave as it will. But we of the Folk have our obligations." The Teutons seemed to have replaced the Latins altogether in Italy, as the Saxons had done the Britons in Everard's world.

"I know how you feel," said the Patrolman. "It is a strange thing, that so many should fight when so few want to."

"Oh, but it is necessary." Almost a whine there. "You don't understand. Carthagalann stole Egypt, our rightful possession."

"*Italia irredenta,*" murmured Everard.

"Huh?"

"Never mind. So you Cimbri are allied with Littorn, and hope to grab off Europe and Africa while the big powers are fighting in the East."

"Not at all!" replied Boierik indignantly. "We are merely asserting our rightful and historic territorial claims. Why, the king himself said—" And so on and so on.

Everard braced himself against the roll of the deck. "It seems to me that you treat us wizards rather hardily," he declared. "Beware lest we get really angered at you."

"All of us are protected against curses and shapings."

"Well—"

"I wish you would help us freely," said Boierik. "I will be happy to demonstrate to you the justice of our cause, if you have a few hours to spare."

Everard shook his head and stopped by Deirdre. Her face was a blur in the thickening dusk, but he caught a forlorn defiance in her voice: "I hope you are telling him what to do with his plans, Manslach."

"No," said Everard heavily. "We are going to help them."

She stood as if struck.

"What are you saying, Manse?" asked van Sarawak.

Everard told him.

"No!" said the Venusian.

"Yes," said Everard.

"By God, no! I'll—"

Everard grabbed his arm and said coldly: "Be still. I know what I'm doing. We can't take sides in this world, we're against everybody and

37

you'd better realize it. The only thing to do is play along with these fellows for a while. And don't tell that to Deirdre."

Van Sarawak bent his head and stood for a moment, thinking. "All right," he said dully.

The Littornian resort was on the southern shore of Nantucket, near a fishing village but walled off from it. The embassy had built in the style of its homeland, long timber houses with roofs arched like a cat's back, a main hall and its outbuildings enclosing a flagged courtyard. Everard finished a night's sleep and a breakfast made miserable by Deirdre's eyes by standing on deck as they came to the private pier. Another, bigger launch was already there, and the grounds swarmed with hard-looking men. Arkonsky's eyes kindled, and he said in Afallonian: "I see the magic engine has been brought. We can go right to work."

When Boierik interpreted, Everard felt his heart slam.

The guests, as the Cimbrian insisted on calling them, were led into a great room where Arkonsky bent the knee to an idol with four faces, that Svantevit which the Danes had chopped up for firewood in the other history. There was a blaze on the hearth against the autumn chill, and guards posted around the walls. Everard had eyes only for the scooter, where it stood gleaming on the floor.

"I hear it was a hard fight in Catuvellaunan," remarked Boierik to him. "Many were killed, but our folk got away without being followed." He touched a handlebar gingerly. "And this wain can truly appear anywhere it wishes, out of thin air?"

"Yes," said Everard.

Deirdre gave him a look of scorn such as he had never known. She stood haughtily away from him and van Sarawak.

Arkonsky spoke to her, something he wanted translated. She spat at his feet. Boierik sighed and gave the word to Everard:

"We wish the engine demonstrated. You and I will go for a ride on it. I warn you, I will have a revolver at your back; you will tell me in advance everything you mean to do, and if aught untoward happens I will shoot. Your friends will remain here as hostages, also to be shot on the first suspicion. But I'm sure we will all be good friends."

Everard nodded. There was a tautness thrumming in him, and his palms felt cold and wet. "First I must say a spell," he answered.

His eyes flicked. One glance memorized the spatial reading of the position meters and the time reading of the clock on the scooter. Another look showed van Sarawak seated on a bench, under Arkonsky's drawn

pistol and the rifles of the guards; Deirdre sat down too, stiffly, as far
from him as she could get. Everard made a close estimate of the bench's
position relative to the scooter's, lifted his arms, and chanted in
Temporal:

"Van, I'm going to try to pull you out of here. Stay exactly where
you are now; repeat, exactly. I'll pick you up on the fly. If all goes well,
that'll happen about one minute after I blink out of here with our shaggy
comrade."

The Venusian sat wooden-faced. There was a thin beading of sweat
on his forehead.

"Very good," said Everard in his pidgin Cimbrian. "Mount on the
rear saddle, Boierik, and we'll put this magic horse through her paces."

The big man nodded and obeyed. As Everard took the front seat, he
felt a gun muzzle held shakily against his back. "Tell Arkonsky we'll be
back in half an hour," he added; they had approximately the same time
units here as in his world, both descended from the Babylonian. When
that had been taken care of, Everard said: "The first thing we will do is
appear in midair over the ocean and hover."

"F-f-ine," said Boierik. He didn't sound very convinced.

Everard set the space controls for ten miles east and a thousand feet
up and threw the main switch.

They sat like witches astride a broom, looking down on a greenish-
gray sweep of waters and the distant blur which was land. The wind was
high, it caught at them and Everard gripped tight with his knees. He
heard Boierik's oath and smiled wanly.

"Well," he asked, "how do you like this?"

"It . . . it is wonderful." As he grew accustomed to the idea, the
Cimbrian gathered enthusiasm. "Why, with machines like this, we can
soar above enemy cities and pelt them with fire."

Somehow, that made Everard feel better about what he was going to
do.

"Now we will fly ahead," he announced, and sent the scooter gliding
through the air. Boierik whooped exuberantly. "And now we will make
the instantaneous jump to your homeland."

Everard threw the maneuver switch. The scooter looped the loop and
dropped at a three-gee acceleration.

Forewarned, the Patrolman could still barely hang on. He never
knew whether the curve or the dive had thrown Boierik; he only had a
moment's hideous glimpse of the man plunging down through windy
spaces to the sea.

For a little while, then, Everard hung above the waves. His first reaction was a cold shudder . . . suppose Boierik had had time to shoot? His second was a gray guilt. Both he dismissed, and concentrated on the problem of rescuing van Sarawak.

He set the space verniers for one foot in front of the prisoners' bench, the time unit for one minute after he had departed. His right hand he kept by the controls—he'd have to work fast—and his left free.

Hang on to your seats, fellahs. Here we go again.

The machine flashed into existence almost in front of van Sarawak. Everard clutched the Venusian's tunic and hauled him close, inside the spatiotemporal field, even as his right hand spun the time dial back and snapped over the main switch.

A bullet caromed off metal. Everard had a moment's glimpse of Arkonsky shouting. And then it was all gone and they were on a grassy hill sloping down to the beach. It was 2,000 years ago.

He collapsed shivering over the handlebars.

A cry brought him back to awareness. He twisted around, looking at van Sarawak where the Venusian sprawled on the hillside. One arm was still around Deirdre's waist.

The wind lulled, and the sea rolled into a broad white strand, and clouds walked high in heaven.

"I can't say I blame you, Van." Everard paced before the scooter and looked at the ground. "But it does complicate matters greatly."

"What was I supposed to do?" There was a raw note in the other's voice. "Leave her there for those bastards to kill—or to be snuffed out with her entire universe?"

"In case you've forgotten, we're conditioned against revealing the Patrol's existence to unauthorized people," said Everard. "We couldn't tell her the truth even if we wanted to . . . and I, for one, don't want to."

He looked at the girl. She stood breathing heavily, with a dawn in her eyes. The wind caressed her hair and the long thin dress.

She shook her head, as if clearing a mist of nightmare, and ran over to clasp their hands. "Forgive me, Manslach," she whispered. "I should have known you'd not betray us."

She kissed him and van Sarawak. The Venusian responded eagerly, but Everard couldn't bring himself to. He would have remembered Judas.

"Where are we?" she chattered. "It looks almost like Llangollen, but no men— Have you taken us to the Happy Isles?" She spun on one foot and danced among summer flowers. "Can we rest here a while before returning home?"

Everard drew a long breath. "I've bad news for you, Deirdre," he said.

She grew silent, and he saw her gather herself.

"We can't go back."

She waited mutely.

"The—the spells I had to use, to save our lives . . . I had no choice, but those spells debar us from returning home."

"There is no hope?" He could barely hear her.

Everard's eyes stung. "No," he said.

She turned and walked away. Van Sarawak moved to follow her, but thought better of it and sat down beside Everard. "What'd you tell her?" he asked.

Everard repeated his words. "It seemed the best compromise," he finished. "I can't send her back to—what's waiting for this world."

"No." Van Sarawak sat quiet for a while, staring across the sea. Then: "What year is this? About the time of Christ? Then we're still upstairs of the turning point."

"Yeh. And we still have to find out what it was."

"Let's go back to the farther past. Lots of Patrol offices. We can recruit help there."

"Maybe." Everard lay back in the grass and regarded the sky. Reaction overwhelmed him. "I think I can locate the key event right here, though, with Deirdre's help. Wake me up when she comes back."

She returned dry-eyed, a desolate calm over her. When Everard asked if she would assist in his own mission, she nodded. "Of course. My life is yours who saved it."

After getting you into that mess in the first place. Everard said carefully: "All I want from you is some information. Do you know about . . . about putting people to sleep, a sleep in which they may believe anything they're told?"

"Y-yes," she said doubtfully. "I've seen medical Druids do that."

"It won't harm you. I only wish to make you sleep so you can remember everything you know, things you believe forgotten. It won't take long."

Her trustfulness was hard to endure. Using Patrol techniques, Everard put her in a hypnotic state of total recall and dredged out all she had ever read or heard about the Second Punic War. That added up to enough for his purposes.

Roman interference with Carthaginian enterprise south of the Ebro, in direct violation of treaty, had been the last roweling. In 219 B.C. Hannibal Barca, governor of Carthaginian Spain, laid siege to Saguntum. After eight months he took it, and thus provoked his long-planned war with Rome. At the beginning of May, 218, he crossed the Pyrenees with 90,000 infantry, 12,000 cavalry, and 37 elephants, marched through Gaul, and went over the Alps. His losses en route were gruesome: only 20,000 foot and 6,000 horse reached Italy late in the year. Nevertheless, near the Ticinus River he met and broke a superior Roman force. In the course of the following year, he fought several bloodily victorious battles and advanced into Apulia and Campania.

The Apulians, Lucaninas, Bruttians, and Samnites went over to his side. Quintus Fabius Maximus fought a grim guerrilla war, which laid Italy waste and decided nothing. But meanwhile Hasdrubal Barca was organizing Spain, and in 211 he arrived with reinforcements. In 210 Hannibal took and burned Rome, and in 207 the last cities of the confederacy surrendered to him.

"That's it," said Everard. He stroked the coppery hair of the girl lying beside him. "Go to sleep now. Sleep well and wake up glad of heart."

"What'd she tell you?" asked van Sarawak.

"A lot of detail," said Everard—the whole story had required more than an hour. "The important thing is this: her knowledge of history is good, but never mentions the Scipios."

"The who's?"

"Publius Cornelius Scipio commanded the Roman army at Ticinus, and was beaten there. But later he had the intelligence to turn westward and gnaw away the Carthaginian base in Spain. It ended with Hannibal being effectively cut off in Italy, and the Iberian help which could be sent was annihilated. Scipio's son of the same name also held a high command, and was the man who finally whipped Hannibal at Zama; that's Scipio Africanus the Elder.

"Father and son were by far the best leaders Rome had—but Deirdre never heard of them."

"So—" Van Sarawak stared eastward across the sea, where Gauls and Cimbri and Parthians were ramping through the shattered Classical world. "What happened to them in this time line?"

"My own total recall tells me that both the Scipios were at Ticinus, and very nearly killed; the son saved his father's life during the retreat, which I imagine was more like a stampede. One gets you ten that in *this* history the Scipios died there."

"Somebody must have knocked them off," said van Sarawak on a rising note. "Some time traveler . . . it could only have been that."

"Well, it seems probable, anyhow. We'll see." Everard looked away from Deirdre's slumbrous face. "We'll see."

At the Pleistocene resort—half an hour after having left it—the Patrolmen put the girl in charge of a sympathetic Greek-speaking matron and summoned their colleagues. Then the message capsules began jumping through space-time.

All offices prior to 218 B.C.—the closest was Alexandria, 250 - 230—were "still" there, two hundred or so agents altogether. Written contact with the future was confirmed to be impossible, and a few short jaunts upstairs clinched the proof. A worried conference met at the Academy, back in the Oligocene Period. Unattached agents ranked those with steady assignments but not each other; on the basis of his own experience, Everard found himself the chairman of a committee of top-bracket officers.

It was a frustrating job. These men and women had leaped centuries and wielded the weapons of gods; but they were still human, with all the ingrained orneriness of their race.

Everyone agreed that the damage would have to be repaired. But there was fear for those agents who had gone ahead into time before being warned; if they weren't back when history was re-altered, they would never be seen again. Everard deputized parties to attempt rescue, but doubted there'd be much success; he warned them sternly to return in a day or face the consequences.

A man from the Scientific Renaissance had another point to make. Granted, it was the survivors' plain duty to restore the original time track. But they had a duty to knowledge as well. Here was a unique chance to study a whole new phase of humankind; there should be several years' anthropological work done before— Everard slapped him down with difficulty. There weren't so many Patrolmen left that they could take the risk.

Study groups had to determine the exact moment and circumstances of the change. The wrangling over methods went on interminably.

Everard glared out the window, into the prehuman night, and wondered if the sabertooths weren't doing a better job after all than their simian successors.

When he had finally gotten his bands dispatched, he broke out a bottle and got drunk with van Sarawak.

Reconvening the next day, the steering committee heard from its deputies, who had run up a total of years in the future. A dozen Patrolmen had been rescued from more or less ignominious situations; another score would simply have to be written off. The spy group's report was more interesting. It seemed that there had been two Helvetian mercenaries who joined Hannibal in the Alps and won his confidence. After the war, they had risen to high positions in Carthage; under the names of Phrontes and Himilco, they had practically run the government, engineered Hannibal's murder, and set new records for luxurious living. One of the Patrolmen had seen their homes and the men themselves. "A lot of improvements that hadn't been thought of in Classical times. The fellows looked to me like Neldorians, 205th Millennium."

Everard nodded. That was an age of bandits who had "already" given the Patrol a lot of work. "I think we've settled the matter," he said. "It makes no difference whether they were with Hannibal before Ticinus or not. We'd have hell's own time arresting them in the Alps without tipping our hand and changing the future ourselves. What counts is that they seem to have rubbed out the Scipios, and that's the point we'll have to strike at."

A Nineteenth-Century Britisher, competent but with elements of Colonel Blimp, unrolled a map and discoursed on his aerial observations of the battle. He'd used an infra-red telescope to look through low clouds. "And here the Romans stood—"

"I know," said Everard. "A thin red line. The moment when they took flight is the crucial one, but the confusion then also gives us our chance. Okay, we'll want to surround the battlefield unobtrusively, but I don't think we can get away with more than two agents actually on the scene. The Alexandria office can supply Van and me with costumes."

"I say," exclaimed the Englishman. "I thought I'd have the privilege."

"No. Sorry." Everard smiled with one corner of his mouth. "It's no privilege, anyway. Risk your neck, and all to wipe out a world of people like yourself."

"But dash it all—"

Everard rose. "I've got to go," he said flatly. "I don't know why, but I've got to."

Van Sarawak nodded.

They left their scooter in a clump of trees and started across the field. Around the horizon and up in the sky waited a hundred armed Patrolmen, but that was small consolation here among spears and arrows. Lowering clouds hurried before a cold whistling wind, there was a spatter of rain, sunny Italy was enjoying its late fall.

The cuirass was heavy on Everard's shoulders as he trotted across blood-slippery mud. He had helmet, greaves, a Roman shield on his left arm, and a sword at his waist; but his right hand gripped a stunner. Van Sarawak loped behind, similarly equipped, eyes shifting under the wind-ruffled officer's plume.

Trumpets howled and drums stuttered. It was all but lost among the yells of men and tramp of feet, screaming horses and whining arrows. The legion of Carthage was pressing in, hammering edged metal against the buckling Roman lines. Here and there the fight was already breaking up into small knots, where men cursed and cut at strangers.

The combat had passed over this area and swayed beyond. Death lay around him. Everard hurried behind the Roman force, toward the distant gleam of the eagles. Across helmets and corpses, he made out a banner that fluttered triumphant, vivid red and purple against the unrestful sky. And there, looming gray and monstrous, lifting their trunks and bellowing, came a squad of elephants.

He had seen war before. It was always the same—not a neat affair of lines across maps, nor a hallooing gallantry, but men who gasped and sweated and bled in bewilderment.

A slight, dark-faced youth squirmed nearby, trying feebly to pull out the javelin which had pierced his stomach. He was a cavalryman from Carthage, but the burly Italian peasant who sat next to him, staring without belief at the stump of an arm, paid no attention.

A flight of crows hovered overhead, riding the wind and waiting.

"This way," muttered Everard. "Hurry up, for God's sake! That line's going to break any minute."

The breath was raw in his throat as he panted toward the standards of the Republic. It came to him that he'd always rather wished Hannibal had won. There was something repellent about the cold, unimaginative greed of Rome. And here he was, trying to save the city. Well-a-day, life was often an odd business.

It was some consolation that Scipio Africanus was one of the few decent men left after the war.

Screaming and clangor lifted, and the Italians reeled back. Everard saw something like a wave smashed against a rock. But it was the rock which advanced, crying out and stabbing, stabbing.

He began to run. A legionary went past, howling his panic. A grizzled Roman veteran spat on the ground, braced his feet, and stood where he was till they cut him down. Hannibal's elephants squealed and lifted curving tusks. The ranks of Carthage held firm, advancing to the inhuman pulse of their drums. Cavalry skirmished on the wings in a toothpick flash of lances.

Up ahead, now! Everard saw men on horseback, Roman officers. They held the eagles aloft and shouted, but nobody could hear them above the din.

A small group of legionaries came past and halted. Their leader hailed the Patrolmen: "Over here! We'll give them a fight, by the belly of Venus!"

Everard shook his head and tried to go past. The Roman snarled and sprang at him. "Come here, you cowardly—" A stun beam cut off his words and he crashed into the muck. His men shuddered, someone screamed, and the party broke into flight.

The Carthaginians were very near, shield to shield and swords running red. Everard could see a scar livid on the cheek of one man, and the great hook nose of another. A hurled spear clanged off his helmet, he lowered his head and ran.

A combat loomed before him. He tried to go around, and tripped on a gashed corpse. A Roman stumbled over him in turn. Van Sarawak cursed and dragged him away. A sword furrowed the Venusian's arm.

Beyond, Scipio's men were surrounded and battling without hope. Everard halted, sucking air into starved lungs, and looked into the thin rain. Armor gleamed wetly, Roman horsemen galloping in with mud up to their mounts' noses—that must be the son, Scipio Africanus to be, hastening to his father. The hoofbeats were like thunder in the earth.

"Over there!"

Van Sarawak cried it out and pointed. Everard crouched where he was, rain dripping off his helmet and down his face. A small troop of Carthaginians was riding toward the battle around the eagles, and at their head were two men with the height and craggy features of Neldor. They were clad in the usual G.I. armor, but each of them held a slim-barreled gun.

"This way!" Everard spun on his heel and dashed toward them. The leather in his cuirass creaked as he ran.

They were close to the newcomers before they were seen. A Carthaginian face swung to them and called the warning. Everard saw how he grinned in his beard. One of the Neldorians scowled and aimed his blast-rifle.

Everard went on his stomach, and the vicious blue-white beam sizzled where he had been. He snapped a shot and one of the African horses went over in a roar of metal. Van Sarawak stood his ground and fired steadily. Two, three, four—and there went a Neldorian, down in the mud!

Men hewed at each other around the Scipios. The Neldorians' escort yelled with terror. They must have had the blasters demonstrated, but these invisible blows were something else. They bolted. The second of the bandits got his horse under control and turned to follow.

"Take care of the one you potted," gasped Everard. "Haul him off the battlefield—we'll want to question—" He himself scrambled to his feet and made for a riderless horse. He was in the saddle and after the remaining Neldorian before he was fully aware of it.

They fled through chaos. Everard urged speed from his mount, but was content to pursue. Once they'd got out of sight, a scooter could swoop down and make short work of his quarry.

The same thought must have occurred to the time rover. He reined in and took aim. Everard saw the blinding flash and felt his cheek sting with a near miss. He set his pistol to wide beam and rode in shooting.

Another fire-bolt took his horse full in the breast. The animal toppled and Everard went out of the saddle. Trained reflexes softened the fall, he bounced dizzily to his feet and staggered toward his enemy. His stunner was gone, no time to look for it. Never mind, it could be salvaged later, if he lived. The widened beam had found its mark; it wasn't strong enough to knock a man out, but the Neldorian had dropped his rifle and the horse stood swaying with closed eyes.

Rain beat in Everard's face. He slogged up to the mount. The Neldorian jumped to earth and drew a sword. Everard's own blade rasped forth.

"As you will," he said in Latin. "One of us will not leave this field."

The moon rose over mountains and turned the snow to a sudden wan glitter. Far in the north, a glacier threw back the light in broken shards, and a wolf howled. The Cro-Magnons chanted in their cave, it drifted faintly through to the veranda.

Deirdre stood in darkness, looking out. Moonlight dappled her face and caught a gleam of tears. She started as Everard and van Sarawak came up behind her.

"Are you back so soon?" she asked. "You only came here and left me this morning."

"It didn't take long," said van Sarawak. He had gotten a hypno in Attic Greek.

"I hope . . ." She tried to smile. "I hope you have finished your task and can rest from your labors."

"Yes," said Everard. "Yes, we finished it."

They stood side by side for a while, looking out on a world of winter.

"Is it true what you said, that I can never go home?" asked Deirdre.

"I'm afraid so. The spells—" Everard shrugged and swapped a glance with van Sarawak.

They had official permission to tell the girl as much as they wished and take her wherever they thought she could live best. Van Sarawak maintained that that would be Venus in his century, and Everard was too tired to argue.

Deirdre drew a long breath. "So be it," she said. "I'll not waste a life weeping for it . . . but the Baal grant that they have it well, my people at home."

"I'm sure they will," said Everard.

Suddenly he could do no more. He only wanted to sleep. Let van Sarawak say what had to be said, and reap whatever rewards there might be.

He nodded at his companion. "I'm turning in," he declared. "Carry on, Van."

The Venusian took the girl's arm. Everard went slowly back to his room.

The Wheels of If

L. Sprague de Camp

*K*ing Oswiu of Northumbria squirmed in his chair. *In the first place these synods bored him. In the second, his mathematics comprised the ability to add and subtract numbers under twenty on his fingers. Hence all this argument among the learned clerics, assembled in Whitby in the year of Our Lord 664, about the date of Easter and the phases of the moon and cycles of 84 and 532 years, went over the King's head completely.*

What did the exact date of Easter matter, anyhow? If they wanted to, why couldn't the Latins celebrate their Easter when they wanted, and the Ionans celebrate theirs? The Ionans had been doing all right, as far as Oswiu could see. And then this Wilfrid of York had to bring in his swarms of Latin priests, objecting to this and that as schismatic, heretical, etc. They were abetted by Oswiu's queen, Eanfled, which put poor Oswiu in an awkward position. He not only wanted peace in the family, but also hoped to attain to Heaven some day. Moreover, he liked the Abbot Colman, leader of the Ionans. And he certainly didn't want any far-off Bishop of Rome sticking his nose into his affairs. On the other hand . . .

King Oswiu came to with a jerk. Father Wilfrid was speaking to him directly: ". . . the arguments of my learned friend—" *he indicated the Abbot Colman of Lindisfarne* "—are very ingenious, I admit. But that is not the fundamental question. The real decision is, shall we accept the authority of His Holiness of Rome, like good Christians, or—"

"Wait a minute, wait a minute," *interrupted Oswiu.* "Why must we accept Gregory's authority to be good Christians? I'm a good Christian, and I don't let any foreign—"

"*The question, my lord, is whether one can be a good Christian and a rebel against—*"

"*I am too a good Christian!*" bristled Oswiu.

Wilfrid of York smiled. "*Perhaps you remember the statement of our Savior to Peter, the first Bishop of Rome?* 'Thou art Peter; and upon this rock I will build my Church; and the gates of Hell shall not prevail against it. And I will give unto thee the keys of the Kingdom of Heaven; and whatsoever thou shalt bind on earth shall be bound in heaven; and whatsoever thou shalt loose on earth shall be loosed in Heaven.' You see?"

Oswiu thought. *That put a different light on the matter. If this fellow Peter actually had the keys of Heaven . . .*

He turned to the Abbot Colman and asked: "*Is that a correct quotation?*"

"*It is, my lord. But—*"

"*Just a minute, just a minute. You'll get me all confused again if you start arguing. Now, can you quote a text showing that equivalent powers were granted to Saint Columba?*"

The grave Irishman's face registered sudden dismay. He frowned in concentration so intense that one could almost hear the wheels.

"*Well?*" said Oswiu. "*Speak up!*"

Colman sighed. "*No, my lord, I cannot. But I can show that it is the Latins, not we, who are departing from—*"

"*That's enough, Colman!*" Oswiu's single-track mind, once made up, had no intention of being disturbed again. "*I have decided that from this day forth the Kingdom of Northumbria shall follow the Latin practice concerning Easter. And that we shall declare our allegiance to the Roman Bishop Gregory, lest, when I come to the gates of Heaven, there would be none to open them for me—he being my adversary who has the keys. The synod is adjourned.*"

King Oswiu went out, avoiding the reproachful look that the Abbot sent after him. It was a dirty trick on Colman, who was a very decent chap. But after all, it wouldn't do to antagonize the heavenly doorman. And maybe now Eanfled would stop nagging him . . .

Allister Park rubbed his eyes and sat up in bed, as he usually did. He noticed nothing wrong until he looked at the sleeve of his pajamas.

He could not recall ever having had a pair of pajamas of that singularly repulsive green. He couldn't recall having changed to clean pajamas the night before. In short, he couldn't account for these pajamas at all.

Oh, well, probably, Eunice or Mary had given them to him, and he'd put them on without thinking. He yawned, brushing his mouth with the back of his hand.

He jerked his hand away. Then he cautiously felt his upper lip.

He got out of bed and made for the nearest mirror. There was no doubt about it. He had a mustache. He had not had a mustache when he went to bed the night before.

'Abd-ar-Rahman, Governor of Cordoba for the Khalifah Hisham ibn 'Abd-al-Malik, Lord of Damascus, Protector of the Faithful, etc., etc., paced his tent like a caged leopard with claustrophobia. He hated inactivity, and to him the last six days of tentative skirmishing had been just that.

He glowered over his pepper-and-salt beard at his chiefs, sitting cross-legged in an ellipse on the rugs. "Well?" he barked.

Yezid spoke up. "But a little longer, Commander-in-Chief, and the Franks will melt away. The infidels have little cavalry, save Gothic and Aquitanian refugees. Without cavalry, they cannot keep themselves fed. Our horse can range the country, supplying us and cutting off help from our enemies. There is no God but God."

Ya'qub snorted. "How long do you think our men will abide this fearful Frankish climate? The winter is almost upon us. I say strike now, while their spirits are still up. This rabble of Frankish farmers on foot will show some rare running. Have the armies of the Faithful come this far by sitting in front of their enemies and making grimaces at them?"

Yezid delivered an impressive snort of his own. "Just the advice one would expect from a dog of a Ma'ddite. This Karel, who commands the infidels, is no fool—"

"Who's a dog?" yelped Ya'qub, jumping up. "Pig of a Yemenite—"

'Abd-ar-Rahman yelled at them until they subsided. One major idea of this foray into Francia was to bury the animosity between members of the two parties. Yezid's starting a quarrel on political grounds put the Governor in an embarrassing position, as he was a Yemenite himself. He was still undecided. An intelligent man, he could see the sense to Yezid's Fabian advice. Emotionally, however, he burned to get to grips with the army of Charles, Mayor of Austrasia. And Yezid should be punished for his insulting remark.

"I have decided," said 'Abd-ar-Rahman, "that, while there is much to be said on both sides, Ya'qub's advice is the sounder. Nothing hurts an army's spirit like waiting. Besides, God has planned the outcome of the battle anyway. So why should we fear? If He decides that we shall win, we shall win.

"Therefore tomorrow, Saturday, we shall strike the Franks with all our force. God is God, and Mohammed is His prophet . . ."

But the next night 'Abd-ar-Rahman lay dead by the banks of the River Vienne, near Tours, with his handsome face waxy in the starlight and blood in his pepper-and-salt beard. The Austrasian line had held. Yezid, who had been right, was dead likewise, and so was Ya'qub, who had been wrong. And the surviving Arabs were fleeing back to Narbonne and Barcelona.

Allister Park opened the door of his apartment and grabbed up his *Times.* Sure enough, the date was Monday, April eleventh, just as it ought to have been. The year was right, too. That ruled out the possibility of amnesia.

He went back to the mirror. He was still a slightly stout man in his middle thirties, with pale-blue eyes and thinning sandy hair. But he wasn't the same man. The nose was different. So were the eyebrows. The scar under the chin was gone . . .

He gave up his self-inspection and got out his clothes. At that juncture he got another shock. The clothes weren't his. Or rather, they were clothes for a man of his size, and of the quality that a self-indulgent bachelor with an income of $12,000 a year would buy. Park didn't object to the clothes. It was just that they weren't *his* clothes.

Park gave up speculation about his sanity for the nonce; he had to get dressed. Breakfast? He was sick of the more cardboard-like cereals. To hell with it; he'd make himself some French toast. If it put another inch on his middle, he'd sweat it off Sunday at the New York Athletic Club.

The mail was thrust under his door. He finished knotting his necktie and picked it up. The letters were all addressed to a Mr. Arthur Vogel.

Then Allister Park, really awake, did look around. The apartment was built on the same plan as his own, but it wasn't the same. The furniture was different. Lots of little things were different, such as a nick in the wall that shouldn't be there.

Park sat down and smoked a cigarette while he thought. There was no evidence of kidnapping, which, considering his business, was not too unlikely a possibility. He'd gone to bed Sunday night sober, alone, and reasonably early. Why should he wake up in another man's apartment? He forgot for the moment that he had also awakened with another man's face. Before he had time to remember it, the sight of the clock jostled him into action. No time for French toast—it would have to be semi-edible cardboard after all.

But the real shock awaited him when he looked for his briefcase. There was none. Neither was there any sign of the sheaf of notes he had so carefully drawn up on the conduct of the forthcoming Antonini case. That was more than important. On his convicting the Antonini gang depended his nomination for District Attorney for the County of New York next fall. The present DA was due to get the bipartisan nomination to the Court of General Sessions at the same time.

He was planning, with thoroughly dishonorable motives, to invite Martha up for dinner. But he didn't want to have dinner with her until he'd cleared this matter up. The only trouble with calling her up was that the address-book didn't have her name in it—or indeed the name of anybody Park had ever heard of. Neither was he listed in the 'phone book.

He dialed CAnal 6-5700. Somebody said: "Department of Hospitals."

"Huh? Isn't this CAnal 6-5700?"

"Yes, this is the Department of Hospitals."

"Well what's the District Attorney's office then? Hell, I ought to know my own office 'phone."

"The District Attorney's office is WOrth 2-2200."

Park groggily called WOrth 2-2200. "Mr. Park's office, please."

"What office did you ask for, please?"

"The office of Assistant District Attorney Park!" Park's voice took on the metallic rasp. "Racket Bureau to you, sister."

"I'm sorry, we have no such person."

"Listen, young lady, have you got a Deputy Assistant DA named Frenczko? John Frenczko? You spell it with a z."

Silence. "No, I'm sorry, we have no such person."

Allister Park hung up.

The old building at 137 Center was still there. The Racket Bureau was still there. But they had never heard of Allister Park. They already had an Assistant DA of their own, a man named Hutchison, with whom they seemed quite well satisfied. There was no sign of Park's two deputies, Frenczko and Burt.

As a last hope, Park went over to the Criminal Courts Building. If he wasn't utterly mad, the case of *People* v. *Cassidy,* extortion, ought to come up as soon after ten as it would take Judge Segal to read his calendar. Frenczko and Burt would be in there, after Cassidy's hide.

But there was no Judge Segal, no Frenczko, no Burt, no Cassidy . . .

"Very interesting, Mr. Park," soothed the psychiatrist. "Very interesting indeed. The most hopeful feature is that you quite realize your difficulty, and come to me now—"

"What I want to know," interrupted Park, "is: was I sane up to yesterday, and crazy since then, or was I crazy up to then and sane now?"

"It seems hard to believe that one could suffer from a coherent set of illusions for thirty-six years," replied the psychiatrist. "Yet your present account of your perceptions seems rational enough. Perhaps your memory of what you saw and experienced today is at fault."

"But I want to get straightened out! My whole political future depends on it! At least—" he stopped. *Was* there such an Antonini gang? *Was* there a nomination awaiting an Allister Park if they were convicted?

"I know," said the psychiatrist gently. "But this case isn't like any I ever heard of. You go ahead and wire Denver for Allister Park's birth-certificate. We'll see if there is such a person. Then come back tomorrow . . ."

Park awoke, looked around, and groaned. The room had changed again. But he choked off his groan. He was occupying a twin bed. In its mate lay a fair-to-middling handsome woman of about his own age.

His groan had roused her. She asked: "How are you feeling, Wally?"

"I'm feeling fine," he mumbled. The significance of his position was soaking in. He had some trouble suppressing another groan. About marriage, he was an adherent of the why-buy-a-cow philosophy, as he had had occasion to make clear to many women by way of fair warning.

"I hope you are," said the woman anxiously. "You acted so queer yesterday. Do you remember your appointment with Dr. Kerr?"

"I certainly do," said Park. Kerr was not the name of the psychiatrist with whom he had made the appointment.

The woman prepared to dress. Park gulped a little. For years he'd managed to get along without being mixed up with other men's wives, ever since . . .

And he wished he knew her name. A well-mannered man, under those circumstances, wouldn't refer to the woman as "Hey, you."

"What are we having for breakfast, sweetie-pie?" he asked with a sickly grin. She told him, adding: "You never called me that before, dear." When she started toward him with an expectant smile, he jumped out of bed and dressed with frantic haste.

He ate silently. When the woman inquired why, he pointed to his mouth and mumbled: "Canker sore. It hurts to talk."

He fled as soon as he decently could, without learning his "wife's" name. His wallet told him his name was Wallace Heineman, but little else about himself. If he wanted to badly enough, he could no doubt find out whom he worked for, who his friends were, which if any bank he had money in, etc. But if these daily changes were going to continue, it hardly seemed worthwhile. The first thing was to get back to that psychiatrist.

Although the numbers of the streets were different, the general layout was the same. Half an hour's walking brought him to the block where the psychiatrist's office had been. The building had been on the southeast corner of Fifty-seventh and Eighth. Park could have sworn the building that now occupied that site was different.

However, he went up anyway. He had made a careful note of the office number. His notebook had been missing that morning, like all the rest of his (or rather Arthur Vogel's) things. Still, he remembered the number.

The number turned out to be that of a suite of offices occupied by Williamson, Ostendorff, Cohen, Burke, and Williamson, Attorneys. No, they had never heard of Park's brain-man. Yes, Williamson, Ostendorff, Cohen, Burke, and Williamson had occupied those offices for years.

Park came out into the street and stood a long time, thinking. A phenomenon that he had hitherto noticed only vaguely now puzzled him: the extraordinary number of Union Jacks in sight.

He asked the traffic cop about it. The cop looked at him. "King's buithday," he said.

"What king?"

"Why, *our* king of course. David the Fuist." The cop touched his finger to the peak of his cap.

Park settled himself on a park bench with a newspaper. The paper was full of things like references to the recent Anglo-Russian war, the launching of the *Queen Victoria,* His Majesty's visit to a soap factory ("where he displayed a keen interest in the technical problems involved in . . ."), the victory of Massachusetts over Quebec in the Inter-Colonial football matches (Massachusetts a colony? And football in April?), the trial of one Diedrichs for murdering a man with a cross-cut saw . . .

All this was very interesting, especially the Diedrichs case. But Allister Park was more concerned with the whereabouts and probable fate of the Antonini gang. He also thought with gentle melancholy of Mary and Eunice and Dorothy and Martha and Joan and. . . . But that was less important than the beautiful case he had dug up against such a slimy set of public enemies. Even Park, despite the cynical view of humanity that public prosecutors get, had felt a righteous glow when he tallied up the evidence and knew he had them.

And the nomination was not to be sneezed at either. It just happened that he was available when it was a Protestant's turn at that nomination. If he missed out, he'd have to wait while a Catholic and a Jew took theirs. Since you had to be one or the other to get nominated at all, Park had become perforce a church member and regular if slightly hypocritical goer.

His plan was, after a few terms as DA, to follow the incumbent DA onto the bench. You would never have guessed it, but inside Allister Park lingered enough of the idealism that as a young lawyer he had brought from Colorado to give the bench an attractiveness not entirely comprised of salary and social position.

He looked in his pockets. There was enough there for one good bender.

Of the rest of the day, he never could remember much afterwards. He did remember giving a pound note to an old woman selling shoe-laces, leading a group of drunks in a song about one Columbo who knew the world was round-o (unexpurgated), and trying to take a fireman's hose away from him on the ground that the city was having a water shortage.

He awoke in another strange room, without a trace of a hangover. A quick look-around assured him that he was alone.

It was time, he thought, that he worked out a system for the investigation of his identity on each successive morning. He learned that his name was Wadsworth Noe. The pants of all the suits in his closet were baggy knee-pants, plus-fours.

Something was going *ping, ping, ping,* like one of those tactful alarm clocks. Park located the source of the noise in a goose-necked gadget on the table, which he finally identified as a telephone. As the transmitter and receiver were built into a single unit on the end of the goose-neck, there was nothing to lift off the hook. He pressed a button in the base. A voice spoke: "Waddy?"

"Oh—yeah. Who's this?"

"This is your little bunnykins."

Park swore under his breath. The voice sounded female and young, and had a slight indefinable accent. He stalled: "How are you this morning?"

"Oh, I'm fine. How's my little butter-ball?"

Park winced. Wadsworth Noe had a figure even more portly than Allister Park's. Park, with effort, infused syrup into his voice: "Oh, I'm fine too, sweetie-pie. Only I'm lonesome as all hell."

"Oh, isn't that too bad! Oo poor little thing! Shall I come up and cook dinner for my precious?"

"I'd love it." A plan was forming in Park's mind. Hitherto all these changes had taken place while he was asleep. If he could get somebody to sit around and watch him while he stayed up . . .

The date was made. Park found he'd have to market.

On the street, aside from the fact that all the men wore plus-fours and wide-brimmed hats, the first thing that struck him was the sight of two dark men in uniform. They walked in step down the middle of the sidewalk. Their walk implied that they expected people to get out of their way. People got. As the soldiers passed him, Park caught a sentence in a foreign language, sounding like Spanish.

At the market everyone spoke with that accent Park had heard over the 'phone. They fell silent when another pair of soldiers entered. These loudly demanded certain articles of food. A clerk scurried around and got the order. The soldiers took the things and departed without paying.

Park thought of going to a library to learn about the world he was in. But if he were going to shift again, it would hardly be worth while. He bought a *New York Record,* noticing that the stand also carried a lot of papers in French and Spanish.

Back in his apartment he read of His Majesty Napoleon V, apparently emperor of New York City and God knew what else!

His little bunnykins turned out to be a smallish dark girl, not bad-looking, who kissed him soundly. She said: "Where have you been the last few days, Waddy? I haven't heard from you for simply *ages*! I was beginning to think you'd forgotten me. Oo hasn't forgotten, has oo?"

"Me forget? Why, sweetie-pie, I couldn't any more forget you than I could forget my own name." (And what the hell's that? he asked himself. Wordsworth—no, Wadsworth Noe. Thank God.) "Give us another kiss."

She looked at him. "What makes you talk so funny, Waddy?"

"Canker sore," said Allister Park.

"O-o-o, you poor angel. Let me see it."

"It's all right. How about that famous dinner?"

At least Wadsworth Noe kept a good cellar. After dinner Park applied himself cautiously to this. It gave an excuse for just sitting. Park asked the girl about herself. She chattered on happily for some hours. Then the conversation began to run dry. There were long silences. She looked at him quizzically. "Are you worrying about something, Waddy? Somehow you seem like a different man."

"No," he lied. "I'm not worrying."

She looked at the clock. "I suppose I ought to go," she said hesitantly.

Park sat up. "Oh, please don't!"

She relaxed and smiled. "I didn't *think* you'd let me. Just wait." She disappeared into the bedroom and presently emerged in a filmy nightgown.

Allister Park was not surprised. But he was concerned. Attractive as the girl was, the thought of solving his predicament was more so. Besides, he was already sleepy from the liquors he had drunk.

"How about making some coffee, sweetie-pie?" he asked.

She acquiesced. The making and drinking of the coffee took another hour. It was close to midnight. To keep the ball rolling, Park told some stories. Then the conversation died down again. The girl yawned. She seemed puzzled and a bit resentful.

She asked: "Are you going to sit up all night?"

That was just what Park intended to do. But while he cast about for a plausible reason to give, he stalled: "Ever tell you about that man Wugson I met last week? Funniest chap you ever saw. He has a big bunch of hairs growing out the end of his nose . . ."

He went on in detail about the oddities of the imaginary Mr. Wugson. The girl had an expression of what-did-I-do-to-deserve-this. She yawned again.

Click! Allister Park rubbed his eyes and sat up. He was on a hard knobby thing that might, by gross misuse of the language, be called a mattress. His eyes focussed on a row of iron bars.

He was in jail.

Allister Park's day in jail proved neither interesting nor informative. He was marched out for meals and for an hour of exercise. Nobody spoke to him except a guard who asked: "Hey there, chief, who ja think you are today, huh? Julius Caesar?"

Park grinned. "Nope. I'm God, this time."

This was getting to be a bore. If one could do this flitting about from existence to existence voluntarily, it might be fun. As it was, one didn't stay put long enough to adjust oneself to any of these worlds of—illusion?

The next day he was a shabby fellow sleeping on a park bench. The city was still New York—no it wasn't; it was a different city built on the site of New York.

He had money for nothing more than a bottle of milk and a loaf of bread. These he bought and consumed slowly, while reading somebody's discarded newspaper. Reading was difficult because of the queer spelling. And the people had an accent that required the closest attention to understand.

He spent a couple of hours in an art museum. The guards looked at him as if he were something missed by the cleaners. When it closed he went back to his park bench and waited. Night came.

A car—at least, a four-wheeled power vehicle—drew up and a couple of cops got out. Park guessed they were cops because of their rhinestone epaulets. One asked: "Are you John Gilby?" He pronounced it: "Air yew Zhawn Gilbü?"

But Allister Park caught his drift. "Damned if I know, brother. Am I?"

The cops looked at each other. "He's him, all right," said one. To Park: "Come along."

Park learned, little by little, that he was not wanted for anything more serious than disappearance. He kept his own counsel until they arrived at the stationhouse.

Inside was a fat woman. She jumped up and pointed at him, crying raucously: "That's him! That's the dirty deserter, running off and leaving his poor wife to starve! The back of me hand to you, you dirty—"

"Please, Mrs. Gilby!" said the desk sergeant.

The woman was not to be silenced. "Heaven curse the day I met you! Sergeant darlin', what can I do to put the dirty loafer in jail where he belongs?"

"Well," said the sergeant uncomfortably, "you can charge him with desertion, of course. But don't you think you'd better go home and talk it over? We don't want to—"

"Hey!" cried Park. They looked at him. "I'll take jail, if you don't mind—"

Click! Once again he was in bed. It was a real bed this time. He looked around. The place had the unmistakable air of a sanitarium or hospital.

Oh, well. Park rolled over and went to sleep. The next day he was still in the same place. He began to have hopes. Then he remembered that, as the transitions happened at midnight, he had no reason for assuming that the next one would not happen the following midnight.

He spent a very boring day. A physician came in, asked him how he was, and was gone almost before Park could say "Fine." People brought him his meals. If he'd been sure he was going to linger, he'd have made vigorous efforts to orient himself and to get out. But as it was, there didn't seem any point.

The next morning he was still in bed. But when he tried to rub his eyes and sit up, he found that his wrists and ankles were firmly tied to the four posts. This wasn't the same bed, nor the same room; it looked like a room in somebody's private house.

And at the foot of the bed sat the somebody; a small gray-haired man with piercing black eyes that gleamed over a sharp nose.

For a few seconds Allister Park and the man looked at each other. Then the man's expression underwent a sudden and alarming change, as if internal pain had gripped him. He stared at his own clothes as if he had never seen them before. He screamed, jumped up, and dashed out of the room. Park heard his feet clattering down stairs, and the slam of a front door; then nothing.

Allister Park tried pulling at his bonds, but the harder he pulled, the tighter they gripped. So he tried not pulling, which brought no results either.

He listened. There was a faint hiss and purr of traffic outside. He must be still in a city, though, it seemed, a fairly quiet one.

A stair creaked. Park held his breath. Somebody was coming up, and without unnecessary noise. More than one man, Park thought, listening to the creaks.

Somebody stumbled. From far below a voice called up a question that Park couldn't catch. There were several quick steps and the smack of a fist.

The door of Park's room was ajar. Through the crack appeared a vertical strip of face, including an eye. The eye looked at Park and Park looked at the eye.

The door jerked open and three men pounced into the room. They wore floppy trousers and loose blouses that might have come out of a Russian ballet. They had large, flat, pentagonal faces, red-brown skins and straight black hair. They peered behind the door and under the bed.

"What the hell?" asked Allister Park.

The largest of the three men looked at him. "You're not hurt, Hallow?"

"No. But I'm damn sick of being tied up."

The large man's face showed a flicker of surprise. The large man cut Park's lashings. Park sat up, rubbing his wrists, and learned that he was wearing a suit of coarse woolen underwear.

"Where's the rascally Noggle?" asked the large brown man. Although he rolled his r's like a Scot, he did not look like a Scot. Park thought he might be an Asiatic or an American Indian.

"You mean the little gray-haired bird?"

"Sure. You know, the scoundrel." He pronounced the "k" in "know."

"Suppose I do. When I woke up he was in that chair. He looked at me and beat it out of here as if all the bats of Hell were after him."

"Maybe he's gone daft. But the weighty thing is to get you out." One of the men got a suit out of the closet, resembling the three men's clothes, but somber gray.

Allister Park dressed. The tenseness of the men made him hurry, though he didn't take all this very seriously yet.

Working his feet into the elastic-sided shoes with the big metal buckles, Park asked: "How long have I been here?"

"You dropped from the ken of a man a week ago today," replied the large man with a keen look.

A week ago today he had been Allister Park, assistant district attorney. The next day he hadn't been. It was probably not a mere coincidence.

He started to take a look at his new self in the mirror. Before he could do more than glimpse a week's growth of beard, two of the men were gently pulling his arms toward the door. There was something deferential about their urgency. Park went along. He asked: "What do I do now?"

"That takes a bit of thinking on," said the large man. "It might not be safe for you to go home. Shh!" He stole dramatically down the stairs ahead of them. "Of course," he continued, "you could put in a warrant against Joseph Noggle."

"What good would that do?"

"Not much, I fear. If Noggle was put up to this by MacSvensson, you can be sure the lazy knicks wouldn't find him."

Park had more questions, but he didn't want to give himself away any sooner than he had to.

The house was old, decorated in a curious geometrical style, full of hexagons and spirals. On the ground floor sat another brown man in a rocking chair. In one hand he held a thing like an automobile grease-gun, with a pistol grip. Across the room sat another man, with a black eye, looking apprehensively at the gun-thing.

The one in the chair got up, took off his bonnet, and made a bow toward Park. He said: "Haw, Hallow. Were you hurt?"

"He'll live over it, glory be to Patrick," said the big one, whom the others addressed as "Sachem." This person now glowered at the man with the black eye. "Nay alarums, understand? Or—" he drew the tip of his forefinger in a quick circle on the crown of his head. It dawned on Park that he was outlining the part of the scalp that an Indian might remove as a trophy.

They went quickly out, glancing up and down the street. It was early morning; few people were visible. Park's four companions surrounded him in a way that suggested that, much as they respected him, he had better not make a break.

The sidewalk had a wood-block paving. At the curb stood a well-streamlined automobile. The engine seemed to be in the rear. From the size of the closed-in section, Park guessed it to be huge.

They got in. The instrument board had more knobs and dials than a transport plane. The Sachem started the car noiselessly. Another car blew a resonant whistle, and passed them wagging a huge tail of water-vapor. Park grasped the fact that the cars were steam-powered. Hence the smooth, silent operation; hence also the bulky engine and the complex controls.

The buildings were large but low; Park saw none over eight or ten stories. The traffic-signals had semaphore arms with "STAI" and "COM" on them.

"Where are you taking me?" asked Park.

"Outside the burg bounds, first," said the Sachem. "Then we'll think on the next."

Park wondered what was up; they were still respectful as all Hell, but there was something ominous about their haste to get outside the "burg bounds," which Park took to be the city limits. He said, experimentally, "I'm half starved."

A couple of the brown men echoed these sentiments, so the Sachem presently stopped the car at a restaurant. Park looked around it; except for that odd geometric style of decoration, it was much like other restaurants the world over.

"What's the program?" he asked the Sachem. Park had known some heavy drinkers in his time, but never one who washed his breakfast pancakes down with whiskey, as the large brown man was now doing.

"That'll be seen," said the Sachem. "What did Noggle try to do to you?"

"Never did find out."

"There's been an under talk about the swapping of minds. I wonder if—where are you going?"

"Be right back," said Park, heading for the men's room. In another minute the Sachem would have cornered him on the question of identity. They watched him go. Once in the men's room, he climbed onto a sink, opened a window, and squirmed out into the adjacent alley. He put several blocks between himself and his convoyers before he slowed down.

His pockets failed to tell him whose body he had. His only mark of identification was a large gold ring with a Celtic cross. He had a few coins in one pocket, wherewith he bought a newspaper.

Careful searching disclosed the following item:

BISJAP STILL MISSING

At a laet aur jestrdai nee toocan had ben faund of yi mising Bisjap Ib Scoglund of yi Niu Belfast Bisjapric of yi Celtic Cristjan Tjortj, hwuuz vanisjing a wiik agoo haz sterd yi borg. Cnicts sai yai aar leeving nee steen ontornd in yaeir straif tu faind yi hwarabouts of yi mising preetjr, hwuuz losti swink on bihaaf of yi Screlingz haz bimikst him in a furs yingli scofal . . .

It looked to Park as though some German or Norwegian had tried to spell English—or what passed for English in this city—phonetically according to the rules of his own language, with a little Middle English or Anglo-Saxon thrown in. He made a tentative translation:

BISHOP STILL MISSING

At a late hour yesterday no token (sign?) had been found of the missing Bishop Ib Scoglund of the New Belfast Bishopric of the Celtic Christian Church, whose vanishing a week ago has stirred the burg (city?). Cnicts (police?) say they are leaving no stone

63

unturned in their strife (effort?) to find the whereabouts of the missing preacher . . .

It sounded like him, all right. What a hell of a name, Ib Scoglund! The next step was to find where he lived. If they had telephones, they ought to have telephone directories . . .

Half an hour later Park approached the bishop's house. If he were going to change again at midnight, the thing to do would be to find some quiet place, relax, and await the change. However, he felt that the events of the week made a pattern, of which he thought he could see the beginnings of an outline. If his guesses were right, he had arrived at his destination.

The air was moderately warm and a bit sticky, as New York City air might well be in April. A woman passed him, leading a floppy-eared dog. She was stout and fiftyish. Although Park did not think that a skirt that cleared her knees by six inches became her, that was what was being worn.

As he turned the corner onto what ought to be his block, he sighted a knot of people in front of a house. Two men in funny steeple-crowned hats sat in an open car. They were dressed alike, and Park guessed they were policemen.

Park pulled his bonnet—a thing like a Breton peasant's hat—over one side of his face. He walked past on the opposite side of the street, looking unconcerned. The people were watching No. 64, his number.

There was an alley on one side of the house. Park walked to the next corner, crossed, and started back toward No. 64. He had almost reached the entrance to the alley when one of the men spotted him. With a cry of "There's the bishop himself!" the men on the sidewalk—there were four—ran toward him. The men in the funny hats got out of their vehicle and followed.

Park squared his shoulders. He had faced down wardheelers who invaded his apartment to tell him to lay off certain people, or else. However, far from being hostile, these shouted: "Wher-r-re ya been Halloy?" "Were you kidnapped?" "Ja lose your recall?" "How about a wording?" All produced pads and pencils.

Park felt at home. He asked: "Who's it for?"

One of the men said: "I'm from the *Sooth*."

"The what?"

"The *New Belfast Sooth*. We've been upholding you on the Skrelling question."

Park looked serious. "I've been investigating conditions."
The men looked puzzled. Park added: "You know, looking into things."

"Oh," said the man from the *Sooth.* "Peering the kilters, eh?"
The men in the funny hats arrived. One of the pair asked: "Any wrongdoings, Bishop? Want to mark in a slur?"

Park, fumbling through the mazes of this dialect, figured that he meant "file a complaint." He said: "No, I'm all right. Thanks anyway."

"But," cried the hat, "are you *sure* you don't want to mark in a slur? We'll take you to the lair if you do."

"No, thank you," said Park. The hats sidled up to him, one on either side. In the friendliest manner they took his arms and gently urged him toward the car, saying: "Sure you want to mark in a slur. We was sent special to get you so you could. If somebody kidnapped you, you must, or it's helping wrongdoing, you know. It's just a little way to the lair—"

Park had been doing some quick thinking. They had an ulterior reason for wanting to get him to the "lair" (presumably a police-station); but manhandling a bishop, especially in the presence of reporters, just wasn't done. He wrenched loose and jumped into the doorway of No. 64. He snapped: "I haven't got any slurs, and I'm not going to your lair, get me?"

"Aw, but Hallow, we wasn't going to hurt you. Only if you have a slur, you have to mark it in. That's the law, see?" The man, his voice a pleading whine, came closer and reached for Park's sleeve. Park cocked a fist, saying: "If you want me for anything, you can get a warrant. Otherwise the *Sooth*'ll have a story about how you tried to kidnap the bishop, and how he knocked the living bejesus out of you!" The reporters made encouraging noises.

The hats gave up and got back in their car. With some remark about ". . . he'll sure give us hell," they departed.

Park pulled the little handle on the door. Something went *bong, bong* inside. The reporters crowded around, asking questions. Park, trying to look the way a bishop should, held up a hand. "I'm very tired, gentlemen, but I'll have a statement for you in a few days."

They were still pestering him when the door opened. Inside, a small monkeylike fellow opened his mouth. "Hallow Colman keep us from harm!" he cried.

"I'm sure he will," said Park gravely, stepping in. "How about some food?"

"Surely, surely," said Monkey-face. "But—but what on earth has your hallowship been doing? I've been fair sick with worry."

"Peering the kilters, old boy, peering the kilters." Park followed Monkey-face upstairs, as if he had intended going that way of his own accord. Monkey-face doddered into a bedroom and busied himself with getting out clean clothes.

Park looked at a mirror. He was—as he had been throughout his metamorphoses—a stocky man with thinning light hair, in his middle thirties. While he was not Allister Park, neither was he very different from him.

The reddish stubble on his face would have to come off. In the bathroom Park found no razor. He stumbled on a contraption that might be an electric razor. He pushed the switch experimentally, and dropped the thing with a yell. It had bitten a piece out of his thumb. Holding the injured member, Park cut loose with the condemnatory vocabulary that ten years of work among New York City's criminal class had given him.

Monkey-face stood in the doorway, eyes big. Park stopped his swearing long enough to rasp: "Damn your lousy little soul, don't stand there! Get me a bandage!"

The little man obeyed. He applied the bandage as though he expected Park to begin the practice of cannibalism on him at any moment.

"What's the matter?" said Park. "I won't bite you!"

Monkey-face looked up. "Begging pardon, your hallowship, but I thock you wouldn't allow the swearing of aiths in your presence. And now such frickful aiths I never did hear."

"Oh," said Park. He remembered the penetrating look the Sachem had given his mild damns and hells. Naturally a bishop would not use such language—at least not where he could be overheard.

"You'd better finish my shave," he said.

Monkey-face still looked uneasy. "Begging your forgiveness again, Hallow, but what makes you talk such a queer speech?"

"Canker sore," growled Park.

Shaved, he felt better. He bent a kindly look on Monkey-face. "Listen," he said, "your bishop has been consorting with low uncouth persons for the past week. So don't mind it if I fall into their way of speaking. Only don't tell anybody, see? Sorry I jumped on you just now. D'you accept my apology?"

"Yes—yes, of course, Hallow."

"All right, then. How about that famous breakfast?"

After breakfast he took his newspaper and the pile of mail into the bishop's well-equipped library. He looked up "Screling" in the "Wördbuk" or dictionary. A "Screling" was defined as one of the aboriginal inhabitants of Vinland.

"Vinland" stirred a faint chord; something he'd learned in school. The atlas contained a map of North America. A large area in the north and east thereof, bounded on the west and south by an irregular line running roughly from Charleston to Winnipeg, was labeled the Bretwaldate of Vinland. The remaining two-thirds of the continent comprised half a dozen political areas, with such names as Dacoosja, Tjeroogia, Aztecia. Park, referring back to the dictionary, derived these from Dakota, Cherokee, Aztec, etcetera.

In a couple of hours telephone calls began coming in. Monkey-face, according to his instructions, told one and all that the bishop was resting up and couldn't be disturbed. Park meanwhile located a pack of pipes in the library, and a can of tobacco. He got out several pads of paper and sharpened a dozen pencils.

Monkey-face announced lunch. Park told him to bring it in. He announced dinner. Park told him to bring it in. He announced bed-time. Park told him to go soak his head. He went, clucking. He had never seen a man work with such a fury of concentration for so long at a stretch, let alone his master. But then, he had never seen Allister Park reviewing the evidence for a big criminal case.

History, according to the encyclopedia, was much the same as Park remembered it down to the Dark Ages. Tracing down the point at which the divergence took place, he located the fact that King Oswiu of Northumbria had decided in favor of the Celtic Christian Church at the Synod of Whitby, 644 A.D. Park had never heard of the Synod or of King Oswiu. But the encyclopedia ascribed to this decision the rapid spread of the Celtic form of Christianity over Great Britain and Scandinavia. Hence it seemed to Park that probably, in the history of the world *he* had come from, the king had decided the other way.

The Roman Christian Church had held most of its ground in northern Europe for a century more. But the fate of its influence there had been sealed by the defeat of the Franks by the Arabs at Tours. The Arabs had occupied all southern Gaul before they were finally stopped, and according to the atlas they were still there. The Pope and the Lombard duchies of Italy had at once placed themselves under the protection of the

Byzantine emperor Leo the Iconoclast. (A Greek-speaking "Roman" Empire still occupied Anatolia and the Balkans, under a Serbian dynasty.) A Danish king of England named Gorm had brought both the British Isles and Scandinavia under his rule, as Knut had done in Park's world. But Gorm's kingdom proved more durable than Knut's; the connection between England and Scandinavia had survived, despite intervals of disunion and civil war, down to the present. North America was discovered by one Ketil Ingolfsson in 989 A.D. Enough Norse, English, and Irish colonists had migrated thither during the Eleventh Century to found a permanent colony, from which the Bretwaldate of Vinland had grown. Their language, while descended from Anglo-Saxon, naturally contained fewer words of Latin and French origin than Park's English.

The Indians—"Screlingz" or Skrellings—had not proved a pushover, as the colonists had neither the gunpowder nor the numbers that the whites of Park's history had had. By the time the whites had reached the present boundaries of Vinland, expelling or enslaving the Skrellings as they went, the remaining natives had acquired enough knowledge of ferrous metallurgy and organized warfare to hold their own. Those that remained in Vinland were no longer slaves, but were still a suppressed class suffering legal and economic disabilities. He, Bishop Ib Scoglund, was a crusader for the removal of these disabilities. ("Hallow" was simply a respectful epithet, meaning about the same as "Reverend.")

An Italian named Caravello had invented the steam engine about 1790, and the Industrial Revolution had followed as a matter of course . . .

It was the following morning, when Park, having caught the three hours of sleep that sufficed for him when necessary, was back at the books, that Monkey-face (right name: Eric Dunedin) came timidly in. He coughed deferentially. "The pigeon came with a writing from Thane Callahan."

Park frowned up from his mountain of printed matter. "Who? Never mind; let's see it." He took the note. It read (spelling conventionalized):

> Dear Hallow: Why in the name of the Blood Witnesses of Belfast did you run away from us yesterday? The papers say you have gone back home; isn't that risky? Must have a meeting with you forthwith; shall be at Bridget's Beach this noon, waiting. Respectfully, RC

Park asked Dunedin: "Tell me, is Callahan a tall heavy guy who looks like an In—a Skrelling?"

Dunedin looked at him oddly. By this time Park was getting pretty well used to being looked at oddly. Dunedin said: "But he *is* a Skrelling, Hallow; the Sachem of all the Skrellings of Vinland."

"Hm. So he'll meet me at this beach—why the devil can't he come here?"

"Ooooh, but Hallow, bethink what happened to him the last time the New Belfast knicks caught him!"

Whatever that was, Park reckoned he owed the Sachem something for the rescue from the clutches of the mysterious Mr. Noggle. The note didn't sound like one from a would-be abductor to his escaped prey. But just in case, Park went out to the modest episcopal automobile (Dunedin called it a "wain") and put a wrench in his pocket. He told Dunedin: "You'll have to drive this thing; my thumb's still sore."

It took a few minutes to get steam up. As they rolled out of the driveway, a car parked across the street started up too. Park got a glimpse of the men therein. While they were in civilian clothes, as he was, they had a grim plainclothesman look about them.

After three blocks the other car was still behind them. Park ordered Dunedin to go around the block. The other car followed.

Park asked: "Can you shake those guys?"

"I—I don't know, your hallowship. I'm not very good at fast driving."

"Slide over then. How in hell do you run this thing?"

"You mean you don't know—"

"Never mind!" roared Park. "Where's the accelerator or throttle or whatever you call it?"

"Oh, the strangle. There." Dunedin pointed a frankly terrified finger. "And the brake—"

The wain jumped ahead with a rush. Park spun it around a couple of corners, getting the feel of the wheel. The mirror showed the other car still following. Park opened the "strangle" and whisked around the next corner. No sooner had he straightened out than he threw the car into another dizzy turn. The tires screeched and Dunedin yelped as they shot into an alleyway. The pursuers whizzed by without seeing them.

An egg-bald man in shirtsleeves popped out of a door in the alley. "Hi," he said, "this ain't no hitching place." He looked at Park's left front fender, clucking. "Looks like you took off some paint."

Park smiled. "I was just looking for a room, and I saw your sign. How much are you asking?"

"Forty-five a month."

Park made a show of writing this down. He asked: "What's the address, please?"

"One twenty-five Isleif."

"Thanks. I'll be back, maybe." Park backed out, with a scrape of fender against stone, and asked Dunedin directions. Dunedin, gray of face, gave them. Park looked at him and chuckled. "Nothing to be scared of, old boy. I knew I had a good two inches clearance on both sides."

The Sachem awaited Park in the shade of the bathhouse. He swept off his bonnet with a theatrical flourish. "Haw, Hallow! A fair day for our tryst." Park reflected that on a dull day you could smell Rufus Callahan's breath almost as far as you could see Rufus Callahan. He continued: "The west end's best for talk. I have a local knick watching in case Greenfield sends a prowler. Did they follow you out?"

Park told him, meanwhile wondering how to handle the interview so as to make it yield the most information. They passed the end of the bath-house, and Allister Park checked his stride. The beach was covered with naked men and women. Not *quite* naked; each had a gaily colored belt of elastic webbing around his or her middle. Just that. Park resumed his walk at Callahan's amused look.

Callahan said: "If the head knick, Lewis, weren't a friend of mine, I shouldn't be here. If I ever did get pulled up—well, the judges are all MacSvensson's men, just as Greenfield is." Park remembered that Offa Greenfield was mayor of New Belfast. Callahan continued: "While MacSvensson's away, the pushing eases a little."

"When's he due back?" asked Park.

"In a week maybe." Callahan waved an arm toward distant New Belfast. "What a fair burg, and what a wretched wick to rule it! How do you like it?"

"Why, I live there, don't I?"

Callahan chuckled. "Wonderful, my dear Hallow, wonderful. In another week nobody'll know you aren't his hallowship at all."

"Meaning what?"

"Oh, you needn't look at me with that wooden face. You're nay mair Bishop Scoglund than I am."

"Yeah?" said Park noncommittally. He lit one of the bishop's pipes.

"How about a jinn?" asked Callahan.

Park looked at him, until the Sachem got out a cigarette.

Park lit it for him, silently conceding one to the opposition. How was he to know that a jinn was a match? He asked: "Suppose I was hit on the head?"

The big Skrelling grinned broadly. "That mick spoil your recall, in spots, but it wouldn't give you that frickful word-tone you were using when we befreed you. I see you've gotten rid of most of it, by the way. How did you do that in thirty-some hours?"

Park gave up. The man might be just a slightly drunken Indian with a conspiratorial manner, but he had the goods on Allister. He explained: "I found a bunch of records of some of my sermons, and played them over and over on the machine."

"My, my, you are a cool one! Joe Noggle mick have done worse when he picked your mind to swap with the bishop's. Who are you, in sooth? Or perhaps I should say who *were* you?"

Park puffed placidly. "I'll exchange information, but I won't give it away."

When Callahan agreed to tell Park all he wanted to know, Park told his story. Callahan looked thoughtful. He said: "I'm nay brain-wizard, but they do say there's a theory that every time the history of the world hinges on some decision, there are two worlds, one that which would happen if the card fell one way, the other that which would follow fro the other."

"Which is the *real* one?"

"That I can't tell you. But they do say Noggle can swap minds with his thocks, and I don't doubt it's swapping between one of these possible worlds and another they mean."

He went on to tell Park of the bishop's efforts to emancipate the Skrellings, in the teeth of the opposition of the ruling Diamond Party. This party's strength was mainly among the rural squirearchy of the west and south, but it also controlled New Belfast through the local boss, Ivor MacSvensson. If Scoglund's amendment to the Bretwaldate's constitution went through at the next session of the national Thing, as seemed likely if the Ruby Party ousted the Diamonds at the forthcoming election, the squirearchy might revolt. The independent Skrelling nations of the west and south had been threatening intervention on behalf of their abused minority. (That sounded familiar to Park, except that, if he took what he had read and heard at its face value, the minority really had something to kick about this time.) The Diamonds wouldn't mind a war, because in that case the elections, which they expected to lose, would be called off . . .

"You're not listening, Thane Park, or should I say Hallow Scoglund?"

"Nice little number," said Park, nodding toward a pretty blonde girl on the beach.

Callahan clucked. "Such a wording from a strict wedless!"

71

"What?"

"You're a pillar of the church, aren't you?"

"Oh, my Lord!" Park hadn't thought of that angle. The Celtic Christian Church, despite its libertarian tradition, was strict on the one subject of sex.

"Anyhow," said Callahan, "what shall we do with you? For you're bound to arouse mistrust."

Park felt the wrench in his pocket. "*I* want to get *back*. Got a whole career going to smash in my own world."

"Unless the fellow who's running your body knows what to do with it."

"Not much chance." Park could visualize Frenczko or Burt frantically calling his apartment to learn why he didn't appear; the unintelligible answers they would get from the bewildered inhabitant of his body; the cops screaming up in the struggle-buggy to cart the said body off to Belleview; the headline: "PROSECUTOR BREAKS DOWN." So they yanked me here as a bit of dirty politics, eh? I'll get back, but meantime I'll show 'em some *real* politics!

Callahan continued: "The only man who could unswap you is Joseph Noggle, and he's in his own daffy-bin."

"Huh?"

"They found him wandering about, clean daft. It's a good deed you didn't put in a slur against him; they'd have stripped you in court in nay time."

"Maybe that's what they wanted to do."

"That's an idea! That's why they were so anxious for you to go to the lair. I don't doubt they'll be watching for to pull you up on some little charge; it won't matter whether you're guilty or not. Once they get hold of you, you're headed for Noggle's inn. What a way to get rid of the awkward bishop without pipe or knife!"

When Callahan had departed with another flourish, Park looked for the girl. She had gone too. The day was blistering, and the water inviting. Since you didn't need a bathing-suit to swim in Vinland, why not try it?

Park returned to the bath-house and rented a locker. He stowed his clothes, and looked at himself in the nearest mirror. The bishop didn't take half enough exercise, he thought, looking at the waistline. He'd soon fix *that*. No excuse for a man's getting out of shape that way.

He strolled out, feeling a bit exposed with his white skin among all these bronzed people, but not showing it in his well-disciplined face. A few stared. Maybe it was his whiteness; maybe they thought they recognized the bishop. He plunged in and headed out. He swam like a porpoise, but shortness of breath soon reminded him that the bishop's body wasn't up to Allister Park's standards. He cut loose with a few casual curses, since there was nobody to overhear, and swam back.

As he dripped out onto the sand, a policeman approached, thundering: "You! You're under stoppage!"

"What for?"

"Shameful outputting!"

"But look at those!" protested Park, waving at the other bathers.

"That's just it! Come along, now!"

Park went, forgetting his anger in concern as to the best method of avoiding trouble. If the judges were MacSvensson men, and MacSvensson was out to expose him . . . He dressed under the cop's eagle eye, thanking his stars he'd had the foresight to wear nonclerical clothes.

The cop ordered: "Give your name and address to the bookholder."

"Allister Park, 125 Isleif Street, New Belfast."

The clerk filled out a blank; the cop added a few lines to it. Park and the cop went and sat down for a while, waiting. Park watched the legal procedure of this little court keenly.

The clerk called: "Thane Park!" and handed the form up to the judge. The cop went over and whispered to the judge. The judge said: "All women will kindly leave the courtroom!" There were only three; they went out.

"Allister Park," said the judge, "you are marked with shameful outputting. How do you plead?"

"I don't understand this, your honor—I mean your aerness," said Park. "I wasn't doing anything the other people on the beach weren't."

The judge frowned. "Knick Woodson says you afterthockly exposed—uh—" The judge looked embarrassed. "You afterthockly output your—uh—" He lowered his voice. "Your navel," he hissed. The judge blushed.

"Is that considered indecent?"

"Don't try to be funny. It's not in good taste. I ask you again, how do you plead?"

Park hesitated a second. "Do you recognize the plea of *non vult*?"

"What's that? Latin? We don't use Latin here."

"Well then—a plea that I didn't mean any harm, and am throwing myself on the mercy of the court."

"Oh, you mean a plea of good will. That's not usually used in a freerighter's court, but I don't see why you can't. What's your excuse?"

"You see, your honor, I've been living out in Dakotia for many years, and I've rather gotten out of civilized habits. But I'll catch on quickly enough. If you want a character reference, my friend Ivor MacSvensson will give me one."

The judge's eyebrows went up, like a buzzard hoisting its wings for the take-off. "You ken Thane MacSvensson?"

"Oh, sure."

"Hrrrmph. Well. He's out of town. But—uh—if that's so, I'm sure you're a good burger. I hereby sentence you to ten days in jail, sentence withheld until I can check your mooding, and thereafter on your good acting. You are free."

Like a good thane's thane, Eric Dunedin kept his curiosity to himself. This became a really heroic task when he was sent out to buy a bottle of soluble hairdye, a false mustache, and a pair of phoney spectacles with flat glass panes in them.

There was no doubt about it; the boss was a changed man since his reappearance. He had raised Dunedin's salary, and except for occasional outbursts of choler treated him very considerately. The weird accent had largely disappeared; but this hard, inscrutable man wasn't the bishop Dunedin had known . . .

Park presented himself in his disguise to the renting agent at 125 Isleif. He said: "Remember me? I was here this morning asking about a room." The man said sure he remembered him; he never forgot a face. Park rented a small two-room apartment, calling himself Allister Park. Later in the evening he took some books, a folder of etchings, and a couple of suitcases full of clothes over. When he returned to the bishop's house he found another car with a couple of large watchful men waiting at the curb. Rather than risk contact with a hostile authority, he went back to his new apartment and read. Around midnight he dropped in at a small hash-house for a cup of coffee. In fifteen minutes he was calling the waitress "sweetie-pie." The etchings worked like a charm.

Dunedin looked out the window and announced: "Two wains and five knicks, Hallow. The twoth wain drew up just now. The men in it look as if they'd eat their own mothers without salt."

Park thought. He had to get out somehow. He had looked into the subject of search warrants, illegal entry, and so forth, as practiced in the Bretwaldate of Vinland, and was reasonably sure the detectives wouldn't

74

invade his house. The laws of Vinland gave what Park thought was an impractically exaggerated sanctity to a man's home, but he was glad of that as things were. However, if he stepped out, the pack would be all over him with charges of drunken driving, conspiracy to violate the tobacco tax, and anything else they could think of.

He telephoned the "knicks' branch," or police department, and spoke falsetto: "Are you the knicks? Glory be to Patrick and Bridget! I'm Wife Caroline Chisholm, at 79 Mercia, and we have a crazy man running up and down the halls naked with an ax. Sure he's killed my poor husband already; spattered his brains all over the hall he did, and I'm locked in my room and looking for him to break in any time." Park stamped on the floor, and continued: "Eeek! That's the monster now, trying to break the door down. Oh, hurry, I pray. He's shouting that he's going to chop me in little bits and feed me to his cat! . . . Yes, 79 Mercia. Eeeee! Save me!"

He hung up and went back to the window. In five minutes, as he expected, the gongs of the police wains sounded, and three of the vehicles skidded around the corner and stopped in front of No. 79, down the block. Funny hats tumbled out like oranges from a burst paper bag, and raced up the front steps with guns and ropes enough to handle Gargantua. The five who had been watching the house got out of their cars too and ran down the block.

Allister Park lit his pipe, and strode briskly out the front door, down the street away from the disturbance, and around the corner.

Park was announced, as Bishop Scoglund, to Dr. Edwy Borup. The head of the Psychophysical Institute was a smallish, bald, snaggly-toothed man, who smiled with an uneasy cordiality.

Park smiled back. "Wonderful work you've been doing, Dr. Borup." After handing out a few more vague compliments, he got down to business. "I understand that poor Dr. Noggle is now one of your patients?"

"Umm—uh—yes, Reverend Hallow. He is. Uh—his lusty working seems to have brock on a brainly breakdown."

Park sighed. "The good Lord will see him through, let us hope. I wonder if I could see him? I had some small kenning of him before his trouble. He once told me he'd like my spiritual guidance, when he got around to it."

"Well—umm—I'm not sure it would be wise—in his kilter—"

"Oh, come now, Dr. Borup, surely thocks of hicker things would be good for him . . ."

The sharp-nosed, gray-haired man who had been Joseph Noggle sat morosely in his room, hardly bothering to look up when Park entered. "Well, my friend," said Park, "what have they been doing to you?" "Nothing," said the man. His voice had a nervous edge. "That's the trouble. Every day I'm a different man in a different sanitarium. Each day they tell me that two days previously I got violent and tried to poke somebody in the nose. *I* haven't poked *nobody* in the nose. Why in God's name don't they *do* something? Sure, I know I'm crazy. I'll cooperate, if they'll *do* something."

"There, there," said Park. "The good Lord watches over all of us. By the way, what were you before your trouble started?"

"I taught singing."

Park thought several "frickful aiths." If a singing-teacher, or somebody equally incompetent for his kind of work, were in his body now . . .

He lit a pipe and talked soothingly and inconsequentially to the man, who though not in a pleasant mood, was too grateful for a bit of company to discourage him. Finally he got what he was waiting for. A husky male nurse came in to take the patient's temperature and tell Park that his time was up.

Park hung around, on one excuse or another, until the nurse had finished. Then he followed the nurse out and grasped his arm.

"What is it, Hallow?" asked the nurse.

"Are you poor Noggle's regular attendant?"

"Yes."

"Got any kinfolk, or people you like specially, in the priesthood?"

"Yes, there's my Aunt Thyra. She's a nun at the New Lindisfarne Abbey."

"Like to see her advanced?"

"Why—I guess so; yes. She's always been pretty good to me."

"All right. Here's what you do. Can you get out, or send somebody out, to telephone Noggle's condition to me every morning before noon?" The nurse guessed he could. "All right," snapped Park. "And it won't do anybody any good if anybody knows you're doing it, understand?" He realized that his public-prosecutor manner was creeping back on him. He smiled benignly. "The Lord will bless you, my son."

Park telephoned Dunedin; asked him to learn the name of somebody who dwelt on the top floor of the apartment-house next door, and to collect one ladder, thirty feet of rope, and one brick. He made him call back the name of the top-floor tenant. "But Hallow, what in the name of Patrick do you want a brick for . . ."

Park, chuckling, told him he'd learn. When he got off the folk-wain at Mercia Street, he didn't walk boldly up to his own house. He entered the apartment-house next door and said he was calling on Mrs. Figgis, his clericals constituting adequate credentials. When the elevator-man let him out on the top floor, he simply climbed to the roof and whistled for Monkey-face. He directed Dunedin in the tieing of the end of the rope to the brick, the heaving thereof to the roof of the apartment-house, and the planting of the ladder to bridge the ten-foot gap. After that it was a simple matter for Park to lower himself to his own roof, without being intercepted by the watch-dogs in front of his house.

As soon as he got in, the 'phone rang. A sweetness-and-light voice at the other end said: "This is Cooley, Hallow. Every time I've called your man has said you were out or else that you couldn't be bothered!"

"That's right," said Park. "I was."

"Yes? Anyway, we're all giving praises to the Lord that you were spared."

"That's fine," said Park.

"It surely is a wonderful case of how His love watches over us—"

"What's on your mind, Cooley?" said Park, sternly repressing a snarl of impatience.

"Oh—uh—what I meant was, will you give your usual sermon next Sunday?"

Park thought quickly. If he could give a sermon and get away with it, it ought to discourage the people who were trying to prove the bishop loony. "Sure I will. Where are you calling from?"

"Why—uh—the vestry." Some damned assistant, thought Park. "But, Hallow, won't you come up tonight? I'm getting some of the parishioners together in the chapel for a homish thanksgiving stint—with hymns of—"

"I'm afraid not," said Park. "Give 'em my love anyway. There goes my doorbell. 'Bye."

He marched into the library, muttering. Dunedin asked: "What is it, Hallow?"

"Gotta prepare a goddam sermon," said Park, taking some small pleasure at his thane's thane's expression of horror.

Fortunately the bishop was an orderly man. There were manuscripts of all his sermons for the past five years, and phonograph records (in the form of magnetized wire) of several. There was also plenty of information about the order of procedure in a Celtic Christian service. Park set about concocting a sermon out of fragments and paragraphs of those the bishop had delivered during the past year, playing the spools of wire over and over to learn the bishop's inflections. He wished he had some way of getting the bishop's gestures, too.

He was still at it next day when he dimly heard his doorbell. He thought nothing of it, trusting to Dunedin to turn the visitor away, until Monkey-face came in and announced that a pair of knicks awaited without.

Park jumped up. "Did you let 'em in?"

"No, Hallow, I thought—"

"Good boy! I'll take care of 'em."

The larger of the two cops smiled disarmingly. "Can we come in, Hallow, to use your wiretalker?"

"Nope," said Park. "Sorry."

The knick frowned. "In that case we gotta come in anyway. Mistrust of unlawful owning of pipe." He put his foot in the door-crack.

A pipe, Park knew, was a gun. He turned and stamped on the toe of the shoe, hard; then slammed the door shut as the foot was jerked back. There were some seconds of "frickful aiths" wafting through the door, then the pounding of a fist against it.

"Get a warrant!" Park yelled through the door. The noise subsided. Park called Dunedin and told him to lock the other entrances. Presently the knicks departed. Park's inference, based upon what he had been able to learn of Vinland law, that they would not force an entrance without a warrant, had proved correct. However, they would be back, and there is nothing especially difficult about "finding" an illegal weapon in a man's house, whether he had one before or not.

So Park packed a suitcase, climbed to the roof of the adjoining apartment, and went down the elevator. The elevator man looked at him in a marked manner. Once in the street, he made sure nobody was looking, and slapped on his mustache and glasses. He pulled his bonnet well down to hide his undyed hair, and walked over to Allister Park's place. There he telephoned Dunedin, and directed him to call the city editors of all the pro-bishop newspapers and tip them off that an attempt to frame the bishop impended. He told Dunedin to let the reporters in when they came; the more the better. Preferably there should be at least one in every room. Now, he thought, let those flatfeet try to sneak a gun into one of my bureau drawers so they can "find" it and raise a stink.

He spent the night at the apartment, and the next day, having gotten his sermon in shape, he paid a visit to his church. He found a functionary of some sort in an office, and told him that he, Allister Park, was considering getting married in St. Columbanus', and would the functionary (a Th. Morgan) please show him around? Th. Morgan was pleased to; Dr. Cooley usually did that job, but he was out this afternoon. Park looked sharply through his phoney spectacles, memorizing the geography of the place. He wished now he'd passed up the sermon for one more week, and had instead attended next Sunday's service as Allister Park, so that he could see how the thing was done. But it was too late now. Morgan broke in on his thoughts: "There's Dr. Cooley now, Thane Park; wouldn't you like to meet him?"

"*Ulp,*" said Park. "Sorry; got to see a man. Thanks a lot." Before the startled cleric could protest, Park was making for the door as fast as he could go without breaking into a run. The plump rosy young man in pince-nez, whom Park saw out of the corner of his eye, must be Cooley. Park had no intention of submitting his rather thin disguise to his assistant's inspection.

He telephoned the bishop's home. The other people in the lunch-room were startled by the roar of laughter that came through the glass of his telephone booth as Dunedin described the two unhappy cops trying to plant a gun in his house under the noses of a dozen hostile wise-cracking reporters. Monkey-face added: "I—I took the freedom, your hallowship, of finding out that two of the newsers live right near here. If the knicks try that again, and these newsers are at home, we could wirecall them over."

"You're learning fast, old boy," said Park. "Guess I can come home now."

It was Saturday when Dunedin answered a call from the Psychophysical Institute. He cocked an eye upward, whence came a series of irregular whams as if trunks were being tossed downstairs. "Yes," he said, "I'll get him." As he wheezed upstairs, the whams gave way to a quick, muffled drumming. If anything were needed to convince him that something drastic had happened to his master's mind, the installation and regular use of a horizontal bar and a punching-bag in a disused room was it.

Park, in a pair of sweat-soaked shorts, turned his pale eyes. Good old Monkey-face. Park, who treated subordinates with great consideration, never told Dunedin what he thought he looked like.

"It's the man at the Psychophysical Institute," announced Dunedin. The male nurse announced that, for a change, Joseph Noggle was claiming to be Joseph Noggle.

Park grabbed his bonnet and drove the steamer over. Borup asked: "But, my dear, dear Hallow, why must you—uh—see this one patient? There are plenty mair who could use your ghostly guidance."

Fool amateur, thought Park. If he doesn't want me to know why he wants to keep Noggle locked up, why doesn't he say he's violent or something? This way he's giving away his whole game. But aloud he gave a few smooth, pious excuses, and got in to see his man.

The original, authentic Noggle had a quick, nervous manner. It didn't take him more than a minute to catch on to who Park-Scoglund was.

"Look here," he said. "Look here. I've got to get out. I've got to get at my books and onmarkings. If I don't get out now, while I'm in my own body, I shan't be able to stop this damned merry-go-round for another six days!"

"You mean, my son, that you occupy your own body every six days? What happens the rest of the time?"

"The rest of the time I'm going around the wheel, indwelling ane after another of the bodies of the other men on my wheel. And the minds of these other men are following me around likewise. So every ane of the six bodies has each of our six minds in it in turn every six days."

"I see." Park smiled benignly. "And what's this wheel you talk about?"

"I call it my wheel of if. Each of the other five men on it are the men I should most likely have been *if* certain things had been otherwise. For instance, the man in whose body my mind dwelt yesterday was the man I should most likely have been if King Egbert had fallen off his horse in 1781."

Park didn't stop to inquire about King Egbert or the sad results of his poor equestrianism. He asked softly: "How did your wheel get started in the first place?"

"It was when I tried to stop yours! Law of keeping of psychic momentum, you know. I got careless, and the momentum of your wheel was overchanged to mine. So I've been going around ever since. Now look here, whatever your name is, I've got to get out of here, or I'll never get stopped. I ordered them to let me out this morning, but all they'd say was that they'd see about it tomorrow. Tomorrow my body'll be occupied by some other wheel-mate, and they'll say I'm crazy again. Borup won't let me go anyway if he can help it; he likes my job. But you've got to use your inflowing as bishop—"

"Oh," said Park silkily, "I've got to use my influence, eh? Just one more question. Are we all on wheels? And how many of these possible worlds are there?"

"Yes, we're all on wheels. The usual number of rooms on a wheel is fourteen—that's the number on yours—though it sometimes varies. The number of worlds is infinite, or almost, so that the chances that anybody on my wheel would be living in the same world as anybody on yours is pretty small. But that's not weightful. The weightful thing is to get me out so—"

"Ah yes, that's the weightful thing, isn't it? But suppose you tell me why you started my wheel in the first place?"

"It was just a forseeking in the mental control of wheels."

"You're lying," said Park softly.

"Oh, I'm lying, am I? Well then, reckon out your own reason."

"I'm sorry that you take this attitude, my son. How can I help you if you won't put your trust in me and in God?"

"Oh, come on, don't play-act. You're not the bishop, and you know it."

"Ah, but I *was* a churchman in my former being." Park fairly oozed holiness. "That's not odd, is it? Since I was the man the bishop would most likely have been if King Oswiu had chosen for the Romans, and the Arabs had lost the battle of Tours."

"You'd hold yourself bound by professional confidence?"

Park looked shocked. "What a thock! Of course I would."

"All right. I'm something of a sportsman, you know. About a month ago I got badly pinched by the ponies, and I—ah—borrowed a little heading on my pay from the Institute's funds. Of course I'd have paid it back; it was really quite an honest deed. But I had to make a few little—ah—rightings in the books, because otherwise one who didn't understand the conditions might have drawn the wrong thocks from them.

"Ivor MacSvensson somehow found out, and threatened to put me in jail if I didn't use my mental powers to start your wheel of if going until it had made a half-turn, and then stop it. With another man's mind in the bishop's body, it ought to be easy to prove the bishop daft; in any event his inflowing would be destroyed. But as you know, it didn't work out quite that way. You seemingly aren't in anybody's custody. So you'll have to do something to get me out."

Park leaned forward and fixed Noggle with the bishop's fish-pale eyes. He said harshly: "You know, Noggle, I admire you. For a guy who robs his hospital, and then to get out of it goes and starts fourteen men's minds spinning around, ruining their lives and maybe driving some of them crazy or to self-killing, you have more gall than a barn-rat. You sit there and tell me, one of your victims, that I'll have to do something to get you out. Why, damn your lousy little soul, if you ever *do* get out I'll give you a case of lumps that'll make you think somebody dropped a mountain on you!"

Noggle paled a bit. "Then—then you weren't a churchman in your own world?"

"Hell, no! My business was putting lice like you in jail. And I still ock to be able to do that here, with what you so kindly told me just now."

Noggle swallowed as this sank in. "But—you promised—"

Park laughed unpleasantly. "Sure I did. I never let a little thing like a promise to a crook keep me awake nights."

"But you want to get back, don't you? And I'm the only one who can send you back, and you'll have to get me out of here before I can do anything—"

"There is that," said Park thoughtfully. "But I don't know. Maybe I'll like it here when I get used to it. I can always have the fun of coming around here every sixth day and giving you the horse-laugh."

"You're—a devil!"

Park laughed again. "Thanks. You thought you'd get some poor bewildered dimwit in Scoglund's body, didn't you? Well, you'll learn just how wrong you were." He stood up. "I'll let you stay here a while more as Dr. Borup's prize looney. Maybe when you've been taken down a peg we can talk business. Meanwhile, you might form a club with those other five guys on your wheel. You could leave notes around for each other to find. So long, Dr. Svengali!"

Ten minutes later Park was in Borup's office, with a bland episcopal smile on his face. He asked Borup, apropos of nothing in particular, a lot of questions about the rules involving commitment and release of inmates.

"Nay," said Edwy Borup firmly. "We could—uh—parole a patient in your care only if he were rick most of the time. Those that are wrong most of the time, like poor Dr. Noggle, have to stay here."

It was all very definite. But Park had known lots of people who were just as definite until pressure was brought to bear on them from the right quarter.

The nearer the Sunday service came, the colder became Allister Park's feet. Which, for such an aggressive, self-confident man, was peculiar. But when he thought of all the little details, the kneeling and getting up again, the facing this way and that . . . He telephoned Cooley at the cathedral. He had, he said, a cold, and would Cooley handle everything but the sermon? "Surely, Hallow, surely. The Lord will see to it that you're fully restored soon, I hope. I'll say a special prayer for you . . ."

It was also time, Park thought, to take Monkey-face into his confidence. He told him all, whereat Dunedin's eyes grew very large. "Now, old boy," said Park briskly, "if you ever want to get your master back into his own body, you'll have to help me out. For instance, here's that damned sermon. I'm going to read it, and you'll correct my pronunciation and gestures."

Sunday afternoon, Park returned wearily to the bishop's house. The sermon had gone off easily enough; but then he'd had to greet hundreds of people he didn't know, as if they were old friends. And he'd had to parry scores of questions about his absence. He had, he thought, earned a drink.

"A highball?" asked Dunedin. "What's that?"

Park explained. Dunedin looked positively shocked. "But Thane P—I mean Hallow, isn't it bad for your insides to drink such cold stuff?"

"Never mind my insides! I'll—hullo, who's that?"

Dunedin answered the doorbell, and reported that a Th. Figgis wanted to see the bishop. Park said to show him in. There was something familiar about that name. The man himself was tall, angular, and grim-looking. As soon as Dunedin had gone, he leaned forward and hissed dramatically: "I've got you now, Bishop Scoglund! What are you going to do about it?"

"What am I going to do about *what*?"

"My wife!"

"What about your wife?"

"You know well enough. You went up to my rooms last Tuesday, while I was away, and came down again Wednesday."

"Don't be an ass," said Park. "I've never been in your rooms in my life, and I've never met your wife."

"Oh, yes? Don't try to fool me, you wolf in priest's clothing! I've got witnesses. By God, I'll fix you, you seducer!"

"Oh, that!" Park grinned, and explained his ladder-and-rope procedure.

"Think I believe that?" sneered Figgis. "If you weren't a priest I'd challenge you and cut your liver out and eat it. As it is, I can make things so hot for you—"

"Now, now," interrupted Park. "Be reasonable. I'm sure we can come to an understanding—"

"Trying to bribe me, huh?"

"I wouldn't put it just that way."

"So you think you can buy my honor, do you? Well, what's your offer?"

Park sighed. "I thought so. Just another goddam blackmailer. Get out, louse!"

"But aren't you going to—"

Park jumped up, spun Figgis around, and marched him toward the door. "Out, I said! If you think you can get away with spreading your little scandal around, go to it. You'll learn that you aren't the only one who knows things about other people." Figgis tried to wriggle loose. Park kicked him into submission, and sent him staggering down the front steps with a final shove.

Dunedin looked awedly at this formidable creature into which his master had been metamorphosed. "Do you really know something to keep him quiet, Hallow?"

"Nope. But my experience is that most men of his age have something they'd rather not have known. Anyway, you've got to take a strong line with these blackmailers, or they'll raise no end of hell. Of course, my son, *we* hope the good Lord will show our erring brother the folly of his sinful ways, don't we?" Park winked.

Being a bishop entailed much more than putting on a one-hour performance at the cathedral every Sunday, as Park soon learned. But he transacted as much of his episcopal business as he could at home, and put the rest onto Cooley. He didn't yet feel that his impersonation was good enough to submit to close-range examination by his swarm of subordinates.

While he was planning his next step, an accident unexpectedly opened the way for him. He had just settled himself in the Isleif Street apartment the evening of Tuesday, April 26th, when a young man rang his doorbell. It took about six seconds to diagnose the young man as a

fledgling lawyer getting a start on a political career as a precinct worker.
"No," said Park, "I won't sign your petition to nominate Thane
Hammer, because I don't know him. I've just moved here from Dakotia.
But I'd like to come around to the clubhouse and meet the boys."

The young man glowed. "Why don't you? There's a meeting of the
precinct workers tomorrow night, and voters are always welcome . . ."

The clubhouse walls were covered with phoney Viking shields and
weapons. "Who's he?" Park asked his young lawyer through the haze of
smoke. "He" was a florid man to whom several were paying obsequious
attention.

"That's Trigvy Darling, Brahtz's parasite." Park caught a note of
dislike, and added it to the new card in his mental index file. Brahtz was a
Diamond thing-man from a western province, the leader of the squirearchy. In this somewhat naive culture, a gentleman had to demonstrate
his financial standing by supporting a flock of idle friends, or deputy
gentlemen. The name of the parasite was not merely accurate, but was
accepted by these hangers-on without any feeling of derogation.

Through the haze wove an unpleasantly familiar angular figure.
Park's grip on the edge of the table automatically tightened. "Haw,
Morrow," said Figgis, and looked at Park. "Haven't I met you
somewhere?"

"Maybe," said Park. "Ever live in Dakotia?"

Morrow, the young lawyer, introduced Park as Park. Park fervently
hoped his disguise was thick enough. Figgis acknowledged the introduction, but continued to shoot uneasy little glances at Park. "I could
swear—" he said. Just then the meeting was called. Although it would
have driven a lot of people to suicide from boredom, Park enjoyed the
interplay of personalities, the quick fencing with parliamentary rules by
various factions. These rules differed from those he was used to, being
derived from those of the ancient Icelandic Thing instead of the English
Parliament. But the idea was the same. The local members wanted to
throw a party for the voters of the hide (district). A well-knit minority
led by the parasite Darling wanted to save the money for contribution to
the national war-chest.

Park waited until the question was just about to be put to a vote, then
snapped his fingers for the chairman's attention. The chairman, an elderly
dodderer, recognized him.

"My friends," said Park, lurching to his feet, "of course I don't know
that I really ock to say anything, being just a new incomer from the wilds

of Dakotia. But I've always voted Diamond, and so did my father, and his father before him, and so on back as far as there *was* any Diamond Party. So I think I can claim as solid a party membership as some folks who live in New Belfast three months out of the year, and spend the rest of their time upholding the monetary repute of certain honorable country thanes." Park, with satisfaction, saw Darling jerk his tomato-colored face around, and heard a few snickers. "Though," he continued, "taking the healthy skin you get from country life, I don't know but what I envy such people." (More snickers.) "Now it seems to me that . . ."

Twenty minutes later the party had been voted: Park was the chairman (since he alone seemed really anxious to assume responsibility); and Trigvy Darling, at whose expense Park had acquired a frothy popularity by his jibes, had turned from vermillion to magenta.

After the meeting, Park found himself in a group of people including the chairman and Figgis. Figgis was saying something about that scoundrel Scoglund, when his eye caught Park's. He grinned his slightly sepulchral grin. "I know now why I thock I'd meet you! You remind me of the bishop!"

"Know him?"

"I met him once. Say, Dutt," (this was to the aged chairman) "what date's set for your withdrawal?"

"Next meeting," quavered the ancient one. "Ah, here is our crown prince, heh, heh!" Darling, his face back to normal tomato-color, advanced. "Do you ken Thane Park?"

"I ken him well enough," growled Darling with the look of one who has found a cockroach in his ice cream. "It seems to me, Thane Dutt, that part of a chairman's duty is to stop use of personalities on the part of speakers."

"You can always plead point of personal privilege, heh, heh."

Darling did something in his throat that was not quite articulate speech. Figgis murmured: "He knows the boys would laugh him down if he tried it."

"Yeah?" said Darling. "We'll see about that when I'm chairman." He stalked off.

Park wasted no time in exploiting his new job. Knowing that Ivor MacSvensson was due back in New Belfast the next day, he went around—as Allister Park—to the law office used by the boss as a front for his activities. The boss was already in, but the outer office was jammed with favor-seekers. Park, instead of preparing to spend the morning awaiting his turn, bribed the office boy to tell him when and where

MacSvensson ate his lunch. Then he went to the nearby public library—movies not having been invented in this world—and took his ease until one o'clock.

Unfortunately, Ivor MacSvensson failed to show up at the restaurant indicated, though Park stretched one tunafish lunch out for half an hour. Park cursed the lying office-boy. Plain bribery he was hardened to, but he really became indignant when the bribee failed to deliver. So he set about it the hard way. A nearby knick gave him the locations of the five highest-priced restaurants in the neighborhood, and in the third he found his man. He recognized him from the pictures he had studied before starting his search—a big, good-looking fellow with cold blue eyes and prematurely white hair.

Park marched right up. "Haw, Thane MacSvensson. Bethink you me?"

MacSvensson looked puzzled for a fraction of a second, but he said smoothly: "Sure, of course I bethink me of you. Your name is—uh—"

"Allister Park, chairman of the amusement committee of the Tenth Hide," Park rattled off. "I only met you recently, just before you left."

"Sure, of course. I'd know you anywhere—let's see, Judge Vidolf of Bridget's Beach wirecalled me this morning; wanted to know if I kenned you. Told him I'd call him back." He gripped Park's hand. "Come on, sit down. Sure, of course, any good party worker is a friend of mine. What's the Tenth Hide doing?"

Park told of the party. MacSvensson whistled. "Saturday the thirtieth? That's the day after tomorrow."

"I can manage it," said Park. "Maybe you could tell me where I could pick up some sober bartenders."

"Sure, of course." Under Park's deferential prodding, the boss gave him all the information he needed. MacSvensson finished with the quick, vigorous handshake cultivated by people who have to shake thousands of hands and who don't want to develop a case of greeter's cramp. He urged Park to come around and see him again. "Especially after that fellow Darling gets the chairmanship of your committee."

Park went, grinning a little to himself. He knew just what sort of impression he had made, and could guess how the boss was reacting to it. He'd be glad to get a vigorous, aggressive worker in the organization; at the same time he'd want to keep a close watch on him to see that *his* power wasn't undermined.

Park congratulated himself on having arrived in a world where the political set-up had a recognizable likeness to that of his own. In an absolute monarchy, for instance, he'd have a hell of a time learning the particular brand of intrigue necessary to become a king's favorite. As it was . . .

The Bridget's Beach knicks stood glowering at a safe distance from the throng of picknickers. Although they were anti-MacSvensson, the judges were pro, so what could they do about it if the party violated the ordnances regarding use of the beach? Since Park's fellow-committeemen were by now too sodden with beer to do anything at all, Park was dashing around, clad in a pair of tennis-shoes and the absurd particolored belt that constituted the Vinland bathing-suit, running everything himself. Everybody seemed to be having a good time—party workers, the more influential of the voters and their families, everybody but a morose knot of Darling & followers at one end.

Near this knot a group of anti-Darlings was setting up a song:

"Trig Darling, he has a foul temper;
"Trig Darling's as red as can be;
"Oh, nobody here loves Trig Darling,
"Throw Trigvy out into the sea!
"Throw—Trig,
"Throw—Trig,
"Throw Trigvy out into the sea!"

Park hurried up to shush them. Things were going fine, and he didn't want a fight—yet, at any rate. But his efforts were lost in the next stanza:

"Trig Darling, he has a pot-bellee;
"Trig Darling's as mean as can be . . ."

At that moment, apparently, a giant hit Allister Park over the head with a *Sequoia sempervirens*. He reeled a few steps, shook the tears out of his eyes, and faced Trigvy Darling, advancing with large fists cocked.

"Hey," said Park, "this isn't—" He brought up his own fists. But Darling, instead of trying to hit him again, faced him for three seconds and then spat at him.

Park glanced at the drop of saliva trickling down his chest. So did everyone else. One of Darling's friends asked: "Do you make that a challenge, Trig?"

"Yes!" boomed the parasite.

Park didn't really catch on to what was coming until he was surrounded by his own party. He and Darling were pushed together until their bare chests were a foot apart. Somebody called the knicks over;

these stationed themselves around the couple. Somebody else produced a long leather belt, which he fastened around the middles of both men at once, so they could not move farther apart. Darling, his red face expressionless, grabbed Park's right wrist with his left hand, and held out his own right forearm, evidently expecting Park to do the same.

It was not until a big sheath-knife was pressed into each man's right hand that Park knew he was in a duel. Somehow he had missed this phase of Vinland custom in his reading.

Park wondered frantically whether his mustache would come off in the struggle. One knick stepped up and said: "You know the rules: no kicking, biting, butting, or scratching. Penalty for a foul is one free stab. Ready?"

"Yes," said Darling. "Yes," said Park, with more confidence than he felt.

"Go," said the policeman.

Park felt an instant surge of his opponent's muscles. Darling had plenty of these under the fat. If he'd only had longer to train the bishop's body . . . Darling wrenched his wrist loose from Park's grip, threw a leg around one of Park's to trip him, and brought his fist down in a lightning overhand stab.

It was too successful. Park's leg went out from under him and he landed with a thump on his back, dragging Darling down on top of him. Darling drove his knife up to the hilt in the sand. When he jerked it up for another stab, Park miraculously caught his wrist again. A heave, and Darling toppled onto the sand beside him. For seconds they strained and panted, a tangle of limbs.

Park, his heart laboring and sand in his eyes, wrenched his own knife-arm free. But when he stabbed at Darling, the parasite parried with a curious twisting motion of his left arm, and gathered Park's arm into a bone-crushing grip. Park in agony heaved himself to his knees, pulling Darling up too. They faced each other on their knees, the belt still around them. Darling wrenched his knife-arm loose again, whipped it around as for a backhand stab, then back for an overhand. Park, trying to follow the darting blade, felt as if something had exploded in his own left arm. Darling's point was driven into it and into the bone. Before it had a chance to bleed, Darling tried to pull it out. It didn't yield the first pull. Park leaned forward suddenly. Darling unwound his left arm from Park's right to catch himself as he swayed backwards. Park stabbed at him. Darling blocked the stab with his forearm, making Park feel as if his wrist was broken. He played his last improvised trick: tossed up the knife, caught it the other way to, and brought it around in a quick up-and-out thrust. To his surprise, Darling failed to block it at all—the blade slid up under the parasite's ribs to the hilt. Park, warm blood running over his hand, twisted and sliced his way across Darling's abdomen . . .

Trigvy Darling lay on his back, mouth open and sand in his sightless eyeballs. The spectators looked in awe at the ten-inch wound. Park, feeling a bit shaken, stood while they bandaged his arm. The knicks gravely took down the vital information about the dead man, filling the last line in the blank with: "Killed in fair fight with Allister Park, 125 Isleif St., N.B."

Then people were shaking his hand, slapping his bare back, and babbling congratulations at him. "Had it coming to him . . ." ". . . never liked him anyway, only we had to take him on account of Brahtz . . ." "You'll make a better chairman . . ."

Park stole a hand to his upper lip. His mustache was a little loose on one side, but a quick press fixed that. He gradually became aware that the duel, so far from spoiling the party, had made a howling success of it.

Leading a double life is a strenuous business at best. It is particularly difficult when both one's identities are fairly prominent people. Nevertheless, Allister Park managed it, with single-minded determination to let nothing stop his getting the person of Joseph Noggle in such a position that he could make him give his, Park's, wheel of if another half-spin. It might not be too late, even if the Antonini case was washed up, to rehabilitate himself.

His next step was to cultivate Ivor MacSvensson, burg committee chairman for the Diamond Party of the Burg of New Belfast. This was easy enough, as the chairman of the hide committee was ex-officio a member of the burg committee.

They were dining in one of the small but expensive restaurants for which MacSvensson had a weakness. The burg chairman said: "We'll have to get Anlaaf off, that's all there is to it. Those dim knicks should have known better than to pull him in it in the first place."

Park looked at the ceiling. "Even if it was Penda's daughter?"

"Even if it was Penda's daughter."

"After all, spoiling the morals of a ten-year-old—"

"I know, I know," said MacSvensson impatiently. "I know he's a dirty bustard. But what can I do? He's got the twenty-sixth hide in his fist, so I've got to play cards with him. Especially with the thingly choosing coming up in three months. It'll be close, even with Bishop

Scoglund lying low the way he has been. I had a little plan for shushing the dear bishop; it didn't work, but it seems to have scared him into keeping quiet about the ricks of the Skrellings. And the Thing meeting next month . . . If that damned equal-ricks changelet goes through, it'll split the party wide open."

"If it doesn't?" asked Park.

"That'll be all right."

"How about the Dakotians and the rest?"

MacSvensson shrugged. "No trouble for fifty years. They talk a lot, but I never saw a Skrelling that would stand up and fick yet. And what if they did try a war? New Belfast is a long way from the border; and the choosing would be called off. Maybe by the time it was over people would get some sense."

Park had his own ideas. His researches had told him something about the unprepared state of the country. New Belfast had hundreds of miles between it and the independent Skrellings; in case of a sea attack, they could count on the friendly Northumbrian fleet, one of the world's largest, to come over and help out. Hence the New Belfast machine had consistently plugged for more money for harbor improvements and merchant-marine subsidies and less for military purposes. . . . However, if the Northumbrian fleet were immobilized by the threat of the navy of the Amirate of Cordova, and the Skrellings overran the hinterland of Vinland . . .

MacSvensson was speaking: ". . . you know, that youngest daughter of mine, she wants to marry a *schoolteacher*? Craziest idea . . . And that boy of mine has the house full of his musical friends; at least that's what he calls 'em. They'll play their flugelhorns and yell and stamp all night."

"Why not come up to my place?" asked Park with the studied nonchalance of an experienced dry-fly fisherman making a cast.

"Sure, of course. Glad to. I've got three appointments, thinging, but hell with 'em."

There was no doubt about it; Ivor MacSvensson was good company even if he did have a deplorable scale of moral values. Park, having made the necessary soundings, finally suggested getting some company. The chairman's blue eyes lit up a bit; there was some lechery in the old war-horse yet. Park telephoned his little waitress friend. Yes, she had a friend who was just *dying* to meet some big political pipes . . .

Many residents of New Belfast were wont to say of Ivor MacSvensson: "He may be a serpent (crook), but at least he leads a spotless home life." MacSvensson was at pains to encourage this legend, however insubstantial its basis. These people would have been pained to see the boss an hour later, smeared with lipstick, bouncing Park's friend's friend on his knee. The friend's friend was undressed to a degree that would have shocked Vinlanders anywhere but on a beach.

"Stuffy, isn't it?" said Park, and got up to open a window. The unsuspecting MacSvensson was having too good a time to notice Park thrust his arm out the window and wag it briefly.

Five minutes later the doorbell rang. By the time MacSvensson had snapped out of his happy daze, Park had admitted a small, wrinkled man who pointed at the friend's friend and cried: "Fleda!"

"Oswald!" shrieked the girl.

"Sir!" shouted Dunedin at the boss, "what have you been doing with my wife? What have you been doing with my wife?"

"Oh," sobbed Fleda, "I didn't mean to be unfaithful! Truly I didn't! If I'd only thought of you before it was too late . . ."

"Huh?" mumbled MacSvensson. "Too late? Unfaithful? Your wife?"

"Yes, you snake, you scoundrel, you bustard, my wife! You'll suffer for this, Boss MacSvensson! Just wait till I—"

"Here, here, my man!" said Park, taking Dunedin by the arm and pulling him into the vestibule. For ten minutes the boss listened in sweaty apprehension to Park's and Dunedin's voices, rising and falling, the former soothing, the latter strained with rage. Finally the door slammed.

Park came back, and said: "I got him to promise not to put in any slurs or tell any newspapers for a while, until we talk things over again. I know who he is, and I *think* I can squelch him through the company he works for. I'm not sure that'll work, though. He's mad as a wet hen; won't believe that this was just an innocent get-together."

The imperturbable boss looked badly shaken. "You've got to stop him, Al! The story would raise merry hell. If you can do it, you can have just about anything I can give you."

"How about the secretaryship of the burg committee?" asked Park promptly.

"Surely, of course. I can find something else for Ethelbald to do. Only keep that man shut up!"

"All right, old boy. Right now you'd better get home as soon as you can."

When MacSvensson had been gone a few minutes, Eric Dunedin's ugly face appeared in the doorway. "All clear, Hal—I mean Thane Park?"

The Wheels of If

"Come on in, old boy. That was a neat piece of work. You did well too, Fleda. Both you girls did. And now—" Park started to drive a corkscrew into another cork, "we can have a *real* party!"

"Damn it, Dunedin," said Park, "when I say put your breakfast down on the table and eat it, I mean it!"

"But Hallow, it simply isn't done for a thane's thane to eat with his master—"

"To hell with what's done and what isn't. I've got more for you to do than stand around and treat me as if I were God Almighty. We've got work, brother. Now get busy on that mail."

Dunedin sighed and gave up. When Park chose to, he could by now put on what Dunedin admitted was a nearly perfect imitation of Bishop Scoglund. But unless there were somebody present to be impressed thereby, he chose instead to be his profane and domineering self.

Dunedin frowned over one letter, and said: "Thane Callahan wants to know why you haven't been doing anything to push the glick-ricks changelet."

Park mentally translated the last to "equal-rights amendment." "Why should I? It isn't my baby. Oh, well, tell him I've been too busy, but I'll get around to it soon. That's always the stock excuse."

Dunedin whistled suddenly. "The kin of the late Trigvy Darling have filed a wergild claim of a hundred and fifty thousand crowns against you."

"What? What? Let's see that! . . . What's that all about? Have they got the right to sue me, when I killed him in self-defense?"

"Oh, but of course, Hallow. There's nay criminal penalty for killing a man in fair fight. But his heirs can claim two years' earnings from you. Didn't you know that when you took up his challenge?"

"Good lord, no! What can I do about it?"

"Oh, deary me, glory be to Patrick. You can try to prove the claim too big, as this one may be. I don't know, though; Darling got a big stipend from Brahtz as a parasite."

"I can always withdraw Allister Park from circulation and be just the bishop. Then let 'em try to collect!"

It would be wearisome to follow Allister Park's political activities in detail for the three weeks after his use of the badger-game on MacSvensson. But lest his extraordinary rise to power seem improbable, consider that it was not until the 1920's in Park's original world that a certain Josef Vissarianovitch Dzugashvili, better known as Joseph Stalin, discovered what could really be done with the executive secretaryship of a political

93

committee. So it is not too surprising that, whereas Park knew what could be done with his office, the politicians of Vinland did not. They learned. Among other things, the secretary makes up the agenda of meetings. He puts motions in "proper" form, since a motion is seldom intelligible in the form in which it is presented from the floor. He prompts the chairman—the nominal head of the organization—on parliamentary procedure. He is the interim executive officer; wherefore all appointments go through his hands, and he has custody of all records. He is ex-officio member of all committees. Since a committee seldom has any clear idea of what it wants to do or how it wants to do it, an aggressive secretary can usually run as many committees as he has time for. Whereas the chairman can't speak at meetings, the secretary can not only speak but speak last. He gets the gavel when an appeal is made from the chair . . .

At least, that is how it is done in *this* world. In Vinland, the rules were not quite the same, but the similarity was close enough for Park's purpose—which was still to get back to good old New York and that judgeship, if there was still any chance of getting it.

It was after the burg committee meeting on the first of June that Park faced Ivor MacSvensson in the latter's office. Park intended to start needling the boss about the body of Joseph Noggle. But MacSvensson got there first, demanding: "What's all this about your making up to the committeemen?"

"What's that?" asked Park blandly. "I've been seeing them on routine duties only."

"Yeah? Not according to what I've been told. And I've found out that that girl you had up for me wasn't wedded at all. Trying to put one down on the boss, eh? Well, you can go back to hide-walking. You'll call a special committee-meeting for Friday night. Get those seeings out today without fail. That's all."

"Suits me," grinned Park. The chairman can demand special meetings, but the secretary's the man who sends out the notices.

When Friday evening arrived, two-thirds of the seats in the committee-room in Karlsefni Hall remained empty. MacSvensson, blue eyes glacial, fretted. Park, sending out thunder-heads of smoke from the bishop's largest pipe, lolled in a chair, glancing surreptitiously at his watch. If MacSvensson were down at the far end of the hall when the hand touched sixty, Park would simply arise and say: "In the absence of the chairman, and of any other officers authorized to act as such, I, Allister Park, acting as chairman, hereby call this meeting to order . . ."

But MacSvensson, looking at him, divined his intention. He snatched out his own watch, and dashed to the chair. He made it by one and a half seconds.

Park was not disturbed. He took his place, hearing the boss's growl: "Did you send out all those seeings when I told you to, Park? There's just barely a quorum here."

"Absolutely. I can't help it if they go astray in the mail." Park neglected to add that, with the proper cooperation from a postal clerk, it is sometimes possible to make sure that certain of the notices, though duly postmarked as of the time they are received, are accidentally misplaced in the post office and completely overlooked until the day after the meeting.

"The meeting will kindly come to order," snapped MacSvensson. He did not like the look of the quorum at all; not one of his tried and true friends was in sight, except Sleepy Ethelbald.

He continued: "This is a special meeting called to hold in mind the good and welfare of the committee. As such there will be no reading of the minutes. The meeting will now consider items for the agenda."

MacSvensson caught the eye of Sleepy Ethelbald, who had been primed for just this occasion. Before Ethelbald could rouse himself, another committeeman popped up with: "I move that we take up the fitness of Chairman MacSvensson to last in his present office." "Twothed." "I move the agenda be closed." "Twothed."

MacSvensson sat up for a few seconds with his mouth open. He had had revolts before—plenty of them—but never one with the devastating speed and coordination of this. He finally mumbled: "All in favor—"

"Aye!" roared most of the quorum.

MacSvensson ran fingers through his hair, then squared his shoulders. He wasn't licked yet, by any means. There were more tricks . . . "The meeting will now consider the first item on the agenda."

"I move the impeachment of Chairman MacSvensson!" "Twothed!"

For the second time the chairman sat with his mouth open. Park said gently: "You take up the motion and give me the gavel."

"But—" wailed MacSvensson.

"No buts. A motion to impeach the chairman self-movingly shifts the gavel to the secretary. Come on, old boy."

An hour later Ivor MacSvensson stalked out, beaten. Park could have had the chairmanship himself, but he astutely preferred to keep the secretaryship and put the ancient of days, Magnus Dutt, in that exposed position.

95

Mayor Offa Greenfield knew his own mind, such as it was. He banged his fist on his desk, making all his chins quiver. "Nay!" he shouted. "I don't know what you're up to, Allister Park, but by the right ear of Hallow Gall, it's something! The freedom of a free people—"

"Now, now, we're not talking about the freedom of a free people. I'm sure we agree on that matter. It's just a question of the person of Joseph Noggle—"

"I won't be dictated to! I won't take orders from anybody!"

"Except Ivor MacSvensson?"

"Except Iv—nay! I said anybody! Go practice your snaky trick on somebody else, Allister Park; you'll get nothing from me! I won't interfere with Borup's running of his Institute. Unless, of course" (Greenfield lowered his voice to normal), "you can get MacSvensson to back you up."

Greenfield, it seemed, had the one virtue of loyalty. He intended to stick by the fallen boss to the bitter end, even though nearly all the rest of MacSvensson's staunch supporters had deserted him when the effectiveness of Park's coup had become patent.

But Greenfield was not elected, as were the members of the burg thing. He was appointed by a committee of the Althing, the national legislative body. So Park, for all his local power, could not displace Greenfield at the coming elections by putting up a rival candidate. He could only do it by acquiring sufficient power in the Althing. He set himself to study how to do this.

New Belfast elected six members to the Althing. As the city was firmly Diamond, nomination implied election. Therefore the six thingmen, however much they bragged about their independence in public, were careful to obey the whims of the boss of New Belfast.

The repeated efforts of Yon Brahtz to impose his control on the New Belfast Diamonds, by planting stooges like the late Trigvy Darling in their hide committees, had aroused some resentment. Park decided that he could trust his most active supporters, and the six thingmen, to back him in a gigantic double-cross: to desert the Diamond Party altogether and join the Rubies. The goats would be, not merely Brahtz and his squirearchy, but the local Ruby politicians of New Belfast. However, as these had never accomplished anything but draw some patronage from the Althing in the periods when the Rubies were in power there, Park thought he would not find much resistance to their sacrifice on the part of the Ruby leaders. And so it proved.

Twenty men, though, seldom keep a secret for long. The morning of June 9th, Park opened his paper to find the report of a defiant speech by

Yon Brahtz, in which he announced bluntly that "the thanes of the Cherogian March of Vinland will defend the ricks they inherited from their heroic forebears, by any means needful, and moreover the means for such defense are ready and waiting!" Park translated this to mean that if the Scoglund amendment were passed by a coalition of Rubies and insurgent New Belfast Diamonds, the squirearchy would secede.

But that would mean civil war, which in turn would mean postponement of the elections. What was even more serious, the Diamond thingmen from the seceding provinces would automatically lose their seats, giving the Rubies a clear majority. Since the Rubies would no longer need the support of Park's insurgents, they would be disinclined to make a deal with him to appoint a mayor of his choice.

Park privately thought that, while in theory he supposed he believed in the Scoglund amendment, in practice both his and the Ruby leaders' interests would be better served by dropping it for the present, despite the growls of the Dakotians and Cherogians. However, the Ruby leaders were firm; that huge block of Skrelling votes they would get by emancipating the aborigines was worth almost any risk.

As for such questions as the rights of the Skrellings as human beings, or the unfortunate Vinlanders who would be killed or haggled up in a civil war, they were not considered at all.

Park, holed up in the Isleif Street apartment with a couple of bodyguards, answered a call from Dunedin. "Haw, Hallow? Thane Callahan is here to see you."

"Send him over here. Warn him ahead of time who I—" Park remembered the guards, and amended: "warn him about everything. You know."

Lord, he thought, all this just to get hold of Noggle, still shut up in the Psychophysical Institute! Maybe it would have been simpler to organize a private army like Brahtz's and storm that fortress-like structure. A long-distance call for the mobilization of his Sons of the Vikings, as he called his storm-troopers. Kedrick, the Bretwald of Vinland, had refused to mobilize the army because, he explained, such an action would be "provocative." . . . Maybe he secretly favored the squirearchy, whose man he was; maybe he was just a pacific civilian who found the whole subject of soldiers, guns, and such horrid things too repulsive to discuss; maybe he really believed what he said . . .

Callahan arrived with a flourish. Since MacSvensson was no longer boss of New Belfast, the Sachem went openly about the city without fear of arrest and beating-up by the police.

He told Park: "It would be worth my life if some of my fellow-Skrellings knew I'd told you. But the Dakotians have an army secretly assembled on the bounds. If the Vinlanders start fickting among themselves, the Dakotians'll jump in to grab the northwestern provinces."

Park whistled. "How about the Cherogians?"

"They're holding back, waiting to see how things are turning out. If the war seems to be fruitbearing, they'll try a little rickting of the bounds themselves."

"And what will your Skrellings do then?"

"That depends. If the Scoglund changelet is lost, they'll join the foe to a man. If it goes through, I think I can hold most of them in line."

"Why do you tell me this, Callahan?"

The Sachem grinned his large disarming grin. "Two reasons. First, the bishop and I have been friends for years, and I'll stick to his body no matter where his soul may be. Twoth, I'm not fooled, as some of my Skrellings are, by talk of what fine things the Dakotians'll do for us if we help them overthrow the palefaces. The Dakotian realm is even less a folkish one than the Bretwaldate's. I know a thing or two about how they treat their ain folk. So if you'll stick to me, I'll stick to you."

Park would have liked to appear at the opening of the Althing as Bishop Scoglund. But, as too many people there knew him as Allister Park, he attended in his mustache, hair-dye, and spectacles.

The atmosphere was electric. Even Park, with all his acumen, had been unable to keep up with events. The risks were huge, whichever way he threw his insurgents' votes.

He kept them shut up in a committee-room with him until the last possible minute. He did not yet know himself whether he would order them to vote for or against the amendment.

The clock on the wall ticked around.

A boy came in with a message for Park. It said, in effect, that the Sons of the Vikings had received a report that the amendment had already been passed, had mobilized and seized the town of Olafsburg.

Who had sent that mistaken message and why, there was no way of finding out. But it was too late for anybody to back down. Park looked up and said, very seriously: "We're voting for the Scoglund Amendment." That was all; with his well-trained cogs no more was necessary.

The bell rang; they filed out. Park took his seat in the visitors' gallery. He said nothing but thought furiously as the session of the Althing was opened with the usual formalities. The chairman and the speaker and the chaplain took an interminable time about their business, as if afraid to come to grips with the fearful reality awaiting their attention.

When the first motions came up, a dead silence fell as Park's men got up and walked over to the Rubies' side of the house. Then the Rubies let out a yell of triumph. There was no more need of stalling or delicate angling for marginal votes. Motion after motion went through with a roar. Out went the Diamond chairman and speaker, and in went Rubies in their place.

In an hour the debate had been shut off, despite howls from Diamonds and their sympathizers about "gag law" and "high-handed procedure."

The amendment came up for its first vote. It fell short of the two-thirds required by eleven votes.

Park scribbled a note and had it delivered to the speaker. The speaker handed it to the chairman. Park watched the little white note drift around the Ruby side of the house. Then the Ruby leader got up and solemnly moved the suspension of thingmen Adamson, Arduser, Beurwulf, Dahl, Fessenden, Gilpatrick, Holmquist . . . all the thingmen from the seceding area.

Most of those named didn't wait; they rose and filed out, presumably to catch airwains for their home provinces.

The amendment passed on the second vote.

Park looked up the Ruby leader after the Althing adjourned. He said: "I hear Kedrick still won't order motion. Talks about 'Letting the erring brethren go in peace.' What's your party line on the matter?"

The Ruby leader, a thin cool man, blew smoke through his nose. "We're going to fight. If Kedrick won't go along, there are ways. The same applies to *you,* Thane Park."

Park suddenly realized that events had put him in a suspect position. If he didn't want himself and his cogs to be damned as copperheads, or the Vinland equivalent, he'd have to outshout the Rubies for unity, down with the rebels, etcetera.

Well, he might as well do a good job of it.

That afternoon the guards at the Psychophysical Institute were astonished to have their sanctuary invaded by a squad of uniformed knicks with the notorious Allister Park at their head flourishing a search-warrant. The charge was violation of the fire-ordnances—in a building made almost entirely of tile, glass, and reinforced concrete.

"But, but, but!" stuttered Dr. Edwy Borup. Park merely whisked out another warrant, this time for the arrest of Joseph Noggle.

"But, but, you can't stop one of my patients! It's—uh—illegal! I'll call Mayor Greenfield!"

"Go ahead," grinned Park. "But don't be surprised if you get a busy signal." He had taken the precaution of seeing that all the lines to the mayor's office would be occupied at this time.

"Hello, Noggle," said Park.

"Haw. Who are you? I think I've met you—let me see—"

Park produced an air pistol. "I'm Allister Park. You'll figure out where you met me soon enough, but you won't talk about it. I'm glad to see my figuring came out right. Can you start a man's wheel today? Now?"

"I suppose I could. Oh, *I* know who you are now—"

"Nay comments, I said. You're coming along, brother, and doing just as you're told."

The next step was when Park walked arm in arm with Noggle into the imposing executive building. Park's standing as a powerful boss saw him through the guards and flunkeys that guarded the Bretwald's office on the top floor.

The Bretwald looked up from his desk. "Oh, haw, Thane Park. If you're going to nag me about that mobilization order, you're wasting your time. Who's—eeee! Where am I? What's happened to me? Help! Help!"

In bounded the guards, guns ready. Park faced them sadly. "Our respected Bretwald seems to have had a mental seizure," he said.

The guards covered the two visitors and asked Kedrick what was the matter. All they could get out of Kedrick was: "Help! Get away from me! Let me out! I don't know who you're talking about. My name's not Kedrick, it's O'Shaughnessy!"

They took him away. The guards kept Park and Noggle until a message from the acting Bretwald said to let them go.

"By the brazen gates of Hell!" cried Park. "Is *that* all?"

"Yep," said the new Secretary of War. "Douglas was a Brahtz man; hence he saw to it that the army was made as harmless as possible before he skipped out."

Park laughed grimly. "The Secretary of War sabotages—"

"He does what?"

"Never mind. He raises hell with, if you want a more familiar expression. Raises hell with the army for the benefit of his party, with the Dakotians about to come whooping in. I suppose it oughtn't to surprise me, though. How many can we raise?"

"About twenty thousand in the burgish area, but we can arm only half of them rickly. Most of our quick-fire pipes and warwains have been hurt so it'll take a month to fix them."

"How about a force of Skrellings?"

The Secretary shrugged. "We can raise 'em, but we can't arm them."

"Go ahead and raise 'em anyway."

"All right, if you say so. But hadn't you better have a rank? It would look better."

"All right. You make me your assistant."

"Don't you want a commission?"

"Not on your life! Your generals would go on strike, and even if they didn't I'd be subject to military law."

The army was not an impressive one, even when its various contingents had all collected at what would have been Pittsburgh if its name hadn't been the lovely one of Guggenvik. The regulars were few and unimpressive; the militia were more numerous but even less prepossessing; the Skrelling levy was the most unmilitary of all. They stood around with silly grins on their flat brown faces, and chattered and scratched. Park thought disgustedly, so these are the descendants of the noble red man and the heroic viking! Fifty years of peace had been a blessing to Vinland, but not an altogether unmitigated one.

The transport consisted of a vast fleet of private folkwains and goodwains (busses and trucks to you). It had been possible to put only six warwains in the field. These were a kind of steam-driven armored car carrying a compressor and a couple of pneumatic machine-guns. There was one portable liquid-air plant for charging shells and air-bombs.

The backwardness of Vinland chemistry compared with its physics caused a curious situation. The only practical military explosives were a rather low-grade black powder, and a carbon-liquid-oxygen-mixture. Since the former was less satisfactory as a propellant, considering smoke, flash, and barrel-fouling, than compressed air, and was less effective as a detonant than the liquid-air explosive, its military use was largely confined to land mines. Liquid oxygen, however, while as powerful as trinitrotoluol, had to be manufactured on the spot, as there was no way of preventing its evaporation. Hence it was a very awkward thing to use in mobile warfare.

Park walked into the intelligence tent, and asked the Secretary of War: "What do you think our chances are?"

The Secretary looked at him. "Against the squires, about even. Against the Dakotians, one to five. Against both, none." He held out a

101

handful of dispatches. These told of the success of the Sons of the Vikings in extending their hold in the southwest, not surprising considering that the only division of regulars in that area were natives of the region and had gone over to the rebels. More dispatches described in brief fragments the attack of a powerful and fast-moving Dakotian army west of Lake Yanktonai (Michigan). The last of these was dated 6 P.M., June 26th, the preceding day.

"What's happened since then?" asked Park.

"Don't know," said the Secretary. Just then a message came in from the First Division. It told little, but the dateline told much. It had been sent from the city of Edgar, at the south of Lake Yanktonai.

Park looked at his map, and whistled. "But an army *can't* retreat fifty miles in one day!"

"The staff can," said the Secretary. "They ride."

Further speculation about the fate of the First Division seemed unnecessary. The one-eyed Colonel Montrose was dictating an announcement for the press to the effect that: "Our army has driven off severe Dakotian attacks in the Edgar area, with heavy losses to the foe. Nine Dakotian warwains were destroyed and five were captured. Other military booty included twenty-six machine-pipes. Two foeish airwains were shot down . . ."

Park thought, this Montrose has a good imagination, which quality seems sadly lacking in most of the officers. Maybe we can do something with him—if we're still here long enough . . .

The Secretary pulled Park outside. "Looks as though they had us. We haven't anything to fick with. Not even brains. General Higgins is just an easygoing paradeground soldier who never expected to have to shoot at anybody in his life. For that matter neither did I. Got any ideas?"

"Still thinking, brother," said Park, studying his map. "I'm nay soldier either, you know; just a thingman. If I could give you any help it would be political."

"Well, if we can't win by ficking, politics would seem to be the only way left."

"Maybe." Park was still looking at the map. "I begin to have a thock. Let's see Higgins."

Fortunately for Park's idea, General Higgins was not merely easygoing; he was positively comatose. He sat in his tent with his blouse unbuttoned and a bottle of beer in front of him, serene in the midst of worry and confusion.

"Come in, thanes, come in," he said. "Have some beer. Pfff. Got any ideas? Blessed if I know where to turn next. Nay artillery, nay airwains to speak of, nay real soldiers. Pfff. Do you guess if we started fortifying New Belfast now, it'd be strong enough to hold when we were pushed back there? Nobody knows anything, pfff. I'm supposed to have a staff, but half of 'em have got lost or sneaked off to join the rebels. Blessed if I know what to do next."

Park thought General Higgins would make a splendid Salvation Army general. But there was no time for personalities. He sprang his plan.

"Goodness gracious!" said Higgins. "It sounds very risky—get Colonel Callahan."

The Sachem filled the tent-opening when he arrived, weaving lightly. "Somebody want me?" Belatedly he remembered to salute.

Higgins barked at him: "Colonel Callahan, do you ken you have your blouse on *backwards*?"

Callahan looked down. "So I have, ha-ha, sir."

"That's a very weighty matter. Very weighty. No, don't change it here. You're drunk, too."

"So are—" Callahan suppressed an appalling violation of discipline just in time. "Maybe I had a little, sir."

"That's very weighty, very weighty. Just think of it. I ought to have you shot."

Callahan grinned. "What would my regiment do then?"

"I don't know. What would they do?"

"Give you three guesses, sir. *Hic.*"

"Run away, I suppose."

"Right the first time, sir. Congratulations."

"Don't congratulate me, you fool! The Secretary has a plan."

"A plan, really? Haw, Thane Park; I didn't see you. How do you like our army?"

Park said: "I think it's the goddamndest thing I ever saw in my life. It's a galloping nightmare."

"Oh, come now," said Higgins. "Some of the brave boys are a little green, but it's not as bad as all that."

A very young captain entered, gave a heel-click that would have echoed if there had been anything for it to echo against, and said: "Sir, the service company, twentieth regiment, third division, has gone on strike."

"What?" said the general. "Why?"

"No food, sir. The goodwains arrived empty."

"Have them all shot. No, shoot one out of ten. No, wait a minute. Arrived empty, you say? Somebody stole the food to sell to the local grocers. Take a platoon and clean out all the goods shops in Guggenvik. Pay them in thingly IOU's."

The Secretary interjected: "The Althing will never pay those off, you know."

"I know they won't, ha-ha. Now let's get down to that plan of yours."

The names were all different; Allister Park gave up trying to remember those of the dozens of small towns through which they rolled. But the gently rolling stretches of southern Indiana were much the same, cut up into a checkerboard of fields with woodlots here and there, and an occasional snaky line of cottonwoods marking the course of a stream. The Vinlanders had not discovered the beauties of billboard advertising, which, to Park's mind, was something. Not having a businessman's point of view, he had no intention of introducing this charming feature of his own civilization into Vinland. The Vinlanders did have their diabolical habit of covering the landscape with smoke from faulty burners in their wains, and that was bad enough.

A rising whistle and a shattering bang from the rear made Park jump around in the seat of his wain. A mushroom of smoke and dust was rising from a hillside. The airwain that had dropped the bomb was banking slowly to turn away. The pneumatics clattered all along the column, but without visible effect. A couple of their own machines purred over and chased the bomber off.

Those steam-turbine planes were disconcertingly quiet things. On the other hand the weight of their power plants precluded them from carrying either a heavy bomb load or a lot of fuel, so they were far from a decisive arm. They rustled across the sky with the dignity of dowagers, seldom getting much over 150 miles an hour, and their battles had the deliberation of a duel between sailing ships-of-the-line.

They wound down to the sunny Ohio (they called it the Okeeyo, both derived from the same Iroquois word) in the region where the airwains had reported the rebel army. A rebel airwain—a converted transport ship—came to look them over, and was shot down. From across the river came faintly the rebel yells and the clatter of pneumatics, firing at targets far out of range. Park guessed that discipline in Brahtz's outfit was little if any better than in his own.

Now, if they wanted to, the stage was set for an interminable campaign of inaction. Either side could try to sneak its men across the river without being caught in the act by the other. Or it could adopt a defensive program, contenting itself with guarding all the likely crossings. That sort of warfare would have suited General Higgins fine, minimizing as it did the chance that most of his musical-comedy army would do a lightning advance to the rear as soon as they came under fire.

It would in fact have been sound tactics, if they could have counted on the rebels' remaining on the south bank of the Okeeyo in that region, instead of marching east toward Guggenvik, and if the Dakotians were not likely to descend on their rear at any moment.

The Secretary of War had gone back to New Belfast, leaving Park the highest-ranking civilian with Higgins's army. He had the good sense to keep out of sight as much as possible, taking into account the soldier's traditional dislike of the interfering politician.

General Etheling, commanding the rebel army, got a message asking if he would hold a parley with a civilian envoy of General Higgins's army. General Etheling, wearing a military blouse over a farmer's overalls and boots, pulled his long mustache and said no, if Higgins wants to parley with me he can come himself. Back came the answer: This is a *very* high-ranking civilian; in fact he out-ranks Higgins himself. Would that island in the middle of the Okeeyo do? Etheling pulled his mustache some more and decided it would do.

So, next morning General Etheling, wearing the purely ornamental battle-ax that formed part of the Vinland officer's dress uniform, presented himself off the island. As he climbed out of his rowboat, he saw his opposite number's boat pull away from the far side of the little island. He advanced a way among the cottonwoods and yelled: "Haw!"

"Haw." A stocky blond man appeared.

"You all alone, Thane?"

"Yes."

"Well, I'll be jiggered! You boys kin go along back; I'll holler when I need you. Now, Thane, who be you?"

"I'm Bishop Ib Scoglund, General."

"*What?* But ain't you the wick who started the whole rumpus with all that silly talk about ricks for the Skrellings?"

The bishop sighed. "I did what I believed right in the sight of the Lord. But now a greater danger threatens us. The Dakotians are sweeping across our fair land like the hosts of Midian, of old! Surely it were wise to sink our little bickerings in the face of this peril?"

"You say the lousy redskins is doing an invasion? Well, now, that's the first I heered of that. What proof you got?"

Park produced an assortment of papers: dispatches, a copy of the *Edgar Daily Tidings,* etcetera.

The general was at last convinced. He said: "Well, I'll be tarnally damned. Begging your pardon, Hallow; I forgot as how you were a preacher."

"That's all rick, my son. There are times when, even in a cleric like me, the baser passions rise, and it is all I can do to refrain from saying 'damn' myself."

"Well, now, that's rick handsome of you. But what does old Cotton-head Higgins want me to do? I got my orders, you know."

"I know, my son. But don't you see the Divine will in these events? When we His children fall out and desecrate the soil of Vinland with our brothers' blood, He chastises us with the scourge of invasion. Let us unite to hurl back the heathen before it is too late! General Higgins has a plan for joint doing all worked out. If you take it up, he will prove his good faith by letting you cross the Okeeyo unopposed."

"What kind of plan is it? I never knew Cottonhead had enough brains to plan a barn-dance, not to mention a campaign."

"I couldn't give you all the details; they're in this paper. But I know they call for your army to put itself in the path of the invaders, and when you are engaged with them for our army to attack their left flank. If we lose, our brotherly quarrel with be one with Sodom and Gomorrah. If we win, it will be surely possible to settle our strife without further bloodshed. You will be a great man in the sight of the people and a good one in the sight of Heaven, General."

"Well, I guess maybe as how you're right. Give me the rest of the day to study these here plans . . ."

They shook hands; the general made a fumbling salute, and went over to his side of the island to call his boat. Thus, he did not see the bishop hastily don his mustache and spectacles.

When General Etheling's rebels crossed the river next morning, they found no trace of Higgins's force except for the usual camp-litter. Following directions, they set out for Edgar.

General Higgins, goaded to hurry by Allister Park, sent his army rolling northward. People in dust-colored workclothes came out to hang over fences and stare at them.

Park asked one of these, a strapping youth with some Skrelling blood, if he had heard of the invasion.

"Sure," said the man. "Reckon they won't git this fur, though. So we ain't worrying." The young man laughed loudly at the suggestion of volunteering. "Me go off and git shot up so some other wick can sit on his rump and get rich? Not me, Thane! If the folks in Edgar gets scalped, it serves 'em right for not paying us mair for our stuff."

As the army moved farther and farther toward Edgar, the expressions of the civilians grew more anxious. As they approached the Piankishaw (Wabash) River, they passed wains parked by the roads, piled with household goods. However, when the army had passed, many of these reversed their direction and followed the army back north toward their homes. Park was tempted to tell some of these people what idiots they were, but that would hardly have been politic. The army had little enough self-confidence as it was.

Higgins's army spread out along the south bank of the Piankishaw. All those in the front line had, by order, stained their hands and faces brown. The genuine Skrellings were kept well back.

Park took an observation post overlooking the main crossing of the river. He had just settled himself when there was a tremendous purring hum from the other side of the bridge. An enemy warwain appeared. Its ten tires screeched in unison as it stopped at the barrier on the road. Pneumatics began to pop on all sides. The forward turret swung back and forth, its gun clattering. Then a tremendous bang sent earth, bridge, and wain into the air. The wain settled into the water on its side, half out. Some men crawled out and swam for the far shore, bullets kicking up little splashes around their bobbing heads.

Up the river, Park could see a pontoon boat putting out from the north shore. It moved slowly by poling, passed out of sight. In a few minutes it reappeared, drifting downstream. It came slowly past Park and stopped against a ruined bridge-abutment. Water gradually leaked through the bullet-holes in the canvas, until only one corner was above water. A few arms and faces bobbed lazily just below the surface.

The firing gradually died down. Park could imagine the Dakotians scanning the position with their field-glasses and planning their next move. If their reputation was not exaggerated, it would be something devastating.

He climbed down from his perch and trotted back to headquarters, where he found Rufus Callahan, sober for once.

Ten minutes later the two, preceded by an army piper, exposed themselves at the east end of the bridge. Park carried a white flag, and the piper squealed "parlay" on his instrument. Nobody shot at them, so they picked their way across the bridge, climbing along the twisted girders. Callahan got stuck.

"I'm scared of high places," he said through his teeth, clinging to the ironwork.

Park took out his air-pistol. "You'll be worse scared of me," he growled. The huge man was finally gotten under way again.

At the far end, a Skrelling soldier jumped out of the bushes, rifle ready. He crackled something at them in Dakotian. Callahan answered in the same language, and the man took them in tow.

As the road curved out of sight of the river, Park began to see dozens of warwains pulled up to the side of the road. Some had their turrets open, and red men sat in them, smoking or eating sandwiches. There were other vehicles, service cars of various kinds, and horse cavalry with lances and short rifles. They stopped by one warwain. Their escort snapped to a salute that must have jarred his bones. An officer climbed out. He wore the usual mustard-colored Dakotian uniform, topped off with the feathered warbonnet of the Sioux Indian. After more chattering, Park and Callahan were motioned in.

It was crowded inside. Park burned the back of his hand against a steam-pipe, and cut loose with a string of curses that brought admiring grins to the red-brown faces of the crew. Everything was covered with coal-soot.

The engineer opened the throttle, and the reciprocating engine started to chug. Park could not see out. They stopped presently and got out and got into another warwain, a very large one.

Inside the big machine were a number of Dakotian officers in the red-white-and-black war-bonnets. A fat one with a little silver war-club hanging from his belt was introduced to Park and Callahan as General Tashunkanitko, governor of the Oglala and commander-in-chief of the present expedition.

"Well?" snapped this person in a high-pitched, metallic voice.

Callahan gave his sloppy salute—which at first glance looked alarmingly as though he were thumbing his nose—and said: "I'm representing the commander of the Skrelling Division—"

"The *what?*"

"The Skrelling Division. We've been ordered by the Althing to put down the uprising of the Diamonds in the southwest of Vinland. They have a big army, and are likely to win all Vinland if not stopped. We can't stop them, and on the other hand we can't let them take all the south while you take all the north of Vinland.

"My commander humbly suggests that it is hardly proper for two armies of men of the same race to fick each other while their joint foe takes over all Vinland, as Brahtz's army will do unless we join against it." General Tashunkanitko crackled something to one of his men, who rattled back. The general said: "It *was* taled that your men looked like Skrellings, but we could not get close enough to be sure, and did not believe the tale. What do you offer?"

Callahan continued: "My commander will not try to push the Dakotians from the area west of the Piankishaw, if you will help him against the rebels."

"Does that offer bind your thing?"

"Nay. But, as our army is the only real one at present under their command, they will have nay way of enforcing their objections. To prove our good faith we will, if you agree, let you cross the Piankishaw without fickting."

The general thought for some seconds. He said: "That offer ock to be put up to my government."

"Nay time, sir. The rebels are moving north from the Okeeyo already. Anyway, if we make a truce aside from our thing, you should be willing to do the same. After we've overthrown the Brahtz army, I'm sure we can find some workable arrangement between our armies."

Tashunkanitko thought again. "I will do it. Have you a plan worked out?"

"Yes, sir. Right here . . ."

When the Dakotians crossed the Piankishaw the next day, there was no sign of the large and supposedly redskin army that had held the passage against them.

Across the rolling Indiana plain came the rattle of pneumatic rifles and the crack of air- and mortar-bombs. General Higgins told Park: "We just got a message from General Etheling; says he's hard pressed, and it's about time we did our flank attack on the Dakotians. And this General Tush—Tash—General Mad-Horse wants to know why we haven't attacked the flank of the rebels. Says he's still pushing 'em back, but they outnumber him twa to ane and he's had a lot of mechanical breakdowns. Says if we'll hit them now they'll run."

"We don't want to let either side win," said Park. "Guess it's time to start."

With considerable confusion—though perhaps less than was to be expected—the Army of New Belfast got under way. It was strung out on a five-mile front at right angles to the line of contact of the Dakotian and rebel armies. The right wing was the stronger, since it would meet stronger resistance from Tashunkanitko's hardened professionals than from Etheling's armed hayseeds.

Park squeezed into the observation turret of the headquarters wain beside Higgins. They went slowly so as not to outrun the infantry, lurching and canting as the huge rubber doughnut-shaped wheels pulled them over walls and fences. They crunched through one corner of a farmyard, and the countryside was at once inundated by fleeing pigs and chickens. Park had a glimpse of an overalled figure shaking a fist at the wain. He couldn't help laughing; it was too bad about the farmer's livestock, but there was something ultra-rural about the man's indignation over a minor private woe when a battle was going on next door.

Men began to appear ahead; horsemen leaping fences and ditches scattered scouts dodging from tree to fence, firing at unseen targets, then frantically working the pump-levers of their rifles to compress the air for the next shot. One of them was not a hundred yards away when he saw the advancing wains. He stared stupidly at them until the forward machine-gunner in the headquarters wain fired a burst that sent the gravel flying around the scout's feet. The scout jumped straight up and came down running. Others ran when they saw the wains looming out of the dust. A few who didn't see soon enough ran toward the advancing line with their hands up.

They met larger groups of redskins, crawling or running from right to left with faces set. Each time there would be one face the first to turn; then they would all turn. The group would lose its form and purpose, sublimating into its component human atoms. Some stood; some ran in almost any direction.

Then they were in a half-plowed field. The plow and the steam tractor stood deserted among the brown furrows. On the other side of the field crouched a hostile wain. Park felt the engine speed up as the two machines lumbered toward each other. Bullets pattered about his cupola. It gratified him to see the general wince when they struck on and around the glass.

The wains came straight at each other. Park gripped the hand-holds tight. The other wain stopped suddenly, backed swiftly, and tried to run in at them from the side. Their own jumped ahead with a roar. Its ram dug into the side of the other machine with a terrible crash. They backed away; Park could see lubricating oil running out of the wound in the other machine. It still crawled slowly. His own mechanical rhinoceros charged again. This time the other machine heaved up on its far wheels and fell over . . .

The fight went out of the Dakotians all of a sudden. They had made a terrific assault on twice their number; then had fought steadily for two days. Their wains were battered, their horses hungry, and their infantry exhausted from pumping up their rifles. And to have a horde of strangers roll up their flank, just when victory was in sight—no wonder General Tashunkanitko, and his officers, let a tear or two trickle when they were rounded up.

General Etheling's rebels fared no better, rather worse, in fact. The Skrelling regiment ran wild among the rural Vinlanders, doing what they had wanted to do for generations—scalp the palefaces. Having somewhat hazy ideas about that ancestral ritual, they usually made the mistake of trying to take off the whole top of a man's head instead of the neat little two-inch circle of scalp. When they started in on the prisoners, they had to be restrained by a few bursts of machine-gun fire from one of Higgins's wains.

The train back to New Belfast stopped at every crossroads so the people could come out and whoop. They cheered Allister Park well enough; they cheered Rufus Callahan; they yelled for Bishop Scoglund. The story had gone ahead, how Park and General Higgins had devised a scheme for the entrapment of both the rebel and Dakotian armies; how the brave bishop had talked Etheling into it; how Etheling had treacherously shot the brave bishop; how Callahan had swum the Okeeyo with Bishop Scoglund on his back. . . . It was rumored that the city politician Allister Park had had something to do with these developments, but you never want to believe anything good of these politicians. Since he was Assistant Secretary of War, though, it was only polite to give him a cheer too . . .

Park did not think it would be prudent to show himself to the same audience both as Park and as the bishop, so they were all informed that his hallowship was recuperating.

As they rolled into New Belfast, Park experienced the let-down feeling that comes at such moments. What next? By now Noggle would have been rescued from Park's knicks and returned to Edwy Borup's hatch. That was bound to happen anyway, which was why Park hadn't tried to use that method of getting Noggle into his power before. The whirling of the wheel of if was a delicate business, not to be interrupted, by people with warrants, and he would have to see to it that somebody were left behind to force Noggle to stop the wheel when the right point had been reached.

It ought not to be difficult now, though. If he couldn't use his present power and position to get hold of Noggle, he'd have enough after election—which would come off as scheduled after all. First he'd make Noggle stop poor old Kedrick's wheel. Then he'd have Callahan or somebody stand over Noggle with a gun while he spun his, Park's, wheel through another half-turn. Then, maybe, Noggle would be allowed to halt his own carousel.

For the first three days after his return he was too busy to give attention to this plan. Everybody in New Belfast seemingly had written him or telephoned him or called at one of his two homes to see him. Although Monkey-face was a lousy secretary, Park didn't dare hire another so long as he had his double identity to maintain.

But the Antonini trials were due in a week, back in that other world. And the heirs and assigns of Trigvy Darling had had a date set for a hearing on their damage claim. And, if Park knew his history, there would probably be a "reconstruction" period in the revolted territories, of which he wanted no part.

For the second time Edwy Borup had his sanctuary invaded by Allister Park and a lot of tough-looking official persons, including Rufus Callahan. Borup was getting resigned if not reconciled to this. If they didn't let his prize patient Noggle escape before, they weren't likely to this time.

"Haw, Noggle," said Park. "Feel a little more withdoing?"

"Nay," snapped Noggle. "But since you have me by the little finger, I suppose I'll have to do what you say."

"All right. You're honest, anyway. First you're going to stop Bretwald Kedrick's wheel. Bring him in, boys."

"But I daren't stop a wheel without my downwritings. You bethink last time—"

"That's all right; we brought your whole damn library over."

There was nothing to it. Noggle stared at the fidgety Bretwald—the period of whose cycle was fortunately just twice his, so that both were in their own bodies at the same time. Then he said: "Whew. Had a lot of psychic momentum, that ane; I just did stop him. He'll be all rick now. What next?"

Park told everybody but Callahan to go out. Then he explained that Noggle was to give his wheel another half turn.

"But," objected Noggle, "that'll take seven days. What's going to be done with your body in the meantime?"

"It'll be kept here, and so will you. When the half-cycle's done, you'll stop my wheel, and then we'll let you stop your own whenever you like. I've made sure that you'll stay here until you do the right thing by my wheel, whether you cure your own case or not."

Noggle sighed. "And MacSvensson thock he'd get some simple-minded idealist like the bishop! How is it that your pattern of acting is otherly from his, when by the laws of luck you started out with much the same forebearish make-up?"

Park shrugged. "Probably because I've had to fick every step of the way, while he was more or less born into his job. We're not so otherly, at that; his excess energy went into social crusading, while mine's gone into politics. I *have* an ideal or two kicking around somewhere. I'd like to meet Bishop Scoglund some time; think I'd like him."

"I'm afraid that's undoable," said Noggle. "Even sending you back is risky. I don't know what would happen if your body died while his mind indwelt it. You might land in still another doable world instead of in your ain. Or you mick not land anywhere."

"I'll take a chance," said Park. "Ready?"

"Yes." Dr. Joseph Noggle stared at Park . . .

"Hey, Thane Park," said a voice from the doorway. "A wick named Dunedin wants to see you. Says it's weighty."

"Tell him I'm busy—no, I'll see him."

Monkey-face appeared, panting. "Have you gone yet? Have you changed? Glory to Bridget! You—I mean his hallowship—what I mean is, the Althing signed a treaty with the Dakotians and Cherogians and such, setting up an International Court for the Continent of Skrelleland, and the bishop has been chosen one of the judges! I thock you ock to know before you did anything."

"Well, well," said Park. "That's interesting, but I don't know that it changes anything."

Callahan spoke up: "I think you'd make a better judge, Allister, than *he* would. He's a fine fellow, but he will believe that everybody else is as uprick as he. They'd pull the wool over his eyes all the time."

Park pondered. After all, what had he gone to all this trouble for—why had he helped turn the affairs of half the continent upside down—except to resume a career as public prosecutor which, he hoped, would some day land him on the bench? And here was a judgeship handed him on a platter.

"I'll stay," he said.

"But," objected Noggle, "how about those thirteen other men on your wheel? Are you going to leave them out of their rick rooms?"

Park grinned. "If they're like me, they're adaptable guys who've probably got started on new careers by now. If we shift 'em all again, it'll just make more trouble for them. Come along, Rufus."

The funeral of Allister Park, assistant Secretary of War, brought out thousands of people. Some were politicians who had been associated with Park; some came for the ride. A few came because they liked the man.

In an anteroom of the cathedral, Bishop Scoglund waited for that infernal music to end, whereupon he would go out and preach the swellest damn funeral oration New Belfast had ever heard. It isn't given to every man to conduct that touching ceremony for his own corpse, and the bishop intended to give his alter-ego a good send-off.

In a way he was sorry to bid Allister Park good-bye. Allister had a good deal more in common with his natural, authentic self than did the bishop. But he couldn't keep up the two identities forever, and with the judgeship on one hand and the damage-suit on the other there wasn't much question of which of the two would have to be sacrificed. The pose of piety would probably become natural in time. The judgeship would give him an excuse for resigning his bishopric. Luckily the Celtic Christian Church had a liberal attitude toward folk who wished to leave the church. Of course he'd still have to be careful—girlfriends and such. Maybe it would even be worth while getting married . . .

"What the devil—what do you wish, my son?" said the bishop, looking up into Figgis's unpleasant face.

"You know what I wish, you old goat! What are you going to do about my wife?"

"Why, friend, it seems that you have been subject to a monstrous fooling!"

"You bet I—"

"Please, do not shout in the house of God! What I was saying was that the guilty man was none other than the late Allister Park, may the good Lord forgive his sins. He has been impersonating me. As you know, we looked much alike. Allister Park upowned to me on his deathbed two days ago. No doubt his excesses brought him to his untimely end. Still, for all his human frailties, he was a man of many good qualities. You will forgive him, will you not?"

"But—but I—"

"Please, for my sake. You would not speak ill of the dead, would you?"

"Oh, hell. Your forgiveness, Bishop. I thock I had a good thing, that's all. G'bye. Sorry."

The music was coming to an end. The bishop stood up, straightened his vestments, and strode majestically out. If he could only count on that drunken nitwit Callahan not to forget himself and bust out laughing . . .

The coffin, smothered in flowers, was, like all coffins in Vinland, shaped like a Viking longboat. It was also filled with pine planks. Some people were weeping a bit. Even Callahan, in the front row, was appropriately solemn.

"Friends, we have gathered here to pay a last gild to one who has passed from among us . . ."

In the Circle
of Nowhere

Irving E. Cox, Jr.

Pretend, yes. Let them think they had succeeded. Anything, so he could get away. The hard core of scientific reality was still intact. They hadn't destroyed it. Mora-Ta-Kai still believed in the old science, as firmly as they had tried to make him believe in—this.

"On the whole, we've made remarkable progress, Mr. Smith." The doctor was smiling and shaking his hand. Smith was the name they had given him. Mora-Ta-Kai had used his own only once, in the first shock of panic, before he understood the detailed internal structure of the nightmare.

"It's all very clear now," Mora-Ta-Kai said, because he knew he was expected to. "There is the Conrad Hilton and the Blackstone Hotel, and beyond them I can see Lake Michigan."

The doctor's car slid smoothly into the stream of Michigan Avenue traffic. "Excellent, Smith! We still have the amnesia to take care of, but we've conquered the other thing." The doctor pulled at his pipe, his face glowing with satisfaction. "You've earned your vacation, Smith."

"Have you arranged for me to have a room of my own?"

"Everything you asked for. Relax; enjoy yourself. The amnesia may clear up of its own accord."

"This Mrs. Armbruster—is she—"

"A personal friend of mine. You won't have any trouble. She'll leave you alone, or talk with you by the hour—whatever you ask."

And make a record of everything I do, Mora-Ta-Kai thought bitterly; but the expression on his face did not change. He must do nothing

117

now to betray himself. It made very little difference what Mrs. Armbruster chose to set down in her case study; she would never have an opportunity to make her report. All Mora-Ta-Kai needed was a room of his own, a place to work; and the doctor had promised him that. The material he had to use was available everywhere. His belief in the old science was not strong enough to restore reality; but he could at least use it to sweep the universe of the nightmare into oblivion.

The doctor's car rolled to a stop before a comfortable, brick house, decorously withdrawn from the street behind a mask of shrubs which partly concealed the high, wire fence. Mrs. Armbruster met Mora-Ta-Kai at the door—a pleasant, gracious, gray-haired lady dressed in white. A nurse! Mora-Ta-Kai had merely exchanged one form of imprisonment for another, slightly more subtle.

But they kept their promise. Mrs. Armbruster gave him a room of his own. When the door was shut, he sat down slowly on the bed. In the glass above the bureau he saw his reflection: tall, gaunt, hollow-cheeked. His skin was a dusky, reddish-brown. His glossy, black hair was brushed back from his forehead, emphasizing the wasted, skull-like shape of his face. His black eyes were enormous, glittering pools of ebony.

It was his clothing that held his attention, that fantastic costume which nearly covered his whole body: a white shirt, open at the throat; brown slacks; hard leather shoes that hurt his feet. He would have ripped off the shirt, but he dared not. He must conform to the taboos of the White Savages. Only then would they allow him the freedom he needed.

The bedroom window was open. Outside Mora-Ta-Kai saw the rows of green buds marching on the bare branches of the trees, the young spears of sprouting bulbs breaking through the black, garden soil. The air sang with the fresh-earth smell of spring.

Spring! The word hit him with the force of a warclub. The nightmare had started in the dead of winter. He had been trapped in this weird dream for three months, maybe longer. Three months ago the nightmare had started . . .

Mora-Ta-Kai was quarreling with Lassai. He couldn't remember why. Lassai was his squaw; he loved her very much. He had just returned from a trip across the Eastern Sea to slave plantations. It should have been a joyous homecoming. But something came between them—the memory was vague, overlaid by the powerful sorcery of the dream.

Pyrn-Ute had been there, too. Ten months before, Mora-Ta-Kai had won Lassai from him; now Pyrn-Ute was back, his arm draped around

Lassai's shoulder. He sneered at Mora-Ta-Kai. Seething with anger, Mora-Ta-Kai flung out of the house. Snow was falling. A crying wind swept in from the lake, heaping snow in drifts along the walk.

(Why had they quarreled? Mora-Ta-Kai probed desperately into the tormented recesses of his mind, but the memory eluded him.)

He strode in long strides over the slippery walks. The streets were snarled with vehicles, trapped by the sudden storm. At every crossing Mora-Ta-Kai had to pick his way through a mass of stalled moto-canoes. Only the new degravs were moving. They rode comfortably above the turmoil, driven by their whirring roto-paddles. Mora-Ta-Kai observed the performance of the machines critically, and with satisfaction. The degrav was his own invention; this storm was its first real test in a commercial situation.

The quarrel with Lassai and Pyrn-Ute crowded his mind, poisoning everything else. He saw the bulk of the Council House, rising out of the gray mist of the storm, and the beckoning lights of the Teepee Room. Mora-Ta-Kai needed a drink; not one, but a dozen. If he made himself roaring drunk, he could wash the memory of the quarrel away. He turned to cross through the traffic.

A noise-warner blared behind him. He heard the grind of wheels, the skid of safety grips on the slush ice. He dodged. For a moment, a shiver of sharp pain lashed his spine. The snow, the traffic, the light from the Teepee Room swirled together in a tortuous pattern.

Then everything was gone. Instead of the Council House, a different structure rose before him. The letters on the building were strange—foolish marks he had never seen before—yet Mora-Ta-Kai knew and read them!

The building was called the Conrad Hilton.

Mora-Ta-Kai had never before seen any of the peculiar vehicles which cluttered the street. Yet he recognized them all. He saw the faces of the people: White Savages! White Savages walking the streets of— of— Their name for the place was Chicago. Mora-Ta-Kai knew it, just as he was able to read their printed words.

In terror he began to run, fighting his way back to reality. But the nightmare closed on his mind. Hands reached out of the depths of his fear—the pale hands of white Savages. They dragged him down deep into a black, choking chaos, down into a world of quivering pain.

And out of it they brought him to this—the pretense of conformity. From winter to spring, from one sort of prison to another. But Mora-Ta-Kai could end the dream. The old science was more powerful than the sorcery of the White Savages.

119

He opened the bedroom door and called Mrs. Armbruster.
A young, yellow-haired squaw came into the hall. "Mrs. Armbruster is in the sun room. Can I help? I'm Lydia Rand, Mrs. Armbruster's assistant."

He stood staring at the woman. She resembled someone he knew, but he couldn't remember. Not Lassai; Lassai's hair was long and black, braided in a coil at the back of her head. Lydia Rand was like another female, a woman somehow associated with the beginning of the nightmare. The ghost of a new memory tugged at his mind. But it eluded him.

"I need some things," he said.

"Give me a list, Mr. Smith, and I'll—"

"No, I have to buy them myself."

"You came to us for a rest." She put her hand gently on his arm. "If there's any work that needs to be done, leave it to us." She smiled at him warmly. The White Savages had all been kind and attentive; and for that Mora-Ta-Kai was grateful. The nightmare was terror enough; if he had peopled it with real plantation barbarians—he shuddered.

"I'm not permitted to leave the house?" he asked. "Is that it?" His voice choked. He had conformed; he had done all they asked. Surely, now, he would be able to escape!

Lydia Rand looked steadily into his eyes. "In your case, it might be a good thing," she decided. "But I'll have to go with you."

Mora-Ta-Kai sighed with relief. She would be no real hindrance. If she were with him, he would not be able to buy the pure elements he needed, because that would arouse curiosity, but he knew the chemicals were incorporated in common compounds—tooth-powder, cosmetics, patent medicines.

(How did he know? The knowledge was a part of the dream, like his facility in using their language. He thought in terms of his own semantic symbols; but he spoke and read theirs.)

Lydia Rand walked with him to a drugstore a block from the house. She made no comment when he bought the assortment of drugs. From the point of view of her science, they were harmless. However, three vital items presented something of a problem: the copper wire, the foil aluminum, and the magnets. The aluminum he found in a roll. In that form it was sold to White Savage squaws for wrapping left-over foods. The copper wire and the magnets were both available as parts of toys.

"What in the world do you want with these things?" Lydia asked.

"I—these seem to be—" He was in a panic, without an excuse.

Then she helped him out. "They're familiar to you, Mr. Smith? Good! Perhaps you were a toy manufacturer before you—before you came to us. By all means buy them. They may help restore your memory."

They paid for his purchases and left the store. She put her arm through his and they walked back to the rest home. It was dusk and long shadows fell on the street. The sky overhead flamed scarlet with the light of the setting sun.

Lydia laughed pleasantly. "It's a good thing you didn't send me out with a list of what you wanted, Mr. Smith." She gestured at the bulky package under his arm. "Such a conglomeration! Anyone would think you were going to play around with witchcraft or sorcery."

He looked at her squarely. The red blaze of the sun touched her face, like the light of a blazing fire. Her hair was transformed into a fragile crown of gold; her eyes were lost in shadow. He recognized her, then. The memory leaped into clarity, against a background of fear.

Lydia Rand was the Sorceress.

He knew now why he had quarreled with Lassai; he remembered the real beginning of the dream.

Weak with fear, he went back to his room. He shut the door, but there was no way he could lock it. He put his package, unopened, on the bureau and dropped limply on the bed. The full pattern emerged from his memory, complete and unbroken.

The beginning of the dream: not the sudden winter storm; not the ritual of the plantation savages across the Eastern Sea; not even the chant of the Sorceress. The dream began in the eccentric scientific theorizing of his own mind . . .

"You're joking," Pyrn-Ute said.

"No; I've already asked for leave and bought my ticket," Mora-Ta-Kai responded. "I'm going on the *Iroquois* this afternoon."

"But why? You've no reason to go out to the plantations. You're a scientist, a chosen brave—"

"I'm going because I am a scientist. I have a theory; I want to prove it."

"You're a number-man, not a tribalist!"

"The same method is used in both fields."

"Don't tell me your fantastic notion of equality—"

"Red superiority is a myth. Given our opportunities, our environment, the White Savages could have equaled our civilization."

This was too much for Pyrn-Ute. His thin, sardonic face seethed with laughter. It was the reaction Mora-Ta-Kai expected.

"The White Savages are slaves, Mora-Ta-Kai," Pyrn-Ute said. "They always have been. They don't have the mentality to be anything else."

"Slaves only because a quirk of history caused our war canoes to stray across the Eastern Sea. We discovered the dark continent of the White Savages when they still lived in scattered, stone-walled villages, savage tribes constantly at war with each other. Suppose our canoes had arrived two centuries later? In that time, if the Whites had been left alone, they might have learned to live together as one nation, as we did ourselves."

"Oh, I know the radicals trot that nonsense out whenever they find a willing audience. They tell us the yellow-hairs are noble, beautiful people." Pyrn-Ute's lip curled in disgust. "I've seen the plantations. I've seen the filth and the disease, the barbaric rituals!"

"Our basic science was stolen from them, Pyrn-Ute."

"By accident; and we improved it so—"

"Our explorers brought back the number system, the astrology, and the philosophy of science which an earlier culture of White Savages had developed."

"But they had forgotten it themselves."

"Nevertheless, the knowledge was originally theirs."

"In a way, I suppose, we owe their remote ancestors a debt, but that doesn't mean the savages of today. Neither history nor the ranting of the radicals can explain away one obvious fact. At the time when we discovered the dark continent, our races stood on equal footing. They even had the advantage, because the science was theirs. Their land was as rich as ours and as fertile. Our two races started at the same place, from scratch. Yet only the Red Man learned how to build a civilization. The answer, Mora-Ta-Kai, is obvious: we have superior mental ability."

"I think I can prove otherwise."

"How?"

"I want to visit the plantation stations and examine the records on station help. We've taught them to use our language and numbers the way we do. I think I can demonstrate that their rate of learning is no slower than ours."

"But the station help is less than one percent of the population. They're chosen for their superiority—"

"Because we've made them seem so by teaching them what we know."

Pyrn-Ute chuckled. "You've never seen the slave plantations. It'll be different when you stand face to face with the truth. Are you going alone?"

"Lassai isn't the kind of squaw who can rough it on a plantation. She'll stay here. I may want to push into the interior, you know."

"You've been married for three moons, Mora-Ta-Kai. You have strong convictions, if you'll leave your bride so soon. But no sense."

"It's good sense if I can prove—"

"Who cares? When you come back, you'll write a learned monograph for the tribalist files; they'll put it in the archives and forget it."

"I won't let the issue die like that. Pyrn-Ute, our system of slave plantations has to be revised. Think what we might accomplish, if our two races could work together in equality."

"Follow the implications of equality to its logical end, Mora-Ta-Kai. Then ask yourself this: would you let your own sister become the squaw of a White Savage?"

"Intermarriage has nothing to do with it. The two races can live together, as brothers, without it."

Pyrn-Ute held out his hand. "You have enough good sense to change your mind after you see the yellow-hairs in their native setting. How long will you be away?"

"Six moons."

"Enjoy yourself. I'll look in on Lassai occasionally. By the way, this new invention of yours, the degrav unit—"

"I've ironed out all the bugs, I think. They're going into commercial production at once. If you will, Pyrn-Ute, I'd like you to handle the royalty contracts."

"Of course."

"If anything like an emergency comes up, contact me at the slave station on Angle Island. I'll make that my headquarters."

Two hours later Mora-Ta-Kai set sail in the *Iroquois*. It was an enormous sky freighter on the food run, making tri-weekly trips between the Angle Island Plantations and the Lake Cities. Mora-Ta-Kai sat in the cabin as the sphere shot up from the field. Below him were the five lakes, lying like a giant hand placed upon the heart of the continent. Girdling the shores of the lakes were the towers of the interlocked Lake Cities.

As the sphere moved eastward, the pattern of cities on the earth below did not change. No mountain, no valley, no river bank stood unoccupied. The continent was one vast city, teeming with activity. It was Mora-Ta-Kai's civilization, crowded, complex, dynamic. Built solidly on scientific knowledge, the culture seemed eternally enduring. Yet its foundation was riddled with the slow, moral decay of slavery. The food, the heavy labor, the key resources of Mora-Ta-Kai's world were produced by White Savage slaves on the plantations across the Eastern Sea.

The *Iroquois* was an old ship. It had neither the speed nor the comfort of the modern pleasure liners which sailed the routes to the Ethiopian Republic or to the Shogun Union across the Western Sea. It was strange, Mora-Ta-Kai thought, that the black men of Ethiopia should live so much closer to the continent of the White Savages, yet practice so little racial hatred. The Ethiopian Republic had encouraged the growth of free colonies of whites within the republic. In some areas whites and blacks had intermarried, with no loss of social status to the black man.

In ten hours the *Iroquois* settled into the landing crib on Angle Island. Precision-trained natives swarmed into the hatches and the job of loading foodstuffs aboard the sphere began immediately.

This was the first time Mora-Ta-Kai had seen the yellow-hairs. They wore gray, crudely woven tunics; their feet and arms were bare. When he came close to them, he had to admit that, in one particular at least, Pyrn-Ute had been right. The White Savages were filthy. Vermin crawled in their matted hair. Their bodies were covered with sores and scabs.

When he went to the plantation station, Mora-Ta-Kai found the native station personnel somewhat more attractive. They were relatively clean. They wore cheap imitations of the Red Man's civilized costume—leather loin cloths, jeweled chest straps, soft sandals. But they had no pride, no bearing. Their manner was abject, beaten. Once more it seemed that Pyrn-Ute had been right. How could such fawning things be considered the equals of the free Red Man?

Mora-Ta-Kai believed that slavery had made the whites adopt the attitudes of slaves. If they were born in freedom and reared in freedom, they would be no different from their masters. He was convinced of it because he knew that the dependence of the Red Man on the slaves was inexorably destroying civilization, weakening the incentive and the ambition of his people.

Mora-Ta-Kai doggedly assembled his data from the educational records of the station personnel. For five moons he traveled from one plantation to another, collecting statistics. He made three excursions to the interior stations. The Red Men who were station directors gave him no help. They derided the idea of racial equality. The White Savages themselves were afraid when Mora-Ta-Kai tried to talk to them. They would take his orders, yes; they would wait on his wants. But simply to sit and chat with a Red Man was an unheard of violation of established relations with their masters.

At the end of the fifth moon Mora-Ta-Kai sat in his room at the Angle Island station tentatively outlining the report he would make when he returned to the Lake Cities. The regular station personnel were in the recreation room, watching a command performance of a native ritual. Many of the Red Men were very drunk. Mora-Ta-Kai had discovered that many station directors were never sober.

His door creaked open. A yellow-hair slid into the room. Mora-Ta-Kai felt sure he recognized the man, although it was hard to distinguish one savage from another.

"The Red Master is busy? He not wish to be disturbed?"

Mora-Ta-Kai patiently set his papers aside. "I always have time to talk with friends." He studied the white face carefully. "Your name is—Harold?"

"I am proud you remember me, master." The yellow-hair glanced at the desk. "You are making a study of my people; that, too, gives me pride."

"I wish I had more information, Harold."

"The heart of the White Savage cannot be found in a plantation house."

"But where else—"

"Would you be willing, Red master, to visit a Sorceress?"

Mora-Ta-Kai laughed uneasily. "I've heard the legends, Harold; but you're an intelligent man and surely you don't believe the sorcery-makers really exist!"

"The Red Man has never seen one."

"And you have, Harold?"

"The Sorceress says, Red master, that you are honest."

Mora-Ta-Kai stood up and drew his pleated animal hide around his naked shoulders, for the night was cold. "Would you take me to a Sorceress, Harold?"

"She has sent the call; I obey. But, master—" The yellow-hair hesitated, wringing his hands nervously. "There is danger."

"I will be armed, Harold."

"No physical danger, master; but to the soul. Your protection must be honesty, as true and unwavering as fire flaming in a deep well."

Mora-Ta-Kai suppressed a smile. This was the typical superstitious mumbo jumbo of savages everywhere. The ancient ritual of his own people had been no different. "We can go now, Harold," he said. "The others are busy downstairs; we'll not disturb them."

"This is as the Sorceress arranged it, master."

Mora-Ta-Kai followed Harold away from the plantation house. They slipped past the noisy, cluttered slave pens in the forest. And then the Red Man felt the first pang of fear. The night seemed alive with unseen things. Frost lay heavy on the ground, in white shadows, which leered at Mora-Ta-Kai like grinning masks. The darkness pulsed with a clamorous sound. There was a slow rhythm to his fear, like a heartbeat.

In the distance they saw a fire glowing among the trees. Naked white men swirled in a circle around the flame, their bodies contorted in a ritual dance. Yet they made no sound. Mora-Ta-Kai heard nothing but the muted beat of a skin-drum and the low-keyed melody of a reed pipe.

The fear exploded in his mind. The feeling was sensuous, hypnotic. Vaguely he wondered if they had somehow drugged him when he ate that evening. Despite his civilization, his training as a scientist, he was powerless to hold the fear back. The White Savages had wiped away his superiority and reduced him to their level. This, then, was equality!

He would have gone back, but he could not.

He followed Harold to the fire. He saw the Sorceress standing above the flames, her arms raised to the night sky, her pale face red in the glare. His fear dissolved into pure terror . . .

Mora-Ta-Kai felt the same terror as he sat weak and exhausted on the bed in Mrs. Armbruster's house. The Sorceress had made this dream. She had created the nightmare world and condemned him to it: this strange world where a city called Chicago took the place of the beautiful Lake Cities, where an ugly thing called the Conrad Hilton stood on the site of the Council House. Why? Mora-Ta-Kai did not know. His intention had been to help the White Savages, yet they had destroyed him.

He knew only this: he could wipe out the thing the Sorceress had made.

This distortion existed only in his mind. The Sorceress had put it there. But she had not entirely destroyed the real substance of himself. Mora-Ta-Kai was a scientist and his scientific knowledge was intact, unharmed.

The universe of the Sorceress, perhaps as a result of her scientific ignorance, had physical laws different from reality, less complex. In the structure of the dream world, mechanical degravitation was a mathematical absurdity. But in the real science which Mora-Ta-Kai knew, degravs had been popular toys for centuries. Mora-Ta-Kai himself had invented a practical application of the degrav to commercial transportation.

To end the dream, he would apply the science he knew to the distortion. He would set up a degrav core which would activate the planet itself. The dream universe, held together by a clock-like balance of opposing gravities, would fall in upon itself. Perhaps, in the process, Mora-Ta-Kai would also destroy himself. He didn't know. At least he would escape, if only to oblivion.

He got up and opened his package of drugs and toys. He laid the material out on the bed, carefully separating the items he needed. He spread the aluminum sheet in the correct pattern on the floor and began to compute the angle of magnetization.

There was a knock on the door.

Mora-Ta-Kai's throat went cold with panic. He could not hide the aluminum. The sheet was too fragile. If he wrinkled the surface, the distortion angle would be too complex for him to compute without a calculator.

The door swung open. Lydia Rand came into his room.

"Your dinner's ready, Mr. Smith," she said cheerfully. "But if you'd rather eat in here—" Then she saw the aluminum. "What is it, Mr. Smith?"

"A—a toy," he muttered.

"And you want to build it?"

"I—I've made one before."

"Then you're beginning to remember!" Her eyes glowed with pleasure. When he saw her face in the light, he realized that her resemblance to the Sorceress had been superficial. All the yellow-hairs looked so much alike. "Could you tell me about it, Mr. Smith?"

He had recovered poise enough to lie. "It's very vague, like a shadow in my mind. I thought it was something I remembered." He shrugged, and pretended to lose interest. "I'm wrong, of course; it's rather foolish, isn't it?"

"I'm sure it isn't. Please finish it. It may help you find yourself. You stay here and work on it; I'll bring you a sandwich and a glass of milk." She was gone again. With trembling fingers he went back to building the degrav core. Lydia Rand was very naive. It had not occurred to her that his innocent toy could sweep her world into oblivion. Slowly Mora-Ta-Kai stopped and sat down on the bed. They had given him nothing but kindness, these dream people. Was it worth destroying their world, even on the chance that he might regain his own?

All reality, all truth were subjective phenomena. To the doctor, to Lydia Rand, to all the White Savages, this dream was real; his was the abnormality. Universe upon universe, the Sorceress had said, as infinite as the complexity of human thought . . .

The black night, the throbbing, primitive forest closed in on Mora-Ta-Kai. He stood looking into the eyes of the Sorceress, sapphire orbs framed by the wild filigree of her wind-blown, yellow hair.

"Mora-Ta-Kai, you come among us on a quest, and the thing you seek is within yourself. All possible worlds lie dormant in the soul of every man, all possible good and all possible evil. Take my hand, Mora-Ta-Kai, and look with me into the fire. We go on a journey, you and I, a long journey in the circle of nowhere, to other worlds and other faces—"

The lilting chant faded, like the dying whisper of a summer wind, as he took her hand. Her fingers were light, fragile, the feather touch of a ghost; yet they held him like bands of steel. He looked into the fire.

Like the turning pages of an open book, Mora-Ta-Kai saw the kaleidoscope of possible time. He saw yellow people, who lived across the Western Sea, stray from the drive that had created the Shogun Union, and sink slowly into the stalemate of a decayed dictatorship. He saw the proud Republic of Ethiopia lost in savagery, splintered into a hundred helpless tribes, enslaved by other men. And he saw the White Savages rise up and claim the world. He saw them flow in a restless flood into the continent of the Red Man. Mora-Ta-Kai's people were debased, debauched, cheated and murdered, driven slowly into extinction, while a proud culture of White Savages was built on the face of the land.

The picture vanished. The fire died. Mora-Ta-Kai was alone in the clearing with the yellow-haired Sorceress.

"What does the vision mean?" he asked her.

"Meaning you must find for yourself, just as the things you saw came from your own mind, Mora-Ta-Kai. The worlds are all there, universe upon universe, as infinite as the complexity of human thought. I have shown you how to reach them. At another time, you will find the way for yourself."

She turned and disappeared into the forest.

A week later Mora-Ta-Kai took the *Iroquois* back to the Lake Cities. He published his report through the tribalist institute. He called it *The Myth*. The opening sentence set his theme, "All men are brothers." The monograph caused a mild sensation; it was bought and read like a piece of pornographic literature.

But Pyrn-Ute and Lassai met Mora-Ta-Kai with rage and revulsion.

"I suppose you took a squaw among the yellow-hairs!" Lassai cried. "Filthy, vermin-ridden beasts. And you prefer them to me!"

"Of course I don't, Lassai. Even if I had done that, it wouldn't matter. The idea of brotherhood—"

"Don't touch me!" She fled to Pyrn-Ute, and he put his arm around her shoulder.

"Brotherhood," Pyrn-Ute said in his aloof, sardonic way, "is a very dangerous concept, Mora-Ta-Kai. We use it among ourselves. We always have. But to suggest that we include—"

Suddenly Mora-Ta-Kai understood what the Sorceress had meant; he read the fire pictures. "It was brotherhood that made us strong," he said. "Nothing else. When our war canoes first discovered the continent of White Savages, the Red Men were a united people. We had learned how to live together in peace. The White Savages had not. It was not their science that made us great, but the thing we were ourselves!"

"This I know, Mora-Ta-Kai: the idea of brotherhood that you have given us would destroy the world."

"If we are so weak, we deserve destruction!"

Mora-Ta-Kai stormed angrily out of the house, into the winter storm. Five minutes later he had lost his universe. The chant of the Sorceress sang at him: other worlds, other faces—a journey in the circle of nowhere.

He sat on the bed looking at his degrav machine; and he knew now that he would never complete it.

Lydia Rand returned and put a sandwich and a glass of milk on his bureau.

129

"You haven't finished your toy, Mr. Smith!"

"I have no reason to. In this universe or in that, all men are brothers—the rest doesn't matter."

She sat down beside him and took his hand. "You were saying that when we brought you in, Mr. Smith. Have you remembered anything else?"

"All of it." He began to laugh. Very slowly he picked up the sheet of aluminum and crumpled it into a tight ball.

"What were you making?"

"A degravitation core."

"Oh, come now, Mr. Smith. We know better than that, don't we? Degravitation is a physical impossibility."

"In your world, yes, and to Mr. Smith, yes. But in the circle of nowhere, there is a time, there is a place— Sit beside me, Miss Rand, and I will tell you about it."

As he talked he embraced the dream and the dream became real. Lassai, Pyrn-Ute, the White Savages: they were gone, exorcised from his mind like demons. Here, in this new reality, he was a Red Man in a culture of White Savages; but they treated him kindly and with understanding. He had found the thing he sought in the forest; the Sorceress had shown him the way to brotherhood. He asked for nothing else.

The *Lady Margaret*

Keith Roberts

T

Durnovaria, England. 1968.

he appointed morning came, and they buried Eli Strange. The coffin, black and purple drapes twitched aside, eased down into the grave; the white webbings slid through the hands of the bearers in nomine Patris, et Filii, et Spiritus Sancti . . . *The earth took back her own. And miles away* Iron Margaret *cried cold and wreathed with steam, drove her great sea voice across the hills.*

At three in the afternoon the engine sheds were already gloomy with the coming night. Light, blue and vague, filtered through the long strips of the skylights, showing the roof ties stark like angular metal bones. Beneath, the locomotives waited brooding, hulks twice the height of a man, their canopies brushing the rafters. The light gleamed in dull spindle shapes, here from the strappings of a boiler, there from the starred boss of a flywheel. The massive road wheels stood in pools of shadow.

Through the half-dark a man came walking. He moved steadily, whistling between his teeth, boot studs rasping on the worn brick floor. He wore the jeans and heavy reefer jacket of a hauler; the collar of the jacket was turned up against the cold. On his head was a woolen cap, once red, stained now with dirt and oil. The hair that showed beneath it was thickly black. A lamp swung in his hand, sending cusps of light flicking across the maroon livery of the engines.

He stopped by the last locomotive in line and reached up to hang the lamp from her hornplate. He stood a moment gazing at the big shapes of the engines, chafing his hands unconsciously, sensing the faint ever-present stink of smoke and oil. Then he swung onto the footplate of the loco and opened the firebox doors. He crouched, working methodically. The rake scraped against the fire bars; his breath jetted from him, rising in wisps over his shoulder. He laid the fire carefully, wadding paper, adding a crisscrossing of sticks, shoveling coal from the tender with rhythmic swings of his arms. Not too much fire to begin with, not under a cold boiler. Sudden heat meant sudden expansion and that meant cracking, leaks round the fire-tube joints, endless trouble. For all their power, the locos had to be cosseted like children, coaxed and persuaded to give of their best.

The hauler laid the shovel aside and reached into the firebox mouth to sprinkle paraffin from a can. Then a soaked rag, a match. . . . The lucifer flared brightly, sputtering. The oil caught with a faint *whoomph.* He closed the doors, opened the damper handles for draft. He straightened up, wiped his hands on cotton waste, then dropped from the footplate and began mechanically rubbing the brightwork of the engine. Over his head, long name-boards carried the style of the firm in swaggering, curlicued letters: *Strange and Sons of Dorset, Haulers.* Lower, on the side of the great boiler, was the name of the engine herself. The *Lady Margaret.* The hulk of rag paused when it reached the brass plate; then it polished it slowly, with loving care.

The *Margaret* hissed softly to herself, cracks of flame light showing round her ash pan. The shed foreman had filled her boiler and the belly and tender tanks that afternoon; her train was linked up across the yard, waiting by the warehouse loading bays. The hauler added more fuel to the fire, watched the pressure building slowly toward working head; lifted the heavy oak wheel scotches, stowed them in the steamer alongside the packaged water-gauge glasses. The barrel of the loco was warming now, giving out a faint heat that radiated toward the cab.

The driver looked above him broodingly at the skylights. Mid-December; and it seemed as always God was stinting the light itself so the days came and vanished like the blinking of a dim gray eye. The frost would come down hard as well, later on. It was freezing already; in the yard the puddles had crashed and tinkled under his boots, the skin of ice from the night before barely thinned. Bad weather for the haulers; many of them had packed up already. This was the time for the wolves to leave their shelter, what wolves there were left. And the *routiers* . . . this was their season right enough, ideal for quick raids and swoopings, rich hauls from the last road trains of the winter. The man shrugged under his coat.

This would be the last run to the coast for a month or so at least, unless that old goat Serjeantson across the way tried a quick dash with his vaunted Fowler triple compound. In that case the *Margaret* would go out again; because Strange and Sons made the last run to the coast. Always had, always would . . .

Working head, a hundred and fifty pounds to the inch. The driver hooked the hand lamp over the push-pole bracket on the front of the smokebox, climbed back to the footplate, checked gear for neutral, opened the cylinder cocks, inched the regulator across. The *Lady Margaret* woke up, pistons thumping, cross-heads sliding in their guides, exhaust beating sudden thunder under the low roof. Steam whirled back and smoke, thick and cindery, catching at the throat. The driver grinned faintly and without humor. The starting drill was a part of him, burned on his mind. Gear check, cylinder cocks, regulator. . . . He'd missed out just once, years back when he was a boy; opened up a four-horse Roby traction with her cocks shut, let the condensed water in front of the piston knock the end out of the bore. His heart had broken with the cracking iron; but old Eli had still taken a studded belt and whipped him till he thought he was going to die.

He closed the cocks, moved the reversing lever to forward full, and opened the regulator again. Old Dickon, the yard foreman, had materialized in the gloom of the shed; he hauled back on the heavy doors as the *Margaret,* jetting steam, rumbled into the open air, swung across the yard to where her train was parked.

Dickon, coatless despite the cold, snapped the linkage onto the *Lady Margaret*'s drawbar, clicked the brake unions into place. Three freight cars and the water tender; a light enough haul this time. The foreman stood, hands on hips, in breeches and grubby, ruffed shirt, grizzled hair curling over his collar. "Best let I come with 'ee, Master Jesse . . ."

Jesse shook his head somberly, jaw set. They'd been through this before. His father had never believed in overstaffing; he'd worked his few men hard for the wages he paid, and got his money's worth out of them. Though how long that would go on was anybody's guess with the Guild of Mechanics stiffening its attitude all the time. Eli had stayed on the road himself up until a few days before his death; Jesse had steered for him not much more than a week before, taking the *Margaret* round the hill villages topside of Bridport to pick up serge and worsted from the combers there; part of the load that was now outward bound for Poole. There'd been no sitting back in an office chair for old Strange, and his death had left the firm badly shorthanded; pointless taking on fresh drivers now, with the end of the season only days away. Jesse gripped Dickon's shoulder. "We can't spare thee, Dick. Run the yard, see my mother's all right. That's what he'd have wanted." He grimaced briefly. "If I can't take *Margaret* out by now, 'tis time I learned." He walked back along the train pulling at the lashings of the tarps. The tender and numbers one and two were shipshape, all fast. No need to check the trail load; he'd packed it himself the day before, taken hours over it. He checked it all the same, saw the taillights and number-plate lamp were burning before taking the cargo manifest from Dickon. He climbed back to the footplate, working his hands into the heavy driver's mitts with their leather-padded palms.

The foreman watched him stolidly. "Take care for the *routiers*. Norman bastards . . ."

Jesse grunted. "Let 'em take care for themselves. See to things, Dickon. Expect me tomorrow."

"God be with 'ee . . ."

Jesse eased the regulator forward, raised an arm as the stocky figure fell behind. The *Margaret* and her train clattered under the arch of the yard gate and into the rutted streets of Durnovaria.

Jesse had a lot to occupy his mind as he steered his load into the town; for the moment, the *routiers* were the least of his worries. Now, with the first keen grief just starting to lose its edge, he was beginning to realize how much they'd all miss Eli. The firm was a heavy weight to have hung around his neck without warning; and it could be there were awkward times ahead. With the Church openly backing the clamor of the guilds for shorter hours and higher pay, it looked as if the haulage companies were going to have to tighten their belts again, though God knew profit margins were thin enough already. And there were rumors of more restrictions on the road trains themselves; a maximum of six trailers it would be this time, and a water cart. Reason given had been the increasing congestion round the big towns. That, and the state of the roads; but what else could you expect, Jesse asked himself sourly, when half the tax levied in the country went to buy gold plate for its churches? Maybe, though, this was just the start of a new trade recession like the one engineered a couple of centuries back by Gisevius. The memory of that still rankled in the West at least. The economy of England was stable now, for the first time in years; stability meant wealth, gold reserves. And gold, stacked anywhere but in the half-legendary coffers of the Vatican, meant danger . . .

Months back, Eli, swearing blue fire, had set about getting around the new regulations. He'd had a dozen trailers modified to carry fifty gallons of water in a galvanized tank just abaft the drawbar. The tanks took up next to no space and left the rest of the bed for payload; but they'd be enough to satisfy the sheriff's dignity. Jesse could imagine the old devil cackling at his victory; only he hadn't lived to see it. His thoughts slid back to his father, as irrevocably as the coffin had slid into the earth. He remembered his last sight of him, the gray wax nose peeping above the drapes as the visitors, Eli's drivers among them, filed through the mourning room of the old house. Death hadn't softened Eli Strange; it had ravaged the face but left it strong, like the side of a quarried hill.

Queer how when you were driving you seemed to have more time to think. Even driving on your own when you had to watch the boiler gauge, steam head, fire. . . . Jesse's hands felt the familiar thrilling in the wheel rim, the little stresses that on a long run would build and build till countering them brought burning aches to the shoulders and back. Only this was no long run; twenty, twenty-two miles, across to Wool, then over the Great Heath to Poole. An easy trip for the *Lady Margaret,* with an easy load; thirty tons at the back of her, and flat ground most of the way. The loco had only two gears; Jesse had started off in high, and that was where he meant to stay. The *Margaret*'s nominal horsepower was ten, but that was on the old rating; one horsepower to be deemed equal to ten circular inches of piston area. Pulling against the brake the Burrell would clock seventy, eighty horse; enough to shift a rolling load of a hundred and thirty tons. Old Eli had pulled a train that heavy once for a wager. And won . . .

Jesse checked the pressure gauge, eyes performing their work nearly automatically. Ten pounds under max. All right for a while; he could stoke on the move, he'd done it times enough before, but as yet there was no need. He reached the first crossroads, glanced right and left and wound at the wheel, looking behind him to see each car of the train turning sweetly at the same spot. Good; Eli would have liked that turn. The trail load would pull across the road crown, he knew, but that wasn't his concern. His lamps were burning, and any drivers who couldn't see the bulk of *Margaret* and her load deserved the smashing they would get. Forty-odd tons, rolling and thundering; bad luck on any butterfly cars that got too close.

Jesse had all the haulers' ingrained contempt for internal combustion, though he'd followed the arguments for and against it keenly enough. Maybe one day petrol propulsion might amount to something, and there was that other system, what did they call it, *diesel.* . . . But the hand of the Church would have to be lifted first. The Bull of 1910, *Petroleum Veto,* had limited the capacity of IC engines to 150 cc's, and since then the haulers had had no real competition. Petrol vehicles had been forced to fit gaudy sails to help tow themselves along; load hauling was a singularly bad joke. Mother of God, but it was cold! Jesse shrugged himself deeper into his jacket. The *Lady Margaret* carried no spectacle plate; a lot of other steamers had installed them now, even one or two in the Strange fleet, but Eli had sworn not the *Margaret*, not on the *Margaret*. . . . She was a work of art, perfect in herself; as her makers had built her, so she would stay. Decking her out with gewgaws—the old man had been half sick at the thought. It would make her look like one of the railway engines Eli so despised. Jesse narrowed his eyes, forcing them to see against the searing bite of the wind. He glanced down at the tachometer. Road speed fifteen miles an hour, revs one fifty. One gloved hand pulled back on the reversing lever. Ten was the limit through towns, fixed by the laws of the realm; and Jesse had no intention of being run in for exceeding it. The firm of Strange had always kept well in with the JPs and sergeants of police; it partially accounted for their success.

Entering the long High Street, he cut his revs again. The *Margaret*, balked, made a frustrated thunder; the sound echoed back, clapping from the fronts of the gray stone buildings. Jesse felt through his boot soles the slackening pull on the drawbar and spun the brake wheel; a jackknifed train was about the worst blot on a driver's record. Reflectors behind the tail-lamp flames clicked upward, momentarily doubling their glare. The brakes bit; compensators pulled the trail load first, straightening the cars. He eased back another notch on the reversing lever; steam admitted in front of the pistons checked *Margaret*'s speed. Ahead were the gas lamps of town center, high on their standards; beyond, the walls and the East Gate.

The sergeant on duty saluted easily with his halberd, waving the Burrell forward. Jesse shoved at the lever, wound the brakes away from the wheels. Too much stress on the shoes and there could be a fire somewhere in the train. That would be bad; most of the load was inflammable this time.

He ran through the manifest in his mind. The *Margaret* was carrying bale on bale of serge; bulkwise it accounted for most of her cargo. English woolens were famous on the Continent; correspondingly, the serge combers were among the most powerful industrial groups in the Southwest. Their factories and storing sheds dotted the villages for miles around; monopoly of the trade had helped keep old Eli out ahead of his rivals. Then there were dyed silks from Anthony Harcourt at Mells; Harcourt shifts were sought after as far abroad as Paris. And crate after crate of turned ware, products of the local bodgers, Erasmus Cox and Jed

Roberts of Durnovaria, Jeremiah Stringer out at Martinstown. Specie, under the county lieutenant's seal; the last of the season's levies, outward bound for Rome. And machine parts, high-grade cheeses, all kinds of oddments. Clay pipes, horn buttons, ribbons and tape; even a shipment of cherrywood Madonnas from that New World-financed firm over at Beaminster. What did they call themselves—*Calmers of the Soul, Inc.* . . . ? Woolens and worsteds atop the water tender and in car number one, turned goods and the rest in number two. The trail load needed no consideration. That would look after itself.

The East Gate showed ahead, and the dark bulk of the wall. Jesse slowed in readiness. There was no need; the odd butterfly cars that were still braving the elements on this bitter night were already stopped, held back out of harm's way by the signals of the halberdiers. The *Margaret* hooted, left behind a cloud of steam that hung glowing against the evening sky. Passed through the ramparts to the heath and hills beyond.

Jesse reached down to twirl the control of the injector valve. Water, preheated by its passage through an extension of the smokebox, swirled into the boiler. He allowed the engine to build up speed. Durnovaria vanished, lost in the gloom astern; the light was fading fast now. To right and left the land was featureless, dark; in front of him was the half-seen whirling of the crankshaft, the big thunder of the engine. The hauler grinned, still exhilarated by the physical act of driving. Flame light striking round the firebox doors showed the wide, hard jaw, the deep-set eyes under brows that were level and thickly black. Just let old Serjeant-son try and sneak in a last trip. The *Margaret* would take his Fowler, uphill or down; and Eli would churn with glee in his fresh-made grave . . .

The *Lady Margaret*. A scene came unasked into Jesse's mind. He saw himself as a boy, voice half broken. How long ago was that—eight seasons, ten? The years had a way of piling themselves one atop the next, unnoticed and uncounted; that was how young men turned into old ones. He remembered the morning the *Margaret* first arrived in the yard. She'd come snorting and plunging through Durnovaria, fresh from Burrell's works in far-off Thetford, paintwork gleaming, whistle sounding, brasswork a-twinkle in the sun; a compound locomotive of ten nhp, all her details specified from flywheel decoration to static-discharge chains. Spud pan, belly pan, water lifts; Eli had got what he wanted, all right, one of the finest steamers in the West. He'd fetched her himself, making the awkward journey across many counties to Norfork; nobody else had been trusted to bring back the pride of the fleet. And she'd been his steamer ever since; if the old granite shell that had called itself Eli Strange ever loved anything on earth, it had been the huge Burrell.

Jesse had been there to meet her, and his kid brother Tim and the others, James and Micah, dead now—God rest their souls—of the plague that had taken them both that time in Bristol. He remembered how his father had swung off the footplate, looked up at the loco standing shaking like a live thing still and spewing steam. The firm's name had been painted there already, the letters glowing along the canopy edge, but as yet the Burrell had no name of her own. "What be 'ee gwine call en?" his mother had shouted, over the noise of her idling; and Eli had rumpled his hair, puckered his red face. "Danged if I knows. . . ." They had *Thunderer* already and *Apocalypse, Oberon* and *Ballard Down* and *Western Strength;* big-sounding names, right for the machines that carried them. "Danged if I *knows,*" said old Eli, grinning; and Jesse's voice had spoken without his permission, faltering up in its adolescent yodel. "The *Lady Margaret, sir* . . . *Lady Margaret* . . ."

A bad thing that, speaking without being addressed. Eli had glared, shoved up his cap, scrubbed at his hair again and burst into a roar of laughter. "I *like* en . . . bugger me if I *don't* like en. . . ." And the *Lady Margaret* she had become, over the protests of his drivers, even over old Dickon's head. He claimed it "were downright luck" to call a loco after "some bloody 'oman. . . ." Jesse remembered his ears burning, he couldn't tell whether with shame or pride. He'd unwished the name a thousand times, but it had stuck. Eli liked it; and nobody crossed old Strange, not in the days of his strength.

So Eli was dead. There'd been no warning; just the coughing, the hands gripping the chair arms, the face that suddenly wasn't his father's face, staring. Quick dark spattering of blood, the lungs sighing and bubbling; and a clay-colored old man lying abed, one lamp burning, the priest in attendance, Jesse's mother watching empty-faced. Father Thomas had been cold, disapproving of the old sinner; the wind had soughed round the house vicious with frost while the priest's lips absolved and mechanically blessed . . . but that hadn't been death. A death was more than an ending; it was like pulling a thread from a richly patterned cloth. Eli had been a part of Jesse's life, as much a part as his bedroom under the eaves of the old house. Death disrupted the processes of memory, jangled old chords that were maybe best left alone. It took so little imagination for Jesse to see his father still, the craggy face, weathered hands, hauler's greasy buckled cap pulled low over his eyes. The knotted muffler, ends anchored round the braces, the greatcoat, old thick working corduroys.

It was here he missed him, in the clanking and the darkness, with the hot smell of oil, smoke blowing back from the tall stack to burn his eyes. This was how he'd known it would be. Maybe this was what he'd wanted. Time to feed the brute. Jesse took a quick look at the road stretching out straight in front of him. The steamer would hold her course, the worm steering couldn't kick back. He opened the firebox doors, grabbed the shovel. He stoked the fire quickly and efficiently, keeping it dished for maximum heat. Swung the doors shut, straightened up again. The steady thunder of the loco was part of him already, in his bloodstream. Heat struck up from the metal of the footplate, working through his boots; the warmth from the firebox blew back, breathed against his face. Time later for the frost to reach him, nibbling at his bones.

Jesse had been born in the old house on the outskirts of Durnovaria soon after his father started up in business there with a couple of plowing engines, a thresher, and an Aveling and Porter tractor. The third of four brothers, he'd never seriously expected to own the fortunes of Strange and Sons. But God's ways were as inscrutable as the hills; two Strange boys had gone black-faced to Abraham's bosom, now Eli himself. . . . Jesse thought back to long summers spent at home, summers when the engine sheds were boiling hot and reeking of smoke and oil. He'd spend his days there, watching the trains come in and leave, helping unload on the warehouse steps, climbing over the endless stacks of crates and bales. There too were scents; richness of dried fruits in their boxes, apricots and figs and raisins; sweetness of fresh pine and deal, fragrance of cedarwood, thick headiness of twist tobacco cured in rum. Champagne and Oporto for the luxury trade, cognac, French lace; tangerines and pineapples, rubber and saltpeter, jute and hemp . . .

Sometimes he'd cadge rides on the locos, down to Poole or Bourne Mouth, across to Bridport, Wey Mouth; or west down to Isca, Lindinis. He went to Londinium once, and northeast again to Camulodunum. The Burrells and Claytons and Fodens ate miles; it was good to sit on the trail load of one of those old trains, the engine looking half a mile away, hooting and jetting steam. Jesse would pant on ahead to pay the toll keepers, stay behind to help them close the gates with their long white-and-red-striped bars. He remembered the rumbling of the many wheels, the thick rising of dust from the rutted trackways. The dust lay on the verges and hedges, making the roads look like white scars crossing the land. Odd nights he'd spend away from home, squatting in some corner of a tavern bar while his father caroused. Sometimes Eli would turn morose, and cuff Jesse upstairs to bed; at others he'd get expansive and sit and spin tall tales about when he himself was a boy, when the locos had shafts in front of their boilers and horses between them to steer. Jesse had been a brakeboy at eight, a steersman at ten for some of the shorter runs. It had been a wrench when he'd been sent away to school.

He wondered what had been in Eli's mind. "Get some bliddy eddycation" was all the old man had said. "That's what counts, lad. . . ." Jesse remembered how he'd felt; how he'd wandered in the orchards behind the house, seeing the cherry plums hanging thick on the old trees that were craggy and leaning, just right to climb. The apples, Bramleys and Lanes and Haley's Orange; Commodore pears hanging like rough-skinned bombs against walls mellow with September sunlight. Always before, Jesse had helped bring in the crop; but not this year, not anymore. His brothers had learned to write and read and figure in the little village school, and that was all; but Jesse had gone to Sherborne, and stayed on to college in the old university town. He'd worked hard at his languages and sciences, and done well; only there had been something wrong. It had taken him years to realize his hands were missing the touch of oiled steel, his nostrils needed the scent of steam. He'd packed up and come home and started work like any other hauler; and Eli had said not a word. No praise, no condemnation. Jesse shook his head. Deep down he'd always known without any possibility of doubt just what he was going to do. At heart, he was a hauler; like Tim, like Dickon, like old Eli. That was all; and it would have to be enough.

The *Margaret* topped a rise and rumbled onto a downslope. Jesse glanced at the long gauge glass by his knee and instinct more than vision made him open the injectors, valve water into the boiler. The loco had a long chassis; that meant caution descending hills. Too little water in her barrel and the forward tilt would uncover the firebox crown, melt the fusable plug there. All the steamers carried spares, but fitting one was a job to avoid. It meant drawing the fire, a crawl into a baking-hot firebox, an eternity of wrestling overhead in darkness. Jesse had burned his quota of plugs in his time, like any other tyro; it had taught him to keep his firebox covered. Too high a level, on the other hand, meant water reaching the steam outlets, descending from the stack in a scalding cloud. He'd had that happen too.

He spun the valve and the hissing of the injectors stopped. The *Margaret* lumbered at the slope, increasing her speed. Jesse pulled back on the reversing lever, screwed the brakes on to check the train; heard the altered beat as the loco felt the rising gradient, and gave her back her steam. Light or dark, he knew every foot of the road; a good driver had to.

A solitary gleam ahead of him told him he was nearing Wool. The *Margaret* shrieked a warning to the village, rumbled through between the shuttered cottages. A straight run now, across the heath to Poole. An hour to the town gates, say another half to get down to the quay. If the traffic holdups weren't too bad . . . Jesse chafed his hands, worked his shoulders inside his coat. The cold was getting to him now, he could feel it settling in his joints.

He looked out to either side of the road. It was full night, and the Great Heath was pitch black. Far off he saw or thought he saw the glimmer of a will-o'-the-wisp, haunting some stinking bog. A chilling wind moaned in from the emptiness. Jesse listened to the steady pounding of the Burrell and as often before the image of a ship came to him. The *Lady Margaret,* a speck of light and warmth, forged through the waste like some vessel crossing a vast and inimical ocean.

This was the twentieth century, the age of reason; but the heath was still the home of superstitious fears. The haunt of wolves and witches, werethings and fairies; and the *routiers.* . . . Jesse curled his lip. "Norman bastards" Dickon had called them. It was as accurate a description as any. True, they claimed Norman descent; but in this Catholic England of more than a thousand years after the Conquest bloodlines of Norman, Saxon, and original Celt were hopelessly mixed. What distinctions existed were more or less arbitrary, reintroduced in accordance with the racial theories of Gisevius the Great a couple of centuries ago. Most people had at least a smattering of the five tongues of the land; the Norman French of the ruling classes, Latin of the Church, Modern English of commerce and trade, the outdated Middle English and Celtic of the churls. There were other languages, of course; Gaelic, Cornish, and Welsh, all fostered by the Church, kept alive centuries after their use had worn thin. But it was good to chop a land piecemeal, set up barriers of language as well as class. "Divide and rule" had long been the policy, unofficially at least, of Rome.

The *routiers* themselves were surrounded by a mass of legend. There had always been gangs of footpads in the Southwest, probably always would be; they smuggled, they stole, they looted the road trains. Usually, but not invariably, they stopped short at murder. Some years the haulers suffered worse than others; Jesse could remember the *Lady Margaret* limping home one black night with her steersman dead from a crossbow quarrel, half her train ablaze, and old Eli swearing death and destruction. Troops from as far off as Sorviodunum had combed the heath for days, but it had been useless. The gang had dispersed; gone to their homes if Eli's theories had been correct, turned back into honest God-fearing citizens. There'd been nothing on the heath to find; the rumored strong-holds of the outlaws just didn't exist.

Jesse stoked again, shivering inside his coat. The *Margaret* carried no guns; you didn't fight the *routiers* if they came, not if you wanted to stay alive. At least not by conventional methods; Eli had had his own ideas on the matter, though he hadn't lived long enough to see them carried out. Jesse set his mouth. If they came, they came; but all they'd get from the firm of Strange they'd be welcome to keep. The business hadn't been built on softness; in this England, haulage wasn't a soft trade.

A mile or so ahead a brook, a tributary of the Frome, crossed the road. On this run the haulers usually stopped there to replenish their tanks. There were no waterholes on the heath; the cost of making them would be prohibitive. Water standing in earth hollows would turn brackish and foul, unsafe for the boilers; the splashes would have to be concrete lined, and a job like that would set somebody back half a year's profits. Cement manufacture was controlled rigidly by Rome, its price prohibitive. The embargo was deliberate, of course; the stuff was far too handy for the erection of quick strongpoints. Over the years there had been enough revolts in the country to teach caution even to the Popes.

Jesse, watching ahead, saw the sheen of water or ice. His hand went to the reversing lever and the train brakes. The *Margaret* stopped on the crown of a little bridge. Its parapets bore solemn warnings about "ponderous carriages" but few of the haulers paid much attention to them, after dark at least. He swung down and unstrapped the heavy armored hose from the side of the boiler, slung its end over the bridge. Ice broke with a clatter. The water lifts hissed noisily, steam pouring from their vents. A few minutes and the job was done. The *Margaret* would have made Poole and beyond without trouble; but no hauler worth his salt ever felt truly secure with his tanks less than brimming full. Especially after dark, with the ever-present chance of attack. The steamer was ready now if need be for a long, hard flight.

Jesse recoiled the hose and took the running lamps out of the tender. Four of them—one for each side of the boiler, two for the front axle. He hung them in place, turning the valves over the carbide, lifting the front glasses to sniff for acetylene. The lamps threw clear white fans of light ahead and to each side, making the frost crystals on the road surface sparkle. Jesse moved off again. The cold was bitter; he guessed several degrees of frost already, and the worst of the night was still to come. This was the part of the journey where you started to think of the cold as a personal enemy. It caught at your throat, drove glassy claws into your back; it was a thing to be fought, continuously, with the body and brain. Cold could stun a man, freeze him on the footplate till his fire burned low and he lost steam and hadn't the sense to stoke. It had happened before; more than one hauler had lost his life like that out on the road. It would happen again.

The *Lady Margaret* bellowed steadily; the wind moaned in across the heath.

On the landward side, the houses and cottages of Poole huddled behind a massive rampart and ditch. Along the fortifications, cressets burned; their light was visible for miles across the waste ground. The *Margaret* raised the line of twinkling sparks, closed with them slowly. In sight of the West Gate, Jesse spun the brake wheel and swore. Stretching out from the walls, dimly visible in torchlight, was a confusion of traffic: Burrells, Avelings, Claytons, Fowlers, each loco with a massive train. Officials scurried about; steam plumed into the air; the many engines made a muted thundering. The *Lady Margaret* slowed, jetting white clouds like exhaled breath, edged into the turmoil alongside a ten-horse Fowler liveried in the colors of the Merchant Adventurers.

Jesse was fifty yards from the gates, and the jam looked as if it would take an hour or more to sort out. The air was full of din; the noise of the engines, shouts from the steersmen and drivers, the bawling of town marshals and traffic wardens. Bands of Pope's Angels wound between the massive wheels, chanting carols and holding up their cups for offerings. Jesse hailed a harassed-looking peeler. The sergeant grounded his halberd, looked back at the *Lady Margaret*'s load and grinned.

"Bishop Blaize's benison again, friend?"

Jesse grunted an affirmative; alongside, the Fowler let fly a deafening series of hoots.

"Belay that," roared the policeman. "What've ye got up there that needs so much hurry?"

The driver, a little sparrow of a man muffled in scarf and greatcoat, spat a cigarette butt overboard. "Shellfish for 'is 'oliness," he quipped. "They're burning Rome tonight. . . ." The story of Pope Orlando dining on oysters while his mercenaries sacked Florence had already passed into legend.

"Any more of that," shouted the sergeant furiously, "and you'll find the gates shut in your face. You'll lie on the heath all night, and the *routiers* can have their pick of you. Now roll that pile of junk—*roll* it, I say . . ."

A gap had opened ahead; the Fowler thundered contemptuously and moved into it. Jesse followed. An age of shunting and hooting and he was finally past the bottleneck, guiding his train down the long main street of Poole.

Strange and Sons maintained a bonded store on the quay, not far from the old customs house. The *Margaret* threaded her way to it, inching between piles of merchandise that had overflowed from loading bays. The docks were busy for so late in the season; Jesse passed a Scottish collier, a big German freighter, a Frenchman, a New Worlder, an ex-slaver by her raking lines, a handsome Swedish clipper still defiantly under sail, and an old Dutch tramp, the *Groningen,* that he knew to be still equipped with the antiquated and curious mercury boilers. He swung his train eventually into the company warehouse, nearly an hour overdue.

The return load had already been made up; Jesse ditched the freight cars thankfully, handed over the manifest to the firm's agent and backed onto the new haul. He saw again to the securing of the trail load, built steam and headed out. The cold was deep inside him now, the windows of the waterfront pubs tempting with their promise of warmth, drink, and hot food; but tonight the *Margaret* wouldn't lie in Poole. It was nearly eight of the clock by the time she reached the ramparts, and the press of traffic was gone. The gates were opened by a surly faced sergeant; Jesse guided his train through to the open road. The moon was high now, riding a clear sky, and the cold was intense.

A long drag southwest, across the top of Poole harbor to where the Wareham turn branched left from the road to Durnovaria. Jesse coaxed the cars around it. He gave the *Margaret* her head, clocking twenty miles an hour on the open road. Then into Wareham, the awkward bend by the railway crossing; past the Black Bear with its monstrous carved sign and over the Frome where it ran into the sea, limning the northern boundary of Purbeck Island. After that the heaths again: Stoborough, Slepe, Middlebere, Norden, empty and vast, full of droning wind. Finally a twinkle of light showed ahead, high off the road and to the right; the *Margaret* thundered into Corvesgeat, the ancient pass through the Purbeck hills. Foursquare in the cutting and commanding the road, the great castle of Corfe squatted atop its mound, windows blazing light like eyes. My Lord of Purbeck must be in residence then, receiving his guests for Christmas.

The steamer circled the high flanks of the motte, climbed to the village beyond. She crossed the square, wheels and engine reflecting a hollow clamor from the front of the Greyhound Inn, climbed again through the long main street to where the heath was waiting once more, flat and desolate, haunted by wind and stars.

The Swanage road. Jesse, doped by the cold, fought the idea that the *Margaret* had been running through this void fuming her breath away into blackness like some spirit cursed and bound in a frozen hell. He would have welcomed any sign of life, even of the *routiers;* but there was nothing. Just the endless bitterness of the wind, the darkness stretching out each side of the road. He swung his mittened hands, stamping on the footplate, turning to see the tall shoulders of the load swaying against the night, way back the faint reflection of the tail lamps. He'd long since given up cursing himself for an idiot. He should have laid up at Poole, moved out again with the dawn; he knew that well enough. But tonight he felt obscurely that he was not driving but being driven.

He valved water through the preheater, stoked, valved again. One day they'd swap these solid burners for oil-fueled machines. The units had been available for years now; but oil firing was still a theory in limbo, awaiting the Papal verdict. Might be a decision next year, or the year after; or maybe not at all. The ways of Mother Church were devious, not to be questioned by the herd.

Old Eli would have fitted oil burners and damned the priests black to their faces, but his drivers and steersmen would have balked at the excommunication that would certainly have followed. Strange and Sons had bowed the knee there, not for the first time and not for the last. Jesse found himself thinking about his father again while the *Margaret* slogged upward, back into the hills. It was odd; but *now* he felt he could talk to the old man. *Now* he could explain his hopes, his fears. . . . Only now was too late; because Eli was dead and gone, six foot of Dorset muck on his chest. Was that the way of the world? Did people always feel they could talk, and talk, when it was just that bit too late?

The big mason's yard outside Long Tun Matravers. The piles of stone thrust up, dimly visible in the light of the steamer's lamps, breaking at last the deadly emptiness of the heath. Jesse hooted a warning; the voice of the Burrell rushed across the housetops, mournful and huge. The place was deserted, like a town of the dead. On the right the King's Head showed dim lights; its sign creaked uneasily, rocking in the wind. The *Margaret*'s wheels hit cobbles, slewed; Jesse spun the brakes on, snapping back the reversing lever to cut the power from the pistons. The frost had gathered thickly here; in places the road was like glass. At the crest of the hill into Swanage he twisted the control that locked his differentials. The loco steadied and edged down, groping for her haven. The wind skirled, lifting a spray of snow crystals across her headlights.

The roofs of the little town seemed to cluster under their mantle of frost. Jesse hooted again, the sound enormous between the houses. A gang of kids appeared from somewhere, ran yelling alongside the train. Ahead was a crossroads, and the yellow lamps on the front of the George Hotel. Jesse aimed the loco for the yard entrance, edged forward. The smoke-stack brushed the passageway overhead. Here was where he needed a mate; the steam from the Burrell, blowing back in the confined space, obscured his vision. The children had vanished; he gentled the reversing lever, easing in. The exhaust beats thrashed back from the walls, then the *Margaret* was clear, rumbling across the yard. The place had been enlarged years back to take the road trains; Jesse pulled across between a Garrett and a six-horse Clayton and Shuttleworth, neutralized the reversing lever and closed the regulator. The pounding stopped at last.

The hauler rubbed his face and stretched. The shoulders of his coat were beaded with ice; he brushed at it and got down stiffly, shoved the scotches under the engine's wheels, valved off her lamps. The hotel yard was deserted, the wind booming in the surrounding roofs; the boiler of the loco seethed gently. Jesse blew her excess steam, banked his fire and shut the dampers, stood on the front axle to set a bucket upside down atop the chimney. The *Margaret* would lie the night now safely. He stood back and looked at the bulk of her still radiating warmth, the faint glint of light from round the ash pan. He took his haversack from the cab and walked to the George to check in.

They showed him his room and left him. He used the loo, washed his face and hands, and left the hotel. A few yards down the street the windows of a pub glowed crimson, light seeping through the drawn curtains. Its sign proclaimed it the Mermaid Inn. He trudged down the alley that ran alongside the bars. The back room was full of talk, the air thick with the fumes of tobacco. The Mermaid was a haulers' pub; Jesse saw half a score of men he knew: Tom Skinner from Powerstock, Jeff Holroyd from Wey Mouth, two of old Serjeantson's boys. On the road, news travels fast; they crowded round him, talking against each other. He grunted answers, pushing his way to the bar. Yes, his father had had a sudden hemorrhage; no, he hadn't lived long after it. Five of the clock the next afternoon. . . . He pulled his coat open to reach his wallet, gave his order, took the pint and the double Scotch. A poker, thrust glowing into the tankard, mulled the ale; creamy froth spilled down the sides of the pot. The spirit burned Jesse's throat, made his eyes sting. He was fresh off the road; the others made room for him as he crouched knees apart in front of the fire. He swigged at the pint, feeling heat invade his crotch, move into his stomach. Somehow his mind could still hear the pounding of the Burrell; the vibration of her wheel was still in his fingers. Time later for talk and questioning; first the warmth. A man had to be warm.

She managed somehow to cross and stand behind him, spoke before he knew she was there. He stopped chafing his hands and straightened awkwardly, conscious now of his height and bulk.

"Hello, Jesse . . ."

Did she know? The thought always came. All those years back when he'd named the Burrell; she'd been a gawky stripling then, all legs and eyes, but she was the Lady he'd meant. She'd been the ghost that haunted him those hot, adolescent nights, trailing her scent among the scents of the garden flowers. He'd been on the steamer when Eli took that monstrous bet, sat and cried like a fool because when the Burrell breasted the last slope she wasn't winning fifty golden guineas for his father, she was panting out the glory of Margaret. But Margaret wasn't a stripling now, not anymore; the lamps put bright highlights on her brown hair, her eyes flickered at him, the mouth quirked . . .

He grunted at her. "Evenin', Margaret . . ."

She brought him his meal, set a corner table, sat with him awhile as he ate. That made his breath tighten in his throat; he had to force himself to remember it meant nothing. After all, you don't have a father die every week of your life. She wore a chunky costume ring with a bright blue stone; she had a habit of turning it restlessly between her fingers as she talked. The fingers were thin, with flat, polished nails, the hands wide across the knuckles like the hands of a boy. He watched her hands now touching her hair, drumming at the table, stroking the ash of a cigarette sideways into a saucer. He could imagine them sweeping, dusting, cleaning, as well as doing the other things, the secret things women must do to themselves.

She asked him what he'd brought down. She always asked that. He said "*Lady*" briefly, using the jargon of the haulers. Wondering again if she ever watched the Burrell, if she knew she was the *Lady Margaret;* and whether it would matter to her if she did. Then she brought him another drink and said it was on the house, told him she must go back to the bar now and that she'd see him again.

He watched her through the smoke, laughing with the men. She had an odd laugh, a kind of flat chortle that drew back the top lip and showed the teeth while the eyes watched and mocked. She was a good barmaid, was Margaret. Her father was an old hauler; he'd run the house this twenty years. His wife had died a couple of seasons back, the other daughters had married and moved out but Margaret had stayed. She knew a soft touch when she saw one; leastways that was the talk among the haulers. But that was crazy; running a pub wasn't an easy life. The long hours seven days a week, the polishing and scrubbing, mending and sewing and cooking—though they did have a woman in the mornings for the rough work. Jesse knew that like he knew most other things about his Margaret. He knew her shoe size, and that her birthday was in May; he knew she was twenty-four inches around the waist and that she liked Chanel and had a dog called Joe. And he knew she'd sworn never to marry; she'd said running the Mermaid had taught her as much about men as she wanted to learn; five thousand down on the counter would buy her services but nothing else. She'd never met anybody that could raise the half of that; the ban was impossible. But maybe she hadn't said it at all; the village air swam with gossip, and among themselves the haulers yacked like washerwomen.

Jesse pushed his plate away. Abruptly he felt the rising of a black self-contempt. Margaret was the reason for nearly everything; she was why he'd detoured miles out of his way, pulled his train to Swanage for a couple of boxes of *iced* fish that wouldn't repay the hauling back. Well, he'd wanted to see her and he'd seen her. She'd talked to him, sat by him; she wouldn't come to him again. Now he could go. He remembered again the raw sides of a grave, the spattering of earth on Eli's coffin. That was what waited for him, for all God's so-called children; only he'd wait for his death alone. He wanted to drink now, wash out the image in a warm brown haze of alcohol. But not here, not here . . . He headed for the door.

He collided with the stranger, growled an apology, walked on. He felt his arm caught; he turned back, stared into liquid brown eyes set in a straight-nosed, rakishly handsome face. "No," said the newcomer. "No, I don' believe it. By all tha's unholy, *Jesse Strange* . . ."

For a moment the other's jaunty fringe of a beard baffled him; then Jesse started to grin in spite of himself. "Colin," he said slowly. "Col de la Haye . . ."

Col brought his other arm around to grip Jesse's biceps. "Well, hell," he said. "Jesse, you're lookin' well. This calls f'r a drink, ol' boy. What you bin doin' with yourself? Hell, you're lookin' well . . ."

They leaned in a corner of the bar, full pints in front of them. "God damn, Jesse, tha's lousy luck. Los' your ol' man, eh? Tha's rotten. . . ." He lifted his tankard. "To you, ol' Jesse. Happier days . . ."

At college in Sherborne Jesse and Col had been fast friends. It had been the attraction of opposites: Jesse slow-talking, studious, and quiet; de la Haye the rake, the man-about-town. Col was the son of a west country businessman, a feminist and rogue at large; his tutors had always sworn that like the Fielding character he'd been born to be hanged. After college Jesse had lost touch with him. He'd heard vaguely Col had given up the family business; importing and warehousing just hadn't been fast enough for him. He'd apparently spent a time as a strolling *jongleur,* working on a book of ballads that had never got written, had six months on the boards in Londinium before being invalided home the victim of a brawl in a brothel. "A'd show you the scar," said Col, grinning hideously, "but it's a bit bloody awkward in mixed comp'ny, ol' boy. . . ." He'd later become, of all things, a hauler for a firm in Isca. That hadn't lasted long; halfway through his first week he'd howled into Bristol with an eight-horse Clayton and Shuttleworth, unreeled his hose, and drained the corporation horse trough in town center before the peelers ran him in. The Clayton hadn't quite exploded but it had been a near go. He'd tried again, up in Aquae Sulis, where he wasn't so well known; that time he lasted six months before a broken gauge glass stripped most of the skin from his ankles. De la Haye had moved on, seeking, as he put it, "less lethal employment." Jesse chuckled and shook his head. "So what be 'ee doin' now?"

The insolent eyes laughed back at him. "A' trade," said Col breezily. "A' take what comes; a li'l here . . . Times are hard, we must all live how we can. Drink up, ol' Jesse, the next one's mine . . ."

They chewed over old times while Margaret served up pints and took the money, raising her eyebrows at Col. The night de la Haye, pot-valiant, had sworn to strip his professor's cherished walnut tree . . . "A' remember that like it was yes'day," said Col happily. "Lovely ol' moon there was, bright as day. . . ." Jesse had held the ladder while Col climbed; but before he reached the branches the tree was shaken as if by a hurricane. "Nuts comin' down like bloody hailstones," chortled Col. "Y' remember, Jesse, y' must remember. . . . An' there was that—that bloody ol' rogue of a peeler Toby Warrilow sittin' up there with his big ol' boots stuck out, shakin' the hell out of that bloody tree. . . ." For weeks after that, even de la Haye had been able to do nothing wrong in the eyes of the law; and a whole dormitory had gorged themselves on walnuts for nearly a month.

There'd been the business of the two nuns stolen from Sherborne Convent; they'd tried to pin that on de la Haye and hadn't quite managed it, but it had been an open secret who was responsible. Girls in Holy Orders had been removed odd times before, but only Col would have taken two at once. And the affair of the Poet and Peasant. The landlord of that inn, thanks to some personal quirk, kept a large ape chained in the stables; Col, evicted after a singularly rowdy night, had managed to slit the creature's collar. The godforsaken animal caused troubles and panics for a month; men went armed, women stayed indoors. The thing had finally been shot by a militiaman who caught it in his room drinking a bowl of soup.

"So what you goin' to do now?" asked de la Haye, swigging back his sixth or seventh beer. "Is your firm now, no?"

"Aye." Jesse brooded, hands clasped, chin touching his knuckles. "Goin' to run it, I guess . . ."

Col draped an arm around his shoulders. "You be OK," he said. "You be OK, pal; why so sad? Hey, tell you what. You get a li'l girl now, you be all right then. Tha's what you need, ol' Jesse; a' known the signs." He punched his friend in the ribs and roared with laughter. "Keep you warm nights better'n a stack of extra blankets. An' stop you getting fat, no?"

Jesse looked faintly startled. "Dunno 'bout *that* . . ."

"Ah, hell," said de la Haye. "Tha's the thing, though. Ah, there's nothin' like it. *Mmmmyowwhh . . .*" He wagged his hips, shut his eyes, drew shapes with his hands, contrived to look rapturous and lascivious at the same time. "Is no trouble now, ol' Jesse," he said. "You loaded now, you know that? Hell, man, you're *eligible*. . . . They come runnin' when they hear, you have to fight 'em off with a—a pushpole couplin', no?" He dissolved again in merriment.

Eleven of the clock came round far too quickly. Jesse struggled into his coat, followed Col up the alley beside the pub. It was only when the cold air hit him he realized how stoned he was. He stumbled against de la Haye, then ran into the wall. They reeled along the street laughing, parted company finally at the George. Col, roaring out promises, vanished into the night.

Jesse leaned against the *Margaret*'s rear wheel, head laid back on its struts, and felt the beer fume in his brain. When he closed his eyes, a slow movement began; the ground seemed to tilt forward and back under his feet. Man, but that last hour had been good. It had been college all over again; he chuckled helplessly, wiped his forehead with the back of his hand. De la Haye was a no-good bastard, all right, but a nice guy, nice guy. . . . Jesse opened his eyes blearily, looked up at the road train. Then he moved carefully, hand over hand, along the engine, to test her boiler temperature with his palm. He hauled himself to the footplate, opened the firebox doors, spread coal, checked the dampers and water gauge. Everything secure. He tacked across the yard, feeling the odd snow crystals sting his face.

He fiddled with his key in the lock, swung the door open. His room was black and icily cold. He lit the single lantern, left its glass ajar. The candle flame shivered in a draft. He dropped across the bed heavily, lay watching the one point of yellow light sway forward and back. Best get some sleep, make an early start tomorrow. . . . His haversack lay where he'd slung it on the chair but he lacked the strength of will to unpack it now. He shut his eyes.

Almost instantly the images began to swirl. Somewhere in his head the Burrell was pounding; he flexed his hands, feeling the wheel rim thrill between them. That was how the locos got you, after a while; throbbing and throbbing hour on hour till the noise became a part of you, got in the blood and brain so you couldn't live without it. Up at dawn, out on the road, driving till you couldn't stop; Londinium, Aquae Sulis, Isca; stone from the Purbeck quarries, coal from Kimmeridge, wool and grain and worsted, flour and wine, candlesticks, Madonnas, shovels, butter scoops, powder and shot, gold, lead, tin; out on contract to the Army, the Church . . . Cylinder cocks, dampers, regulator, reversing lever; the high iron shaking of the footplate . . .

He moved restlessly, muttering. The colors in his brain grew sharper. Maroon and gold of livery, red saliva on his father's chin, flowers bright against fresh earth; steam and lamplight, flames, the hard sky clamped against the hills.

His mind toyed with memories of Col, hearing sentences, hearing him laugh; the little intake of breath, squeaky and distinctive, then the sharp machine-gun barking while he screwed his eyes shut and hunched his shoulders, pounded with his fist on the counter. Col had promised to look him up in Durnovaria, reeled away shouting he wouldn't forget. But he would forget; he'd lose himself, get involved with some woman, forget the whole business, forget the meeting. Because Col wasn't like Jesse. No planning and waiting for de la Haye, no careful working out of odds; he lived for the moment, vividly. He would never change.

The locos thundered, cranks whirling, crossheads dipping, brass gleaming and tinkling in the wind.

Jesse half sat up, shaking his head. The lamp burned steady now, its flame thin and tall, just vibrating slightly at the tip. The wind boomed, carrying with it the striking of a church clock. He listened, counting.

Twelve strokes. He frowned. He'd slept, and dreamed; he'd thought it was nearly dawn. But the long, hard night had barely begun. He lay back with a grunt, feeling drunk but queerly wide awake. He couldn't take his beer anymore; he'd had the horrors. Maybe there were more to come. He started revolving idly the things de la Haye had said. The crack about getting a woman. That was crazy, typical of Col. No trouble maybe for him, but for Jesse there had only ever been one little girl. And she was out of reach.

His mind, spinning, seemed to check and stop quite still. Now, he told himself irritably, forget it. You've got troubles enough, let it go . . . but a part of him stubbornly refused to obey. It turned the pages of mental ledgers, added, subtracted, thrust the totals insistently into his consciousness. He swore, damning de la Haye. The idea, once implanted, wouldn't leave him. It would haunt him now for weeks, maybe years.

He gave himself up, luxuriously, to dreaming. She knew all about him, that was certain; women knew such things unfailingly. He'd given himself away a hundred times, a thousand; little things, a look, a gesture, a word, were all it needed. He'd kissed her once, years back. Only the one time; that was maybe why it had stayed so sharp and bright in his mind, why he could still relive it. It had been a nearly accidental thing; a New Year's Eve, the pub bright and noisy, a score or more of locals seeing the new season in. The church clock striking, the same clock that marked the hours now, doors in the village street popping undone, folk eating mince pies and drinking wine, shouting to each other across the dark, kissing; and she'd put down the tray she was holding, watching him. "Let's not be left out, Jesse," she said. "Us too . . ."

He remembered the sudden thumping of his heart, like the fussing of a loco when her driver gives her steam. She'd turned her face up to him, he'd seen the lips parting; then she was pushing hard, using her tongue, making a little noise deep in her throat. He wondered if she made the sound every time automatically, like a cat purring when you rubbed its fur. And somehow too she'd guided his hand to her breast; it lay cupped there, hot under her dress, burning his palm. He'd tightened his arm across her back then, pulling her onto her toes till she wriggled away gasping. "*Whoosh,*" she said. "Well done, Jesse. *Ouch.* . . well done. . . ." Laughing at him again, patting her hair; and all past dreams and future visions had met in one melting point of Time.

He remembered how he'd stoked the loco all the long haul back, tireless, while the wind sang and her wheels crashed through a glowing landscape of jewels. The images were back now; he saw Margaret at a thousand sweet moments, patting, touching, undressing, laughing. And he remembered, suddenly, a haulers' wedding; the ill-fated marriage of his brother Micah to a girl from Sturminster Newton. The engines burnished to their canopies, beribboned and flag-draped, each separate plank of their flatbed trailers gleaming white and scoured; drifts of confetti like bright-colored snow, the priest standing laughing with his glass of wine, old Eli, hair plastered miraculously flat, incongruous white collar clamped round his neck, beaming and red-faced, waving from the *Margaret*'s footplate a quart of beer. Then, equally abruptly, the scene was gone; and Eli, in his Sunday suit, with his pewter mug and his polished hair, was whirled away into a dark space of wind.

"*Father . . . !*"

Jesse sat up, panting. The little room showed dim, shadows flicking as the candle flame guttered. Outside, the clock chimed for twelve-thirty. He stayed still, squatting on the edge of the bed with his head in his hands. No weddings for him, no gayness. Tomorrow he must go back to a dark and still mourning house; to his father's unsolved worries and the family business and the same ancient, dreary round . . .

In the darkness, the image of Margaret danced like a solitary spark.

He was horrified at what his body was doing. His feet found the flight of wooden stairs, stumbled down them. He felt the cold air in the yard bite at his face. He tried to reason with himself but it seemed his legs would no longer obey him. He felt a sudden gladness, a lightening. You didn't stand the pain of an aching tooth forever; you took yourself to the barber, changed the nagging for a worse quick agony and then for blessed peace. He'd stood this long enough; now it too was to be finished. Instantly, with no more waiting. He told himself ten years of hoping and dreaming, of wanting dumbly like an animal—that has to count. He asked himself: What had he expected her to do? She wouldn't come running to him pleading, throw herself across his feet; women weren't made like that; she had her dignity too. . . . He tried to remember when the gulf between him and Margaret had been fixed. He told himself never; by no token, no word. . . . He'd never given her a chance. What if she'd been waiting too all these years? Just waiting to be *asked*. . . It had to be true. He knew, glowingly, it was true. As he tacked along the street, he started to sing.

The watchman loomed from a doorway, a darker shadow, gripping a halberd short.

"You all right, sir?"

The voice, penetrating as if from a distance, brought Jesse up short. He gulped, nodded, grinned. "Yeah. Yeah, sure. . . ." He jerked a thumb behind him. "Brought a . . . train down. Strange, Durnovaria . . ."

The man stood back. His attitude said plainly enough, "One o' they beggars. . . ." He said gruffly, "Best get along then, sir, don't want to have to run 'ee in. 'Tis well past twelve o' the clock, y' know . . ."

"On m' way, officer," said Jesse. "On m' way. . . ." A dozen steps along the street, he turned back. "Officer . . . you m–married?"

The voice was uncompromising. "Get along now, sir. . . ." Its owner vanished in blackness.

The little town, asleep. Frost glinting on the rooftops, puddles in the road ruts frozen to iron, houses shuttered blind. Somewhere an owl called; or was it the noise of a far-off engine, out there somewhere on the road? . . . The Mermaid was silent, no lights showing. Jesse hammered at the door. Nothing. He knocked louder. A light flickered on across the street. He started to sob for breath. He'd done it all wrong; she wouldn't open. They'd call the watch instead. . . . But she'd know, she'd know who was knocking, women always knew. He beat at the wood, terrified. "*Margaret* . . ."

A shifting glint of yellow; then the door opened with a suddenness that sent him sprawling. He straightened up, still breathing hard, trying to focus his eyes. She was standing holding a wrap across her throat, hair tousled. She held a lamp high; then, "*You . . . !*" She shut the door with a thump, snatched the bolt across and turned to face him. She said in a low, furious voice, "What the devil do you think you're doing?"

He backed up. "I . . ." he said, "I . . ." He saw her face change. "Jesse," she said, "what's wrong? Are you hurt? What happened?"

"I . . . Sorry," he said. "Had to see you, Margaret. Couldn't leave it no more . . ."

"Hush," she said. Hissed. "You'll wake my father, if you haven't done it already. *What are you talking about?*"

He leaned on the wall, trying to stop the spinning in his head. "Five thousand," he said thickly. "It's . . . nothing, Margaret. Not anymore. Margaret, I'm . . . rich, God help me. It don't matter no more . . ."

"*What?*"

"On the roads," he said desperately. "The . . . haulers' talk. They said you wanted five thousand. Margaret, I can do ten . . ."

A dawning comprehension. And for God's sake, she was starting to laugh. "Jesse Strange," she said, shaking her head. "What are you trying to say?"

And it was out, at last. "I love you, Margaret," he said simply. "Reckon I always have. And I . . . want you to be my wife."

She stopped smiling then, stood quite still and let her eyes close as if suddenly she was very tired. Then she reached forward quietly and took his hand. "Come on," she said. "Just for a little while. Come and sit down."

In the back bar the firelight was dying. She sat by the hearth curled like a cat, watching him, her eyes big in the dimness; and Jesse talked. He told her everything he'd never imagined himself speaking. How he'd wanted her, and hoped, and known it was no use; how he'd waited so many years he'd nearly forgotten a time when she hadn't filled his mind. She stayed still, holding his fingers, stroking the back of his hand with her thumb, thinking and brooding. He told her how she'd be mistress of the house and have the gardens, the orchards of cherry plums, the rose terraces, the servants, her drawing account in the bank; how she'd have nothing to do anymore ever but be Margaret Strange, his wife.

The silence lengthened when he'd finished, till the ticking of the big bar clock sounded loud. She stirred her foot in the warmth of the ashes, wriggling her toes; he gripped her instep softly, spanning it with finger and thumb. "I do love you, Margaret," he said. "I truly do . . ."

She still stayed quiet, staring at nothing visible, eyes opaque. She'd let the shawl fall off her shoulders; he could see her breasts, the nipples pushing against the flimsiness of the nightdress. She frowned, pursed her mouth, looked back at him. "Jesse," she said, "when I've finished talking, will you do something for me? Will you promise?"

Quite suddenly, he was no longer drunk. The whirling and the warmth faded, leaving him shivering. Somewhere he was sure the loco hooted again. "Yes, Margaret," he said. "If that's what you want."

She came and sat by him. "Move up," she whispered. "You're taking all the room." She saw the shivering; she put her hand inside his jacket, rubbed softly. "Stop it," she said. "Don't do that, Jesse. Please . . ."

The spasm passed; she pulled her arm back, flicked at the shawl, gathered her dress around her knees. "When I've said what I'm going to, will you promise to go away? Very quietly, and not . . . make trouble for me? Please, Jesse. I did let you in . . ."

"That's all right," he said. "Don't worry, Margaret, that's all right." His voice, talking, sounded like the voice of a stranger. He didn't want to hear what she had to say; but listening to it meant he could stay close just a little longer. He felt suddenly he knew what it would be like to be given a cigarette just before you were hanged; how every puff would mean another second's life.

She twined her fingers together, looked down at the carpet. "I . . . want to get this just right," she said. "I want to . . . say it properly, Jesse, because I don't want to hurt you. I . . . like you too much for that."

155

"I . . . knew about it, of course, I've known all the time. That was why I let you in. Because I . . . like you very much, Jesse, and didn't want to hurt. And now you see I've . . . trusted you, so you mustn't let me down. I can't marry you, Jesse, because I don't love you. I never will. Can you understand that? It's terribly hard knowing . . . well, how you feel and all that and still having to say it to you but I've got to because it just wouldn't work. I . . . knew this was going to happen sometime; I used to lie awake at night thinking about it, thinking all about you, honestly I did, but it wasn't any good. It just . . . wouldn't work, that's all. So . . . no. I'm terribly sorry but . . . no."

How can a man balance his life on a dream, how can he be such a fool? How can he live when the dream gets knocked apart? . . .

She saw his face alter and reached for his hand again. "Jesse, *please . . .* I think you've been terribly sweet waiting all this time and I . . . know about the money, I know why you said that, I know you just wanted to give me a . . . good life. It was terribly sweet of you to think like that about me and I . . . know you'd do it. But it just wouldn't work. . . . Oh, God, isn't this awful . . ."

You try to wake from what you know is a dream, and you can't. Because you're awake already, this is the dream they call life. You move in the dream and talk, even when something inside you wants to twist and die. He rubbed her knee, feeling the firm smoothness. "Margaret," he said. "I don't want you to rush into anything. Look, in a couple of months I shall be comin' back through . . ."

She bit her lip. "I knew you were . . . going to say that as well. But . . . no, Jesse. It isn't any use thinking about it; I've tried to and it wouldn't work. I don't want to . . . have to go through this again and hurt you all over another time. Please don't ask me again. Ever."

He thought dully: He couldn't buy her. Couldn't win her, and couldn't buy. Because he wasn't man enough, and that was the simple truth. Just not quite what she wanted. That was what he'd known all along, deep down, but he'd never faced it; he'd kissed his pillows nights, and whispered love for Margaret, because he hadn't dared bring the truth into the light. And now he'd got the rest of time to try and forget . . . this.

She was still watching him. She said, "Please understand . . ."

And he felt better. God preserve him, some weight seemed to shift suddenly and let him talk. "Margaret," he said, "this sounds damn stupid, don't know how to say it . . ."

"Try . . ."

He said, "I don't want to . . . hold you down. It's . . . selfish, like somehow having a . . . bird in a cage, owning it. . . . Only I didn't think on it that way before. Reckon I . . . really love you because I don't want that to happen to you. I wouldn't do anything to hurt. Don't you worry, Margaret, it'll be all right. It'll be all right now. Reckon I'll just . . . well, get out o' your way like . . ."

She put a hand to her head. "God, this is awful. I knew it would happen. . . . Jesse, don't just . . . well, vanish. You know, go off an' . . . never come back. You see I . . . like you so very much, as a friend, I should feel terrible if you did that. Can't things be like they . . . were before; I mean can't you just sort of . . . come in and see me, like you used to? Don't go right away, please . . ."

Even that, he thought. *God, I'll do even that.*

She stood up. "And now go. Please . . ."

He nodded dumbly. "It'll be all right . . ."

"Jesse," she said. "I don't want to . . . get in any deeper. But . . ." She kissed him, quickly. There was no feeling there this time. No fire. He stood until she let him go; then he walked quickly to the door.

He heard, dimly, his boots ringing on the street. Somewhere a long way off from him was a vague sighing, a susurration; could have been the blood in his ears, could have been the sea. The house doorways and the dark-socketed windows seemed to lurch toward him of their own accord, fall away behind. He felt as a ghost might feel grappling with the concept of death, trying to assimilate an idea too big for its consciousness. There was no Margaret now, not anymore. No Margaret. Now he must leave the grown-up world where people married and loved and mated and mattered to each other, go back for all time to his child's universe of oil and steel. And the days would come, and the days would go, till on one of them he would die.

He crossed the road outside the George; then he was walking under the yard entrance, climbing the stairs, opening again the door of his room. Putting out the light, smelling Goody Thompson's fresh-sour sheets.

The bed felt cold as a tomb.

The fishwives woke him, hawking their wares through the streets. Somewhere there was a clanking of milk churns; voices crisped in the cold air of the yard. He lay still, face down, and there was an empty time before the cold new fall of grief. He remembered he was dead; he got up and dressed, not feeling the icy air on his body. He washed, shaved the blue-chinned face of a stranger, went out to the Burrell. Her livery glowed in weak sunlight, topped by a thin bright icing of snow. He opened her firebox, raked the embers of the fire and fed it. He felt no desire to eat; he went down to the quay instead, haggled absentmindedly for the fish he was going to buy, arranged for its delivery to the George. He saw the boxes stowed in time for late service at the church, stayed on for confession. He didn't go near the Mermaid; he wanted nothing now but to leave, get back on the road. He checked the *Lady Margaret* again, polished her nameplates, hubs, flywheel boss. Then he remembered seeing something in a shop window, something he'd intended to buy: a little tableau, the Virgin, Joseph, the Shepherds kneeling, the Christ child in the manger. He knocked at the shop door, bought it, and had it packed; his mother set great store by such things, and it would look well on the sideboard over Christmas.

By then it was lunchtime. He made himself eat, swallowing food that tasted like string. He nearly paid his bill before he remembered. Now it went on account; the account of Strange and Sons of Dorset. After the meal he went to one of the bars of the George, drank to try and wash the sour taste from his mouth. Subconsciously he found himself waiting; for footsteps, a remembered voice, some message from Margaret to tell him not to go, she'd changed her mind. It was a bad state of mind to get into, but he couldn't help himself. No message came.

It was nearly three of the clock before he walked out to the Burrell and built steam. He uncoupled the *Margaret* and turned her, shackled the load to the push-pole lug and backed it into the road. A difficult feat, but he did it without thinking. He disconnected the loco, brought her around again, hooked on, shoved the reversing lever forward, and inched open on the regulator. The rumbling of the wheels started at last. He knew once clear of Purbeck he wouldn't come back. Couldn't, despite his promise. He'd send Tim or one of the others. The thing he had inside him wouldn't stay dead; if he saw her again it would have to be killed all over. And once was more than enough.

He had to pass the pub. The chimney smoked, but there was no other sign of life. The train crashed behind him, thunderously obedient. Fifty yards on, he used the whistle, over and again, waking *Margaret*'s huge iron voice, filling the street with steam. Childish, but he couldn't stop himself. Then he was clear. Swanage dropping away behind as he climbed toward the heath. He built up speed. He was late; in that other world he seemed to have left so long ago, a man called Dickon would be worrying.

Way off on the left a semaphore stood stark against the sky. He hooted to it, the two pips followed by the long call that all the haulers used. For a moment the thing stayed dead; then he saw the arms flip an acknowledgment. Out there he knew Zeiss glasses would be trained on the Burrell. The Guildsmen had answered; soon a message would be streaking north along the little local towers. *The* Lady Margaret, *locomotive, Strange and Sons, Durnovaria; out of Swanage routed for Corvesgeat, fifteen thirty hours. All well . . .*

Night came quickly; night, and the burning frost. Jesse swung west well before Wareham, cutting straight across the heath. The Burrell thundered steadily, gripping the road with her seven-foot drive wheels, leaving thin wraiths of steam behind her in the dark. He stopped once, to fill his tanks and light the lamps, then pushed on again into the heathland. A light mist or frost smoke was forming now; it clung to the hollows of the rough ground, glowing oddly in the light from the side lamps. The wind soughed and threatened. North of the Purbecks, off the narrow coastal strip, the winter could strike quick and hard; come morning the heath could be impassable, the trackways lost under two feet or more of snow.

An hour out from Swanage, and the *Margaret* still singing her tireless song of power. Jesse thought, blearily, that she at least kept faith. The semaphores had lost her now in the dark; there would be no more messages till she made her base. He could imagine old Dickon standing at the yard gate under the flaring cressets, worried, cocking his head to catch the beating of an exhaust miles away. The loco passed through Wool. Soon be home now; home, to whatever comfort remained . . .

The boarder took him nearly by surprise. The train had slowed near the crest of a rise when the man ran alongside, lunged for the footplate step. Jesse heard the scrape of a shoe on the road; some sixth sense warned him of movement in the darkness. The shovel was up, swinging for the stranger's head, before it was checked by an agonized yelp. "Hey' ol' boy, don' you know your friends?"

Jesse, half off balance, grunted and grabbled at the steering. "*Col. . .* What the hell are you doin' here?"

De la Haye, still breathing hard, grinned at him in the reflection of the sidelights. "Jus' a fellow traveler, my friend. Happy to see you come along there, I tell you. Had a li'l bit of trouble, thought a'd have to spend the night on the bloody heath . . ."

"What trouble?"

"Oh, I was ridin' out to a place a' know," said de la Haye. "Place out by Culliford, li'l farm. Christmas with friends. Nice daughters. Hey, Jesse, you know?" He punched Jesse's arm, started to laugh. Jesse set his mouth. "What happened to your horse?"

"Bloody thing foundered, broke its leg."

159

"Where?"

"On the road back there," said de la Haye carelessly. "A' cut its throat an' rolled it in a ditch. Din' want the damn *routiers* spottin' it, gettin' on my tail. . . ." He blew his hands, held them out to the firebox, shivered dramatically inside his sheepskin coat. "Damn cold, Jesse, cold as a bitch . . . How far you go?"

"Home. Durnovaria."

De la Haye peered at him. "Hey, you don' sound good. You sick, ol' Jesse?"

"No."

Col shook his arm insistently. "Whassamatter, ol' pal? Anythin' a friend can do to help?"

Jesse ignored him, eyes searching the road ahead. De la Haye bellowed suddenly with laughter. "Was the beer. The beer, no? Ol' Jesse, your stomach has shrunk!" He held up a clenched fist. "Like the stomach of a li'l baby, no? Not the old Jesse anymore; ah, life is hell . . ."

Jesse glanced down at the gauge, turned the belly tank cocks, heard water splash on the road, touched the injector controls, saw the burst of steam as the lifts fed the boiler. The pounding didn't change its beat. He said steadily, "Reckon it must have been the beer that done it. Reckon I might go on the wagon. Gettin' old."

De la Haye peered at him, intently. "Jesse," he said. "You got problems, my son. You got troubles. What gives? C'mon, spill . . ."

That damnable intuition hadn't left him, then. He'd had it right through college; seemed somehow to know what you were thinking nearly as soon as it came into your head. It was Col's big weapon; he used it to have his way with women. Jesse laughed bitterly; and suddenly the story was coming out. He didn't want to tell it; but he did, down to the last word. Once started, he couldn't stop.

Col heard him in silence; then he started to shake. The shaking was laughter. He leaned back against the cab side, holding onto a stanchion. "Jesse, Jesse, you are a lad. Christ, you never change. . . . Oh, you bloodly Saxon . . ." He went off into fresh peals, wiped his eyes. "So . . . so she show you her pretty li'l scut, heh? Jesse, you are a lad; when will you learn? What, you go to her with—with this. . . ." He banged the *Margaret*'s hornplate. "An' your face so earnest an' black—oh, Jesse, a' can see that face of yours. Man, she don't want your great iron *destrier*. Christ above no . . . But a'—a' tell you what you do . . ."

Jesse turned down the corners of his lips. "Why don't you just *shut up* . . ."

De la Haye shook his arm. "Nah, listen. Don' get mad, listen. You . . . woo her, Jesse; she like that, that one. You know? Get the ol' glad rags on, man, get a butterfly car, mak' its wings of cloth of gold. She like that. . . . Only don' stand no shovin', ol' Jesse. An' don' ask her nothin', not no more. You tell her what you want, say you goin' to get it. . . . Pay for your beer with a golden guinea, tell her you'll tak' the change upstairs, no? She's worth it, Jesse, she's worth havin', is that one. Oh, but she's nice . . ."

"Go to hell . . ."

"You don' want her?" De la Haye looked hurt. "A' jus' try to help, ol' pal. . . . You los' interest now?"

"Yeah," said Jesse. "I lost interest."

"Ahhh . . ." Col sighed. "Ah, but is a shame. Young love all blighted . . . Tell you what, though." He brightened. "You given me a great idea, ol' Jesse. You don' want her, a' have her myself. OK?"

When you hear the wail that means your father's dead, your hands go on wiping down a crosshead guide. When the world turns red and flashes, and drums roll inside your skull, your eyes watch ahead at the road, your fingers stay quiet on the wheel. Jesse heard his own voice speak dryly. "You're a lying bastard, Col, you always were. She wouldn't fall for you . . ."

Col snapped his fingers, danced on the footplate. "Man, a' got it halfway made. Oh, but she's nice. . . . Those li'l eyes, they were flashin' a bit las' night, no? Is easy, man, easy. . . . A' tell you what: a' bet she be sadistic in bed. But nice, ahhh, *nice* . . ." His gestures somehow suggested rapture. "I tak' her five ways in a night," he said. "An' send you proof. OK?"

Maybe he doesn't mean it. Maybe he's lying. But he isn't. I know Col; and Col doesn't lie. Not about this. What he says he'll do, he'll do. . . . Jesse grinned, just with his teeth. "You do that, Col. Break her in. Then I take her off you. OK?"

De la Haye laughed and gripped his shoulder. "Jesse, you are a lad. Eh . . . ? Eh . . . ?

A light flashed briefly, ahead and to the right, way out on the heathland. Col spun around, stared at where it had been, looked back to Jesse. "You see that?"

Grimly. "I saw."

De la Haye looked around the footplate nervously. "You got a gun?"

"Why?"

"The bloody light. The *routiers* . . ."

"You don't fight the *routiers* with a gun."

Col shook his head. "Man, I hope you know what you're doin'. . ."

Jesse wrenched at the firebox doors, letting out a blaze of light and heat. "Stoke . . ."

"What?"

"*Stoke!*"

"OK, man," said de la Haye. "All right, OK . . ." He swung the shovel, building the fire. Kicked the doors shut, straightened up. "A' love you an' leave you soon," he said. "When we pass the light. If we pass the light . . ."

The signal, if it had been a signal, was not repeated. The heath stretched out empty and black. Ahead was a long series of ridges; the *Lady Margaret* bellowed heavily, breasting the first of them. Col stared round again uneasily, hung out the cab to look back along the train. The high shoulders of the tarps were vaguely visible in the night. "What you carryin', Jesse?" he asked. "You got the goods?"

Jesse shrugged. "Bulk stuff. Cattle cake, sugar, dried fruit. Not worth their trouble."

De la Haye nodded worriedly. "Wha's in the trail load?"

"Brandy, some silks. Bit of tobacco. Veterinary supply. Animal castrators." He glanced sideways. "Cord grip. Bloodless."

Col looked startled again, then started to laugh. "Jesse, you are a lad. A right bloody lad. . . But tha's a good load, ol' pal. Nice pickings . . ."

Jesse nodded, feeling empty. "Ten thousand quid's worth. Give or take a few hundred."

De la Haye whistled. "Yeah. Tha's a good load . . ."

They passed the point where the light had appeared, left it behind. Nearly two hours out now, not much longer to run. The *Margaret* came off the downslope, hit the second rise. The moon slid clear of a cloud, showed the long ribbon of road stretching ahead. They were almost off the heath now, Durnovaria just over the horizon. Jesse saw a track running away to the left before the moon, veiling itself, gave the road back to darkness.

De la Haye gripped his shoulder. "You be fine now," he said. "We passed the bastards. . . . You be all right. I drop off now, ol' pal; thanks for th' ride. An' remember, 'bout the li'l girl. You get in there punchin', you do what a' say. OK, ol' Jesse?"

Jesse turned to stare at him. "Look after yourself, Col," he said.

The other swung onto the step. "A' be OK. A' be great." He let go, vanished in the night.

He'd misjudged the speed of the Burrell. He rolled forward, somer-saulted on rough grass, sat up grinning. The lights on the steamer's trail load were already fading down the road. There were noises around him; six mounted men showed dark against the sky. They were leading a seventh horse, its saddle empty. Col saw the quick gleam of a gun barrel, the bulky shape of a crossbow. *Routiers* . . . He got up, still laughing, swung onto the spare mount. Ahead the train was losing itself in the low fogbanks. De la Haye raised his arm. "The last car . . ." He rammed his heels into the flanks of his horse, and set off at a flat gallop.

Jesse watched his gauges. Full head, a hundred and fifty pounds in the boiler. His mouth was still grim. It wouldn't be enough; down this next slope, halfway up the long rise beyond, that was where they would take him. He moved the regulator to its farthest position; the *Lady Margaret* started to build speed again, swaying as her wheels found the ruts. She hit the bottom of the slope at twenty-five, slowed as her engine felt the dead pull of the train.

Something struck the nearside hornplate with a ringing crash. An arrow roared overhead, lighting the sky as it went. Jesse smiled, because nothing mattered anymore. The *Margaret* seethed and bellowed; he could see the horsemen now, galloping to either side. A pale gleam that could have been the edge of a sheepskin coat. Another concussion, and he tensed himself for the iron shock of a crossbow bolt in his back. It never came. But that was typical of Col de la Haye; he'd steal your woman but not your dignity, he'd take your trail load but not your life. Arrows flew again, but not at the loco. Jesse, craning back past the shoulders of the freight cars, saw flames running across the sides of the last tarp.

Halfway up the rise; the *Lady Margaret* laboring, panting with rage. The fire took hold fast, tongues of flame licking forward. Soon they would catch the next trailer in line. Jesse reached down. His hand closed slowly, regretfully, around the emergency release. He eased upward, felt the catch disengage, heard the engine beat slacken as the load came clear. The burning truck slowed, faltered, and began to roll back away from the rest of the train. The horsemen galloped after it as it gathered speed down the slope, clustered around it in a whooping knot and beat upward with their cloaks at the fire. Col passed them at the run, swung from the saddle and leaped. A scramble, a shout; and the *routiers* bellowed their laughter. Poised on top of the moving load, gesticulating with his one free hand, their leader was pissing valiantly onto the flames.

The *Lady Margaret* had topped the rise when the cloud scud overhead lit with a white glare. The explosion cracked like a monstrous whip; the shock wave slapped at the trailers, skewed the steamer off course. Jesse fought her straight, hearing echoes growl back from distant hills. He leaned out from the footplate, stared down past the shoulders of the load. Behind him twinkled spots of fire where the hell-burner, two score kegs of fine-grain powder packed round with bricks and scrap iron, had scythed the valley clear of life.

Water was low. He worked the injectors, checked the gauge. "We must live how we can," he said, not hearing the words. "We must all live how we can." The firm of Strange had not been built on softness; what you stole from it, you were welcome to keep.

Somewhere a semaphore clacked to Emergency Attention, torches lighting its arms. The *Lady Margaret,* with her train behind her, fled to Durnovaria, huddled ahead in the dim silver elbow of the Frome.

He Walked Around the Horses

H. Beam Piper

In November, 1809, an Englishman named Benjamin Bathurst vanished, inexplicably and utterly.

He was en route to Hamburg from Vienna, where he had been serving as his government's envoy to the court of what Napoleon had left of the Austrian Empire. At an inn in Perleburg, in Prussia, while examining a change of horses for his coach, he casually stepped out of sight of his secretary and his valet. He was not seen to leave the inn yard. He was not seen again, ever.

At least, not in this continuum . . .

I

(From Baron Eugen von Krutz, Minister of Police, to His Excellency the Count von Berchtenwald, Chancellor to His Majesty Friedrich Wilhelm III of Prussia.)

25 November, 1809

Your Excellency:

A circumstance has come to the notice of this Ministry, the significance of which I am at a loss to define, but, since it appears to involve matters of state, both here and abroad, I am convinced that it is of sufficient importance to be brought to the personal attention of your Excellency. Frankly, I am unwilling to take any further action in the matter without your Excellency's advice.

Briefly, the situation is this: We are holding, here at the Ministry of Police, a person giving his name as Benjamin Bathurst, who claims to be a British diplomat. This person was taken into custody by the police at Perleburg yesterday, as a result of a disturbance at an inn there; he is being detained on technical charges of causing disorder in a public place, and of being a suspicious person. When arrested, he had in his possession a dispatch case, containing a number of papers; these are of such an extraordinary nature that the local authorities declined to assume any responsibility beyond having the man sent here to Berlin.

After interviewing this person and examining his papers, I am, I must confess, in much the same position. This is not, I am convinced, any ordinary police matter; there is something very strange and disturbing here. The man's statements, taken alone, are so incredible as to justify the assumption that he is mad. I cannot, however, adopt this theory, in view of his demeanor, which is that of a man of perfect rationality, and because of the existence of these papers. The whole thing is mad; incomprehensible!

The papers in question accompany, along with copies of the various statements taken at Perleburg, and a personal letter to me from my nephew, Lieutenant Rudolf von Tarlburg. This last is deserving of your Excellency's particular attention; Lieutenant von Tarlburg is a very level-headed young officer, not at all inclined to be fanciful or imaginative. It would take a good deal to affect him as he describes.

The man calling himself Benjamin Bathurst is now lodged in an apartment here at the Ministry; he is being treated with every consideration, and, except for freedom of movement, accorded every privilege.

I am, most anxiously awaiting your Excellency's advice, etc., etc.,

Krutz

II

(Report of Traugott Zeller, Oberwachtmeister, Staatspolizei, made at Perleburg, 25 November, 1809.)

At about ten minutes past two of the afternoon of Saturday, 25 November, while I was at the police station, there entered a man known to me as Franz Bauer, an inn servant employed by Christian Hauck, at the sign of the Sword & Scepter, here in Perleburg. This man Franz Bauer made complaint to *Staatspolizeikapitan* Ernst Hartenstein, saying that there was a madman making trouble at the inn where he, Franz Bauer, worked.

I was therefore directed by *Staatspolizeikapitan* Hartenstein to go to the Sword & Scepter Inn, there to act at discretion to maintain the peace.

Arriving at the inn in company with the said Franz Bauer, I found a considerable crowd of people in the common room, and, in the midst of them, the innkeeper, Christian Hauck, in altercation with a stranger. This stranger was a gentlemanly appearing person, dressed in traveling clothes, who had under his arm a small leather dispatch case. As I entered, I could hear him, speaking in German with a strong English accent, abusing the innkeeper, the said Christian Hauck, and accusing him of having drugged his, the stranger's, wine, and of having stolen his, the stranger's, coach-and-four, and of having abducted his, the stranger's, secretary and servants. This the said Christian Hauck was loudly denying, and the other people in the inn were taking the innkeeper's part, and mocking the stranger for a madman.

On entering, I commanded everyone to be silent, in the King's name, and then, as he appeared to be the complaining party of the dispute, I required the foreign gentleman to state to me what was the trouble. He then repeated his accusations against the innkeeper, Hauck, saying that Hauck, or, rather, another man who resembled Hauck and who had claimed to be the innkeeper, had drugged his wine and stolen his coach and made off with his secretary and his servants. At this point, the innkeeper and the bystanders all began shouting denials and contradictions, so that I had to pound on the table with my truncheon to command silence.

I then required the innkeeper, Christian Hauck, to answer the charges which the stranger had made; this he did with a complete denial of all of them, saying that the stranger had had no wine in his inn, and that he had not been inside the inn until a few minutes before, when he had burst in shouting accusations, and that there had been no secretary, and no valet, and no coachman, and no coach-and-four, at the inn, and that the gentleman was raving mad. To all this, he called the people who were in the common room to witness.

I then required the stranger to account for himself. He said that his name was Benjamin Bathurst, and that he was a British diplomat, returning to England from Vienna. To prove this, he produced from his dispatch case sundry papers. One of these was a letter of safe-conduct, issued by the Prussian Chancellery, in which he was named and described as Benjamin Bathurst. The other papers were English, all bearing seals, and appearing to be official documents.

167

Accordingly, I requested him to accompany me to the police station, and also the innkeeper, and three men whom the innkeeper wanted to bring as witnesses.

Traugott Zeller
Oberwachtmeister

Report approved,

Ernst Hartenstein
Staatspolizeikapitan

III

(Statement of the self-so-called Benjamin Bathurst, taken at the police station at Perleburg, 25 November, 1809.)

My name is Benjamin Bathurst, and I am Envoy Extraordinary and Minister Plenipotentiary of the Government of His Britannic Majesty to the court of His Majesty Franz I, Emperor of Austria, or, at least I was until the events following the Austrian surrender made necessary my return to London. I left Vienna on the morning of Monday, the 20th, to go to Hamburg to take ship home; I was traveling in my own coach-and-four, with my secretary, Mr. Bertram Jardine, and my valet, William Small, both British subjects, and a coachman, Josef Bidek, an Austrian subject, whom I had hired for the trip. Because of the presence of French troops, whom I was anxious to avoid, I was forced to make a detour west as far as Salzburg before turning north toward Magdeburg, where I crossed the Elbe. I was unable to get a change of horses for my coach after leaving Gera, until I reached Perleburg, where I stopped at the Sword & Scepter Inn.

Arriving there, I left my coach in the inn yard, and I and my secretary, Mr. Jardine, went into the inn. A man, not this fellow here, but another rogue, with more beard and less paunch, and more shabbily dressed, but as like him as though he were his brother, represented himself as the innkeeper, and I dealt with him for a change of horses, and ordered a bottle of wine for myself and my secretary, and also a pot of beer apiece for my valet and the coachman, to be taken outside to them. Then Jardine and I sat down to our wine, at a table in the common room, until the man who claimed to be the innkeeper came back and told us that the fresh horses were harnessed to the coach and ready to go. Then we went outside again.

I looked at the two horses on the off side, and then walked around in front of the team to look at the two nigh-side horses, and as I did, I felt giddy, as though I were about to fall, and everything went black before my eyes. I thought I was having a fainting spell, something I am not at all subject to, and I put out my hand to grasp the hitching bar, but could not find it. I am sure, now, that I was unconscious for some time, because when my head cleared, the coach and horses were gone, and in their place was a big farm wagon, jacked up in front, with the right front wheel off, and two peasants were greasing the detached wheel.

I looked at them for a moment, unable to credit my eyes, and then I spoke to them in German, saying, "Where the devil's my coach-and-four?"

They both straightened, startled; the one who was holding the wheel almost dropped it.

"Pardon, Excellency," he said. "There's been no coach-and-four here, all the time we've been here."

"Yes," said his mate, "and we've been here since just after noon."

I did not attempt to argue with them. It occurred to me—and it is still my opinion—that I was the victim of some plot; that my wine had been drugged, that I had been unconscious for some time, during which my coach had been removed and this wagon substituted for it, and that these peasants had been put to work on it and instructed what to say if questioned. If my arrival at the inn had been anticipated, and everything put in readiness, the whole business would not have taken ten minutes.

I therefore entered the inn, determined to have it out with this rascally innkeeper, but when I returned to the common room, he was nowhere to be seen, and this other fellow, who has also given his name as Christian Hauck, claimed to be the innkeeper and denied knowledge of any of the things I have just stated. Furthermore, there were four cavalrymen, Uhlans, drinking beer and playing cards at the table where Jardine and I had had our wine, and they claimed to have been there for several hours.

I have no idea why such an elaborate prank, involving the participation of many people, should be played on me, except at the instigation of the French. In that case, I cannot understand why Prussian soldiers should lend themselves to it.

Benjamin Bathurst

IV

(Statement of Christian Hauck, innkeeper, taken at the police station at Perleburg, 25 November, 1809.)

May it please Your Honor, my name is Christian Hauck, and I keep an inn at the sign of the Sword & Scepter, and have these past fifteen years, and my father, and his father, before me, for the past fifty years, and never has there been a complaint like this against my inn. Your Honor, it is a hard thing for a man who keeps a decent house, and pays his taxes, and obeys the laws, to be accused of crimes of this sort.

I know nothing of this gentleman, nor of his coach nor his secretary nor his servants; I never set eyes on him before he came bursting into the inn from the yard, shouting and raving like a madman, and crying out, "Where the devil's that rogue of an innkeeper?"

I said to him, "I am the innkeeper; what cause have you to call me a rogue, sir?"

The stranger replied:

"You're not the innkeeper I did business with a few minutes ago, and he's the rascal I have a crow to pick with. I want to know what the devil's been done with my coach, and what's happened to my secretary and my servants."

I tried to tell him that I knew nothing of what he was talking about, but he would not listen, and gave me the lie, saying that he had been drugged and robbed, and his people kidnapped. He even had the impudence to claim that he and his secretary had been sitting at a table in that room, drinking wine, not fifteen minutes before, when there had been four non-commissioned officers of the Third Uhlans at that table since noon. Everybody in the room spoke up for me, but he would not listen, and was shouting that we were all robbers, and kidnappers, and French spies, and I don't know what all, when the police came.

Your Honor, the man is mad. What I have told you about this is the truth, and all that I know about this business, so help me God.

Christian Hauck

V

(Statement of Franz Bauer, inn servant, taken at the police station at Perleburg, 25 November, 1809.)

May it please Your Honor, my name is Franz Bauer, and I am a servant at the Sword & Scepter Inn, kept by Christian Hauck.

This afternoon, when I went into the inn yard to empty a bucket of slops on the dung heap by the stables, I heard voices and turned around, to see this gentleman speaking to Wilhelm Beick and Fritz Herzer, who were greasing their wagon in the yard. He had not been in the yard when I had turned around to empty the bucket, and I thought that he must have come in from the street. This gentleman was asking Beick and Herzer where was his coach, and when they told him they didn't know, he turned and ran into the inn.

Of my own knowledge, the man had not been inside the inn before then, nor had there been any coach, or any of the people he spoke of, at the inn, and none of the things he spoke of happened there, for otherwise I would know, since I was at the inn all day.

When I went back inside, I found him in the common room, shouting at my master, and claiming that he had been drugged and robbed. I saw that he was mad, and was afraid that he would do some mischief, so I went for the police.

Franz Bauer

his (X) mark

VI

(Statements of Wilhelm Beick and Fritz Herzer, peasants, taken at the police station at Perleburg, 25 November, 1809.)

May it please Your Honor, my name is Wilhelm Beick, and I am a tenant on the estate of the Baron von Hentig. On this day, I and Fritz Herzer were sent in to Perleburg with a load of potatoes and cabbages which the innkeeper at the Sword & Scepter had bought from the estate superintendent. After we had unloaded them, we decided to grease our wagon, which was very dry, before going back, so we unhitched and began working on it. We took about two hours, starting just after we had eaten lunch, and in all that time, there was no coach-and-four in the inn yard. We were just finishing when this gentleman spoke to us, demanding to know where his coach was. We told him that there had been no coach in the yard all the time we had been there, so he turned around and ran into the inn. At the time, I thought that he had come out of the inn before speaking to us, for I know that he could not have come in from the street. Now I do not know where he came from, but I know that I never saw him before that moment.

Wilhelm Beick

his (X) mark

I have heard the above testimony, and it is true to my own knowledge, and I have nothing to add to it.

Fritz Herzer
his (X) mark

VII

(From Staatspolizeikapitan *Ernst Hartenstein, to His Excellency, the Baron von Krutz, Minister of Police.)*

25 November, 1809

Your Excellency:

The accompanying copies of statements taken this day will explain how the prisoner, the self-so-called Benjamin Bathurst, came into my custody. I have charged him with causing disorder and being a suspicious person, to hold him until more can be learned about him. However, as he represents himself to be a British diplomat, I am unwilling to assume any further responsibility, and am having him sent to Your Excellency, in Berlin.

In the first place, Your Excellency, I have the strongest doubts of the man's story. The statement which he made before me, and signed, is bad enough, with a coach-and-four turning into a farm wagon, like Cinderella's coach into a pumpkin, and three people vanishing as though swallowed by the earth. Your Excellency will permit me to doubt that there ever was any such coach, or any such people. But all this is perfectly reasonable and credible, beside the things he said to me, of which no record was made.

Your Excellency will have noticed, in his statement, certain allusions to the Austrian surrender, and to French troops in Austria. After his statement had been taken down, I noticed these allusions, and I inquired, what surrender, and what were French troops doing in Austria. The man looked at me in a pitying manner, and said:

"News seems to travel slowly, hereabouts; peace was concluded at Vienna on the 14th of last month. And as for what French troops are doing in Austria, they're doing the same things Bonaparte's brigands are doing everywhere in Europe."

"And who is Bonaparte?" I asked.

He stared at me as though I had asked him, "Who is the Lord Jehovah?" Then, after a moment, a look of comprehension came into his face.

"So; you Prussians concede him the title of Emperor, and refer to him as Napoleon,"he said. "Well, I can assure you that His Britannic Majesty's Government haven't done so, and never will; not so long as one Englishman has a finger left to pull a trigger. General Bonaparte is a usurper; His Britannic Majesty's Government do not recognize any sovereignty in France except the House of Bourbon."This he said very sternly, as though rebuking me.

It took me a moment or so to digest that, and to appeciate all its implications. Why, this fellow evidently believed, as a matter of fact, that the French Monarchy had been overthrown by some military adventurer named Bonaparte, who was calling himself the Emperor Napoleon, and who had made war on Austria and forced a surrender. I made no attempt to argue with him—one wastes time arguing with madmen—but if this man could believe that, the transformation of a coach-and-four into a cabbage wagon was a small matter indeed. So, to humor him, I asked him if he thought General Bonaparte's agents were responsible for his trouble at the inn.

"Certainly,"he replied. "The chances are they didn't know me to see me, and took Jardine for the Minister, and me for the secretary, so they made off with poor Jardine. I wonder, though, that they left me my dispatch case. And that reminds me; I'll want that back. Diplomatic papers, you know."

I told him, very seriously, that we would have to check his credentials. I promised him I would make every effort to locate his secretary and his servants and his coach, took a complete description of all of them, and persuaded him to go into an upstairs room, where I kept him under guard. I did start inquiries, calling in all my informers and spies, but, as I expected, I could learn nothing. I could not find anybody, even, who had seen him anywhere in Perleburg before he appeared at the Sword & Scepter, and that rather surprised me, as somebody should have seen him enter the town, or walk along the street.

In this connection, let me remind Your Excellency of the discrepancy in the statements of the servant, Franz Bauer, and of the two peasants. The former is certain the man entered the inn yard from the street; the latter are just as positive that he did not. Your Excellency, I do not like such puzzles, for I am sure that all three were telling the truth to the best of their knowledge. They are ignorant common folk, I admit, but they should know what they did or did not see.

After I got the prisoner into safe-keeping, I fell to examining his papers, and I can assure Your Excellency that they gave me a shock. I had paid little heed to his ravings about the King of France being dethroned, or about this General Bonaparte who called himself the Emperor Napoleon, but I found all these things mentioned in his papers and dispatches, which had every appearance of being official documents. There was repeated mention of the taking, by the French, of Vienna, last May, and of the capitulation of the Austrian Emperor to this General Bonaparte, and of battles being fought all over Europe, and I don't know what other fantastic things. Your Excellency, I have heard of all sorts of madmen—one believing himself to be the Archangel Gabriel, or Mohammed, or a werewolf, and another convinced that his bones are made of glass, or that he is pursued and tormented by devils—but, so help me God, this is the first time I have heard of a madman who had documentary proof for his delusions! Does Your Excellency wonder, then, that I want no part of this business?

But the matter of his credentials was even worse. He had papers, sealed with the seal of the British Foreign Office, and to every appearance genuine—but they were signed, as Foreign Minister, by one George Canning, and all the world knows that Lord Castlereagh has been Foreign Minister these last five years. And to cap it all, he had a safe-conduct, sealed with the seal of the Prussian Chancellery—the very seal, for I compared it, under a strong magnifying glass, with one that I knew to be genuine, and they were identical—and yet, this letter was signed, as Chancellor, not by Count von Berchtenwald, but by Baron vom und zum Stein, the Minister of Agriculture, and the signature, as far as I could see, appeared to be genuine! This is too much for me, Your Excellency; I must ask to be excused from dealing with this matter, before I become as mad as my prisoner!

I made arrangements, accordingly, with Colonel Keitel, of the Third Uhlans, to furnish an officer to escort this man in to Berlin. The coach in which they come belongs to this police station, and the driver is one of my men. He should be furnished expense money to get back to Perleburg. The guard is a corporal of Uhlans, the orderly of the officer. He will stay with the *Herr Oberleutnant,* and both of them will return here at their own convenience and expense.

I have the honor, Your Excellency, to be, etc., etc.

Ernst Hartenstein
Staatspolizeikapitan

VIII

(From Oberleutnant *Rudolf von Tarlburg, to Baron Eugen von Krutz.)*

26 November, 1809

Dear Uncle Eugen:

This is in no sense a formal report; I made that at the Ministry, when I turned the Englishman and his papers over to one of your officers—a fellow with red hair and a face like a bulldog. But there are a few things which you should be told, which wouldn't look well in an official report, to let you know just what sort of a rare fish has gotten into your net.

I had just come in from drilling my platoon, yesterday, when Colonel Keitel's orderly told me that the colonel wanted to see me in his quarters. I found the old fellow in undress in his sitting room, smoking his big pipe.

"Come in, Lieutenant; come in and sit down, my boy!"he greeted me, in that bluff, hearty manner which he always adopts with his junior officers when he has some particularly nasty job to be done. "How would you like to take a little trip in to Berlin? I have an errand, which won't take half an hour, and you can stay as long as you like, just so you're back by Thursday, when your turn comes up for road patrol."

Well, I thought, this is the bait. I waited to see what the hook would look like, saying that it was entirely agreeable with me, and asking what his errand was.

"Well, it isn't for myself, Tarlburg,"he said. "It's for this fellow Hartenstein, the *Staatspolizeikapitan* here. He has something he wants done at the Ministry of Police, and I thought of you because I've heard you're related to the Baron von Krutz. You are, aren't you?"he asked, just as though he didn't know all about who all his officers are related to.

"That's right, Colonel; the Baron is my uncle,"I said. "What does Hartenstein want done?"

"Why, he has a prisoner whom he wants taken to Berlin and turned over at the Ministry. All you have to do is to take him in, in a coach, and see he doesn't escape on the way, and get a receipt for him, and for some papers. This is a very important prisoner; I don't think Hartenstein has anybody he can trust to handle him. A state prisoner. He claims to be some sort of a British diplomat, and for all Hartenstein knows, maybe he is. Also, he is a madman."

"A madman?"I echoed.

"Yes, just so. At least, that's what Hartenstein told me. I wanted to know what sort of a madman—there are various kinds of madmen, all of whom must be handled differently—but all Hartenstein would tell me was that he had unrealistic beliefs about the state of affairs in Europe."

"Ha! What diplomat hasn't?" I asked.

Old Keitel gave a laugh, somewhere between the bark of a dog and the croaking of a raven.

"Yes, naturally! The unrealistic beliefs of diplomats are what soldiers die of,"he said. "I said as much to Hartenstein, but he wouldn't tell me anything more. He seemed to regret having said even that much. He looked like a man who's seen a particularly terrifying ghost."The old man puffed hard at his famous pipe for a while, blowing smoke up through his mustache. "Rudi, Hartenstein has pulled a hot potato out of the ashes, this time, and he wants to toss it to your uncle, before he burns his fingers. I think that's one reason why he got me to furnish an escort for his Englishman. Now, look; you must take this unrealistic diplomat, or this undiplomatic madman, or whatever in blazes he is, in to Berlin. And understand this."He pointed his pipe at me as though it were a pistol. "Your orders are to take him there and turn him over at the Ministry of Police. Nothing has been said about whether you turn him over alive, or dead, or half one and half the other. I know nothing about this business, and want to know nothing; if Hartenstein wants us to play gaol warders for him, then, *bei Gott,* he must be satisfied with our way of doing it!"

Well, to cut short the story, I looked at the coach Hartenstein had placed at my disposal, and I decided to chain the left door shut on the outside, so that it couldn't be opened from within. Then, I would put my prisoner on my left, so that the only way out would be past me. I decided not to carry any weapons which he might be able to snatch from me, so I took off my saber and locked it in the seat box, along with the dispatch case containing the Englishman's papers. It was cold enough to wear a greatcoat in comfort, so I wore mine, and in the right side pocket, where my prisoner couldn't reach, I put a little leaded bludgeon, and also a brace of pocket pistols. Hartenstein was going to furnish me a guard as well as a driver, but I said that I would take a servant who could act as guard. The servant, of course, was my orderly, old Johann; I gave him my double hunting gun to carry, with a big charge of boar shot in one barrel and an ounce ball in the other.

In addition, I armed myself with a big bottle of cognac. I thought that if I could shoot my prisoner often enough with that, he would give me no trouble.

As it happened, he didn't, and none of my precautions—except the cognac—were needed. The man didn't look like a lunatic to me. He was a rather stout gentleman, of past middle age, with a ruddy complexion and an intelligent face. The only unusual thing about him was his hat, which was a peculiar contraption, looking like the pot out of a close-stool. I put him in the carriage, and then offered him a drink out of my bottle, taking one about half as big myself. He smacked his lips over it and said, "Well, that's real brandy; whatever we think of their detestable politics, we can't criticize the French for their liquor." Then, he said, "I'm glad they're sending me in the custody of a military gentleman, instead of a confounded gendarme. Tell me the truth, Lieutenant; am I under arrest for anything?"

"Why," I said, "Captain Hartenstein should have told you about that. All I know is that I have orders to take you to the Ministry of Police, in Berlin, and not to let you escape on the way. These orders I will carry out; I hope you don't hold that against me."

He assured me that he did not, and we had another drink on it—I made sure, again, that he got twice as much as I did—and then the coachman cracked his whip and we were off for Berlin.

Now, I thought, I am going to see just what sort of a madman this is, and why Hartenstein is making a state affair out of a squabble at an inn. So I decided to explore his unrealistic beliefs about the state of affairs in Europe.

After guiding the conversation to where I wanted it, I asked him:

"What, *Herr* Bathurst, in your belief, is the real, underlying cause of the present tragic situation in Europe?"

That, I thought, was safe enough. Name me one year, since the days of Julius Caesar, when the situation in Europe hasn't been tragic! And it worked, to perfection.

"In my belief," says this Englishman, "the whole damnable mess is the result of the victory of the rebellious colonists in North America, and their blasted republic."

Well, you can imagine, that gave me a start. All the world knows that the American Patriots lost their war for independence from England; that their army was shattered, that their leaders were either killed or driven into exile. How many times, when I was a little boy, did I not sit up long past my bedtime, when old Baron von Steuben was

177

a guest at Tarlburg-Schloss, listening openmouthed and wide-eyed to his stories of that gallant lost struggle! How I used to shiver at his tales of the terrible winter camp, or thrill at the battles, or weep as he told how he held the dying Washington in his arms, and listened to his noble last words, at the Battle of Doylestown! And here, this man was telling me that the Patriots had really won, and set up the republic for which they had fought! I had been prepared for some of what Hartenstein had called unrealistic beliefs, but nothing as fantastic as this.

"I can cut it even finer than that," Bathurst continued. "It was the defeat of Burgoyne at Saratoga. We made a good bargain when we got Benedict Arnold to turn his coat, but we didn't do it soon enough. If he hadn't been on the field that day, Burgoyne would have gone through Gates's army like a hot knife through butter."

But Arnold hadn't been at Saratoga. I know; I have read much of the American war. Arnold was shot dead on New Year's Day of 1776, during the attempted storming of Quebec. And Burgoyne had done just as Bathurst had said; he had gone through Gates like a knife, and down the Hudson to join Howe.

"But, *Herr* Bathurst," I asked, "how could that affect the situation in Europe? America is thousands of miles away, across the ocean."

"Ideas can cross oceans quicker than armies. When Louis XVI decided to come to the aid of the Americans, he doomed himself and his regime. A successful resistance to royal authority in America was all the French Republicans needed to inspire them. Of course, we have Louis's own weakness to blame, too. If he'd given those rascals a whiff of grapeshot, when the mob tried to storm Versailles in 1790, there'd have been no French Revolution."

But he had. When Louis XVI ordered the howitzers turned on the mob at Versailles, and then sent the dragoons to ride down the survivors, the Republican movement had been broken. That had been when Cardinal Talleyrand, who had then been merely Bishop of Autun, had come to the fore and become the power that he is today in France; the greatest King's Minister since Richelieu.

"And, after that, Louis's death followed as surely as night after day," Bathurst was saying. "And because the French had no experience in self-government, their republic was foredoomed. If Bonaparte hadn't seized power, somebody else would have; when the French murdered their King, they delivered themselves to dictatorship. And a dictator, unsupported by the prestige of royalty, has no choice but to lead his people into foreign war, to keep them from turning upon him."

It was like that all the way to Berlin. All these things seem foolish, by daylight, but as I sat in the darkness of that swaying coach, I was almost convinced of the reality of what he told me. I tell you, Uncle Eugen, it was frightening, as though he were giving me a view of Hell. *Gott im Himmel,* the things that man talked of! Armies swarming over Europe; sack and massacre, and cities burning; blockades, and starvation; kings deposed, and thrones tumbling like tenpins! battles in which the soldiers of every nation fought, and in which tens of thousands were mowed down like ripe grain; and, over all, the Satanic figure of a little man in a gray coat, who dictated peace to the Austrian Emperor in Schoenbrunn, and carried the Pope away a prisoner to Savona.

Madman, eh? Unrealistic beliefs, says Hartenstein? Well, give me madmen who drool spittle, and foam at the mouth, and shriek obscene blasphemies. But not this pleasant-seeming gentleman who sat beside me and talked of horrors in a quiet, cultured voice, while he drank my cognac.

But not all my cognac! If your man at the Ministry—the one with red hair and the bulldog face—tells you that I was drunk when I brought in that Englishman, you had better believe him!

Rudi

IX

(From Count von Berchtenwald, to the British Minister.)

28 November, 1809

Honored Sir:

The accompanying *dossier* will acquaint you with the problem confronting this Chancellery, without needless repetition on my part. Please to understand that it is not, and never was, any part of the intentions of the Government of His Majesty Friedrich Wilhelm III to offer any injury or indignity to the Government of His Britannic Majesty George III. We would never contemplate holding in arrest the person, or tampering with the papers, of an accredited envoy of your Government. However, we have the gravest doubt, to make a considerable understatement, that this person who calls himself Benjamin Bathurst is any such envoy, and we do not think that it would be any service to the Government of His Britannic Majesty to allow an imposter to travel about Europe in the guise of a British diplomatic representative. We certainly should not thank the Government of His Britannic Majesty for failing to take steps to deal with some person who, in England, might falsely represent himself to be a Prussian diplomat.

This affair touches us almost as closely as it does your own Government; this man had in his possession a letter of safe-conduct, which you will find in the accompanying dispatch case. It is of the regular form, as issued by this Chancellery, and is sealed with the Chancellery seal, or with a very exact counterfeit of it. However, it has been signed, as Chancellor of Prussia, with a signature indistinguishable from that of the Baron vom und zum Stein, who is the present Prussian Minister of Agriculture. Baron Stein was shown the signature, with the rest of the letter covered, and without hesitation acknowledged it for his own writing. However, when the letter was uncovered and shown to him, his surprise and horror were such as would require the pen of a Goethe or a Schiller to describe, and he denied categorically ever having seen the document before.

I have no choice but to believe him. It is impossible to think that a man of Baron Stein's honorable and serious character would be party to the fabrication of a paper of this sort. Even aside from this, I am in the thing as deeply as he; if it is signed with his signature, it is also sealed with my seal, which has not been out of my personal keeping in the ten years that I have been Chancellor here. In fact, the word "impossible" can be used to describe the entire business. It was impossible for the man Benjamin Bathurst to have entered the inn yard—yet he did. It was impossible that he should carry papers of the sort found in his dispatch case, or that such papers should exist—yet I am sending them to you with this letter. It is impossible that Baron vom und zum Stein should sign a paper of the sort he did, or that it should be sealed by the Chancellery—yet it bears both Stein's signature and my seal.

You will also find in the dispatch case other credentials ostensibly originating with the British Foreign Office, of the same character, being signed by persons having no connection with the Foreign Office, or even with the Government, but being sealed with apparently authentic seals. If you send these papers to London, I fancy you will find that they will there create the same situation as that caused here by this letter of safe-conduct.

I am also sending you a charcoal sketch of the person who calls himself Benjamin Bathurst. This portrait was taken without its subject's knowledge. Baron von Krutz's nephew, Lieutenant von Tarlburg, who is the son of our mutual friend Count von Tarlburg, has a *little friend,* a very clever young lady who is, as you will see, an expert at this sort of work; she was introduced into a room at the Ministry of Police and placed behind a screen, where she could sketch our prisoner's face. If you should send this picture to London, I think that there is a good chance that it might be recognized. I can vouch that it is an excellent likeness.

To tell the truth, we are at our wits' end about this affair. I can not understand how such excellent imitations of these various seals could be made, and the signature of the Baron vom und zum Stein is the most expert forgery that I have ever seen, in thirty years' experience as a statesman. This would indicate careful and painstaking work on the part of somebody; how, then, do we reconcile this with such clumsy mistakes, recognizable as such by any schoolboy, as signing the name of Baron Stein as Prussian Chancellor, or Mr. George Canning, who is a member of the opposition party and not connected with your Government, as British Foreign Secretary?

These are mistakes which only a madman would make. There are those who think our prisoner is a madman, because of his apparent delusions about the great conqueror, General Bonaparte, *alias* the Emperor Napoleon. Madmen have been known to fabricate evidence to support their delusions, it is true, but I shudder to think of a madman having at his disposal the resources to manufacture the papers you will find in this dispatch case. Moreover, some of our foremost medical men, who have specialized in the disorders of the mind, have interviewed this man Bathurst and say that, save for his fixed belief in a nonexistent situation, he is perfectly rational.

Personally, I believe that the whole thing is a gigantic hoax, perpetrated for some hidden and sinister purpose, possibly to create confusion, and undermine the confidence existing between your Government and mine, and to set against one another various persons connected with both Governments, or else as a mask for some other conspiratorial activity. Without specifying any Sovereigns or Governments who might wish to do this, I can think of two groups, namely, the Jesuits, and the outlawed French Republicans, either of whom might conceive such a situation to be to their advantage. Only a few months ago, you will recall, there was a Jacobin plot unmasked at Köln.

But, whatever this business may portend, I do not like it. I want to get to the bottom of it as soon as possible, and I will thank you, my dear Sir, and your Government, for any assistance you may find possible.

I have the honor, sir, to be, etc., etc., etc.,

Berchtenwald

X

FROM BARON VON KRUTZ, TO THE COUNT VON BERCHTENWALD. MOST
URGENT; MOST IMPORTANT. TO BE DELIVERED IMMEDIATELY AND IN
PERSON, REGARDLESS OF CIRCUMSTANCES.

28 November, 1809

Count von Berchtenwald:

Within the past half hour, that is, at about eleven o'clock tonight,
the man calling himself Benjamin Bathurst was shot and killed by a
sentry at the Ministry of Police, while attempting to escape from
custody.

A sentry on duty in the rear courtyard of the Ministry observed a
man attempting to leave the building in a suspicious and furtive
manner. This sentry, who was under the strictest orders to allow no one
to enter or leave without written authorization, challenged him; when
he attempted to run, the sentry fired his musket at him, bringing him
down. At the shot, the Sergeant of the Guard rushed into the courtyard
with his detail, and the man whom the sentry had shot was found to be
the Englishman, Benjamin Bathurst. He had been hit in the chest with
an ounce ball, and died before the doctor could arrive, and without
recovering consciousness.

An investigation revealed that the prisoner, who was confined on
the third floor of the building, had fashioned a rope from his bedding,
his bed cord, and the leather strap of his bell pull; this rope was only
long enough to reach to the window of the office on the second floor,
directly below, but he managed to enter this by kicking the glass out of
the window. I am trying to find out how he could do this without being
heard; I can assure Your Excellency that somebody is going to smart
for this night's work. As for the sentry, he acted within his orders; I
have commended him for doing his duty, and for good shooting, and I
assume full responsibility for the death of the prisoner at his hands.

I have no idea why the self-so-called Benjamin Bathurst, who, until
now, was well behaved and seemed to take his confinement philosophi-
cally, should suddenly make this rash and fatal attempt, unless it was
because of those infernal dunderheads of madhouse doctors who have
been bothering him. Only this afternoon, Your Excellency, they deliberately handed him a bundle of newspapers—Prussian, Austrian,
French, and English—all dated within the last month. They wanted,
they said, to see how he would react. Well, God pardon them, they've
found out!

What does Your Excellency think should be done about giving the body burial?

Krutz

XI

(From the British Minister, to the Count von Berchtenwald.)

December 20th, 1809

My Dear Count von Berchtenwald:

Reply from London to my letter of the 28th *ult.*, which accompanied the dispatch case and the other papers, has finally come to hand. The papers which you wanted returned—the copies of the statements taken at Perleburg, the letter to the Baron von Krutz from the police captain, Hartenstein, and the personal letter of Krutz's nephew, Lieutenant von Tarlburg, and the letter of safe-conduct found in the dispatch case—accompany herewith. I don't know what the people at Whitehall did with the other papers; tossed them into the nearest fire, for my guess. Were I in Your Excellency's place, that's where the papers I am returning would go.

I have heard nothing, yet, from my dispatch of the 29th *ult.* concerning the death of the man who called himself Benjamin Bathurst, but I doubt very much if any official notice will ever be taken of it. Your Government had a perfect right to detain the fellow, and, that being the case, he attempted to escape at his own risk. After all, sentries are not required to carry loaded muskets in order to discourage them from putting their hands in their pockets.

To hazard a purely unofficial opinion, I should not imagine that London is very much dissatisfied with this *dénouement.* His Majesty's Government are a hard-headed and matter-of-fact set of gentry who do not relish mysteries, least of all mysteries whose solution may be more disturbing than the original problem.

This is entirely confidential, Your Excellency, but those papers which were in that dispatch case kicked up the devil's own row in London, with half the Government bigwigs protesting their innocence to high Heaven, and the rest accusing one another of complicity in the hoax. If that was somebody's intention, it was literally a howling success. For a while, it was even feared that there would be Questions in Parliament, but eventually, the whole vexatious business was hushed.

You may tell Count Tarlburg's son that his little friend is a most talented young lady; her sketch was highly commended by no less an

183

authority than Sir Thomas Lawrence, and here, Your Excellency, comes the most bedeviling part of a thoroughly bedeviled business. The picture was instantly recognized. It is a very fair likeness of Benjamin Bathurst, or, I should say, Sir Benjamin Bathurst, who is King's Lieutenant-Governor for the Crown Colony of Georgia. As Sir Thomas Lawrence did his portrait a few years back, he is in an excellent position to criticize the work of Lieutenant von Tarlburg's young lady. However, Sir Benjamin Bathurst was known to have been in Savannah, attending to the duties of his office, and in the public eye, all the while that his double was in Prussia. Sir Benjamin does not have a twin brother. It has been suggested that this fellow might be a half-brother, born on the wrong side of the blanket, but, as far as I know, there is no justification for this theory.

The General Bonaparte, *alias* the Emperor Napoleon, who is given so much mention in the dispatches, seems also to have a counterpart in actual life; there is, in the French army, a Colonel of Artillery by that name, a Corsican who Gallicized his original name of Napolione Buonaparte. He is a most brilliant military theoretician; I am sure some of your own officers, like General Scharnhorst, could tell you about him. His loyalty to the French Monarchy has never been questioned.

This same correspondence to fact seems to crop up everywhere in that amazing collection of pseudo-dispatches and pseudo-state-papers. The United States of America, you will recall, was the style by which the rebellious colonies referred to themselves, in the Declaration of Philadelphia. The James Madison who is mentioned as the current President of the United States is now living, in exile, in Switzerland. His alleged predecessor in office, Thomas Jefferson, was the author of the rebel Declaration; after the defeat of the rebels, he escaped to Havana, and died, several years ago, in the Principality of Lichtenstein.

I was quite amused to find our old friend Cardinal Talleyrand—without the ecclesiastical title—cast in the role of chief adviser to the usurper, Bonaparte. His Eminence, I have always thought, is the sort of fellow who would land on his feet on top of any heap, and who would as little scruple to be Prime Minister to His Satanic Majesty as to His Most Christian Majesty.

I was baffled, however, by one name, frequently mentioned in those fantastic papers. This was the English General, Wellington. I haven't the least idea who this person might be.

I have the honor, Your Excellency, etc., etc., etc.,

Sir Arthur Wellesley

Custer's Last Jump

Steven Utley and
Howard Waldrop

Smithsonian Annals of Flight 39:
The Air War in the West
Chapter 27: "The Krupp Monoplane"

INTRODUCTION

Its wings still hold the tears from many bullets. The ailerons are still scorched black, and the exploded Henry machine rifle is bent awkwardly in its blast port.

The right landing skid is missing, and the frame has been restraightened. It stands in the left wing of the Air Museum today, next to the French Devre jet and the X-FU-5 Flying Flapjack, the world's fastest fighter aircraft.

On its rudder is the swastika, an ugly reminder of days of glory fifty years ago.

A simple plaque describes the aircraft. It reads:

CRAZY HORSE'S KRUPP MONOPLANE
(Captured at the raid on Fort Carson, January 5, 1882)

GENERAL

1. To study the history of this plane is to delve into one of the most glorious eras of aviation history. To begin: the aircraft was manufactured by the Krupp plant in Haavesborg, Netherlands. The airframe was completed August 3, 1862, as part of the third shipment of Krupp aircraft to the Confederate States of America under terms of the Agreement of Atlanta of 1861. It was originally equipped with power plant #311 Zed of 87¼ horsepower, manufactured by the Jumo plant at Nordmung, Duchy of Austria, on May 3 of the year 1862. Wingspan of the craft is twenty-three feet; its length is seventeen feet three inches. The aircraft arrived in the port of Charlotte on September 21, 1862, aboard the transport *Mendenhall,* which had suffered heavy bombardment from GAR picket ships. The aircraft was possibly sent by rail to Confederate Army Air Corps Center at Fort Andrew Mott, Alabama. Unfortunately, records of rail movements during this time were lost in the burning of the Confederate archives at Ittebeha in March 1867, two weeks after the Truce of Haldeman was signed.

2. The aircraft was damaged during a training flight in December 1862. Student pilot was Flight Subaltern (Cadet) Neldoo J. Smith, CSAAC; flight instructor during the ill-fated flight was Air Captain Winslow Homer Winslow, on interservice instructor-duty loan from the Confederate States Navy.

Accident forms and maintenance officer's reports indicate that the original motor was replaced with one of the new 93½ horsepower Jumo engines which had just arrived from Holland by way of Mexico.

3. The aircraft served routinely through the remainder of Flight Subaltern Smith's training. We have records[141] which indicate that the aircraft was one of the first to be equipped with the Henry repeating machine rifle of the chain-driven type. Until December 1862, all CSAAC aircraft were equipped with the Sharps repeating rifles of the motor-driven, low-voltage type on wing or turret mounts.

As was the custom, the aircraft was flown by Flight Subaltern Smith to his first duty station at Thimblerig Aerodrome in Augusta, Georgia. Flight Subaltern Smith was assigned to Flight Platoon 2, 1st Aeroscout Squadron.

4. The aircraft, with Flight Subaltern Smith at the wheel, participated in three of the aerial expeditions against the Union Army in the Second Battle of the Manassas. Smith distinguished himself in the first and third missions. (He was assigned aerial picket duty south of the actual battle

during his second mission.) On the first, he is credited with one kill and one probable (both bi-wing Airsharks). During the third mission, he destroyed one aircraft and forced another down behind Confederate lines. He then escorted the craft of his immediate commander, Air Captain Dalton Trump, to a safe landing on a field controlled by the Confederates. According to Trump's sworn testimony, Smith successfully fought off two Union craft and ranged ahead of Trump's crippled plane to strafe a group of Union soldiers who were in their flight path, discouraging them from firing on Trump's smoking aircraft.

For heroism on these two missions, Smith was awarded the Silver Star and Bar with Air Cluster. Presentation was made on March 3, 1863, by the late General J.E.B. Stuart, Chief of Staff of the CSAAC.

5. Flight Subaltern Smith was promoted to flight captain on April 12, 1863, after distinguishing himself with two kills and two probables during the first day of the Battle of the Three Roads, North Carolina. One of his kills was an airship of the Moby class, with a crew of fourteen. Smith shared with only one other aviator the feat of bringing down one of these dirigibles during the War of Secession.

This was the first action the 1st Aeroscout Squadron had seen since Second Manassas, and Captain Smith seems to have been chafing under inaction. Perhaps this led him to volunteer for duty with Major John S. Mosby, then forming what would later become Mosby's Raiders. This was actually sound military strategy: the CSAAC was to send a unit to southwestern Kansas to carry out harassment raids against the poorly defended forts of the Far West. These raids would force the Union to send men and materiel sorely needed at the southern front far to the west, where they would be ineffectual in the outcome of the war. That this action was taken is pointed to by some[142] as a sign that the Confederate States envisioned defeat and were resorting to desperate measures four years before the Treaty of Haldeman.

At any rate, Captain Smith and his aircraft joined a triple flight of six aircraft each, which, after stopping at El Dorado, Arkansas, to refuel, flew away on a westerly course. This is the last time they ever operated in Confederate states. The date was June 5, 1863.

6. The Union forts stretched from a medium-well-defended line in Illinois to poorly garrisoned stations as far west as the Wyoming Territory and south to the Kansas–Indian Territory border. Southwestern Kansas was both sparsely settled and garrisoned. It was from this area that Mosby's raiders, with the official designation 1st Western Interdiction Wing, CSAAC, operated.

A supply wagon train had been sent ahead a month before from Fort Worth, carrying petrol, ammunition, and material for shelters. A crude landing field, hangars, and barracks awaited the eighteen craft.

After two months of reconnaissance (done by mounted scouts due to the need to maintain the element of surprise, and, more importantly, by the limited amount of fuel available) the 1st WIW took to the air. The citizens of Riley, Kansas, long remembered the day: their first inkling that Confederates were closer than Texas came when motors were heard overhead and the Union garrison was literally blown off the face of the map.

7. Following the first raid, word went to the War Department headquarters in New York, with pleas for aid and reinforcements for all Kansas garrisons. Thus the CSAAC achieved its goal in the very first raid. The effects snowballed; as soon as the populace learned of the raid, it demanded protection from nearby garrisons. Farmers' organizations threatened to stop shipments of needed produce to eastern depots. The garrison commanders, unable to promise adequate protection, appealed to higher military authorities.

Meanwhile, the 1st WIW made a second raid on Abilene, heavily damaging the railways and stockyards with twenty-five-pound fragmentation bombs. They then circled the city, strafed the Army Quartermaster depot, and disappeared into the west.

8. This second raid, and the ensuing clamor from both the public and the commanders of western forces, convinced the War Department to divert new recruits and supplies, with seasoned members of the 18th Aeropursuit Squadron, to the Kansas–Missouri border, near Lawrence.

9. Inclement weather in the fall kept both the 18th AS and the 1st WIW grounded for seventy-two of the ninety days of the season. Aircraft from each of these units met several times; the 1st is credited with one kill, while pilots of the 18th downed two Confederate aircraft on the afternoon of December 12, 1863.

Both aircraft units were heavily resupplied during this time. The Battle of the Canadian River was fought on December 18, when mounted reconnaissance units of the Union and Confederacy met in Indian territory. Losses were small on both sides, but the skirmish was the first of what would become known as the Far Western Campaign.

10. Civilians spotted the massed formation of the 1st WIW as early as 10 A.M. Thursday, December 16, 1863. They headed northeast, making a leg due north when eighteen miles south of Lawrence. Two planes sped ahead to destroy the telegraph station at Felton, nine miles south of Lawrence. Nevertheless, a message of some sort reached

Lawrence; a Union messenger on horseback was on his way to the aerodrome when the first flight of Confederate aircraft passed overhead.

In the ensuing raid, seven of the nineteen Union aircraft were destroyed on the ground and two were destroyed in the air, while the remaining aircraft were severely damaged and the barracks and hangars demolished.

The 1st WIW suffered one loss: during the raid a Union clerk attached for duty with the 18th AS manned an Agar machine rifle position and destroyed one Confederate aircraft. He was killed by machine rifle fire from the second wave of planes. Private Alden Evans Gunn was awarded the Congressional Medal of Honor posthumously for his gallantry during the attack.

For the next two months, the 1st WIW ruled the skies as far north as Illinois and as far east as Trenton, Missouri.

THE FAR WESTERN CAMPAIGN

1. At this juncture, the two most prominent figures of the next nineteen years of frontier history enter the picture: the Oglala Sioux Crazy Horse, and Lieutenant Colonel (Brevet Major General) George Armstrong Custer. The clerical error giving Custer the rank of Brigadier General is well known. It is not common knowledge that Custer was considered by the General Staff as a candidate for Far Western Commander as early as the spring of 1864, a duty he would not take up until May 1869, when the Far Western Command was the only theater of war operations within the Americas.

The General Staff, it is believed, considered Major General Custer for the job for two reasons: they thought Custer possessed those qualities of spirit suited to the warfare necessary in the Western Command, and that the Far West was the ideal place for the twenty-three-year-old Boy General.

Crazy Horse, the Oglala Sioux warrior, was with a hunting party far from Oglala territory, checking the size of the few remaining buffalo herds before they started their spring migrations. Legend has it that Crazy Horse and the party were crossing the prairies in early February 1864 when two aircraft belonging to the 1st WIW passed nearby. Some of the Sioux jumped to the ground, believing that they were looking on the Thunderbird and its mate. Only Crazy Horse stayed on his pony and watched the aircraft disappear into the south.

He sent word back by the rest of the party that he and two of his young warrior friends had gone looking for the nest of the Thunderbird.

189

2. The story of the 1st WIW here becomes the story of the shaping of the Indian wars, rather than part of the history of the last four years of the War of Secession. It is well known that increased alarm over the Kansas raids had shifted War Department thinking: the defense of the Far West changed in importance from a minor matter in the larger scheme of war to a problem of vital concern. For one thing, the Confederacy was courting the emperor Maximilian of Mexico, and through him the French, to entering the war on the Confederate side. The South wanted arms, but most necessarily to break the Union submarine blockade. Only the French navy possessed the capability.

The Union therefore sent the massed 5th Cavalry to Kansas and attached to it the 12th Air Destroyer Squadron and the 2nd Airship Command.

The 2nd Airship Command, at the time of its deployment, was equipped with the small pursuit airships known in later days as the "torpedo ship," from its double-pointed ends. These ships were used for reconnaissance and light interdiction duties, and were almost always accompanied by aircraft from the 12th ADS. They immediately set to work patrolling the Kansas skies from the renewed base of operations at Lawrence.

3. The idea of using Indian personnel in some phase of airfield operations in the west had been proposed by Mosby as early as June 1863. The C of C, CSA, disapproved in the strongest possible terms. It was not a new idea, therefore, when Crazy Horse and his two companions rode into the airfield, accompanied by the sentries who had challenged them far from the perimeter. They were taken to Major Mosby for questioning.

Through an interpreter, Mosby learned they were Oglala, not Crows sent to spy for the Union. When asked why they had come so far, Crazy Horse replied, "To see the nest of the Thunderbird."

Mosby is said to have laughed[143] and then taken the three Sioux to see the aircraft. Crazy Horse was said to have been stricken with awe when he found that men controlled their flight.

Crazy Horse then offered Mosby ten ponies for one of the craft. Mosby explained that they were not his to give, but his Great Father's, and that they were used to fight the Yellowlegs from the Northeast.

At this time, fate took a hand: the 12th Air Destroyer Squadron had just begun operations. The same day Crazy Horse was having his initial interview with Mosby, a scout plane returned with the news that the 12th was being reinforced by an airship combat group; the dirigibles had been seen maneuvering near the Kansas–Missouri border.

Mosby learned from Crazy Horse that the warrior was respected, if not in his own tribe, then with other Nations of the North. Mosby, with an eye toward those reinforcements arriving in Lawrence, asked Crazy Horse if he could guarantee safe conduct through the northern tribes and land for an airfield should the present one have to be abandoned. Crazy Horse answered, "I can talk the idea to the people; it will be for them to decide."

Mosby told Crazy Horse that if he could secure the promise, he would grant him anything within his power.

Crazy Horse looked out the window toward the hangars. "I ask that you teach me and ten of my brother-friends to fly the Thunderbirds. We will help you fight the Yellowlegs."

Mosby, expecting requests for beef, blankets, or firearms, was taken aback. Unlike the others who had dealt with the Indians, he was a man of his word. He told Crazy Horse he would ask his Great Father if this could be done. Crazy Horse left, returning to his village in the middle of March. He and several warriors traveled extensively that spring, smoking the pipe, securing permissions from the other Nations for safe conduct for the Gray white men through their hunting lands. His hardest task came in convincing the Oglala themselves that the airfield could be built in their southern hunting grounds.

Crazy Horse, his two wives, seven warriors, and their women, children, and belongings rode into the CSAAC airfield in June 1864.

4. Mosby had been granted permission from Stuart to go ahead with the training program. Derision first met the request within the southern General Staff when Mosby's proposal was circulated. Stuart, though not entirely sympathetic to the idea, became its champion. Others objected, warning that ignorant savages should not be given modern weapons. Stuart reminded them that some of the good Tennessee boys already flying airplanes could neither read nor write.

Stuart's approval arrived a month before Crazy Horse and his band made camp on the edge of the airfield.

5. It fell to Captain Smith to train Crazy Horse. The Indian became what Smith in his journal[144] describes as "the best natural pilot I have seen or it has been my pleasure to fly with." Part of this seems to have come from Smith's own modesty; by all accounts, Smith was one of the finer pilots of the war.

The operations of the 12th ADS and the 2nd Airship Command ranged closer to the CSAAC airfield. The dogfights came frequently and the fighting grew less gentlemanly. One 1st WIW fighter was pounced by three aircraft of the 12th simultaneously: they did not stop firing even when the pilot signaled that he was hit and that his engine was dead. Nor did they break off their runs until both pilot and craft plunged into the Kansas prairie. It is thought that the Union pilots were under secret orders to kill all members of the 1st WIW. There is some evidence[145] that this rankled with the more gentlemanly of the 12th Air Destroyer Squadron. Nevertheless, fighting intensified.

A flight of six more aircraft joined the 1st WIW some weeks after the Oglala Sioux started their training: this was the first of the ferry flights from Mexico through Texas and Indian territory to reach the airfield. Before the summer was over, a dozen additional craft would join the Wing, this before shipments were curtailed by Juarez's revolution against the French and the ouster and execution of Maximilian and his family.

Smith records[146] that Crazy Horse's first solo took place on August 14, 1864, and that the warrior, though deft in the air, still needed practice on his landings. He had a tendency to come in overpowered and to stall his engine out too soon. Minor repairs were made on the skids of the craft after his flight.

All this time Crazy Horse had flown Smith's craft. Smith, after another week of hard practice with the Indian, pronounced him "more qualified than most pilots the CSAAC in Alabama turned out"[147] and signed over the aircraft to him. Crazy Horse begged off. Then, seeing that Smith was sincere, he gave the captain many buffalo hides. Smith reminded the Indian that the craft was not his: during their off hours, when not training, the Indians had been given enough instruction in military discipline as Mosby, never a stickler, thought necessary. The Indians had only a rudimentary idea of government property. Of the seven other Indian men, three were qualified as pilots; the other four were given gunner positions in the Krupp bi-wing light bombers assigned to the squadron.

Soon after Smith presented the aircraft to Crazy Horse, the captain took off in a borrowed monoplane on what was to be the daily weather flight into northern Kansas. There is evidence[148] that it was Smith who encountered a flight of light dirigibles from the 2nd Airship Command and attacked them singlehandedly. He crippled one airship; the other was rescued when two escort planes of the 12th ADS came to its defense. They raked the attacker with withering fire. The attacker escaped into the clouds.

It was not until 1897, when a group of schoolchildren on an outing found the wreckage, that it was known that Captain Smith had brought his crippled monoplane within five miles of the airfield before crashing into the rolling hills.

When Smith did not return from his flight, Crazy Horse went on a vigil, neither sleeping nor eating for a week. On the seventh day, Crazy Horse vowed vengeance on the men who had killed his white friend.

6. The devastating Union raid of September 23, 1864, caught the airfield unawares. Though the Indians were averse to fighting at night, Crazy Horse and two other Sioux were manning three of the four craft which got off the ground during the raid. The attack had been carried out by the 2nd Airship Command, traveling at twelve thousand feet, dropping fifty-pound fragmentation bombs and shrapnel canisters. The shrapnel played havoc with the aircraft on the ground. It also destroyed the mess hall, enlisted barracks, and three teepees.

The dirigibles turned away and were running fast before a tail wind when Crazy Horse gained their altitude.

The gunners on the dirigibles filled the skies with tracers from their light .30–30 machine rifles. Crazy Horse's monoplane was equipped with a single Henry .41–40 machine rifle. Unable to get in close killing distance, Crazy Horse and his companions stood off beyond the range of the lighter Union guns and raked the dirigibles with heavy machine rifle fire. They did enough damage to force one airship down twenty miles from its base, and to ground two others for two days while repairs were made. The intensity of fire convinced the airship commanders that more than four planes had made it off the ground, causing them to continue their headlong retreat.

Crazy Horse and the others returned and brought off the second windfall of the night; a group of 5th Cavalry raiders were to have attacked the airfield in the confusion of the airship raid and burn everything still standing. On their return flight, the four craft encountered the cavalry unit as it began its charge across open ground.

In three strafing runs, the aircraft killed thirty-seven men and wounded fifty-three, while twenty-nine were taken prisoner by the airfield's defenders. Thus, in his first combat mission for the CSAAC, Crazy Horse was credited with saving the airfield against overwhelming odds.

7. Meanwhile, Major General George A. Custer had distinguished himself at the Battle of Gettysburg. A few weeks after the battle, he enrolled himself in the GAR jump school at Watauga, New York. Howls of outrage came from the General Staff. Custer quoted the standing order: "any man who volunteered and of whom the com-

manding officer approved" could be enrolled. Custer then asked, in a letter to C of S, GAR, "how any military leader could be expected to plan maneuvers involving parachute infantry when he himself had never experienced a drop, or found the true capabilities of the parachute infantryman?"[149] The Chief of Staff shouted down the protest. There were mutterings among the General Staff[150] to the effect that the real reason Custer wanted to become jump-qualified was so that he would have a better chance of leading the invasion of Atlanta, part of whose contingency plans called for attacks by airborne units.

During the three-week parachute course, Custer became acquainted with another man who would play an important part in the Western Campaign, Captain (Brevet Colonel) Frederick W. Benteen. Upon graduation from the jump school, Brevet Colonel Benteen assumed command of the 505th Balloon Infantry, stationed at Chicago, Illinois, for training purposes. Colonel Benteen would remain commander of the 505th until his capture at the Battle of Montgomery in 1866. While he was prisoner of war, his command was given to another, later to figure in the Western Campaign, Lieutenant Colonel Myles W. Keogh.

Custer, upon his successful completion of jump school, returned to his command of the 6th Cavalry Division and participated throughout the remainder of the war in that capacity. It was he who led the successful charge at the Battle of the Cape Fear which smashed Lee's flank and allowed the 1st Infantry to overrun the Confederate position and capture that southern leader. Custer distinguished himself and his command up until the cessation of hostilities in 1867.

8. The 1st WIW, CSAAC, moved to a new airfield in Wyoming Territory three weeks after the raid of September 24. At the same time, the 2nd WIW was formed and moved to an outpost in Indian territory. The 2nd WIW raided the Union airfield, took it totally by surprise, and inflicted casualties on the 12th ADS and 2nd AC so devastating as to render them ineffectual. The 2nd WIW then moved to a second field in Wyoming Territory. It was here, following the move, that a number of Indians, including Black Man's Hand, were trained by Crazy Horse.

9. We leave the history of the 2nd WIW here. It was redeployed for the defense of Montgomery. The Indians and aircraft in which they trained were sent north to join the 1st WIW. The 1st WIW patrolled the skies of Indiana, Nebraska, and the Dakotas. After the defeat of the 12th ADS and the 2nd AC, the Union forestalled attempts to retaliate until the cessation of southern hostilities in 1867.

We may at this point add that Crazy Horse, Black Man's Hand, and the other Indians sometimes left the airfield during periods of long inactivity. They returned to their nations for as long as three months at a time. Each time Crazy Horse returned, he brought one or two pilot or gunner recruits with him. Before the winter of 1866, more than thirty percent of the 1st WIW were Oglala, Sansarc Sioux, or Cheyenne.

The South, losing the war of attrition, diverted all supplies to Alabama and Mississippi in the fall of 1866. None was forthcoming for the 1st WIW, though a messenger arrived with orders for Major Mosby to return to Texas for the defense of Fort Worth, where he would later direct the Battle of the Trinity. That Mosby was not ordered to deploy the 1st WIW to that defense has been considered by many military strategists as a "lost turning point" of the battle for Texas. Command of the 1st WIW was turned over to Acting Major (Flight Captain) Natchitoches Hooley.

10. The loss of Mosby signaled the end of the 1st WIW. Not only did the nondeployment of the 1st to Texas cost the South that territory, it also left the 1st in an untenable position, which the Union was quick to realize. The airfield was captured in May 1867 by a force of five hundred cavalry and three hundred infantry sent from the Battle of the Arkansas, and a like force, plus aircraft, from Chicago. Crazy Horse, seven Indians, and at least five Confederates escaped in their monoplanes. The victorious Union troops were surprised to find Indians at the field. Crazy Horse's people were eventually freed; the army thought them to have been hired by the Confederates to hunt and cook for the airfield. Mosby had provided for this in contingency plans long before; he had not wanted the Plains tribes to suffer for Confederate acts. The army did not know, and no one volunteered the information, that it had been Indians doing the most considerable amount of damage to the Union garrisons lately.

Crazy Horse and three of his Indians landed their craft near the Black Hills. The Cheyenne helped them carry the craft, on travois, to caves in the sacred mountains. Here they mothballed the planes with mixtures of pine tar and resins and sealed up the caves.

11. The aircraft remained stored until February 1872. During this time, Crazy Horse and his Oglala Sioux operated, like the other Plains Indians, as light cavalry, skirmishing with the army and with settlers up and down the Dakotas and Montana. George Armstrong Custer was appointed commander of the new 7th Cavalry in 1869. Stationed first at

Chicago (Far Western Command Headquarters), they later moved to Fort Abraham Lincoln, Nebraska.

A column of troops moved against Indians on the warpath in the winter of 1869. They reported a large group of Indians encamped on the Washita River. Custer obtained permission for the 505th Balloon Infantry to join the 7th Cavalry. From that day on, the unit was officially Company I (Separate Troops), 7th US Cavalry, though it kept its numerical designation. Also attached to the 7th was the 12th Airship Squadron, as Company J.

Lieutenant Colonel Keogh, acting commander of the 505th for the last twenty-one months, but who had never been on jump status, was appointed by Custer as commander of K Company, 7th Cavalry.

It is known that only the 505th Balloon Infantry and the 12th Airship Squadron were used in the raid on Black Kettle's village. Black Kettle was a treaty Indian, "walking the white man's road." Reports have become garbled in transmission: Custer and the 505th believed they were jumping into a village of hostiles.

The event remained a mystery until Kellogg, the Chicago newspaperman, wrote his account in 1872.[151] The 505th, with Custer in command, flew the three (then numbered, after 1872, named) dirigibles No. 31, No. 76, and No. 93, with seventy-two jumpers each. Custer was in the first "stick" on Airship 76. The three sailed silently to the sleeping village. Custer gave the order to hook up at 5:42 Chicago time, 4:42 local time, and the 505th jumped into the village. Black Kettle's people were awakened when some of the balloon infantry crashed through their teepees; others died in their sleep. One of the first duties of the infantry was to moor the dirigibles; this done, the gunners on the airships opened up on the startled villagers with their Gatling and Agar machine rifles. Black Kettle himself was killed while waving an American flag at Airship No. 93.

After the battle, the men of the 505th climbed back up to the moored dirigibles by rope ladder, and the airships departed for Fort Lincoln. The Indians camped downriver heard the shooting and found horses stampeded during the attack. When they came to the village, they found only slaughter. Custer had taken his dead (three, one of whom died during the jump by being drowned in the Washita) and wounded (twelve) away. They left 307 dead men, women, and children, and 500 slaughtered horses.

There were no tracks leading in and out of the village except those of the frightened horses. The other Indians left the area, thinking the white men had magicked it.

Crazy Horse is said[152] to have visited the area soon after the massacre. It was this action by the 7th which spelled their doom seven years later.

12. Black Man's Hand joined Crazy Horse; so did other former 1st WIW pilots soon after Crazy Horse's two-plane raid on the airship hangars at Bismark, in 1872. For that mission, Crazy Horse dropped twenty-five-pound fragmentation bombs tied to petrol canisters. The shrapnel ripped the dirigibles, the escaping hydrogen was ignited by the burning petrol: all—hangars, balloons, and maintenance crews— were lost.

It was written up as an unreconstructed Confederate's sabotage; a somewhat ignominious former Southern major was eventually hanged on circumstantial evidence. Reports by sentries that they heard aircraft just before the explosions were discounted. At the time, it was believed the only aircraft were those belonging to the army, and the carefully licensed commercial craft.

13. In 1874, Custer circulated rumors that the Black Hills were full of gold. It has been speculated that this was used to draw miners to the area so the Indians would attack them; then the cavalry would have unlimited freedom to deal with the red man.[153] Also that year, those who had become agency Indians were being shorted in their supplies by members of the scandal-plagued Indian Affairs Bureau under President Grant. When these left the reservations in search of food, the cavalry was sent to "bring them back." Those who were caught were usually killed.

The Sioux ignored the miners at first, expecting the gods to deal with them. When this did not happen, Sitting Bull sent out a party of two hundred warriors, who killed every miner they encountered. Public outrage demanded reprisals; Sheridan wired Custer to find and punish those responsible.

14. Fearing what was to come, Crazy Horse sent Yellow Dog and Red Chief with a war party of five hundred to raid the rebuilt Fort Phil Kearny. This they did successfully, capturing twelve planes and fuel and ammunition for many more. They hid these in the caverns with the 1st WIW craft.

The army would not have acted as rashly as it did had it known the planes pronounced missing in the reports on the Kearny raid were being given into the hands of experienced pilots.

The reprisal consisted of airship patrols which strafed any living thing on the plains. Untold thousands of deer and the few remaining buffalo were killed. Unofficial counts list as killed a little more than eight hundred Indians who were caught in the open during the next eight months.

Indians who jumped the agencies and who had seen or heard of the slaughter streamed to Sitting Bull's hidden camp on the Little Big Horn. They were treated as guests, except for the Sansarcs, who camped a little way down the river. It is estimated there were no less than ten thousand Indians, including some four thousand warriors, camped along the river for the Sun Dance ceremony of June 1876.

A three-pronged-pincers movement for the final eradication of the Sioux and Cheyenne worked toward them. The 7th Cavalry, under Keogh and Major Marcus Reno, set out from Fort Lincoln during the last week of May. General George Crook's command was coming up the Rosebud. The gunboat *Far West,* with three hundred reserves and supplies, steamed to the mouth of the Big Horn River. General Terry's command was coming from the northwest. All Indians they encountered were to be killed.

Just before the Sun Dance, Crazy Horse and his pilots got word of the movement of Crook's men up the Rosebud, hurried to the caves, and prepared their craft for flight. Only six planes were put in working condition in time. The other pilots remained behind while Crazy Horse, Black Man's Hand, and four others took to the skies. They destroyed two dirigibles, soundly trounced Crook, and chased his command back down the Rosebud in a rout. The column had to abandon its light-armored vehicles and fight its way back, on foot for the most part, to safety.

15. Sitting Bull's vision during the Sun Dance is well known.[154] He told it to Crazy Horse, the warrior who would see that it came true, as soon as the aviators returned to camp.

Two hundred fifty miles away, "Chutes and Saddles" was sounded on the morning of June 23, and the men of the 505th Balloon Infantry climbed aboard the airships *Benjamin Franklin, Samuel Adams, John Hancock,* and *Ethan Allen.* Custer was first man on stick one of the *Franklin.* The *Ethan Allen* carried a scout aircraft which could hook up or detach in flight; the bi-winger was to serve as liaison between the three armies and the airships.

When Custer bade good-bye to his wife Elizabeth that morning, both were in good spirits. If either had an inkling of the fate which awaited Custer and the 7th three days away on the bluffs above a small stream, they did not show it.

The four airships sailed from Fort Lincoln, their silver sides and sharktooth mouths gleaming in the sun, the eyes painted on the noses looking west. On the sides were the crossed sabers of the cavalry; above, the numeral 7, below, the numerals 505. It is said that they looked magnificent as they sailed away for their rendezvous with destiny.[155]

16. It is sufficient to say that the Indians attained their greatest victory over the army, and almost totally destroyed the 7th Cavalry, on June 25–26, 1876, due in large part to the efforts of Crazy Horse and his aviators. Surprise, swiftness, and the skill of the Indians cannot be discounted, nor can the military blunders made by Custer that morning. The repercussions of that summer day rang down the years and the events are still debated. The only sure fact is that the US Army lost its prestige, part of its spirit, and more than four hundred of its finest soldiers in the battle.

17. While the demoralized commands were sorting themselves out, the Cheyenne and Sioux left for the Canadian border. They took their aircraft with them on travois. With Sitting Bull, Crazy Horse and his band settled just across the border. The aircraft were rarely used again until the attack on the camp by the combined Canadian–US Cavalry offensive in 1879. Crazy Horse and his aviators, as they had done so many times before, escaped with their aircraft, using one of the planes to carry their remaining fuel. Two of the nine craft were shot down by a Canadian battery.

Crazy Horse, sensing the end, fought his way, with men on horseback and the planes on travois, from Montana to Colorado. After learning of the deaths of Sitting Bull and Chief Joseph, he took his small band as close as he dared to Fort Carson, where the cavalry was massing to wipe out the remaining American Indians.

He assembled his men for the last time. He made his proposal; all concurred and joined him for a last raid on the army. The five remaining planes came in low, the morning of January 5, 1882, toward the army airfield. They destroyed twelve aircraft on the ground, shot up the hangars and barracks, and ignited one of the two ammunition dumps of the stockade. At this time, army gunners manned the William's machine cannon batteries (improved by Thomas Edison's contract scientists) and blew three of the craft to flinders. The war gods must have smiled on Crazy Horse: his aircraft was crippled, the machine rifle was blown askew, the motor slivered, but he managed to set down intact. Black Man's Hand turned away; he was captured two months later, eating cottonwood bark in the snows of Arizona.

Crazy Horse jumped from his aircraft as most of Fort Carson ran toward him; he pulled two Sharps repeating carbines from the cockpit and blazed away at the astonished troopers, wounding six and killing one. His back to the craft, he continued to fire until more than one hundred infantrymen fired a volley into his body.

The airplane was displayed for seven months at Fort Carson before being sent to the Smithsonian in Pittsburgh, where it stands today. Thus passed an era of military aviation.

Lt. Gen. Frank Luke, Jr.
USAF, Ret.

From the December 2, 1939, issue of *Collier's Magazine*
Custer's Last Jump?
A.R. Redmond

Few events in American history have captured the imagination so thoroughly as the Battle of the Little Big Horn. Lieutenant Colonel George Armstrong Custer's devastating defeat at the hands of Sioux and Cheyenne Indians in June 1876 has been rendered time and again by such celebrated artists as George Russell and Frederic Remington. Books, factual and otherwise, which have been written around or about the battle would fill an entire library wing. The motion-picture industry has on numerous occasions drawn upon "Custer's last jump" for inspiration; latest in a long line of movieland Custers is Errol Flynn, who appears with Olivia de Havilland and newcomer Anthony Quinn in Warner Brothers' soon-to-be-released *They Died with Their Chutes On*.

The impetuous and flamboyant Custer was an almost legendary figure long before the Battle of Little Big Horn, however. Appointed to West Point in 1857, Custer was placed in command of Troop G, 2nd Cavalry, in June 1861, and participated in a series of skirmishes with Confederate cavalry throughout the rest of the year. It was during the First Battle of Manassas, or Bull Run, that he distinguished himself. He continued to do so in other engagements—at Williamsburg, Chancellorsville, Gettysburg—and rose rapidly through the ranks. He was twenty-six years old when he received a promotion to Brigadier General. He was, of course, immediately dubbed the Boy General. He had become an authentic war hero when the Northerners were in dire need of nothing less during those discouraging months between First Manassas and Gettysburg.

With the cessation of hostilities in the East when Bragg surrendered to Grant at Haldeman, the small hamlet about eight miles from

Morehead, Kentucky, Custer requested a transfer of command. He and his young bride wound up at Chicago, which was manned by the new 7th US Cavalry.

The war in the West lasted another few months; the tattered remnants of the Confederate Army staged last desperate stands throughout Texas, Colorado, Kansas, and Missouri. The final struggle at the Trinity River in October 1867 marked the close of conflict between North and South. Those few Mexican military advisers left in Texas quietly withdrew across the Rio Grande. The French, driven from Mexico in 1867 when Maximilian was ousted, lost interest in the Americas when they became embroiled with the newly united Prussian states.

During his first year in Chicago, Custer familiarized himself with the airships and aeroplanes of the 7th. The only jump-qualified general officer of the war, Custer seemed to have felt no resentment at the ultimate fate of mounted troops boded by the extremely mobile flying machines. The Ohio-born Boy General eventually preferred traveling aboard the airship *Benjamin Franklin,* one of the eight craft assigned to the 505th Balloon Infantry (Troop I, 7th Cavalry, commanded by Brevet Colonel Frederick Benteen) while his horse soldiers rode behind the very capable Captain (Brevet Lt. Col.) Myles Keogh.

The War Department in Pittsburgh did not know that various members of the Plains Indian tribes had been equipped with aeroplanes by the Confederates, and that many had actually flown against the Union garrisons in the West. (Curiously enough, those tribes which held out the longest against the army—most notably the Apaches under Geronimo in the deep Southwest—were those that did not have aircraft.) The problems of transporting and hiding, to say nothing of maintaining planes, outweighed the advantages. A Cheyenne warrior named Brave Bear is said to have traded his band's aircraft in disgust to Sitting Bull for three horses. Also, many of the Plains Indians hated the aircraft outright, as they had been used by the white men to decimate the great buffalo herds in the early 1860s.

Even so, certain Oglalas, Minneconjous, and Cheyenne did reasonably well in the aircraft given them by CS Army Air Corps Major John S. Mosby, whom the Indians called the "Gray White Man" or "Many-Feathers-in-Hat." The Oglala war chief Crazy Horse led the raid on the Bismarck hangars (1872) four months after the 7th Cavalry was transferred to Fort Abraham Lincoln, Dakota Territory, and made his presence felt at the Rosebud and Little Big Horn in 1876.

The Cheyenne Black Man's Hand, trained by Crazy Horse himself, shot down two army machines at the Rosebud and was in the flight of planes that accomplished the annihilation of the 505th Balloon Infantry during the first phase of the Little Big Horn fiasco.

After the leveling of Fort Phil Kearny in February 1869, Custer was ordered to enter the Indian territories and punish those who had sought sanctuary there after the raid. Taking with him 150 parachutists aboard three airships, Custer left on the trail of a large band of Cheyenne. On the afternoon of February 25, Lieutenant William van W. Reily, dispatched for scouting purposes in a Studebaker bi-winger, returned to report that he had shot up a hunting party near the Washita River. The Cheyenne, he thought, were encamped on the banks of the river some twenty miles away. They appeared not to have seen the close approach of the 7th Cavalry as they had not broken camp.

Just before dawn the next morning, the 505th Balloon Infantry, led by Custer, jumped into the village, killing all inhabitants and their animals.

For the next five years, Custer and the 7th chased the hostiles of the plains back and forth between Colorado and the Canadian border. Relocated at Fort Lincoln, Custer and an expedition of horse soldiers, geologists, and engineers discovered gold in the Black Hills. Though the Black Hills still belonged to the Sioux according to several treaties, prospectors began to pour into the area. The 7th was ordered to protect them. The Blackfeet, Minneconjous, and Hunkpapa—Sioux who had left the warpath on the promise that the Black Hills, their sacred lands, were theirs to keep for all time—protested, and when protests brought no results, took matters into their own hands. Prospectors turned up in various stages of mutilation, or not at all.

Conditions worsened over the remainder of 1875, during which time the United States Government ordered the Sioux out of the Black Hills. To make sure the Indians complied, airships patrolled the skies of the Dakota Territory.

By the end of 1875, plagued by the likes of Crazy Horse's Oglala Sioux, it was decided that there was but one solution to the Plains Indian problem—total extermination.

At this point, General Phil Sheridan, Commander in Chief of the United States Army, began working on the practical angle of this new policy toward the red men.

In January 1876, delegates from the Democratic Party approached George Armstrong Custer at Fort Abraham Lincoln and offered him the party's presidential nomination on the condition that he pull off a flashy victory over the red men before the national convention in Chicago in July.

On February 19, 1876, the Boy General's brother Thomas, commander of Troop C of the 7th, climbed into the observer's cockpit behind Lieutenant James C. Sturgis and took off on a routine patrol. Their aeroplane, a Whitney pushertype, did not return. Ten days later its wreckage was found sixty miles west of Fort Lincoln. Apparently, Sturgis and Tom Custer had stumbled on a party of mounted hostiles and, swooping low to fire or drop a handbomb, suffered a lucky hit from one of the Indians' firearms. The mutilated remains of the two officers were found a quarter mile from the wreckage, indicating that they had escaped on foot after the crash but were caught.

The shock of his brother's death, combined with the Democrats' offer, was to lead Lieutenant Colonel G.A. Custer into the worst defeat suffered by an officer of the United States Army.

Throughout the first part of 1876, Indians drifted into the Wyoming Territory from the east and south, driven by mounting pressure from the army. Raids on small Indian villages had been stepped up. Waning herds of buffalo were being systematically strafed by the airships. General Phil Sheridan received reports of tribes gathering in the vicinity of the Wolf Mountains, in what is now southern Montana, and devised a strategy by which the hostiles would be crushed for all time.

Three columns were to converge upon the massed Indians from the north, south, and east, the west being blocked by the Wolf Mountains. General George Crook's dirigibles, light tanks, and infantry were to come up the Rosebud River. General Alfred Terry would push from the northeast with infantry, cavalry, and field artillery. The 7th Cavalry was to move from the east. The Indians could not escape.

Commanded by Captain Keogh, Troops A, C, D, E, F, G, and H of the 7th—about 580 men, not counting civilian teamsters, interpreters, Crow and Arikara scouts—set out from Fort Lincoln five weeks ahead of the July 1 rendezvous at the junction of the Big Horn and Little Big Horn rivers. A month later, Custer and 150 balloon infantrymen aboard the airships *Franklin*, *Adams*, *Hancock*, and *Allen* set out on Keogh's trail.

Everything went wrong from that point onward.

The early summer of 1876 had been particularly hot and dry in the Wyoming Territory. Crook, proceeding up the Rosebud, was slowed by the tanks, which theoretically traveled at five miles per hour but kept breaking down from the heat and from the alkaline dust which worked its way into the engines through chinks in the three-inch armor plate. The crews roasted. On June 13, as Crook's column halted beside the Rosebud to let the tanks cool off, six monoplanes dived out of the clouds to attack the escorting airships *Paul Revere* and *John Paul Jones.* Caught by surprise, the two dirigibles were blown up and fell about five miles from Crook's position. The infantrymen watched, astonished, as the Indian aeronauts turned their craft toward them. While the foot soldiers ran for cover, several hundred mounted Sioux warriors showed up. In the ensuing rout, Crook lost forty-seven men and all his armored vehicles. He was still in headlong retreat when the Indians broke off their chase at nightfall.

The 7th Cavalry and the 505th Balloon Infantry linked up by liaison craft carried by the *Ethan Allen* some miles southeast of the hostile camp on the Little Big Horn on the evening of June 24. Neither they, nor Terry's column, had received word of Crook's retreat, but Keogh's scouts had sighted a large village ahead.

Custer did not know that this village contained not the five or six hundred Indians expected, but between eight and ten *thousand,* of whom slightly less than half were warriors. Spurred by his desire for revenge for his brother Tom, and filled with glory at the thought of the Democratic presidential nomination, Custer decided to hit the Indians before either Crook's or Terry's columns could reach the village. He settled on a scaled-down version of Sheridan's tri-pronged movement, and dispatched Keogh to the South and Reno to the east, with himself and the 505th attacking from the north. A small column was to wait downriver with the pack train. On the evening of June 24, George Armstrong Custer waited, secure in the knowledge that he, personally, would deal the Plains Indians their mortal blow within a mere twenty-four hours.

Unfortunately, the Indians amassed on the banks of the Little Big Horn—Oglalas, Minneconjous, Arapaho, Hunkpapas, Blackfeet, Cheyenne, and so forth—had the idea that white men were on the way. During the Sun Dance ceremony the week before, the Hunkpapa chief Sitting Bull had had a dream about soldiers falling into his camp. The hostiles, assured of victory, waited.

On the morning of June 25, the *Benjamin Franklin, Samuel Adams, John Hancock,* and *Ethan Allen* drifted quietly over the hills toward the village. They were looping south when the Indians attacked.

Struck by several spin-stabilized rockets, the *Samuel Adams* blew up
with a flash that might have been seen by the officers and men riding
behind Captain Keogh up the valley of the Little Big Horn. Eight or
twelve Indians had, in the gray dawn, climbed for altitude above the
ships. Still several miles short of their intended drop zone, the balloon
infantrymen piled out of the burning and exploding craft. Though each
ship was armed with two Gatling rifles fore and aft, the airships were
helpless against the aeroplanes' bullets and rockets. Approximately one
hundred men, Custer included, cleared the ships. The Indian aviators
made passes through them, no doubt killing several in the air. The
Franklin and *Hancock* burned and fell to the earth across the river from
the village. The *Allen,* dumping water ballast to gain altitude, turned
for the Wolf Mountains. Though riddled by machine rifle fire, it did
not explode and settled to earth about fifteen miles from where now
raged a full-scale battle between increasingly demoralized soldiers and
battle-maddened Sioux and Cheyenne.

Major Reno had charged the opposite side of the village as soon as
he heard the commotion. Wrote one of his officers later:

A solid wall of Indians came out of the haze which had hidden
the village from our eyes. They must have outnumbered us ten
to one, and they were ready for us . . . . Fully a third of the
column was down in three minutes.

Reno, fearing he would be swallowed up, pulled his men back
across the river and took up a position in a stand of timber on the
riverward slope of the knoll. The Indians left a few hundred braves to
make certain Reno did not escape and moved off to Reno's right to
descend on Keogh's flank.

The hundred-odd parachute infantrymen who made good their
escape from the airship were scattered over three square miles. The
ravines and gullies cutting up the hills around the village quickly filled
with mounted Indians who rode through unimpeded by the random fire
of disorganized balloon infantrymen. They swept them up, on the way
to Keogh. Keogh, unaware of the number of Indians and the rout of
Reno's command, got as far as the north bank of the river before he was
ground to pieces between two masses of hostiles. Of Keogh's
command, less than a dozen escaped the slaughter. The actual battle
lasted about thirty minutes.

The hostiles left the area that night, exhausted after their greatest victory over the soldiers. Most of the Indians went north to Canada; some escaped the mass extermination of their race which was to take place in the American West during the next six years.

Terry found Reno entrenched on the ridge the morning of the twenty-seventh. The scouts sent to find Custer and Keogh could not believe their eyes when they found the bodies of the 7th Cavalry six miles away.

Some of the men were not found for another two days. Terry and his men scoured the ravines and valleys. Custer himself was about four miles from the site of Keogh's annihilation; the Boy General appeared to have been hit by a piece of exploding rocket shrapnel and may have been dead before he reached the ground. His body escaped the mutilation that befell most of Keogh's command, possibly because of its distance from the camp.

Custer's miscalculation cost the army 430 men, four dirigibles (plus the Studebaker scout from the *Ethan Allen*), and its prestige. An attempt was made to make a scapegoat of Major Reno, blaming his alleged cowardice for the failure of the 7th. Though Reno was acquitted, grumblings continued until the turn of the century. It is hoped the matter will be settled for all time by the opening, for private research, of the papers of the late President Phil Sheridan. As Commander in Chief, he had access to a mountain of material which was kept from the public at the time of the court of inquiry of 1879.

Extract from *Huckleberry Among the Hostiles:*
A Journal
by Mark Twain, edited by Bernard van Dyne
Hutton and Company, New York, 1932

EDITOR'S NOTE: In November 1886 Clemens drafted a tentative outline for a sequel to *The Adventures of Huckleberry Finn,* which had received mixed reviews on its publication in January 1885, but which had nonetheless enjoyed a second printing within five months of its release. The proposed sequel was intended to deal with Huckleberry's adventures as a young man on the frontier. To gather research material firsthand, Mark Twain boarded the airship *Peyton* in Cincinnati, Ohio, in mid-December 1886, and set out across the Southwest, amassing copious notes and reams of interviews with soldiers, frontiersmen, law enforcement officers, exhostiles, at least two notorious outlaws, and a number of less readily categorized persons. Twain had intended to spend four months out west. Unfortunately, his wife, Livy, fell gravely ill in late February 1887; Twain returned to her as soon as he received word in Fort Hood, Texas. He lost interest in all writing for two years after her death in April 1887. The proposed novel about Huckleberry Finn as a man was never written: we are left with 110,000 words of interviews and observations and an incomplete journal of the author's second trek across the American West.—BvD.

February 2: A more desolate place than the Indian Territory of Oklahoma would be impossible to imagine. It is flat the year 'round, stingingly cold in winter, hot and dry, I am told, during the summer (when the land turns brown save for scattered patches of greenery which serve only to make the landscape all the drearier; Arizona and New Mexico are devoid of greenery, which is to their credit—when those territories elected to become barren wastelands they did not lose heart halfway, but followed their chosen course to the end).

It is easy to see why the United States Government swept the few Indians into Godforsaken Oklahoma and ordered them to remain there under threat of extermination. The word "Godforsaken" is the vital clue. The white men who "gave" this land to the few remaining tribes for as long as the wind shall blow—which it certainly does in February—and the grass shall grow (which it does, in Missouri, perhaps) were Christians who knew better than to let heathen savages run loose in parts of the country still smiled upon by our heavenly malefactor.

February 4: Whatever I may have observed about Oklahoma from the cabin of the *Peyton* has been reinforced by a view from the ground. The airship was running into stiff winds from the north, so we put in at Fort Sill yesterday evening and are awaiting calmer weather. I have gone on with my work.

Fort Sill is located seventeen miles from the Cheyenne Indian reservation. It has taken me all day to learn (mainly from one Sergeant Howard, a gap-toothed, unwashed Texan who is apparently my unofficial guardian angel for whatever length of time I am to be marooned here) that the Cheyenne do not care much for Oklahoma, which is still another reason why the government keeps them there. One or two exhostiles will leave the reservation every month, taking with them their wives and meager belongings, and Major Rickards will have to send out a detachment of soldiers to haul the erring ones back, either in chains or over the backs of horses. I am told the reservation becomes particularly annoying in the winter months, as the poor boys who are detailed to pursue the Indians suffer greatly from the cold. At this, I remarked to Sergeant Howard that the red man can be terribly inconsiderate, even ungrateful, in view of all the blessings the white man has heaped upon him—smallpox and that French disease, to name two. The good sergeant scratched his head and grinned, and said, "You're right, sir."

I'll have to make Howard a character in the book.

February 5: Today, I was taken by Major Rickards to meet a Cheyenne named Black Man's Hand, one of the participants of the alleged massacre of the 7th Cavalry at the Little Big Horn River in '76. The major had this one Cheyenne brought in after a recent departure from the reservation. Black Man's Hand had been shackled and left to dwell upon his past misdeeds in an unheated hut at the edge of the airport, while two cold-benumbed privates stood on guard before the door. It was evidently feared this one savage would, if left unchained, do to Fort Sill that which he (with a modicum of assistance from four or five thousand of his race) had done to Custer. I nevertheless mentioned to Rickards that I was interested in talking to Black Man's Hand, as the Battle of the Little Big Horn would perfectly climax Huckleberry's adventures in the new book. Rickards was reluctant to grant permission but gave in abruptly, perhaps fearing I would model a villain after him.

Upon entering the hut where the Cheyenne sat, I asked Major Rickards if it were possible to have the Indian's manacles removed, as it makes me nervous to talk to a man who can rattle his chains at me whenever he chooses. Major Rickards said no and troubled himself to explain to me the need for limiting the movement of this specimen of ferocity within the walls of Fort Sill.

With a sigh, I seated myself across from Black Man's Hand and offered him one of my cigars. He accepted it with a faint smile. He appeared to be in his forties, though his face was deeply lined.

He was dressed in ragged leather leggings, thick calf-length woolen pajamas, and a faded army jacket. His vest appeared to have been fashioned from an old parachute harness. He had no hat, no footgear, and no blanket.

"Major Rickards," I said, "this man is freezing to death. Even if he isn't, I am. Can you provide this hut with a little warmth?"

The fretting major summarily dispatched one of the sentries for firewood and kindling for the little stove sitting uselessly in the corner of the hut.

I would have been altogether comfortable after that could I have had a decanter of brandy with which to force out the inner chill. But Indians are notoriously incapable of holding liquor, and I did not wish to be the cause of this poor wretch's further downfall.

Black Man's Hand speaks surprisingly good English. I spent an hour and a half with him, recording his remarks with as much attention paid to accuracy as my advanced years and cold fingers permitted. With luck, I'll be able to fill some gaps in his story before the *Peyton* resumes its flight across this griddlecake countryside.

Extract from *The Testament of Black Man's Hand*
[NOTE: For the sake of easier reading, I have substituted a number of English terms for those provided by the Cheyenne Black Man's Hand.—MT]

I was young when I first met the Oglala mystic Crazy Horse and was taught by him to fly the Thunderbirds which the one called the Gray White Man had given him. [The Gray White Man—John S. Mosby, Major, CSAAC—MT.] Some of the older men among the People [as the Cheyenne call themselves, Major Rickards explains; I assured him that such egocentricity is by no means restricted to savages—MT] did not think much of the flying machines and said, "How will we be able to remain brave men when this would enable us to fly over the heads of our enemies, without counting coup or taking trophies?"

But the Oglala said, "The Gray White Man has asked us to help him."

"Why should we help him?" asked Two Pines.

"Because he fights the blueshirts and those who persecute us. We have known for many years that the men who cheated us and lied to us and killed our women and the buffalo are men without honor, cowards who fight only because there is no other way for them to get what they want. They cannot understand why we fight with the Crows and Pawnees—to be brave, to win honor for ourselves. They fight because it is a means to an end, and they fight us only because we have what they want. The blueshirts want to kill us all. They fight to win. If we are to fight them, we must fight with their own weapons. We must fight to win."

The older warriors shook their heads sorrowfully and spoke of younger days when they fought the Pawnees bravely, honorably, man-to-man. But I and several other young men wanted to learn how to control the Thunderbirds. And we knew Crazy Horse spoke the truth, that our lives would never be happy as long as there were white men in the world. Finally, because they could not forbid us to go with the Oglala, only advise against it and say that the Great Mystery had not intended us to fly, Red Horse and I and some others went with Crazy Horse. I did not see my village again, not even at the big camp on the Greasy Grass [Little Big Horn—MT] where we rubbed out Yellow Hair. I think perhaps the blueshirts came after I was gone and told Two Pines that he had to leave his home and come to this flat dead place.

The Oglala Crazy Horse taught us to fly the Thunderbirds. We learned a great many things about the Gray White Man's machines. With them, we killed yellowleg flyers. Soon I tired of the waiting and the hunger. We were raided once. It was a good fight. In the dark, we chased the Big Fish [the Indian word for dirigibles—MT] and killed many men on the ground.

I do not remember all of what happened those seasons. When we were finally chased away from the landing place, Crazy Horse had us hide the Thunderbirds in the Black Hills. I have heard the yellowlegs did not know we had the Thunderbirds; that they thought they were run by the gray white men only. It did not matter; we thought we had used them for the last time.

Many seasons later, we heard what happened to Black Kettle's village. I went to the place some time after the battle. I heard that Crazy Horse had been there and seen the place. I looked for him but he had gone north again. Black Kettle had been a treaty man: we talked among ourselves that the yellowlegs had no honor.

It was the winter I was sick [1872. The Plains Indians and the US Army alike were plagued that winter by what we would call the influenza. It was probably brought by some itinerant French trapper—MT] that I heard of Crazy Horse's raid on the landing place of the Big Fish. It was news of this that told us we must prepare to fight the yellowlegs.

When I was well, my wives and I and Eagle Hawk's band went looking for Crazy Horse. We found him in the fall. Already the army had killed many Sioux and Cheyenne that summer. Crazy Horse said we must band together, we who knew how to fly the Thunderbirds. He said we would someday have to fight the yellowlegs among the clouds as in the old days. We only had five Thunderbirds which had not been flown many seasons. We spent the summer planning to get more. Red Chief and Yellow Dog gathered a large band. We raided the Fort Kearny and stole many Thunderbirds and canisters of powder. We hid them in the Black Hills. It had been a good fight.

It was at this time Yellow Hair sent out many soldiers to protect the miners he had brought in by speaking false. They destroyed the sacred lands of the Sioux. We killed some of them, and the yellowlegs burned many of our villages. That was not a good time. The Big Fish killed many of our people.

We wanted to get the Thunderbirds and kill the Big Fish. Crazy Horse had us wait. He had been talking to Sitting Bull, the Hunkpapa chief. Sitting Bull said we should not go against the yellowlegs yet, that we could only kill a few at a time. Later, he said, they would all come. That would be a good day to die.

The next year they came. We did not know until just before the Sun Dance [about June 10, 1876—MT] that they were coming. Crazy Horse and I and all those who flew the Thunderbirds went to get ours. It took us two days to get them going again, and we had only six Thunderbirds flying when we flew to stop the blueshirts. Crazy Horse, Yellow Dog, American Gun, Little Wolf, Big Tall, and I flew that day. It was a good fight. We killed two Big Fish and many men and horses. We stopped the Turtles-which-kill [that would be the light armored cars Crook had with him on the Rosebud River—MT] so they could not come toward the Greasy Grass where we camped. The Sioux under Spotted Pony killed more on the ground. We flew back and hid the Thunderbirds near camp.

When we returned, we told Sitting Bull of our victory. He said it was good, but that a bigger victory was to come. He said he had had a vision during the Sun Dance. He saw many soldiers and enemy Indians fall out of the sky on their heads into the village. He said ours was not the victory he had seen.

It was some days later we heard that a yellowlegs Thunderbird had been shot down. We went to the place where it lay. There was a strange device above its wing. Crazy Horse studied it many moments. Then he said, "I have seen such a thing before. It carries Thunderbirds beneath one of the Big Fish. We must get our Thunderbirds. It will be a good day to die."

We hurried to our Thunderbirds. We had twelve of them fixed now, and we had on them, besides the quick rifles [Henry machine rifles of calibers .41–40 or .30–30—MT], the roaring spears [Hale spin-stabilized rockets, of two-and-a-half-inch diameter—MT]. We took off before noonday.

We arrived at the Greasy Grass and climbed into the clouds, where we scouted. Soon, to the south, we saw the dust of many men moving. But Crazy Horse held us back. Soon we saw why; four Big Fish were coming. We came at them out of the sun. They did not see us till we were on them. We fired our roaring sticks, and the Big Fish caught fire and burned. All except one, which drifted away, though it lost all its fat. Wild Horse, in his Thunderbird, was shot but still fought on with us that morning. We began to kill the men on the Big Fish when a new thing happened. Men began to float down on blankets. We began to kill them with our quick rifles as they fell. Then we attacked those who reached the ground, until we saw Spotted Pony and his men were on them. We turned south and killed many horse soldiers there. Then we flew back to the Greasy Grass and hid the Thunderbirds. At camp, we learned that many pony soldiers had been killed. Word came that more soldiers were coming.

I saw, as the sun went down, the women moving among the dead Men-Who-Float-Down, taking their clothes and supplies. They covered the ground like leaves in the autumn. It had been a good fight.

Extract from *The Seventh Cavalry: A History*
Colonel E.R. Burroughs, USA, Ret.

So much has been written about that hot June day in 1876, so much guesswork applied where knowledge was missing. Was Custer dead in his harness before he reached the ground? Or did he stand and fire at the aircraft strafing his men? How many reached the ground alive? Did any escape the battle itself, only to be killed by Indian patrols later that afternoon or the next day? No one really knows, and all the Indians are gone now, so history stands a blank.

Only one thing is certain: for the men of the 7th Cavalry there was only the reality of the exploding dirigibles, the snap of their chutes deploying, the roar of the aircraft among them, the bullets, and those terrible last moments on the bluff. Whatever the verdict of their peers, whatever the future may reveal, it can be said that they did not die in vain.

SUGGESTED READING

Anonymous. *Remember Ft. Sumter!* Washington: War Department Recruiting Pamphlet, 1862.

―――. *Leviathans of the Skies.* Goodyear Publications, 1923.

―――. *The Dirigible in War and Peace.* Goodyear Publications, 1911.

―――. *Sitting Bull, Killer of Custer.* G. E. Putnam's, 1903.

―――. *Comanche of the Seventh.* Chicago: Military Press, 1879.

―――. *Thomas Edison and the Indian Wars.* Menlo Park, N.J.: Edison Press, 1921.

―――. "Fearful Slaughter at Big Horn." *New York Herald-Times,* July 8, 1876, *et passim.*

―――. *Custer's Gold Hoax.* Boston: Barnum Press, 1892.

―――. "Reno's Treachery: New Light on the Massacre at The Little Big Horn." *Chicago Daily News-Mirror,* June 12–19, 1878.

―――. "Grant Scandals and the Plains Indian Wars." *Life,* May 3, 1921.

―――. *The Hunkpapa Chief Sitting Bull,* Famous Indians Series #3. New York: 1937.

Arnold, Henry H. *The Air War in the East,* Smithsonian Annals of Flight, Vol. 38. Four books 1932–1937: 1. *Sumter to Bull Run*; 2. *Williamsburg to Second Manassas*; 3. *Gettysburg to the Wilderness*; 4. *The Bombing of Atlanta to Haldeman.*

Ballows, Edward. *The Indian Ace: Crazy Horse.* G. E. Putnam's, 1903.

Benteen, Capt. Frederick. *Major Benteen's Letters to His Wife.* University of Oklahoma Press, 1921.

Brininstool, A.E. *A Paratrooper with Custer.* n.p.g., 1891.

Burroughs, Col. E.R., Ret. *The Seventh Cavalry: A History.* Chicago: 1931.

Clair-Britner, Edoard. *Haldeman: Where the War Ended.* Frankfort University Press, 1911.

Crook, General George C. *Yellowhair: Custer as the Indians Knew Him.* Cincinnati Press, 1882.

Custer, George A. *My Life on the Plains and in the Clouds.* Chicago: 1874.

―――, and Custer, Elizabeth. *'Chutes and Saddles.* Chicago: 1876.

Custer's Luck, n.a., n.p.g. [1891].

DeCamp, L. Sprague, and Pratt, Fletcher. *Franklin's Engine: Mover of the World.* Hanover House, 1939.

De Voto, Bernard. *The Road from Sumter.* Scribner's, 1931.

Elsee, D.V. *The Last of Crazy Horse.* Random House, 1921.

The 505th: History of the Skies. DA Pamphlet 870-10-3. GPO Pittsburgh, May 12, 1903.

FM 23-13-2 Machine Rifle M3121A1 and M3121A1E1 Cal. .41-40 Operator's Manual, DA FM, July 12, 1873.

Goddard, Robert H. *Rocketry: From 400 B.C. to 1933.* Smithsonian Annals of Flight 31. GPO Pittsburgh, 1934.

Guide to the Custer Battlefield National Monument. U.S. Parks Services, GPO Pittsburgh, 1937.

The Indian Wars. 3 vols. GPO Pittsburgh, 1898.

Kalin, David. *Hook Up! The Story of the Balloon Infantry.* New York: 1932.

Kellogg, Mark W. *The Drop at Washita.* Chicago: Times Press, 1872.

Lockridge, Sgt. Robert. *History of the Airborne: From Shiloh to Ft. Bragg.* Chicago: Military Press, 1936.

Lowe, Thaddeus C. *Aircraft of the Civil War.* 4 vols. 1891-1896.

McCoy, Col. Tim. *The Vanished American.* Phoenix Press, 1934.

McGovern, Maj. William. *Death in the Dakotas.* Sioux Press, 1889.

Morison, Samuel Eliot. *France in the New World 1627-1864.* 1931.

Myren, Gundal. *The Sun Dance Ritual and the Last Indian Wars.* 1901.

Patton, Gen. George C. *Custer's Last Campaigns.* Military House, 1937.

Paul, Winston. *We Were There at the Bombing of Ft. Sumter.* Landmark Books, 1929.

Payley, David. *Where Custer Fell.* New York Press, 1931.

Powell, Maj. John Wesley. *Report on the Arid Lands.* GPO, 1881.

Proceedings, Reno Court of Inquiry. GPO Pittsburgh, 1881.

Report on the U.S.-Canadian Offensive Against Sitting Bull, 1879. GPO Pittsburgh, War Department, 1880.

Sandburg, Carl. *Mr. Lincoln's Airmen.* Chicago: Driftwind Press, 1921.

Settle, Sgt. Maj. Winslow. *Under the Crossed Sabers.* Military Press, 1898.

Sheridan, Gen. Phillip. *The Only Good Indian. . . .* Military House, 1889.

Singleton, William Warren. *J.E.B. Stuart, Attila of the Skies.* Boston, 1871.

Smith, Gregory. *The Gray White Man: Mosby's Expedition to the Northwest 1863-1866.* University of Oklahoma Press, 1921.

Smith, Neldoo. *He Gave Them Wings: Captain Smith's Journal 1861-1864.* Urbana: University of Illinois Press, 1927.

Steen, Nelson. *Opening of the West.* Jim Bridger Press, 1902.

Tapscott, Richard D. *He Came with the Comet.* University of Illinois Press, 1927.

Twain, Mark. *Huckleberry Among the Hostiles: A Journal.* Hutton Books, 1932.

The Curfew Tolls

Stephen Vincent Benét

It is not enough to be the possessor of genius—the time and the man must conjoin. An Alexander the Great, born into an age of profound peace, might scarce have troubled the world—a Newton, grown up in a thieves' den, might have devised little but a new and ingenious picklock. . . .

Diversions of Historical Thought
JOHN CLEVELAND COTTON

(The following extracts have been made from the letters of General Sir Charles William Geoffrey Estcourt, C.B., to his sister Harriet, Countess of Stokely, by permission of the Stokely family. Omissions are indicated by triple dots, thus . . .)

St. Philippe-des-Bains, September 3d, 1788.

MY DEAR SISTER: . . . I could wish that my excellent Paris physician had selected some other spot for my convalescence. But he swears by the water of St. Philip and I swear by him, so I must resign myself to a couple of yawning months ere my constitution mends. Nevertheless, you will get long letters from me, though I fear they may be dull ones. I cannot bring you the gossip of Baden or Aix—except for its baths, St. Philip is but one of a dozen small white towns on this agreeable coast. It has its good inn and its bad inn, its dusty, little square with its dusty, fleabitten beggar, its posting-station and its promenade of scrubby lindens and palms. From the heights one may see Corsica on a clear day, and the Mediterranean is of an unexampled blue. To tell the truth, it is all agreeable enough and an old Indian campaigner, like myself, should not complain. I am well treated at the Cheval Blanc—am I not an English milord?—and my excellent Gaston looks after me devotedly. But there is a blue-bottle drowsiness about small watering places out of season, and our gallant enemies, the French, know how to bore themselves more exquisitely in their provinces than any nation on earth. Would you think that the daily arrival of the diligence from Toulon would be an excitement? Yet it is to me, I assure you, and to all St. Philip. I walk, I take the waters, I read Ossian, I play piquet with Gaston, and yet I seem to myself but half-alive. . . .

. . . You will smile and say to me, "Dear brother, you have always plumed yourself on being a student of human nature. Is there no society, no character for you to study, even in St. Philippe-des-Bains?" My dear sister, I bend myself earnestly to that end, yet so far with little result. I have talked to my doctor—a good man but unpolished; I have talked to the curé—a good man but dull. I have even attempted the society of the baths, beginning with Monsieur le Marquis de la Percedragon, who has ninety-six quarterings, soiled wristbands, and a gloomy interest in my liver, and ending with Mrs. Macgregor Jenkins, a worthy and red-faced lady whose conversation positively cannonades with dukes and duchesses. But, frankly, I prefer my chair in the garden and my Ossian to any of them, even at the risk of being considered a bear. A witty scoundrel would be the veriest godsend to me, but do such exist in St. Philip? I trow not. As it is, in my weakened condition, I am positively agog when Gaston comes in every morning with his budget of village scandal. A pretty pass to come to, you will say, for a man who has served with Eyre Coote and but for the mutabilities of fortune, not to speak of a most damnable cabal. . . . (A long passage dealing with General Estcourt's East Indian services and his personal and unfavorable opinion of Warren Hastings is here omitted from the manuscript.) . . . But, at fifty, a man is either a fool or a philosopher. Nevertheless, unless Gaston provides me with a character to try my wits on, shortly, I shall begin to believe that they too have deteriorated with Indian suns. . . .

216

September 21st, 1788.

MY DEAR SISTER: . . . Believe me, there is little soundness in the views of your friend, Lord Martindale. The French monarchy is not to be compared with our own, but King Louis is an excellent and well-beloved prince, and the proposed summoning of the States-General cannot but have the most salutary effect. . . . (Three pages upon French politics and the possibility of cultivating sugar-cane in Southern France are here omitted.) . . . As for news of myself, I continue my yawning course, and feel a decided improvement from the waters. . . . So I shall continue them though the process is slow. . . .

You ask me, I fear a trifle mockingly, how my studies in human nature proceed?

Not so ill, my dear sister—I have, at least, scraped acquaintance with one odd fish, and that, in St. Philip, is a triumph. For some time, from my chair in the promenade, I have observed a pursy little fellow, of my age or thereabouts, stalking up and down between the lindens. His company seems avoided by such notables of the place as Mrs. Macgregor Jenkins and at first I put him down as a retired actor, for there is something a little theatrical in his dress and walk. He wears a wide-brimmed hat of straw, loose nankeen trousers and a quasi-military coat, and takes his waters with as much ceremony as Monsieur le Marquis, though not quite with the same *ton*. I should put him down as a Meridional, for he has the quick, dark eye, the sallow skin, the corpulence and the rodomontish airs that mark your true son of the Midi, once he has passed his lean and hungry youth.

And yet, there is some sort of unsuccessful oddity about him, which sets him off from your successful bourgeois. I cannot put my finger on it yet, but it interests me.

At any rate, I was sitting in my accustomed chair, reading Ossian, this morning, as he made his solitary rounds of the promenade. Doubtless I was more than usually absorbed in my author, for I must have pronounced some lines aloud as he passed. He gave me a quick glance at the time, but nothing more. But on his next round, as he was about to pass me, he hesitated for a moment, stopped, and then, removing his straw hat, saluted me very civilly.

"Monsieur will pardon me," he said, with a dumpy hauteur, "but surely monsieur is English? And surely the lines that monsieur just repeated are from the great poet, Ossian?"

I admitted both charges, with a smile, and he bowed again.

217

"Monsieur will excuse the interruption," he said, "but I myself have long admired the poetry of Ossian"—and with that he continued my quotation to the end of the passage, in very fair English, too, though with a strong accent. I complimented him, of course, effusively—after all, it is not every day that one runs across a fellow-admirer of Ossian on the promenade of a small French watering place—and after that, he sat down in the chair beside me and we fell into talk. He seems, astonishingly for a Frenchman, to have an excellent acquaintance with our English poets— perhaps he has been a tutor in some English family. I did not press him with questions on this first encounter, though I noted that he spoke French with a slight accent also, which seems odd.

There is something a little rascally about him, to tell you the truth, though his conversation with me was both forceful and elevated. An ill man, too, and a disappointed one, or I miss my mark, yet his eyes, when he talks, are strangely animating. I fancy I would not care to meet him in a *guetapens,* and yet, he may be the most harmless of broken pedagogues. We took a glass of waters together, to the great disgust of Mrs. Macgregor Jenkins, who ostentatiously drew her skirts aside. She let me know, afterward, in so many words, that my acquaintance was a noted bandit, though, when pressed, she could give no better reason than that he lives a little removed from the town, that "nobody knows where he comes from," and that his wife is "no better than she should be," whatever that portentous phrase entails. Well, one would hardly call him a gentleman, even by Mrs. Macgregor's somewhat easy standards, but he has given me better conversation that I have had in a month—and if he is a bandit, we might discuss thuggee together. But I hope for nothing so stimulating, though I must question Gaston about him. . . .

October 11th.

. . . But Gaston could tell me little, except that my acquaintance comes from Sardinia or some such island originally, has served in the French army and is popularly supposed to possess the evil eye. About Madame he hinted that he could tell me a great deal, but I did not labor the point. After all, if my friend has been c-ck-ld-d—do not blush, my dear sister!—that, too, is the portion of a philosopher, and I find his wide range of conversation much more palatable than Mrs. Macgregor Jenkins's rewarmed London gossip. Nor has he tried to borrow money from me yet, something which, I am frank to say, I expected and was prepared to refuse. . . .

November 20th.

. . . Triumph! My character is found—and a character of the first water, I assure you! I have dined with him in his house, and a very bad dinner it was. Madame is not a good housekeeper, whatever else she may be. And what she has been, one can see at a glance—she has all the little faded coquetries of the garrison coquette. Good-tempered, of course, as such women often are, and must have been pretty in her best days, though with shocking bad teeth. I suspect her of a touch of the tarbrush, though there I may be wrong. No doubt she caught my friend young—I have seen the same thing happen in India often enough—the experienced woman and the youngster fresh from England. Well, 'tis an old story—an old one with him, too—and no doubt Madame has her charms, though she is obviously one reason why he has not risen.

After dinner, Madame departed, not very willingly, and he took me into his study for a chat. He had even procured a bottle of port, saying he knew the Englishman's taste for it, and while it was hardly the right Cockburn, I felt touched by the attention. The man is desperately lonely—one reads that in his big eyes. He is also desperately proud, with the quick, touchy sensitiveness of the failure, and I quite exerted myself to draw him out.

And indeed, the effort repaid me. His own story is simple enough. He is neither bandit nor pedagogue, but, like myself, a broken soldier—a major of the French Royal Artillery, retired on half pay for some years. I think it creditable of him to have reached so respectable a rank, for he is of foreign birth—Sardinian, I think I told you—and the French service is by no means as partial to foreigners as they were in the days of the first Irish Brigade. Moreover, one simply does not rise in that service, unless one is a gentleman of quarterings, and that he could hardly claim. But the passion of his life has been India, and that is what interests me. And, 'pon my honor, he was rather astonishing about it.

As soon as, by a lucky chance, I hit upon the subject, his eyes lit up and his sickness dropped away. Pretty soon he began to take maps from a cabinet in the wall and ply me with questions about my own small experiences. And very soon indeed, I am abashed to state, I found myself stumbling in my answers. It was all book knowledge on his part, of course, but where the devil he could have got some of it, I do not know. Indeed, he would even correct me, now and then, as cool as you please. "Eight twelve pounders, I think, on the north wall of the old fortifications of Madras—" and the deuce of it is, he would be right. Finally, I could contain myself no longer.

219

"But, major, this is incredible," I said. "I have served twenty years with John Company and thought that I had some knowledge. But one would say you had fought over every inch of Bengal!"

He gave me a quick look, almost of anger, and began to roll up his maps.

"So I have, in my mind," he said, shortly, "but, as my superiors have often informed me, my hobby is a tedious one."

"It is not tedious to me," I said boldly. "Indeed, I have often marveled at your government's neglect of their opportunities in India. True, the issue is settled now—"

"It is by no means settled," he said, interrupting me rudely. I stared at him.

"It was settled, I believe, by Baron Clive, at a spot named Plassey," I said frigidly. "And afterward, by my own old general, Eyre Coote, at another spot named Wandewash."

"Oh, yes—yes—yes," he said impatiently, "I grant you Clive—Clive was a genius and met the fate of geniuses. He steals an empire for you, and your virtuous English Parliament holds up its hands in horror because he steals a few lakhs of rupees for himself as well. So he blows out his brains in disgrace—you inexplicable English!—and you lose your genius. A great pity. I would not have treated Clive so. But then, if I had been Milord Clive, I would not have blown out my brains."

"And what would you have done, had you been Clive?" I said, for the man's calm, staring conceit amused me.

His eyes were dangerous for a moment and I saw why the worthy Mrs. Macgregor Jenkins had called him a bandit.

"Oh," he said coolly, "I would have sent a file of grenadiers to your English Parliament and told it to hold its tongue. As Cromwell did. Now there was a man. But your Clive—faugh!—he had the ball at his feet and he refused to kick it. I withdraw the word genius. He was a nincompoop. At the least, he might have made himself a rajah."

This was a little too much, as you may imagine. "General Clive had his faults," I said icily, "but he was a true Briton and a patriot."

"He was a fool," said my puffy little major, flatly, his lower lip stuck out. "As big a fool as Dupleix, and that is saying much. Oh, some military skill, some talent for organization, yes. But a genius would have brushed him into the sea! It was possible to hold Arcot, it was possible to win Plassey—look!" and, with that, he ripped another map from his cabinet and began to expound to me eagerly exactly what he would have done in command of the French forces in India, in 1757, when he must have been but a lad in his twenties. He thumped the paper, he strewed corks along the table for his troops—corks taken from a supply in a tin box, so it must be an old game with him. And, as I listened, my irritation faded, for the man's monomania was obvious. Nor was it, to tell the truth, an ill-designed plan of campaign, for corks on a map. Of course these things are different, in the field.

I could say, with honesty, that his plan had features of novelty, and he gulped the words down hungrily—he has a great appetite for flattery.

"Yes, yes," he said. "That is how it should be done—the thickest skull can see it. And, ill as I am, with a fleet and ten thousand picked men—" He dreamed, obviously, the sweat of his exertions on his waxy face—it was absurd and yet touching to see him dream.

"You would find a certain amount of opposition," I said, in an amused voice.

"Oh, yes, yes," he said quickly. "I do not underrate the English. Excellent horse, solid foot. But no true knowledge of cannon, and I am a gunner—"

I hated to bring him down to earth and yet I felt that I must.

"Of course, major," I said, "you have had great experience in the field."

He looked at me for a moment, his arrogance quite unshaken.

"I have had very little," he said, quietly, "but one knows how the thing should be done or one does not know. And that is enough."

He stared at me for an instant with his big eyes. A little mad, of course. And yet I found myself saying, "But surely, major—what happened?"

"Why," he said, still quietly, "what happens to folk who have naught but their brains to sell? I staked my all on India when I was young—I thought that my star shone over it. I ate dirty puddings—*corpo di Bacco!*—to get there—I was no De Rohan or Soubise to win the king's favor! And I reached there indeed, in my youth, just in time to be included in the surrender of Pondicherry." He laughed, rather terribly, and sipped at his glass.

"You English were very courteous captors," he said. "But I was not released till the Seven Years' War had ended—that was in '63. Who asks for the special exchange of an unknown artillery lieutenant? And then ten years odd of garrison duty at Mauritius. It was there that I met Madame—she is a Creole. A pleasant spot, Mauritius. We used to fire the cannon at the sea birds when we had enough ammunition for target practice," and he chuckled drearily. "By then I was thirty-seven. They had to make me a captain—they even brought me back to France. To garrison duty. I have been on garrison duty, at Toulon, at Brest, at—" He ticked off the names on his fingers but I did not like his voice.

"But surely," I said, "the American war, though a small affair—there were opportunities—"

"And who did they send?" he said quickly. "Lafayette—Rochambeau—De Grasse—the sprigs of the nobility. Oh, at Lafayette's age, I would have volunteered like Lafayette. But one should be successful in youth—after that, the spring is broken. And when one is over forty, one has responsibilities. I have a large family, you see, though not of my own begetting," and he chuckled as if at a secret joke. "Oh, I wrote the Continental Congress," he said reflectively, "but they preferred a dolt like Von Steuben. A good dolt, an honest dolt, but there you have it. I also wrote your British War Office," he said in an even voice. "I must show you that plan of campaign—sometime—they could have crushed General Washington with it in three weeks."

I stared at him, a little appalled.

"For an officer who has taken his king's shilling to send to an enemy nation a plan for crushing his own country's ally," I said, stiffly—"well, in England, we would call that treason."

"And what is treason?" he said lightly. "If we call it unsuccessful ambition we shall be nearer the truth." He looked at me, keenly. "You are shocked, General Estcourt," he said. "I am sorry for that. But have you never known the curse"—and his voice vibrated—"the curse of not being employed when you should be employed? The curse of being a hammer with no nail to drive? The curse—the curse of sitting in a dusty garrison town with dreams that would split the brain of a Caesar, and no room on earth for those dreams?"

"Yes," I said, unwillingly, for there was something in him that demanded the truth, "I have known that."

"Then you know hells undreamed of by the Christian," he said, with a sigh, "and if I committed treason—well, I have been punished for it. I might have been a brigadier, otherwise—I had Choiseul's ear for a few weeks, after great labor. As it is, I am here on half pay, and there will not be another war in my time. Moreover, M. de Ségur has proclaimed that all officers now must show sixteen quarterings. Well, I wish them joy of those officers, in the next conflict. Meanwhile, I have my corks, my maps, and my family ailment." He smiled and tapped his side. "It killed my father at thirty-nine—it has not treated me quite so ill, but it will come for me soon enough."

And indeed, when I looked at him, I could well believe it, for the light had gone from his eyes and his cheeks were flabby. We chatted a little on indifferent subjects after that, then I left him, wondering whether to pursue the acquaintance. He is indubitably a character, but some of his speeches leave a taste in my mouth. Yet he can be greatly attractive—even now, with his mountainous failure like a cloak upon him. And yet why should I call it mountainous? His conceit is mountainous enough, but what else could he have expected of his career? Yet I wish I could forget his eyes. . . . To tell the truth, he puzzles me and I mean to get to the bottom of him. . . .

February 12th, 1789.

. . . I have another sidelight on the character of my friend, the major. As I told you, I was half of a mind to break off the acquaintance entirely, but he came up to me so civilly, the following day, that I could find no excuse. And since then, he has made me no embarrassingly treasonable confidences, though whenever we discuss the art of war, his arrogance is unbelievable. He even informed me, the other day, that while Frederick of Prussia was a fair general, his tactics might have been improved upon. I merely laughed and turned the question. Now and then I play a war game with him, with his corks and maps, and when I let him win, he is as pleased as a child. . . . His illness increases visibly, despite the waters, and he shows an eagerness for my company which I cannot but find touching. . . . After all, he is a man of intelligence, and the company he has had to keep must have galled him at times. . . .

Now and then I amuse myself by speculating what might have happened to him, had he chosen some other profession than that of arms. He has, as I have told you, certain gifts of the actor, yet his stature and figure must have debarred him from tragic parts, while he certainly does not possess the humors of the comedian. Perhaps his best choice would have been the Romish church, for there, the veriest fisherman may hope, at least, to succeed to the keys of St. Peter. . . . And yet, Heaven knows, he would have made a very bad priest! . . .

But, to my tale. I had missed him from our accustomed walks for some days and went to his house—St. Helen's it is called; we live in a pother of saints' names hereabouts—one evening to inquire. I did not hear the quarreling voices till the tousle-haired servant had admitted me and then it was too late to retreat. Then my friend bounced down the corridor, his sallow face bored and angry.

223

"Ah, General Estcourt!" he said, with a complete change of expression as soon as he saw me. "What fortune! I was hoping you would pay us a call—I wish to introduce you to my family!"

He had told me previously of his pair of stepchildren by Madame's first marriage, and I must confess I felt curious to see them. But it was not of them he spoke, as I soon gathered.

"Yes," he said. "My brothers and sisters, or most of them, are here for a family council. You come in the nick of time!" He pinched my arm and his face glowed with the malicious naïveté of a child. "They do not believe that I really know an English general—it will be a great blow to them!" he whispered as we passed down the corridor. "Ah, if you had only worn your uniform and your Garters! But one cannot have everything in life!"

Well, my dear sister, what a group, when we entered the salon! It is a small room, tawdrily furnished in the worst French taste, with a jumble of Madame's femininities and souvenirs from the Island of Mauritius, and they were all sitting about in the French after-dinner fashion, drinking tisane and quarreling. And, indeed, had the room been as long as the nave of St. Peter's, it would yet have seemed too small for such a crew! An old mother, straight as a ramrod and as forbidding, with the burning eyes and the bitter dignity one sees on the faces of certain Italian peasants—you could see that they were all a little afraid of her except my friend, and he, I must say, treated her with a filial courtesy that was greatly to his credit. Two sisters, one fattish, swarthy, and spiteful, the other with the wreck of great beauty and the evident marks of a certain profession on her shabby-fine *toilette* and her pinkened cheeks. An innkeeper brother-in-law called Buras or Durat, with a jowlish, heavily handsome face and the manners of a cavalry sergeant—he is married to the spiteful sister. And two brothers, one sheep-like, one fox-like, yet both bearing a certain resemblance to my friend.

The sheep-like brother is at least respectable, I gathered—a provincial lawyer in a small way of business whose great pride is that he has actually appeared before the Court of Appeals at Marseilles. The other, the fox-like one, makes his living more dubiously—he seems the sort of fellow who orates windily in taprooms about the Rights of Man, and other nonsense of M. Rousseau's. I would certainly not trust him with my watch, though he is trying to get himself elected to the States-General. And, as regards family concord, it was obvious at first glance that not one of them trusted the others. And yet, that is not all of the tribe. There are, if you will believe me, two other brothers living, and this family council was called to deal with the affairs of the next-to-youngest, who seems, even in this melange, to be a black sheep.

I can assure you, my head swam, and when my friend introduced me, proudly, as a Knight of the Garters, I did not even bother to contradict him. For they admitted me to their intimate circle at once—there was no doubt about that. Only the old lady remained aloof, saying little and sipping her camomile tea as if it were the blood of her enemies. But, one by one, the others related to me, with an unasked-for frankness, the most intimate and scandalous details of their brothers' and sisters' lives. They seemed united only on two points, jealousy of my friend, the major, because he is his mother's favorite, and dislike of Madame Josephine because she gives herself airs. Except for the haggard beauty—I must say, that, while her remarks anent her sister-in-law were not such as I would care to repeat, she seemed genuinely fond of her brother, the major, and expounded his virtues to me through an overpowering cloud of scent.

It was like being in a nest of Italian smugglers, or a den of quarrelsome foxes, for they all talked, or rather barked at once, even the brother-in-law, and only Madame Mère could bring silence among them. And yet, my friend enjoyed it. It was obvious he showed them off before me as he might have displayed the tricks of a set of performing animals. And yet with a certain fondness, too—that is the inexplicable part of it. I do not know which sentiment was upmost in my mind—respect for this family feeling or pity for his being burdened with such a clan.

For though not the eldest, he is the strongest among them, and they know it. They rebel, but he rules their family conclaves like a petty despot. I could have laughed at the farce of it, and yet, it was nearer tears. For here, at least, my friend was a personage.

I got away as soon as I could, despite some pressing looks from the haggard beauty. My friend accompanied me to the door.

"Well, well," he said, chuckling and rubbing his hands, "I am infinitely obliged to you, general. They will not forget this in a hurry. Before you entered, Joseph"—Joseph is the sheep-like one—"was boasting about his acquaintance with a *sous-intendant,* but an English general, bah! Joseph will have green eyes for a fortnight!" And he rubbed his hands again in a perfect paroxysm of delight.

It was too childlike to make me angry. "I am glad, of course, to have been of any service," I said.

"Oh, you have been a great service," he said. "They will not plague my poor Josie for at least half an hour. Ah, this is a bad business of Louis's—a bad business!"—Louis is the black sheep—"but we will patch

225

it up somehow. Hortense is worth three of him—he must go back to Hortense!"

"You have a numerous family, major," I said, for want of something better to say.

"Oh, yes," he said, cheerfully. "Pretty numerous—I am sorry you could not meet the others. Though Louis is a fool—I pampered him in his youth. Well! He was a baby—and Jerome a mule. Still, we haven't done so badly for ourselves; not badly. Joseph makes a go of his law practice—there are fools enough in the world to be impressed by Joseph—and if Lucien gets to the States-General, you may trust Lucien to feather his nest! And there are the grandchildren, and a little money—not much," he said, quickly. "They mustn't expect that from me. But it's a step up from where we started—if papa had lived, he wouldn't have been so ill-pleased. Poor Elisa's gone, but the rest of us have stuck together, and, while we may seem a little rough, to strangers, our hearts are in the right place. When I was a boy," and he chuckled again, "I had other ambitions for them. I thought, with luck on my side, I could make them all kings and queens. Funny, isn't it, to think of a numskull like Joseph as a king! Well, that was the boy of it. But, even so, they'd all be eating chestnuts back on the island without me, and that's something."

He said it rather defiantly, and I did not know which to marvel at most—his preposterous pride in the group or his cool contempt of them. So I said nothing but shook his hand instead. I could not help doing the latter. For surely, if anyone started in life with a millstone about his neck . . . and yet they are none of them ordinary people. . . .

March 13th, 1789.

. . . My friend's complaint has taken a turn for the worse and it is I who pay him visits now. It is the act of a Christian to do so and, to tell the truth, I have become oddly attached to him, though I can give no just reason for the attachment. He makes a bad patient, by the way, and is often abominably rude to both myself and Madame, who nurses him devotedly though unskillfully. I told him yesterday that I could have no more of it and he looked at me with his strangely luminous eyes. "So," he said, "even the English desert the dying." . . . Well, I stayed; after that, what else might a gentleman do? . . . Yet I cannot feel that he bears me any real affection—he exerts himself to charm, on occasion, but one feels he is playing a game . . . yes, even upon his deathbed, he plays a game . . . a complex character. . . .

April 28th, 1789.

. . . My friend the major's malady approaches its term—the last few days find him fearfully enfeebled. He knows that the end draws nigh; indeed he speaks of it often, with remarkable calmness. I had thought it might turn his mind toward religion, but while he has accepted the ministrations of his Church, I fear it is without the sincere repentance of a Christian. When the priest had left him, yesterday, he summoned me, remarking, "Well, all that is over with," rather more in the tone of a man who has just reserved a place in a coach than one who will shortly stand before his Maker.

"It does no harm," he said, reflectively. "And, after all, it might be true. Why not?" and he chuckled in a way that repelled me. Then he asked me to read to him—not the Bible, as I had expected, but some verses of the poet Gray. He listened attentively, and when I came to the passage, "Hands, that the rod of empire might have swayed," and its successor, "Some mute inglorious Milton here may rest," he asked me to repeat them. When I had done so, he said, "Yes, yes. That is true, very true. I did not think so in boyhood—I thought genius must force its own way. But your poet is right about it."

I found this painful, for I had hoped that his illness had brought him to a juster, if less arrogant, estimate of his own abilities.

"Come, major," I said, soothingly, "we cannot all be great men, you know. And you have no need to repine. After all, as you say, you have risen in the world—"

"Risen?" he said, and his eyes flashed. "Risen? Oh, God, that I should die alone with my one companion an Englishman with a soul of suet! Fool, if I had had Alexander's chance, I would have bettered Alexander! And it will come, too, that is the worst of it. Already Europe is shaking with a new birth. If I had been born under the Sun-King, I would be a Marshal of France; if I had been born twenty years ago, I would mold a new Europe with my fists in the next half-dozen years. Why did they put my soul in my body at this infernal time? Do you not understand, imbecile? Is there no one who understands?"

I called Madame at this, as he was obviously delirious, and, after some trouble, we got him quieted.

May 8th, 1789.

. . . My poor friend is gone, and peacefully enough at the last. His death, oddly enough, coincided with the date of the opening of the

States-General at Versailles. The last moments of life are always painful for the observer, but his end was as relatively serene as might be hoped for, considering his character. I was watching at one side of the bed and a thunderstorm was raging at the time. No doubt, to his expiring consciousness, the cracks of the thunder sounded like artillery, for, while we were waiting the death-struggle, he suddenly raised himself in the bed and listened intently. His eyes glowed, a beatific expression passed over his features. "The army! Head of the army!" he whispered ecstatically, and, when we caught him, he was lifeless. . . . I must say that, while it may not be very Christian, I am glad that death brought him what life could not, and that, in the very article of it, he saw himself at the head of victorious troops. Ah, Fame—delusive spectre. . . . (A page of disquisition by General Estcourt on the vanities of human ambition is here omitted.) . . . The face, after death, was composed, with a certain majesty, even . . . one could see that he might have been handsome as a youth. . . .

May 26th, 1789.
. . . I shall return to Paris by easy stages and reach Stokely sometime in June. My health is quite restored and all that has kept me here this long has been the difficulty I have met with in attempting to settle my poor friend, the major's affairs. For one thing, he appears to have been originally a native of Corsica, not of Sardinia as I had thought, and while that explains much in his character, it has also given occupation to the lawyers. I have met his rapacious family, individually and in conclave, and, if there are further gray hairs on my head, you may put it down to them. . . . However, I have finally assured the major's relict of her legitimate rights in his estate, and that is something—my one ray of comfort in the matter being the behavior of her son by the former marriage, who seems an excellent and virtuous young man. . . .
. . . You will think me a very soft fellow, no doubt, for wasting so much time upon a chance acquaintance who was neither, in our English sense, a gentleman nor a man whose Christian virtues counterbalanced his lack of true breeding. Yet there was a tragedy about him beyond his station, and that verse of Gray's rings in my head. I wish I could forget the expression on his face when he spoke of it. Suppose a genius born in circumstances that made the development of that genius impossible—well, all this is the merest moonshine. . . .
. . . To revert to more practical matters, I discover that the major has left me his military memoirs, papers and commentaries, including his

maps. Heaven knows what I shall do with them! I cannot, in courtesy, burn them *sur-le-champ,* and yet they fill two huge packing cases and the cost of transporting them to Stokely will be considerable. Perhaps I will take them to Paris and quietly dispose of them there to some waste-paper merchant. . . . In return for this unsought legacy, Madame has consulted me in regard to a stone and epitaph for her late husband, and, knowing that otherwise the family would squabble over the affair for weeks, I have drawn up a design which I hope meets with their approval. It appears that he particularly desired that the epitaph should be writ in English, saying that France had had enough of him, living—a freak of dying vanity for which one must pardon him. However, I have produced the following, which I hope will answer.

Here lies

NAPOLEONE BUONAPARTE

Major of the Royal Artillery

of France.

Born August 15th, 1737,

at Ajaccio, Corsica.

Died May 5th, 1789,

at St. Philippe-des-Bains.

"Rest, perturbed spirit . . ."

. . . I had thought, for some hours, of excerpting the lines of Gray's— the ones that still ring in my head. But, on reflection, though they suit well enough, they yet seem too cruel to the dust.

Hush My Mouth

Suzette Haden Elgin

Irst time ever I saw a Silent, I was no more than a tiny child; I might have been five years old. And it meant nothing to me. It was just a woman, and not a very pretty one to look at, with her head shaved. I remember her skull; it had a lumpy look to it that bothered me. I had never before seen a bald woman, nor very many bald men. I wasn't eager to see this one, either, because my sisters had been pushing me on the swing that hung from our black walnut tree, and I had complained bitterly at being made to leave that and go look at this woman passing by.

But my father paid no mind to my fuss, hauling me up onto his shoulder and almost running out to the edge of the street, the other children hurrying along behind us. He stopped at the curb and he shook me a little bit to be sure he had my attention, and he said to me, "Now you *remember* that, boy! You put it away in your heart, and you remember it, that there was a morning a Silent walked by your house so close you could of touched her if you'd had a mind to!" The woman turned to look at us as she passed, and her smile was the only thing about her not black as the inside of our water well, and Daddy squeezed my thighs where he had me braced on his shoulder and added, "And you remember she *smiled* at you, child! See you remember that, forevermore!" And I have remembered it, as he told me to do, all these years.

She smiled at Matthias Darrow, too, him standing down on the corner of our street with his father and his grandmother and his two big brothers. I suppose his mother was busy with her everlasting tending of

231

the sick and with someone she couldn't leave, even for this occasion. Matthias was there, and all my other friends and their parents, lining both sides of the street to watch a Silent go by on her way to somewhere. I don't know where she could have been going; nobody told me to concern myself with that. But we all stood and watched her walk to the end of the street, tall and straight and stake-thin in her long black dress. We watched her turn the corner and go on down the side street. Not until she was out of sight did anybody move to leave the curbs and go back to what they had been doing. I remember there was a little bit of a breeze, and it stirred the branches of the pink mimosa and spread their perfume all around; I remember that smell, mimosa and hot dust and the several smells of sluggish summer river, mixed. I can smell it now, as strong as I smelled it that day.

And I remember Matthias, watching the Silent and shouting out, "Morning, ma'am!" as she went by, and his father clapping a swift hand over his mouth and bending down to tell him that he'd appreciate it if he'd behave like he had good sense, whether he did or not. And Matthias, looking up over Mr. Darrow's huge hand with eyes wide and round and scared, wondering what he'd done.

Matthias broke this morning. I heard it happen. The Lord God help me, please, I'll hear it forever, the sound his head—the sound his head made as he smashed it against the wall of his room. Bare flesh, not a strand of hair to cushion it, smacking against white-washed brick. Seven blows, it took. Seven times, that sound. That unspeakable sound.

How could a human being have the strength to take his life by battering his own head against a wall? Will you tell me that? How could he stay conscious long enough to get to the fatal blow that ended it? And to do it silently! How in the name of God could you do that and *stay silent*?

Matthias did. I could not have done it, but he did. I swear to you, as I shall swear to the judges that come to question me. I will close my eyes three times, signifying NO, when they ask me if Matthias Darrow cried out at the last. His family has no shame coming, for he died without so much as a gasp. And the town we came from, he and I, all those people who were so blazing proud to have *two* of us choose to be Silents, there's no shame coming to them, either. We took our vows together, Matthias and I, both of us just seventeen; and now he is gone.

We were expecting that he would do something. All of us had seen it coming. He had taken to chewing at his lips, so that they were always cracked and bloody. His fingers were forever twitching; he'd notice, and

he'd shove them out of sight into the pockets of his robe. We watched
him day by day as the tension drew his skin tight to his skull, till the bones
strained to shove through the flesh and the whole head gleamed like
polished ebony. When he started wearing the leather gag even in the
daytime, that foul gag that stands witness to our frailty and guards us
from the word spoken in sleep, we knew that he was going to break. If
there had been anything we could have done to help him, we would have
done it, but there was nothing to do. When the lust for language
consumes a man, you can only watch him burn and dedicate your prayers
to him.

We were on our guard on his behalf; we were not just praying. We
had taken to being wary around him. When we walked along the
balconies of the shelterhouse, one of us would walk at his side next the
rail, and two others ahead and behind him, so that he could not throw
himself into the courtyard. The elders had begun tasting his food and
drink at the table openly, so that if he were so mad as to poison either he
would have to take one of them with him into death. We watched what
he picked up and what he put down; we went with him when he walked
out of the building. At least one of us stayed close by no matter what he
was engaged in; we were watchful of our brother. Except in the privacy
of his room, where we could not follow.

I am sure I'm not the only one who wishes we had been more careless.
If Matthias had been able to slip poison into his soup in the diningroom, it
would have been easier for him, and I would not now be hearing in my
soul the wet thud of his skull against brick.

Still. It must be noted that Matthias Darrow *did not give in.* For his
family there will not be the shame of a failed Silent with broken vows,
sent home from the shelterhouse in disgrace. He spared them that. He
spared all his vast family, spared them the scandal that shames the line
down to the cousins many times removed, that is the end of respect and
the beginning of a courteous pity that is like a stone hung round the neck.
Matthias saw to it that his people did not have that shame to endure. The
Lord God help me be as brave if I come to such a pass. The Lord God grant
I never come to such a pass, and let my neverending silent dialogue with
my own foolish self be my worst failing.

All of this, we will be reminded, was born of the sin of pride, beside
which murder and debauchery are no more than childish foibles. First the
white man's pride; and that not being foul enough, the black man's pride
to cap it off. Pride, that is not called the worst of all the sins for idle

reasons. When the preacher comes this Sunday, that will be his sermon, and his text will be "Pride goeth before a fall." There is no room in this house where that text is not burned into a beam or painted over a window. Because of what pride has brought us to.

If the Union Army had let us serve with them in the Civil War, the North would have won; no one disputes that. President Lincoln himself said it was so—they would have won! But they wouldn't allow it. Not them. No black man was going to put on the uniform of a Union soldier, or ride a horse of the Union Cavalry, or march in the least last straggling row of the Union infantry. They were told we'd serve in our own clothes, or serve naked, if they felt that would be sufficient to keep us from being mistaken for their comrades at arms. But they were stiff-necked; it made no difference. No black—Negroes, they called us then— no Negro was going to be able to say he had served in the Union Army. We were not fit even to die beside them; that was their position on the matter, and they would not budge from it.

You'd have thought the Confederates would have had better sense. White and black, we'd played together as children and suckled at the same black breasts as infants and gotten blind drunk together as young men. But the Confederate Army followed the Yankees' lead, bound they'd outdo them. If a Negro was not good enough to soldier for the *Union,* well then bygod he was twice that not good enough to soldier for the South! Damn fools they were, too, for we would have fought to the death beside them and no quarter given, after the way the Union spurned us.

Abraham Lincoln, standing there for all to hear in Washington, and then the words spread across the newspapers for all to read, he said: "We shall not send our women into battle; we shall not send our children. And we shall surely not send our Negroes, who are as children, to shed their blood in a war they are not even able to understand." He said that, and we heard it, and I suppose it was nothing we hadn't heard before. But somehow his saying it made it official. He made it the official public policy of the Disunited States of America, that the blacks had not even the wisdom of children. After that, we would willingly have fought for the South, even if it meant fighting beside a man who'd ordered us whipped by the cruelest black driver in the worst slave state there ever was.

They wouldn't have it. And later, when it got to be obvious that the war could not be won without us, they still would not, for neither side was willing to be the first to say, "Well, we were wrong; I guess the blood of a black man is good enough to spill for this country."

Pride! Thus it was that nobody won that awful war, that dragged on eight terrible years. Oh, the South claimed the victory, in the strict sense of the word; there being so many blacks at home to see to the work of the plantations and the farms and the Southern towns, the South lasted longer. It was the North that first proposed to stop fighting. But there was no victory. The time came when there was nobody left with the will to fight any more, that's all. They just laid down their weapons and went home. What was left of them. To what was left of home.

They didn't last very long. Smallpox and cholera took most of them that didn't die of their battle wounds. A handful came stumbling back to the burned-out ruins that had been the glorious South; and they were ruins, themselves.

We had been prepared to kill every last one of them, with our bare hands if need be. My grandfather swears to that, and I believe him. We had been ready to kill them all. We were four million strong; even half-starved we had more strength than those ragtag men that lived through the Civil War to come home. Our women were ready, and our children, too, to do whatsoever had to be done.

But when it came right down to it we had to kill very few of them. The young men, and the older ones that had gone in when the young men were mostly dead and maimed, they brought their diseases home with them. And they went to sleep and eat with their wives and their children and their old people. The sicknesses went through those families like wildfire through a piney woods.

In another time, we would have nursed them. Some of them would have lived, and many of us would have died, and when it was over we would have been as mixed up as ever. But not this time. They hadn't considered us fit to die with them in their filthy war; we were not willing to die with them in their filthy peace. We lifted no hand either to help or to harm them, we simply waited. And when it was over we rounded up the pitiful remnant that did not die, man or woman or child, and we sent them with all courtesy into the North, out of New Africa forever, beyond the walls at the border.

They went docilely enough. As for the occasional damn Yankee fool that decided he'd ride South and see about bringing New Africa back into the United States, we tried to reason with him. And if he would not be reasonable we took him into our courts and tried him swiftly and carried out the sentence with sufficient dispatch to discourage others from any such hopeless lost notion.

So. There we were. A sovereign nation. Mexico to the south of us, the United States to the north of us, and the oceans at either side. All the land there for our taking, much of it burnt over and scorched black and covered with destruction, but no damage done that we weren't capable of setting to rights. We made the land clean again, and we cleared away the gutted buildings and put up new ones; we laid out farms and streets and set ourselves to live a decent life for the first time since we were torn out of the breast of Africa and flung like cattle onto this land.

We should have been all right. We had everything we wanted, and that one most precious thing of all—we were free. Free! The work of our hands was there to do, and the tools to do it with, and its fruits were for the first time to be *ours*. Hallelujah, it was the Promised Land; praise be to God, it was Eden . . .

And why, then, do we find ourselves, all these years later, with the work only half done, and half our strength and passions still devoted to squabbling? And the North once again eyeing our borders, thinking the time will come when we'll be ripe for conquering?

Pride again. We will be reminded, come Sunday. Pride! We who thought ourselves so fine, watching the white man both Northern and Southern destroy himself and all his kin and all his substance for pride. More fools we, because we were just as human when the time came to test us.

We'd never given the problem any thought, my grandfather says. There'd been no time to think about it, and no reason. Scattered as we were, subjugated as we were, the matter of language had not come up; under the lash, any word will do to scream with.

But we'd brought many dozens of languages with us from Africa, each one of them the language of a proud people with a proud heritage. And when it came time to choose one, to decide which one we would speak now in this New Africa, there was no question in anybody's mind. The only possible choice for the New African tongue was whatsoever language *he* spoke. "Why, *my* language, obviously!" And so said they all.

Bitter. Bitter, the fruit of pride, and harsh in the mouth. Oh God in Heaven, be you black or white or the color of mimosa flowers, it was bitter! That it should come to this . . . our children free to go to school and learn, finally, and every forty or so in a different school learning a different language. You talk of segregation! And in our legislature, and in our churches and our colleges and our publishing houses and all our daily business of life, it is no African language we speak. Pride will not let us choose one. Only in the white man's hated English are we able to govern this land, the very name of which is a white man's name, because our pride would not and will not let us agree on a name in one of our own tongues.

And so there are Silents.

Sworn to use *no* language. Not spoken; not written; not language of the hands. Only that irreducible minimum of all signs that must be used if we are to survive. Four signs a day, we are allowed, if by no other means can we make our brother or our sister understand that the building is on fire or the piece of meat on the table is unsafe to eat or a baby is about to be born. And not even those four, unless we are forced to them.

Before we come into the shelterhouse, before we make our vows, those who serve as liaison between the Silents and the world explain this to us; they make it very certain that we understand, before they let us come.

We will be silent. That is the vow we take. Until death; or until our people can lay aside the pride that destroys them and choose a language that is not a white man's language. Whichever comes first.

Matthias Darrow, the Lord God have mercy on his soul, could not wait any longer.

Interurban Queen

R.A. Lafferty

"It was the year 1907 when I attained my majority and came into a considerable inheritance," the old man said. "I was a very keen young man, keen enough to know that I didn't know everything. I went to knowledgeable men and asked their advice as to how I might invest this inheritance.

"I talked with bankers and cattlemen and the new oilmen. These were not stodgy men. They had an edge on the future, and they were excited and exciting about the way that money might be made to grow. It was the year of statehood and there was an air of prosperity over the new state. I wished to integrate my patrimony into that new prosperity.

"Finally I narrowed my choice to two investments which then seemed about of equal prospect, though you will now smile to hear them equated. One of them was the stock-selling company of a certain Harvey Goodrich, a rubber company, and with the new automobile coming into wider use, it seemed that rubber might be a thing of the future. The other was a stock-selling transportation company that proposed to run an interurban railway between the small towns of Kiefer and Mounds. It also proposed (at a future time) to run branches to Glenpool, to Bixby, to Kellyville, to Slick, to Bristow, to Beggs, even to Okmulgee and Sapulpa. At that time it also seemed that these little interurban railways might be things of the future. An interurban already ran between Tulsa and Sand Springs, and one was building between Tulsa and Sapulpa. There were more than one thousand of these small trolley railroads operating in the nation, and thoughtful men believed that they would come to form a complete national network, might become the main system of transportation."

But now the old man Charles Archer was still a young man. He was listening to Joe Elias, a banker in a small but growing town.

"It is a riddle you pose me, young man, and you set me thinking," Elias said. "We have dabbled in both, thinking to have an egg under every hen. I begin to believe that we were wrong to do so. These two prospects are types of two futures, and only one of them will obtain. In this state with its new oil discoveries, it might seem that we should be partial to rubber, which has a tie-in with the automobile, which has a tie-in with petroleum fuel. This need not be. I believe that the main use of oil will be in powering the new factories, and I believe that rubber is already oversold as to industrial application. And yet there *will be* a new transportation. Between the horse and the main-line railways there is a great gap. I firmly believe that the horse will be eliminated as a main form of transportation. We are making no more loans to buggy or buckboard manufacturers nor to harness makers. I have no faith in the automobile. It destroys something in me. It is the interurbans that will go into the smallest localities, and will so cut into the main-line railroads as to leave no more than a half dozen of the long-distance major lines in America. Young man, I would invest in the interurban with complete confidence."

Charles Archer was listening to Carl Bigheart, a cattleman.

"I ask you, boy, how many head of cattle can you put into an automobile? Or even into what they call a lorry or truck? Then I ask you how many you can put into an honest cattle car which can be coupled onto any interurban on a country run? The interurban will be the salvation of us cattlemen. With the fencing regulations we cannot drive cattle even twenty miles to a railroad; but the little interurbans will go into the deep country, running along every second or third section line.

"And I will tell you another thing, boy: there is no future for the automobile. *We cannot let there be!* Consider the man on horseback, and I have been a man on horseback for most of my life. Well, mostly he is a good man, but there is a change in him as soon as he mounts. Every man on horseback is an arrogant man, however gentle he may be on foot. I know this in myself and in others. He was necessary in his own time, and I believe that time is ending. There was always extreme danger from the man on horseback.

"Believe me, young man, the man in the automobile is one thousand times as dangerous. The kindest man in the world assumes an incredible arrogance when he drives an automobile, and this arrogance will increase still further if the machine is allowed to develop greater power and sophistication. I tell you, it will engender absolute selfishness in mankind if the driving of automobiles becomes common. It will breed violence on a scale never seen before. It will mark the end of the family as we know it, the three or four generations living happily in one home. It will destroy the sense of neighborhood and the true sense of nation. It will create giantized cankers of cities, false opulence of suburbs, ruinized countryside, and unhealthy conglomeration of specialized farming and manufacturing. It will breed rootlessness and immorality. It will make every man a tyrant. I believe the private automobile will be suppressed. *It will have to be!* This is a moral problem, and we are a moral nation and world; we will take moral action against it. And without the automobile, rubber has no real future. Opt for the interurban stock, young man."

Young Charles Archer was listening to Nolan Cushman, an oilman.

"I will not lie to you, young fellow, I love the automobile, the motorcar. I have three, custom-built. I am an emperor when I drive. Hell, I'm an emperor anyhow! I bought a castle last summer that had housed emperors. I'm having it transported, stone by stone, to my place in the Osage. Now, as to the motorcar, I can see how it should develop. It should develop with the roads, they becoming leveled and metaled or concreted, and the cars lower and lower and faster and faster. We would develop them so, if we were some species other than human. It is the logical development, but I hope it will not come, and it will not. That would be to make it common, and the commonality of men cannot be trusted with this power. Besides, I love a high car, and I do not want there to be very many of them. They should only be allowed to men of extreme wealth and flair. How would it be if the workingmen were ever permitted them? It would be murderous if they should come into the hands of ordinary men. How hellish a world would it be if all men should become as arrogant as myself! No, the automobile will never be anything but a rich man's pride, the rubber will never be anything but a limited adjunct to that special thing. Invest in your interurban. It is the thing of the future, or else I dread that future."

Young Charles Archer knew that this was a crossroads of the world. Whichever turning was taken, it would predicate a certain sort of nation

241

and world and humanity. He thought about it deeply. Then he decided. He went out and invested his entire inheritance in his choice.

"I considered the two investments and I made my choice," said Charles Archer, the old man now in the now present. "I put all I had into it, thirty-five thousand dollars, a considerable sum in those days. You know the results."

"I am one of the results, Great-grandfather," said Angela Archer. "If you had invested differently you would have come to different fortune, you would have married differently, and I would be different or not at all. I like me here and now. I like everything as it is."

Three of them were out riding early one Saturday morning, the old man Charles Archer, his great-granddaughter Angela, and her fiancé, Peter Brady. They were riding through the quasiurbia, the rich countryside. It was not a main road, and yet it had a beauty (partly natural and partly contrived) that was as exciting as it was satisfying.

Water always beside the roadway, that was the secret! There were the carp ponds one after another. There were the hatcheries. There were the dancing rocky streams that in a less enlightened age might have been mere gutter runs or roadway runs. There were the small and rapid trout streams, and boys were catching big trout from them.

There were the deep bush-trees, sumac, witch hazel, sassafras—incense trees they might almost have been. There were the great trees themselves, pecan and hickory and black walnut, standing like high backdrops; and between were the lesser trees, willow, cottonwood, sycamore. Catheads and sedge grass and reeds stood in the water itself, and tall Sudan grass and bluestem on the shores. And always the clovers there, and the smell of wet sweet clover.

"I chose the wrong one," said old Charles Archer as they rode along through the textured country. "One can now see how grotesque was my choice, but I was young. In two years, the stock-selling company in which I had invested was out of business and my loss was total. So early and easy riches were denied me, but I developed an ironic hobby: keeping track of the stock of the enterprise in which I did *not* invest. The stock I could have bought for thirty-five thousand dollars would now make me worth nine million dollars."

"Ugh, don't talk of such a thing on such a beautiful day," Angela objected.

"They heard another of them last night," Peter Brady commented. "They've been hearing this one, off and on, for a week now, and haven't caught him yet."

"I always wish they wouldn't kill them when they catch them," Angela bemoaned. "It doesn't seem quite right to kill them."

A goose-girl was herding her white honking charges as they gobbled weeds out of fields of morning onions. Flowering kale was shining green-purple, and okra plants were standing. Jersey cows grazed along the roadway, and the patterned plastic (almost as patterned as the grasses) filled the roadway itself. There were clouds like yellow dust in the air. Bees! Stingless bees they were. But dust itself was not. That there never be dust again!

"They will have to find out and kill the sly klunker makers," said old man Charles Archer. "Stop the poison at its source."

"There's too many of them, and too much money in it," said Peter Brady. "Yes, we kill them. One of them was found and killed Thursday, and three nearly finished klunkers were destroyed. But we can't kill them all. They seem to come out of the ground like snakes."

"I wish we didn't have to kill them," Angela said.

There were brightly colored firkins of milk standing on loading stoas, for this was a milk shed. There were chickens squawking in nine-story-high coops as they waited the pickups, but they never had to wait long. Here were a thousand dozen eggs on a refrigeration porch; there a clutch of piglings, or of red steers.

Tomato plants were staked two meters high. Sweet corn stood, not yet come to tassel. They passed cucumber vines and cantaloupe vines, and the potato hills rising up blue-green. Ah, there were grapevines in their tight acres, deep alfalfa meadows, living fences of Osage orange and whitethorn. Carrot tops zephyred like green lace. Cattle were grazing fields of red clover and of peanuts—that most magic of all clovers. Men mowed hay.

"I hear him now!" Peter Brady said suddenly.

"You couldn't. Not in the daytime. Don't even think of such a thing," Angela protested.

Farm ducks were grazing with their heads under water in the roadway ponds and farm ponds. Bower oaks grew high in the roadway parks. Sheep fed in hay grazer that was higher than their heads; they were small white islands in it. There was local wine and choc beer and cider for sale at small booths, along with limestone sculpture and painted fruitwood carvings. Kids danced on loading stoas to little postmounted music canisters, and goats licked slate outcroppings in search of some new mineral.

The Saturday riders passed a roadway restaurant with its tables out under the leaves and under a little rock overhang. A one-meter-high waterfall gushed through the middle of the establishment, and a two-meter-long bridge of set shale stone led to the kitchen. Then they broke onto view after never-tiring view of the rich and varied quasiurbia. The roadway forms, the fringe farms, the berry patches! In their seasons: Juneberries, huckleberries, blueberries, dewberries, elderberries, highbush cranberries, red raspberries, boysenberries, loganberries, nine kinds of blackberries, strawberries, greenberries.

Orchards! Can there ever be enough orchards? Plum, peach, sand plum and chokecherry, black cherry, apple and crabapple, pear, blue-fruited pawpaw, persimmon, crooked quince. Melon patches, congregations of beehives, pickle patches, cheese farms, flax farms, close clustered towns (twenty houses in each, twenty persons in a house, twenty of the little settlements along every mile of roadway), country honky-tonks, as well as highdog clubs already open and hopping with action in the early morning; roadway chapels with local statuary and with their rich-box-poor-boxes (one dropped money in the top if one had it and the spirit to give it, one tripped it out the bottom if one needed it), and the little refrigeration niches with bread, cheese, beef rolls, and always the broached cask of country wine: that there be no more hunger on the roadways forever!

"I hear it too!" old Charles Archer cried out suddenly. "High-pitched and off to the left. And there's the smell of monoxide and—gah—rubber. Conductor, conductor!"

The conductor heard it, as did others in the car. The conductor stopped the cars to listen. Then he phoned the report and gave the location as well as he might, consulting with the passengers. There was rough country over to the left, rocks and hills, and someone was driving there in broad daylight.

The conductor broke out rifles from the locker, passing them out to Peter Brady and two other young men in the car, and to three men in each of the other two cars. A competent-seeming man took over the communication, talking to men on a line farther to the left, beyond the mad driver, and they had him boxed into a box no more than half a mile square.

"You stay, Angela, and you stay, Great-grandfather Archer," Peter Brady said. "Here is a little thirty carbine. Use it if he comes in range at all. We'll hunt him down now." Then Peter Brady followed the conductor and the rifle-bearing men, ten men on a death hunt. And there were now four other groups out on the hunt, converging on their whining, coughing target.

"Why do they have to kill them, Great-grandfather? Why not turn them over to the courts?"

"The courts are too lenient. All they give them is life in prison."

"But surely that should be enough. It will keep them from driving the things, and some of the unfortunate men might even be rehabilitated."

"Angela, they are the greatest prison breakers ever. Only ten days ago, Mad Man Gudge killed three guards, went over the wall at State Prison, evaded all pursuit, robbed the cheesemakers' cooperative of fifteen thousand dollars, got to a sly klunker maker, and was driving one of the things in a wild area within thirty hours of his breakout. It was four days before they found him and killed him. They are insane, Angela, and the mental hospitals are already full of them. Not one of them has ever been rehabilitated."

"Why is it so bad that they should drive? They usually drive only in the very wild places, and for a few hours in the middle of the night."

"Their madness is infectious, Angela. Their arrogance would leave no room for anything else in the world. Our country is now in balance, our communication and travel is minute and near perfect, thanks to the wonderful trolleys and the people of the trolleys. We are all one neighborhood, we are all one family! We live in love and compassion, with few rich and few poor, and arrogance and hatred have all gone out from us. We are the people with roots, and with trolleys. We are one with our earth."

"Would it hurt that the drivers should have their own limited place to do what they wanted, if they did not bother sane people?"

"Would it hurt if disease and madness and evil were given their own limited place? But they will not stay in their place, Angela. There is the diabolical arrogance in them, the rampant individualism, the hatred of order. There can be nothing more dangerous to society than the man in the automobile. Were they allowed to thrive, there would be poverty and want again, Angela, and wealth and accumulation. And cities."

"But cities are the most wonderful things of all! I love to go to them."

"I do not mean the wonderful Excursion Cities, Angela. There would be cities of another and blacker sort. They were almost upon us once when a limitation was set on them. Uniqueness is lost in them; there would be mere accumulation of rootless people, of arrogant people, of duplicated people, of people who have lost their humanity. Let them

245

never rob us of our involuted countryside, or our quasiurbia. We are not perfect; but what we have, we will not give away for the sake of wild men."

"The smell! I cannot stand it!"

"Monoxide. How would you like to be born in the smell of it, to live every moment of your life in the smell of it, to die in the smell of it?"

"No, no, not that."

The rifleshots were scattered but serious. The howling and coughing of the illicit klunker automobile were nearer. Then it was in sight, bouncing and bounding weirdly out of the rough rock area and into the tomato patches straight toward the trolley interurban.

The klunker automobile was on fire, giving off a ghastly stench of burning leather and rubber and noxious monoxide and seared human flesh. The man, standing up at the broken wheel, was a madman, howling, out of his head. He was a young man, but sunken-eyed and unshaven, bloodied on the left side of his head and the left side of his breast, foaming with hatred and arrogance.

"Kill me! Kill me!" he croaked like clattering broken thunder. "There will be others! We will not leave off driving so long as there is one desolate place left, so long as there is one sly klunker maker left!"

He went rigid. He quivered. He was shot again. But he would die howling.

"Damn you all to trolley heaven! A man in an automobile is worth a thousand on foot! He is worth a million men in a trolley car! You never felt your black heart rise up in you when you took control of one of the monsters! You never felt the lively hate choke you off in rapture as you sneered down the whole world from your bouncing center of the universe! Damn all decent folks! I'd rather go to hell in an automobile than to heaven in a trolley car!"

A spoked wheel broke, sounding like one of the muted volleys of rifle fire coming from behind him. The klunker automobile pitched onto its nose, upended, turned over, and exploded in blasting flames. And still in the middle of the fire could be seen the two hypnotic eyes with their darker flame, could be heard the demented voice:

"The crankshaft will still be good, the differential will still be good, a sly klunker maker can use part of it, part of it will drive again—*ahhhiiii.*"

Some of them sang as they rode away from the site in the trolley cars, and some of them were silent and thoughtful. It had been an unnerving thing.

"It curdles me to remember that I once put my entire fortune into that future," Great-grandfather Charles Archer moaned. "Well, that is better than to have lived in such a future."

A young couple had happily loaded all their belongings onto a baggage trolley and were moving from one of the Excursion Cities to live with kindred in quasiurbia. The population of that Excursion City (with its wonderful theaters and music halls and distinguished restaurants and literary coffeehouses and alcoholic oases and amusement centers) had now reached seven thousand persons, the legal limit for any city. Oh, there were a thousand Excursion Cities and all of them delightful! But a limit must be kept on size. A limit must be kept on everything.

It was a wonderful Saturday afternoon. Fowlers caught birds with collapsible kite-cornered nets. Kids rode free out to the diamonds to play Trolley League ball. Old gaffers rode out with pigeons in pigeon boxes, to turn them loose and watch them race home. Shore netters took shrimp from the semisaline Little Shrimp Lake. Banjo players serenaded their girls in grassy lanes.

The world was one single bronze gong song with the melodious clang of trolley cars threading the country on their green-iron rails, with the sparky fire following them overhead and their copper gleaming in the sun. By law there must be a trolley line every mile, but they were oftener. By law no one trolley line might run for more than twenty-five miles. This was to give a sense of locality. But transfers between the lines were worked out perfectly. If one wished to cross the nation, one rode on some one hundred and twenty different lines. There were no more long-distance railroads. They also had had their arrogance, and they also had had to go.

Carp in the ponds, pigs in the clover, a unique barn-factory in every hamlet and every hamlet unique, bees in the air, pepper plants in the lanes, and the whole land as sparky as trolley fire and right as rails.

The Lucky Strike

Kim Stanley Robinson

War breeds strange pastimes. In July of 1945 on Tinian Island in the North Pacific, Captain Frank January had taken to piling pebble cairns on the crown of Mount Lasso—one pebble for each B-29 takeoff, one cairn for each mission. It was a mindless pastime, but so was poker. The men of the 509th had played a million hands of poker, sitting in the shade of a palm around an upturned crate, sweating in their skivvies, swearing and betting all their pay and cigarettes, playing hand after hand, until the cards got so soft and dog-eared you could have used them for toilet paper. Captain January had gotten sick of it, and after he lit out for the hilltop a few times some of his crewmates started trailing him. When their pilot, Jim Fitch, joined them it became an official pastime, like throwing flares into the compound or going hunting for stray Japs. What Captain January thought of the development he didn't say. The others grouped near Captain Fitch, who passed around his battered flask. "Hey, January," Fitch called. "Come and have a shot."

January wandered over and took the flask. Fitch laughed at his pebble. "Practicing your bombing up here, eh, Professor?"

"Yeah," January said sullenly. Anyone who read more than the funnies was Professor to Fitch. Thirstily January knocked back some rum. He passed the flask on to Lieutenant Matthews, their navigator.

"That's why he's the best," Matthews joked. "Always practicing."

Fitch laughed. "He's best because I make him be best, right, Professor?"

January frowned. Fitch was a bulky youth, thick-featured, pig-eyed—a thug, in January's opinion. The rest of the crew were all in their mid-twenties, like Fitch, and they liked the captain's bossy roughhouse style. January, who was thirty-seven, didn't go for it. He wandered away, back to the cairn he had been building. From Mount Lasso they had an overview of the whole island, from the harbor at Wall Street to the north field in Harlem. January had observed hundreds of B-29s roar off the four parallel runways of the north field and head for Japan. The last quartet of this particular mission buzzed across the width of the island, and January dropped four more pebbles, aiming for crevices in the pile. One of them stuck nicely.

"There they are!" said Matthews. "They're on the taxiing strip."

January located the 509th's first plane. Today, the first of August, there was something more interesting to watch than the usual Superfortress parade. Word was out that General LeMay wanted to take the 509th's mission away from it. Their commander, Colonel Tibbets, had gone and bitched to LeMay in person, and the general had agreed the mission was theirs, but on one condition—one of the general's men was to make a test flight with the 509th to make sure they were fit for combat over Japan. The general's man had arrived, and now he was down there in the strike plane with Tibbets and the whole first team. January sidled back to his mates to view the takeoff with them.

"Why don't the strike plane have a name, though?" Haddock was saying.

Fitch said, "Lewis won't give it a name because it's not his plane, and he knows it." The others laughed. Lewis and his crew were naturally unpopular, being Tibbets's favorites.

"What do you think he'll do to the general's man?" Matthews asked.

The others laughed at the very idea. "He'll kill an engine at takeoff, I bet you anything," Fitch said. He pointed at the wrecked B-29s that marked the end of every runway. "He'll want to show that he wouldn't go down if it happened to him."

"Course he wouldn't!" Matthews said.

"You hope," January said under his breath.

"They let those Wrights out too soon," Haddock said seriously. "They keep busting under the takeoff load."

"Won't matter to the old bull," Matthews said. Then they all started in about Tibbets's flying ability, even Fitch. They all thought Tibbets was the greatest. January, on the other hand, liked Tibbets even less than he liked Fitch. That had started right after he was assigned to the 509th. He had been told he was part of the most important group in the war and then given a leave. In Vicksburg a couple of fliers just back from England had bought him a lot of whiskeys, and since January had spent several months stationed near London they had talked for a good long time and gotten pretty drunk. The two were really curious about what January was up to now, but he had stayed vague on it and kept returning the talk to the blitz. He had seen an English nurse, for instance, whose flat had been bombed, family killed. . . . But they had really wanted to know. So he had told them he was onto something special, and they had flipped out their badges and told him they were Army Intelligence, and that if he ever broke security like that again he'd be transferred to Alaska. It was a dirty trick. January had gone back to Wendover and told Tibbets so to his face, and Tibbets had turned red and threatened him some more. January despised him for that. During their year's training he had bombed better than ever, as a way of showing the old bull he was wrong. Every time their eyes had met it was clear what was going on. But Tibbets never backed off no matter how precise January's bombing got. Just thinking about it was enough to cause January to line up a pebble over an ant and drop it.

"Will you cut that out?" Fitch complained.

January pointed. "They're going."

Tibbets's plane had taxied to runway Baker. Fitch passed the flask around again. The tropical sun beat on them, and the ocean surrounding the island blazed white. January put up a sweaty hand to aid the bill of his baseball cap.

The four props cut in hard, and the sleek Superfortress quickly trundled up to speed and roared down Baker. Three quarters of the way down the strip the outside right prop feathered.

"Yow!" Fitch crowed. "I told you he'd do it!"

The plane nosed off the ground and slewed right, then pulled back on course to cheers from the four young men around January. January pointed again. "He's cut number three, too."

The inside right prop feathered, and now the plane was pulled up by the left wing only, while the two right props windmilled uselessly. "Holy smoke!" Haddock cried. "Ain't the old bull something?"

They whooped to see the plane's power and Tibbets's nervy arrogance.

"By God, LeMay's man will remember this flight," Fitch hooted. "Why, look at that! He's banking!"

Apparently taking off on two engines wasn't enough for Tibbets; he banked the plane right until it was standing on its dead wing, and it curved back toward Tinian.

Then the inside left engine feathered.

War tears at the imagination. For three years Frank January had kept his imagination trapped, refusing to give it any play whatsoever. The dangers threatening him, the effects of the bombs, the fate of the other participants in the war—he had refused to think about any of it. But the war tore at his control. That English nurse's flat. The missions over the Ruhr. The bomber just below him blown apart by flak. And then there had been a year in Utah, and the viselike grip that he had once kept on his imagination had slipped away.

So when he saw the number two prop feather, his heart gave a little jump against his sternum, and helplessly he was up there with Ferebee, the first-team bombardier. He would be looking over the pilots' shoulders . . .

"Only one engine?" Fitch said.

"That one's for real," January said harshly. Despite himself he *saw* the panic in the cockpit, the frantic rush to power the two right engines. The plane was dropping fast and Tibbets leveled it off, leaving them on a course back toward the island. The two right props spun, blurred to a shimmer. January held his breath. They needed more lift; Tibbets was trying to pull it over the island. Maybe he was trying for the short runway on the south half of the island.

But Tinian was too tall, the plane too heavy. It roared right into the jungle above the beach, where Forty-second Street met their East River. It exploded in a bloom of fire. By the time the sound of it struck them they knew no one in the plane had survived.

Black smoke towered into white sky. In the shocked silence on Mount Lasso, insects buzzed and creaked. The air left January's lungs with a gulp. He had been with Ferebee, he had heard the desperate shouts, seen the last green rush, been stunned by the dentist-drill-all-over pain of the impact.

"Oh my God," Fitch was saying. "Oh my God." Matthews was sitting. January picked up the flask, tossed it at Fitch.

"C-come on," he stuttered. He hadn't stuttered since he was sixteen. He led the others in a rush down the hill. When they got to Broadway a jeep careened toward them and skidded to a halt. It was Colonel Scholes, the old bull's exec. "What happened?"

Fitch told him.

"Those damned Wrights," Scholes said as the men piled in. This time one had failed at just the wrong moment; some welder in the States had kept flame to metal a second less than usual—or something equally minor, equally trivial—and that had made all the difference.

They left the jeep at Forty-second and Broadway and hiked east over a narrow track to the shore. A fairly large circle of trees was burning. The fire trucks were already there. Scholes stood beside January, his expression bleak. "That was the whole first team," he said. "I know," said January. He was still in shock, his imagination crushed, incinerated, destroyed. Once as a kid he had tied sheets to his arms and waist, jumped off the roof, and landed right on his chest; this felt like that had. He had no way of knowing what would come of this crash, but he had a suspicion that he had indeed smacked into something hard. Scholes shook his head. A half-hour had passed, the fire was nearly out. January's four mates were over chattering with the Seabees. "He was going to name the plane after his mother," Scholes said to the ground. "He told me that just this morning. He was going to call it *Enola Gay.*"

At night the jungle breathed, and its hot wet breath washed over the 509th's compound. January stood in the doorway of his Quonset barracks hoping for a real breeze. No poker tonight. Noises were hushed, faces solemn. Some of the men had helped box up the dead crew's gear. Now most lay on their bunks. January gave up on the breeze, climbed onto his top bunk to stare at the ceiling.

He observed the corrugated arch over him. Cricket song sawed through his thoughts. Below him a rapid conversation was being carried on in guilty undertones, Fitch at its center. "January is the best bombardier left," he said. "And I'm as good as Lewis was."

"But so is Sweeney," Matthews said. "And he's in with Scholes."

They were figuring out who would take over the strike. January scowled. Tibbets and the rest were less than twelve hours dead, and they were squabbling over who would replace them.

January grabbed a shirt, rolled off his bunk, put the shirt on.

"Hey, Professor," Fitch said, "where you going?"

"Out."

Though midnight was near, it was still sweltering. Crickets shut up as he walked by, started again behind him. He lit a cigarette. In the dark the MPs patrolling their compound were like pairs of walking armbands. Forcefully January expelled smoke, as if he could expel his disgust with it. They were only kids, he told himself. Their minds had been shaped in the war, by the war, and for the war. They knew you couldn't mourn the dead for long; carry around a load like that and your own engines might fail. That was all right with January. It was an attitude that Tibbets had helped to form, so it was what he deserved. Tibbets would *want* to be forgotten in favor of the mission; all he had lived for was to drop the gimmick on the Japs, and he was oblivious to anything else—men, wife, family, anything.

So it wasn't the lack of feeling in his mates that bothered January. And it was natural of them to want to fly the strike they had been training a year for. Natural, that is, if you were a kid with a mind shaped by fanatics like Tibbets, shaped to take orders and never imagine consequences. But January was not a kid, and he wasn't going to let men like Tibbets do a thing to his mind. And the gimmick . . . the gimmick was not natural. A chemical bomb of some sort, he guessed. Against the Geneva convention. He stubbed his cigarette against the sole of his sneaker, tossed the butt over the fence. The tropical night breathed over him. He had a headache.

For months now he had been sure he would never fly a strike. The dislike Tibbets and he had exchanged in their looks (January was acutely aware of looks) had been real and strong. Tibbets had understood that January's record of pinpoint accuracy in the runs over the Salton Sea had been a way of showing contempt. The record had forced him to keep January on one of the four second-string teams, but with the fuss they were making over the gimmick January had figured that would be far enough down the ladder to keep him out of things.

Now he wasn't so sure. Tibbets was dead. He lit another cigarette, found his hand shaking. The Camel tasted bitter. He threw it over the fence at a receding armband and regretted it instantly. A waste. He went back inside.

Before climbing onto his bunk he got a paperback out of his footlocker. "Hey, Professor, what you reading now?" Fitch said, grinning. January showed him the blue cover. *Winter's Tales*, by an Isak Dinesen. Fitch examined the little wartime edition. "Pretty racy, eh?"

"You bet," January said heavily. "This guy puts sex on every page." He climbed onto his bunk, opened the book. The stories were strange, hard to follow. The voices below bothered him. He concentrated harder.

As a boy on the farm in Arkansas, January had read everything he could lay his hands on. On Saturday afternoons he would race his father down the muddy lane to the mailbox (his father was a reader too), grab the *Saturday Evening Post*, and run off to devour every word of it. That meant he had another week with nothing new to read, but he couldn't help it. It was a way off the farm, a way into the world. He had become a man who could slip between the covers of a book whenever he chose.

But not on this night.

The next day the chaplain gave a memorial service, and on the morning after that Colonel Scholes looked in the door of their hut right after mess. "Briefing at eleven," he announced. His face was haggard. "Be there early." He looked at Fitch with bloodshot eyes, crooked a finger. "Fitch, January, Matthews—come with me."

January put on his shoes. The rest of the men sat on their bunks and watched them wordlessly. January followed Fitch and Matthews out of the hut.

"I've spent most of the night on the radio with General LeMay," Scholes said. He looked them each in the eye. "We've decided you're to be the first crew to make a strike."

Fitch was nodding, as if he had expected it.

"Think you can do it?" Scholes said.

"Of course," Fitch replied. Watching him, January understood why they had chosen him to replace Tibbets. Fitch was like the old bull, he had that same ruthlessness. The young bull.

"Yes sir," Matthews said.

Scholes was looking at him. "Sure," January said, not wanting to think about it. "Sure." His heart was pounding directly on his sternum. But Fitch and Matthews looked serious as owls, so he wasn't going to stick out by looking odd. It was big news, after all; anyone would be taken aback by it. Nevertheless, January made an effort to nod.

"Okay," Scholes said. "McDonald will be flying with you as co-pilot." Fitch frowned. "I've got to go tell those British officers that LeMay doesn't want them on the strike with you. See you at the briefing."

"Yes sir."

As soon as Scholes was around the corner Fitch swung a fist at the sky. "Yow!" Matthews cried. He and Fitch shook hands. "We did it!" Matthews took January's hand and wrung it, his face plastered with a goofy grin. "We did it!"

"Somebody did it, anyway," January said.

"Ah, Frank," Matthews said. "Show some spunk. You're always so cool."

"Old Professor Stoneface," Fitch said, glancing at January with a trace of amused contempt. "Come on, let's get to the briefing."

The briefing hut, one of the longer Quonsets, was completely surrounded by MPs holding carbines. "Gosh," Matthews said, subdued by the sight. Inside, it was already smoky. The walls were covered by the usual maps of Japan. Two blackboards at the front were draped with sheets. Captain Shepard, the naval officer who worked with the scientists on the gimmick, was in back with his assistant Lieutenant Stone, winding a reel of film onto a projector. Dr. Nelson, the group psychiatrist, was already seated on a front bench near the wall. Tibbets had recently sicced the psychiatrist on the group—another one of his great ideas, like the spies in the bar. The man's questions had struck January as stupid. He hadn't even been able to figure out that Easterly was a flake, something that was clear to anybody who flew with him or even played him in a single round of poker. January slid onto a bench beside his mates.

The two Brits entered, looking furious in their stiff-upper-lip way. They sat on the bench behind January. Sweeney's and Easterly's crews filed in, followed by the other men, and soon the room was full. Fitch and the rest pulled out Lucky Strikes and lit up; since they had named the plane only January had stuck with Camels.

Scholes came in with several men January didn't recognize and went to the front. The chatter died, and all the smoke plumes ribboned steadily into the air.

Scholes nodded, and two intelligence officers took the sheets off the blackboards, revealing aerial reconnaissance photos.

"Men," Scholes said, "these are the target cities."

Someone cleared his throat.

"In order of priority they are Hiroshima, Kokura, and Nagasaki. There will be three weather scouts—*Straight Flush* to Hiroshima, *Strange Cargo* to Kokura, and *Full House* to Nagasaki. *The Great Artiste* and *Number 91* will be accompanying the mission to take photos. And *Lucky Strike* will fly the bomb."

There were rustles, coughs. Men turned to look at January and his mates, and they all sat up straight. Sweeney stretched back to shake Fitch's hand, and there were some quick laughs. Fitch grinned.

"Now listen up," Scholes went on. "The weapon we are going to deliver was successfully tested stateside a couple weeks ago. And now we've got orders to drop it on the enemy." He paused to let that sink in. "I'll let Captain Shepard tell you more."

Shepard walked to the blackboard slowly, savoring his entrance. His forehead was shiny with sweat, and January realized he was excited or nervous. He wondered what the psychiatrist would make of that.

"I'm going to come right to the point," Shepard said. "The bomb you are going to drop is something new in history. We think it will knock out everything within four miles."

Now the room was completely still. January noticed that he could see a great deal of his nose, eyebrows, and cheeks; it was as if he were receding back into his body, like a fox into its hole. He kept his gaze rigidly on Shepard, steadfastly ignoring the feeling. Shepard pulled a sheet back over a blackboard while someone else turned down the lights. "This is a film of the only test we have made," Shepard said. The film started, caught, started again. A wavery cone of bright cigarette smoke speared the length of the room, and on the sheet sprang a dead gray landscape—a lot of sky, a smooth desert floor, hills in the distance. The projector went *click-click-click-click, click-click-click-click.* "The bomb is on top of the tower," Shepard said, and January focused on the pinlike object sticking out of the desert floor, off against the hills. It was between eight and ten miles from the camera, he judged; he had gotten good at calculating distances. He was still distracted by his face.

Click-click-click-click, click—then the screen went white for a second, filling even their room with light. When the picture returned the desert floor was filled with a white bloom of fire. The fireball coalesced, and then quite suddenly it leaped off the earth all the way into the *stratosphere,* by God, like a tracer bullet leaving a machine gun, trailing a whitish pillar of smoke behind it. The pillar gushed up, and a growing ball of smoke billowed outward, capping the pillar. January calculated the size of the cloud but was sure he got it wrong. There it stood. The picture flickered, and then the screen went white again, as if the camera had melted or that part of the world had come apart. But the flapping from the projector told them it was the end of the film.

January felt the air suck in and out of his open mouth. The lights came on in the smoky room, and for a second he panicked. He struggled to shove his features into an accepted pattern—the psychiatrist would be looking around at them all—and then he glanced around and realized he needn't have worried, that he wasn't alone. Faces were bloodless, eyes were blinky or bugged out with shock, mouths hung open or were clamped whitely shut. For a few moments they all had to acknowledge what they were doing. January, scaring himself, felt an urge to say, "Play it again, will you?" Fitch was pulling his curled black hair off his thug's forehead uneasily. Beyond him January saw that one of the Limeys had already reconsidered how mad he was about missing the flight. Now he looked sick. Someone let out a long *whew,* another whistled. January looked to the front again, where Dr. Nelson watched them, undisturbed.

Shepard said, "It's big, all right. And no one knows what will happen when it's dropped from the air. But the mushroom cloud you saw will go to at least thirty thousand feet, probably sixty. And the flash you saw at the beginning was hotter than the sun."

257

Hotter than the sun. More licked lips, hard swallows, readjusted baseball caps. One of the intelligence officers passed out tinted goggles like welder's glasses. January took his and twiddled the opacity dial. Scholes said, "You're the hottest thing in the armed forces, now. So no talking, even among yourselves." He took a deep breath. "Let's do it the way Colonel Tibbets would have wanted us to. He picked every one of you because you were the best, and now's the time to show he was right. So—so let's make the old man proud."

The briefing was over. Men filed out into the sudden sunlight. Into the heat and glare. Captain Shepard approached Fitch. "Stone and I will be flying with you to take care of the bomb," he said.

Fitch nodded. "Do you know how many strikes we'll fly?"

"As many as it takes to make them quit." Shepard stared hard at all of them. "But it will only take one."

War breeds strange dreams. That night, January writhed over his sheets in the hot, wet, vegetable night, in that frightening half sleep when you sometimes know you are dreaming but can do nothing about it, and he dreamed he was walking . . .

. . . *walking through the streets when suddenly the sun swoops down, the sun touches down and everything is instantly darkness and smoke and silence, a deaf roaring. Walls of fire. His head hurts and in the middle of his vision is a blue-white blur as if God's camera went off in his face. Ah—the sun fell, he thinks. His arm is burned. Blinking is painful. People stumbling by, mouths open, horribly burned—*

He is a priest, he can feel the clerical collar, and the wounded ask him for help. He points to his ears, tries to touch them but can't. Pall of black smoke over everything, the city has fallen into the streets. Ah, it's the end of the world. In a park he finds shade and cleared ground. People crouch under bushes like animals. Where the park meets the river, red and black figures crowd into steaming water. A figure gestures from a copse of bamboo. He enters it, finds five or six faceless soldiers huddling. Their eyes have melted, their mouths are holes. Deafness spares him their words. The sighted soldier mimes drinking. The soldiers are thirsty. He nods and goes to the river in search of a container. Bodies float downstream.

Hours pass as he hunts fruitlessly for a bucket. He pulls people from the rubble. He hears a bird screeching, and he realizes that his deafness is the roar of the city burning, a roar like the blood in his ears, but he is not deaf, he only thought he was because there are no human cries. The people are suffering in silence. Through the dusky night he stumbles back to the river, pain crashing through his head. In a field, men are pulling potatoes out of the ground that have been baked well enough to eat. He shares one with them. At the river everyone is dead—

—and he struggled out of the nightmare drenched in rank sweat, the taste of dirt in his mouth, his stomach knotted with horror. He sat up, and the wet, rough sheet clung to his skin. His heart felt crushed between lungs desperate for air. The flowery rotting-jungle smell filled him, and images from the dream flashed before him so vividly that in the dim hut he saw nothing else. He grabbed his cigarettes and jumped off the bunk, hurried out into the compound. Trembling, he lit up, started pacing around. For a moment he worried that the idiot psychiatrist might see him, but then he dismissed the idea. Nelson would be asleep. They were all asleep. He shook his head, looked down at his right arm, and almost dropped his cigarette—but it was just his stove scar, an old scar. He'd had it most of his life, since the day he'd pulled the frypan off the stove and onto his arm, burning it with oil. He could still remember the round O of fear that his mother's mouth had made as she rushed in to see what was wrong. Just an old burn scar, he thought, let's not go overboard here. He pulled his sleeve down.

For the rest of the night he tried to walk it off, cigarette after cigarette. The dome of the sky lightened until all the compound and the jungle beyond it was visible. He was forced by the light of day to walk back into his hut and lie down as if nothing had happened.

Two days later Scholes ordered them to take one of LeMay's men over Rota for a test run. This new lieutenant colonel ordered Fitch not to play with the engines on takeoff. They flew a perfect run, January put the dummy gimmick right on the aiming point, and Fitch powered the plane down into the violent bank that started their 150-degree turn and flight for safety. Back on Tinian the lieutenant colonel congratulated them and shook each of their hands. January smiled with the rest, palms cool, heart steady. It was as if his body were a shell, something he could manipulate from without, like a bombsight. He ate well, he chatted as much as he ever had, and when the psychiatrist ran him to earth for some questions, he was friendly and seemed open.

"Hello, Doc."

"How do you feel about all this, Frank?"

"Just like I always have, sir. Fine."

"Eating well?"

"Better than ever."

"Sleeping well?"

"As well as I can in this humidity. I got used to Utah, I'm afraid." Dr. Nelson laughed. Actually January had hardly slept since his dream. He was afraid of sleep. Couldn't the man see that?

259

"And how do you feel about being part of the crew chosen to make the first strike?"

"Well, it was the right choice, I reckon. We're the b—— the best crew left."

"Do you feel sorry about Tibbets's crew's accident?"

"Yes sir, I do." You better believe it.

After the jokes that ended the interview, January walked out into the blaze of the tropical noon and lit a cigarette. He allowed himself to feel how much he despised the psychiatrist and his blind profession at the same time he was waving good-bye to the man. Ounce brain. Why couldn't he have seen? Whatever happened it would be his fault. . . . With a rush of smoke out of him January realized how painfully easy it was to fool someone if you wanted to. All action was no more than a mask that could be perfectly manipulated from somewhere else. And all the while in that somewhere else, January lived in a *click-click-click* of film, in the silent roaring of a dream, struggling against images he couldn't dispel. The heat of the tropical sun—ninety-three million miles away, wasn't it?—pulsed painfully on the back of his neck.

As he watched the psychiatrist collar their tail gunner, Kochenski, he thought of walking up to the man and saying *I quit*. I don't want to do this. In imagination he saw the look that would form in the man's eye, in Fitch's eye, in Tibbets's eye, and his mind recoiled from the idea. He felt too much contempt for them. He wouldn't for anything give them a means to despise him, a reason to call him coward. Stubbornly he banished the whole complex of thought. Easier to go along with it.

And so a couple of disjointed days later, just after midnight of August 9, he found himself preparing for the strike. Around him Fitch and Matthews and Haddock were doing the same. How odd were the everyday motions of getting dressed when you were off to demolish a city! January found himself examining his hands, his boots, the cracks in the linoleum. He put on his survival vest, checked the pockets abstractedly for fishhooks, water kit, first-aid package, emergency rations. Then the parachute harness, and his coveralls over it all. Tying his bootlaces took minutes; he couldn't do it when watching his fingers so closely.

"Come on, Professor!" Fitch's voice was tight. "The big day is here."

He followed the others into the night. A cool wind was blowing. The chaplain said a prayer for them. They took jeeps down Broadway to runway Able. *Lucky Strike* stood in a circle of spotlights and men, half of them with cameras, the rest with reporters' pads. They surrounded the crew; it reminded January of a Hollywood premiere. Eventually he escaped up the hatch and into the plane. Others followed. Half an hour passed before Fitch joined them, grinning like a movie star. They started the engines, and January was thankful for their vibrating, thought-smothering roar. They taxied away from the Hollywood scene, and January felt relief for a moment, until he remembered where they were going. On runway Able the engines pitched up to their twenty-three-hundred-RPM whine, and looking out the clear windscreen, he saw the runway paint marks move by ever faster. Fitch kept them on the runway till Tinian had run out from under them, then quickly pulled up. They were on their way.

When they got to altitude, January climbed past Fitch and McDonald to the bombardier's seat and placed his parachute on it. He leaned back. The roar of the four engines packed around him like cotton batting. He was on the flight, nothing to be done about it now. The heavy vibration was a comfort, he liked the feel of it there in the nose of the plane. A drowsy, sad acceptance hummed through him.

Against his closed eyelids flashed a black eyeless face, and he jerked awake, heart racing. He was on the flight, no way out. Now he realized how easy it would have been to get out of it. He could have just said he didn't want to. The simplicity of it appalled him. Who gave a damn what the shrink or Tibbets or anyone else thought, compared to this? Now there was no way out. It was a comfort, in a way. Now he could stop worrying, stop thinking he had any choice.

Sitting there with his knees bracketing the bombsight, January dozed, and as he dozed he daydreamed his way out. He could climb the step to Fitch and McDonald and declare he had been secretly promoted to major and ordered to redirect the mission. They were to go to Tokyo and drop the bomb in the bay. The Jap War Cabinet had been told to watch this demonstration of the new weapon, and when they saw that fireball boil the bay and bounce into heaven they'd run and sign surrender papers as fast as they could write, kamikazes or not. They weren't crazy, after all. No need to murder a whole city. It was such a good plan that the generals were no doubt changing the mission at this very minute, desperately radioing their instructions to Tinian, only to find out it was too late . . . so that when they returned to Tinian, January would become a hero for guessing what the generals really wanted and for risking all to do it. It would be like one of the Hornblower stories he had read in the *Saturday Evening Post*.

Once again January jerked awake. The drowsy pleasure of the fantasy was replaced with desperate scorn. There wasn't a chance in hell that he could convince Fitch and the rest that he had secret orders superseding theirs. And he couldn't go up there and wave his pistol around and *order* them to drop the bomb in Tokyo Bay, because he was the one who had to actually drop it, and he couldn't be down in front dropping the bomb and up ordering the others around at the same time. Pipe dreams.

Time swept on, slow as a second hand. January's thoughts, however, matched the spin of the props; desperately they cast about, now this way now that, like an animal caught by the leg in a trap. The crew was silent. The clouds below were a white scree on the black ocean. January's knee vibrated against the bombsight. He was the one who had to drop the bomb. No matter where his thoughts lunged, they were brought up short by that. He was the one, not Fitch or the crew, not LeMay, not the generals and scientists back home, not Truman and his advisors. Truman—suddenly January hated him. Roosevelt would have done it differently. If only Roosevelt had lived! The grief that had filled January when he learned of Roosevelt's death reverberated through him more strongly than ever. It was unfair to have worked so hard and then not see the war's end. And FDR would have ended it differently. Back at the start of it all he had declared that civilian centers were never to be bombed, and if he had lived, if, if, if. But he hadn't. And now it was smiling bastard Harry Truman, ordering *him,* Frank January, to drop the sun on two hundred thousand women and children. Once his father had taken him to see the Browns play before twenty thousand, a giant crowd— "I never voted for you," January whispered viciously and jerked to realize he had spoken aloud. Luckily his microphone was off. And Roosevelt would have done it differently, he *would have.*

The bombsight rose before him, spearing the black sky and blocking some of the hundreds of little cruciform stars. *Lucky Strike* ground on toward Iwo Jima, minute by minute flying four miles closer to their target. January leaned forward and put his face in the cool headrest of the bombsight, hoping that its grasp might hold his thoughts as well as his forehead. It worked surprisingly well.

His earphones crackled and he sat up. "Captain January." It was Shepard. "We're going to arm the bomb now, want to watch?"

"Sure thing." He shook his head, surprised at his own duplicity. Stepping up between the pilots, he moved stiffly to the roomy cabin behind the cockpit. Matthews was at his desk taking a navigational fix on the radio signals from Iwo Jima and Okinawa, and Haddock stood beside him. At the back of the compartment was a small circular hatch, below the larger tunnel leading to the rear of the plane. January opened it, sat down, and swung himself feetfirst through the hole.

The bomb bay was unheated, and the cold air felt good. He stood facing the bomb. Stone was sitting on the floor of the bay; Shepard was laid out under the bomb, reaching into it. On a rubber pad next to Stone were tools, plates, several cylindrical blocks. Shepard pulled back, sat up, sucked a scraped knuckle. He shook his head ruefully. "I don't dare wear gloves with this one."

"I'd be just as happy myself if you didn't let something slip," January joked nervously. The two men laughed.

"Nothing can blow till I change those wires," Stone said.

"Give me the wrench," Shepard said. Stone handed it to him, and he stretched under the bomb again. After some awkward wrenching inside it he lifted out a cylindrical plug. "Breech plug," he said, and set it on the mat.

January found his skin goose-pimpling in the cold air. Stone handed Shepard one of the blocks. Shepard extended under the bomb again. Watching them, January was reminded of auto mechanics on the oily floor of a garage, working under a car. He had spent a few years doing that himself, after his family moved to Vicksburg. Hiroshima was a river town. One time a flatbed truck carrying bags of cement powder down Fourth Street hill had lost its brakes and careened into the intersection with River Road, where, despite the driver's efforts to turn, it smashed into a passing car. Frank had been out in the yard playing and heard the crash and saw the cement dust rising. He had been one of the first there. The woman and child in the passenger seat of the Model T had been killed. The woman driving was okay. They were from Chicago. A group of folks subdued the driver of the truck, who kept trying to help at the Model T, though he had a bad cut on his head and was covered with white dust.

"Okay, let's tighten the breech plug." Stone gave Shepard the wrench. "Sixteen turns exactly," Shepard said. He was sweating even in the bay's chill, and he paused to wipe his forehead. "Let's hope we don't get hit by lightning." He put the wrench down, shifted onto his knees, and picked up a circular plate. Hubcap, January thought. Stone connected wires, then helped Shepard install two more plates. Good old American know-how, January thought, goose pimples rippling across his skin like cat's-paws over water. There was Shepard, a scientist, putting together a bomb like he was an auto mechanic changing oil. January felt a tight rush of rage at the scientists who had designed the bomb. They had worked on it for over a year. Had none of them in all that time ever stopped to think what they were doing?

But none of them had to drop it. January turned to hide his face from Shepard, stepped down the bay. The bomb looked like a big long trash can, with fins at one end and little antennae at the other. Just a bomb, he thought, damn it, it's just another bomb.

Shepard stood and patted the bomb gently. "We've got a live one now." Never a thought about what it would do. January hurried by the man, afraid that hatred would crack his shell and give him away. The pistol strapped to his belt caught on the hatchway, and he imagined shooting Shepard—shooting Fitch and McDonald and plunging the controls forward so that *Lucky Strike* tilted and spun down into the sea like a spent tracer bullet, like a plane broken by flak, following the arc of all human ambition. Nobody would ever know what had happened to them, and their trash can would be dumped to the bottom of the Pacific. He could even shoot everyone, parachute out, and perhaps be rescued by one of the Superdumbos following them . . .

The thought passed, and remembering it January squinted with disgust. But another part of him agreed that it was a possibility. It could be done. It would solve his problem.

"Want some coffee?" Matthews asked.

"Sure," January said, and took a cup. He sipped—hot. He watched Matthews and Benton tune the loran equipment. As the beeps came in, Matthews took a straightedge and drew lines from Okinawa and Iwo Jima. He tapped a finger on the intersection. "They've taken the art out of navigation," he said to January. "They might as well stop making the navigator's dome," thumbing up at the little Plexiglas bubble over them.

"Good old American know-how," January said.

Matthews nodded. With two fingers he measured the distance between their position and Iwo Jima. Benton measured with a ruler.

"Rendezvous at five thirty-five, eh?" Matthews said. They were to rendezvous with the two trailing planes over Iwo.

Benton disagreed. "I'd say five-fifty."

"What? Check again, guy, we're not in no tugboat here."

"The wind—"

"Yeah, the wind. Frank, you want to add a bet to the pool?"

"Five thirty-six," January said promptly.

They laughed. "See, he's got more confidence in me," Matthews said with a dopey grin.

January recalled his plan to shoot the crew and tip the plane into the sea, and he pursed his lips, repelled. Not for anything would he be able to shoot these men, who, if not friends, were at least companions. They passed for friends. They meant no harm.

Shepard and Stone climbed into the cabin. Matthews offered them coffee. "The gimmick's ready to kick their ass, eh?" Shepard nodded and drank.

January moved forward, past Haddock's console. Another plan that wouldn't work. What to do? All the flight engineer's dials and gauges showed conditions were normal. Maybe he could sabotage something? Cut a line somewhere?

Fitch looked back at him and said, "When are we due over Iwo?"

"Five-forty, Matthews says."

"He better be right."

A thug. In peacetime Fitch would be hanging around a pool table giving the cops trouble. He was perfect for war. Tibbets had chosen his men well—most of them, anyway. Moving back past Haddock, January stopped to stare at the group of men in the navigation cabin. They joked, drank coffee. They were all a bit like Fitch—young toughs, capable and thoughtless. They were having a good time, an adventure. That was January's dominant impression of his companions in the 509th; despite all the bitching and the occasional moments of overmastering fear, they were having a good time. His mind spun forward, and he saw what these young men would grow up to be like as clearly as if they stood before him in businessmen's suits, prosperous and balding. They would be tough and capable and thoughtless, and as the years passed and the great war receded in time they would look back on it with ever-increasing nostalgia, for they would be the survivors and not the dead. Every year of this war would feel like ten in their memories, so that the war would always remain the central experience of their lives—a time when history lay palpable in their hands, when each of their daily acts affected it, when moral issues were simple, and others told them what to do—so that as more years passed and the survivors aged, bodies falling apart, lives in one rut or another, they would unconsciously push harder and harder to thrust the world into war again, thinking somewhere inside themselves that if they could only return to world war then they would magically be again as they were in the last one—young and free and happy. And by that time they would hold the positions of power, they would be capable of doing it.

So there would be more wars, January saw. He heard it in Matthews's laughter, saw it in their excited eyes. "There's Iwo, and it's five thirty-one. Pay up! I win!" And in future wars they'd have more bombs like the gimmick, hundreds of them no doubt. He saw more planes, more young crews like this one, flying to Moscow, no doubt, or to wherever, fireballs in every capital. Why not? And to what end? To what end? So that the old men could hope to become magically young again. Nothing more sane than that. It made January sick.

They were over Iwo Jima. Three more hours to Japan. Voices from *The Great Artiste* and *Number 91* crackled on the radio. Rendezvous accomplished, the three planes flew northwest, toward Shikoku, the first Japanese island in their path. January maneuvered down into the nose. "Good shooting," Matthews called after him.

Forward it seemed quieter. January got settled, put his headphones on, and leaned forward to look out the ribbed Plexiglas.

Dawn had turned the whole vault of the sky pink. Slowly the radiant shade shifted through lavender to blue, pulse by pulse a different color. The ocean below was a glittering blue plane, marbled by a pattern of puffy pink cloud. The sky above was a vast dome, darker above than on the horizon. January had always thought that dawn was the time when you could see most clearly how big the earth was and how high above it they flew. It seemed they flew at the very upper edge of the atmosphere, and January saw how thin it was, how it was just a skin of air really, so that even if you flew up to its top the earth still extended away infinitely in every direction. The coffee had warmed January, he was sweating. Sunlight blinked off the Plexiglas. His watch said six. Plane and hemisphere of blue were split down the middle by the bombsight. His earphones crackled, and he listened in to the reports from the lead planes flying over the target cities. Kokura, Nagasaki, Hiroshima, all of them had six-tenths cloud cover. Maybe they would have to cancel the whole mission because of weather. "We'll look at Hiroshima first," Fitch said. January peered down at the fields of miniature clouds with renewed interest. His parachute slipped under him. Readjusting it, he imagined putting it on, sneaking back to the central escape hatch under the navigator's cabin, opening the hatch. . . . He could be out of the plane and gone before anyone noticed. They could bomb or not but it wouldn't be January's doing. He could float down onto the world like a puff of dandelion, feel cool air rush around him, watch the silk canopy dome hang over him like a miniature sky, a private world.

An eyeless black face. January shuddered; it was as though the nightmare could return any time. If he jumped nothing would change, the bomb would still fall—would he feel any better, floating on his Inland Sea? Sure, one part of him shouted; maybe, another conceded; the rest of him saw that face . . .

Earphones crackled. Shepard said, "Lieutenant Stone has now armed the bomb, and I can now tell you all what we are carrying. Aboard with us is the world's first atomic bomb."

Not exactly, January thought. Whistles squeaked in his earphones. The first one went off in New Mexico. Splitting atoms. January had heard the term before. Tremendous energy in every atom, Einstein had said. Break one, and—he had seen the result on film. Shepard was talking about radiation, which brought back more to January. Energy released in the form of X-rays. Killed by X-rays! It would be against the Geneva convention if they had thought of it.

Fitch cut in. "When the bomb is dropped Lieutenant Benton will record our reaction to what we see. This recording is being made for history, so watch your language." Watch your language! January choked back a laugh. Don't curse or blaspheme God at the sight of the first atomic bomb incinerating a city with X-rays!

Six-twenty. January found his hands clenched together on the headrest of the bombsight. He felt as if he had a fever. In the harsh wash of morning light the skin on the backs of his hands appeared slightly translucent. The whorls in the skin looked like the delicate patterning of waves on the sea's surface. His hands were made of atoms. Atoms were the smallest building blocks of matter. It took billions of them to make those tense, trembling hands. Split one atom and you had the fireball. That meant that the energy contained in even one hand . . . He turned up a palm to look at the lines and the mottled flesh under the transparent skin. A person was a bomb that could blow up the world. January felt that latent power stir in him, pulsing with every hard heart knock. What beings they were, and in what a blue expanse of a world! And here they spun on to drop a bomb and kill a hundred thousand of these astonishing beings.

When a fox or raccoon is caught by the leg in a trap, it lunges until the leg is frayed, twisted, perhaps broken, and only then does the animal's pain and exhaustion force it to quit. Now in the same way January wanted to quit. His mind hurt. His plans to escape were so much crap—stupid, useless. Better to quit. He tried to stop thinking, but it was hopeless. How could he stop? As long as he was conscious he would be thinking. The mind struggles longer than any fox.

Lucky Strike tilted up and began the long climb to bombing altitude. On the horizon the clouds lay over a green island. Japan. Surely it had gotten hotter. The heater must be broken, he thought. Don't think. Every few minutes Matthews gave Fitch small course adjustments. "Two seventy-five, now. That's it." To escape the moment, January recalled his childhood. Following a mule and plow. Moving to Vicksburg (rivers). For a while there in Vicksburg, since his stutter made it hard to gain friends, he had played a game with himself. He had passed the time by imagining that everything he did was vitally important and determined the fate of the world. If he crossed a road in front of a certain car, for instance, then the car wouldn't make it through the next intersection before a truck hit it, and so the man driving would be killed and wouldn't be able to invent the flying boat that would save President Wilson from kidnappers, so he had to wait for that car, oh damn it, he thought, damn it, think of something *different*. The last Hornblower story he had read— how would *he* get out of this? The round O of his mother's face as she ran in and saw his arm— The Mississippi, mud-brown behind its levees— Abruptly he shook his head, face twisted in frustration and despair, aware at last that no possible avenue of memory would serve as an escape for him now; for now there was no part of his life that did not apply to the situation he was in, and no matter where he cast his mind it was going to shore up against the hour facing him.

Less than an hour. They were at thirty thousand feet, bombing altitude. Fitch gave him altimeter readings to dial into the bombsight. Matthews gave him wind speeds. Sweat got in his eye and he blinked furiously. The sun rose behind them like an atomic bomb, glinting off every corner and edge of the Plexiglas, illuminating his bubble compartment with a fierce glare. Broken plans jumbled together in his mind, his breath was short, his throat dry. Uselessly and repeatedly he damned the scientists, damned Truman. Damned the Japanese for causing the whole mess in the first place, damned yellow killers, they had brought this on themselves. Remember Pearl. American men had died under bombs when no war had been declared; they had started it and now it was coming back to them with a vengeance. And they deserved it. And an invasion of Japan would take years, cost millions of lives. End it now, end it, they deserved it, they deserved it, steaming river full of charcoal people silently dying, damned stubborn race of maniacs!

"There's Honshu," Fitch said, and January returned to the world of the plane. They were over the Inland Sea. Soon they would pass the secondary target, Kokura, a bit to the south. Seven-thirty. The island was draped more heavily than the sea by clouds, and again January's heart leaped with the idea that weather would cancel the mission. But they did deserve it. It was a mission like any other mission. He had dropped bombs on Africa, Sicily, Italy, all Germany. . . . He leaned forward to take a look through the sight. Under the X of the cross hairs was the sea, but at the lead edge of the sight was land. Honshu. At two hundred and thirty miles an hour that gave them about a half hour to Hiroshima. Maybe less. He wondered if his heart could beat so hard for that long.

Fitch said, "Matthews, I'm giving over guidance to you. Just tell us what to do."

"Bear south two degrees," was all Matthews said. At last their voices had taken on a touch of awareness.

"January, are you ready?" Fitch asked.

"I'm just waiting," January said. He sat up so Fitch could see the back of his head. The bombsight stood between his legs. A switch on its side would start the bombing sequence—the bomb would not leave the plane immediately upon the flick of the switch but would drop after a fifteen-second radio tone warned the following planes. The sight was adjusted accordingly.

"Adjust to a heading of two sixty-five," Matthews said. "We're coming in directly upwind." This was to make any side-drift adjustments for the bomb unnecessary. "January, dial it down to two hundred and thirty-one miles per hour."

"Two thirty-one."

Fitch said, "Everyone but January and Matthews, get your goggles on."

January took the darkened goggles from the floor. One needed to protect one's eyes or they might melt. He put them on, put his forehead on the headrest. They were in the way. He took them off. When he looked through the sight again there was land under the cross hairs. He checked his watch. Eight o'clock. Up and reading the papers, drinking tea.

"Ten minutes to AP," Matthews said. The aiming point was Aioi Bridge, a T-shaped bridge in the middle of the delta-straddling city. Easy to recognize.

"There's a lot of cloud down there," Fitch noted. "Are you going to be able to see?"

"I won't be sure until we try it," January said.

"We can make another pass and use radar if we need to," Matthews said.

Fitch said, "Don't drop it unless you're sure, January."

"Yes sir."

Through the sight a grouping of rooftops and gray roads was just visible between broken clouds. Around it green forest. "All right," Matthews exclaimed, "here we go! Keep it right on this heading, Captain! January, we'll stay at two thirty-one."

"And same heading," Fitch said. "January, she's all yours. Everyone be ready for the turn."

January's world contracted to the view through the bombsight. A stippled field of cloud and forest. Over a small range of hills and into Hiroshima's watershed. The broad river was mud brown, the land pale hazy green, the growing network of roads flat gray. Now the tiny rectangular shapes of buildings covered almost all the land, and swimming into the sight came the city proper, narrow islands thrusting into a dark blue bay. Under the cross hairs the city moved island by island, cloud by cloud. January had stopped breathing. His fingers were rigid as stone on the switch. And there was Aioi Bridge. It slid right under the cross hairs, a tiny T right in a gap in the clouds. January's fingers crushed the switch. Deliberately he took a breath, held it. Clouds swam under the cross hairs, then the next island. "Almost there," he said calmly into his microphone. "Steady." Now that he was committed his heart was humming like the Wrights. He counted to ten. Now flowing under the cross hairs were clouds alternating with green forest, leaden roads. "I've turned the switch, but I'm not getting a tone!" he croaked into the mike. His right hand held the switch firmly in place. Behind him Fitch was shouting something; Matthews's voice cracked across it. "Flipping it b-back and forth," January shouted, shielding the bombsight with his body from the eyes of the pilots. "But *still*—wait a second—"

He pushed the switch down. A low hum filled his ears. "That's it! It started!"

"But where will it land?" Matthews cried.

"Hold steady!" January shouted.

Lucky Strike shuddered and lofted up ten or twenty feet. January twisted to look down, and there was the bomb, flying just below the plane. Then with a wobble it fell away.

The plane banked right and dove so hard that the centrifugal force threw January against the Plexiglas. Several thousand feet lower, Fitch leveled it out and they hurtled north.

"Do you see anything?" Fitch cried.

From the tail gun Kochenski gasped, "Nothing." January struggled upright. He reached for the welder's goggles, but they were no longer on his head. He couldn't find them. "How long has it been?" he said.

"Thirty seconds," Matthews replied.

January shut his eyes.

The blood in his eyelids lit up red, then white.

On the earphones a clutter of voices— "Oh my God. Oh my God." The plane bounced and tumbled, metallically shrieking. January pressed himself off the Plexiglas. "'Nother shock wave!" Kochenski yelled. The plane rocked again. This is it, January thought, end of the world, I guess that solves my problem.

He opened his eyes and found he could still see. The engines still roared, the props spun. "Those were the shock waves from the bomb," Fitch called. "We're okay now. Look at that! Will you look at that son of a bitch go!"

January looked. The cloud layer below had burst apart, and a black column of smoke billowed up from a core of red fire. Already the top of the column was at their height. Exclamations of shock hurt January's ears. He stared at the fiery base of the cloud, at the scores of fires feeding into it. Suddenly he could see past the cloud, and his fingernails cut into his palms. Through a gap in the clouds he saw it clearly, the delta, the six rivers, there off to the left of the tower of smoke—the city of Hiroshima, untouched.

"We missed!" Kochenski yelled. "We missed it!"

January turned to hide his face from the pilots; on it was a grin like a rictus. He sat back in his seat and let the relief fill him.

Then it was back to it. "Goddamn it!" Fitch shouted down at him. McDonald was trying to restrain him. "January, get up here!"

"Yes sir." Now there was a new set of problems.

January stood and turned, legs weak. His right fingertips throbbed painfully. The men were crowded forward to look out the Plexiglas. January looked with them.

The mushroom cloud was forming. It roiled out as if it might continue to extend forever, fed by the inferno and the black stalk below it. It looked about two miles wide and half a mile tall, and it extended well above the height they flew at, dwarfing their plane entirely. "Do you think we'll all be sterile?" Matthews said.

"I can taste the radiation," McDonald declared. "Can you? It tastes like lead."

Bursts of flame shot up into the cloud from below, giving a purplish tint to the stalk. There it stood—lifelike, malignant, sixty thousand feet tall. One bomb. January shoved past the pilots into the navigation cabin, overwhelmed.

"Should I start recording everyone's reactions, Captain?" asked Benton.

"To hell with that," Fitch said, following January back. But Shepard got there first, descending quickly from the navigation dome. He rushed across the cabin, caught January on the shoulder. "You bastard!" he screamed as January stumbled back. "You lost your nerve, coward!"

271

January went for Shepard, happy to have a target at last, but Fitch cut in and grabbed him by the collar, pulled him around until they were face to face.

"Is that right?" Fitch cried, as angry as Shepard. "Did you screw up on purpose?"

"No," January grunted, and knocked Fitch's hands away from his neck. He swung and smacked Fitch on the mouth, caught him solid. Fitch staggered back, recovered, and no doubt would have beaten January up, but Matthews and Benton and Stone leaped in and held him back, shouting for order. "Shut up! Shut up!" McDonald screamed from the cockpit, and for a moment it was bedlam. But Fitch let himself be restrained, and soon only McDonald's shouts for quiet were heard. January retreated to between the pilot seats, right hand on his pistol holster.

"The city was in the cross hairs when I flipped the switch," he said. "But the first couple of times I flipped it nothing happened—"

"That's a lie!" Shepard shouted. "There was nothing wrong with the switch, I checked it myself. Besides the bomb exploded *miles* beyond Hiroshima, look for yourself! That's *minutes*." He wiped spit from his chin and pointed at January. "You did it."

"You don't know that," January said. But he could see the men had been convinced by Shepard, and he took a step back. "You just get me to a board of inquiry, quick. And leave me alone till then. If you touch me again," glaring venomously at Fitch and then Shepard, "I'll shoot you." He turned and hopped down to his seat, feeling exposed and vulnerable, like a treed racoon.

"They'll shoot *you* for this," Shepard screamed after him. "Disobeying orders—treason—" Matthews and Stone were shutting him up.

"Let's get out of here," he heard McDonald say. "I can taste the lead, can't you?"

January looked out the Plexiglas. The giant cloud still burned and roiled. One atom . . . Well, they had really done it to that forest. He almost laughed but stopped himself, afraid of hysteria. Through a break in the clouds he got a clear view of Hiroshima for the first time. It lay spread over its islands like a map, unharmed. Well, that was that. The inferno at the base of the mushroom cloud was eight or ten miles around the shore of the bay and a mile or two inland. A certain patch of forest would be gone, destroyed—utterly blasted from the face of the earth. The Japs would be able to go out and investigate the damage. And if they

were told it was a demonstration, a warning—and if they acted fast—
well, they had their chance. Maybe it would work.
The release of tension made January feel sick. Then he recalled
Shepard's words, and he knew that whether his plan worked or not he
was still in trouble. In trouble! It was worse than that. Bitterly he cursed
the Japanese. He even wished for a moment that he *had* dropped it on
them. Wearily he let his despair empty him.
A long while later he sat up straight. Once again he was a trapped
animal. He began lunging for escape, casting about for plans. One
alternative after another. All during the long, grim flight home he
considered it, mind spinning at the speed of the props and beyond. And
when they came down on Tinian he had a plan. It was a long shot, he
reckoned, but it was the best he could do.

The briefing hut was surrounded by MPs again. January stumbled
from the truck with the rest and walked inside. He was more than ever
aware of the looks given him, and they were hard, accusatory. He was
too tired to care. He hadn't slept in more than thirty-six hours and had
slept very little since the last time he had been in the hut, a week before.
Now the room quivered with the lack of engine vibration to stabilize it,
and the silence roared. It was all he could do to hold on to his plan. The
glares of Fitch and Shepard, the hurt incomprehension of Matthews, they
had to be thrust out of his focus. Thankfully he lit a cigarette.
In a clamor of question and argument the others described the strike.
Then the haggard Scholes and an intelligence officer led them through
the bombing run. January's plan made it necessary to hold to his story.
". . . and when the AP was under the cross hairs I pushed down the
switch, but got no signal. I flipped it up and down repeatedly until the
tone kicked in. At that point there was still fifteen seconds to the release."
"Was there anything that may have caused the tone to start when it
did?"
"Not that I noticed immediately, but—"
"It's impossible," Shepard interrupted, face red. "I checked the
switch before we flew and there was nothing wrong with it. Besides, the
drop occurred over a minute—"
"Captain Shepard," Scholes said. "We'll hear from you presently."
"But he's obviously lying—"
"Captain Shepard! It's not at all obvious. Don't speak unless
questioned."

273

"Anyway," January said, hoping to shift the questions away from the issue of the long delay, "I noticed something about the bomb when it was falling that could explain why it stuck. I need to discuss it with one of the scientists familiar with the bomb's design."

"What was that?" Scholes asked suspiciously.

January hesitated. "There's going to be an inquiry, right?"

Scholes frowned. "This is the inquiry, Captain January. Tell us what you saw."

"But there will be some proceeding beyond this one?"

"It looks like there's going to be a court-martial, yes, Captain."

"That's what I thought. I don't want to talk to anyone but my counsel, and some scientist familiar with the bomb."

"*I'm* a scientist familiar with the bomb," Shepard burst out. "You could tell me if you really had anything, you—"

"I said I need a scientist!" January exclaimed, rising to face the scarlet Shepard across the table. "Not a g-goddamned mechanic." Shepard started to shout, others joined in, and the room rang with argument. While Scholes restored order January sat down, and he refused to be drawn out again.

"I'll see you're assigned counsel and initiate the court-martial," Scholes said, clearly at a loss. "Meanwhile you are under arrest, on suspicion of disobeying orders in combat." January nodded, and Scholes gave him over to MPs.

"One last thing," January said, fighting exhaustion. "Tell General LeMay that if the Japs are told this drop was a warning, it might have the same effect as—"

"I told you!" Shepard shouted, "I told you he did it on purpose!"

Men around Shepard restrained him. But he had convinced most of them, and even Matthews stared at him with surprised anger.

January shook his head wearily. He had the dull feeling that his plan, while it had succeeded so far, was ultimately not a good one. "Just trying to make the best of it." It took all of his remaining will to force his legs to carry him in a dignified manner out of the hut.

His cell was an empty NCO's office. MPs brought his meals. For the first couple of days he did little but sleep. On the third day he glanced out the office's barred window and saw a tractor pulling a tarpaulin-draped trolley out of the compound, followed by jeeps filled with MPs. It looked like a military funeral. January rushed to the door and banged on it until one of the young MPs came.

"What's that they're doing out there?" January demanded.

Eyes cold and mouth twisted, the MP said, "They're making another strike. They're going to do it right this time."

"No!" January cried, "No!" He rushed the MP, who knocked him back and locked the door. "*No!*" He beat the door until his hands hurt, cursing wildly. "You don't *need* to do it, it isn't *necessary.*" Shell shattered at last, he collapsed on the bed and wept. Now everything he had done would be rendered meaningless. He had sacrificed himself for nothing.

A day or two after that the MPs led in a colonel, an iron-haired man who stood stiffly and crushed January's hand when he shook it. His eyes were a pale icy blue.

"I am Colonel Dray," he said. "I have been ordered to defend you in court-martial." January could feel the dislike pouring from the man. "To do that I'm going to need every fact you have, so let's get started."

"I'm not talking to anybody until I've seen an atomic scientist."

"I am your *defense* counsel—"

"I don't care who you are," January said. "Your defense of me depends on you getting one of the scientists *here.* The higher up he is, the better. And I want to speak to him alone."

"I will have to be present."

So he would do it. But now January's counsel, too, was an enemy.

"Naturally," January said. "You're my counsel. But no one else. Our atomic secrecy may depend on it."

"You saw evidence of sabotage?"

"Not one word more until that scientist is here."

Angrily the colonel nodded and left.

Late the next day the colonel returned with another man. "This is Dr. Forest."

"I helped develop the bomb," Forest said. He had a crew cut and was dressed in fatigues, and to January he looked more Army than the colonel. Suspiciously he stared back and forth at the two men.

"You'll vouch for this man's identity on your word as an officer?" he asked Dray.

"Of course," the colonel said stiffly, offended.

"So," Dr. Forest said. "You had some trouble getting it off when you wanted to. Tell me what you saw."

"I saw nothing," January said harshly. He took a deep breath; it was time to commit himself. "I want you to take a message back to the scientists. You folks have been working on this thing for years, and you must have had time to consider how the bomb should have been used. You know we could have convinced the Japs to surrender by showing them a demonstration—"

"Wait a minute," Forest said. "You're saying you didn't see anything? There wasn't a malfunction?"

"That's right," January said, and cleared his throat. "It wasn't *necessary*, do you understand?"

Forest was looking at Colonel Dray. Dray gave him a disgusted shrug. "He told me he saw evidence of sabotage."

"I want you to go back and ask the scientists to intercede for me," January said, raising his voice to get the man's attention. "I haven't got a chance in that court-martial. But if the scientists defend me then maybe they'll let me live, see? I don't want to get shot for doing something every one of you scientists would have done."

Dr. Forest backed away. Color rising, he said, "What makes you think that's what we would have done? Don't you think we considered it? Don't you think men better qualified than you made the decision?" He waved a hand. "Goddamn it—what made you think you were competent to decide something as important as that!"

January was appalled at the man's reaction; in his plan it had gone differently. Angrily he jabbed a finger at Forest. "Because *I* was the man doing it, *Doctor* Forest. You take even one step back from that and suddenly you can pretend it's not your doing. Fine for you, but *I was there.*"

At every word the man's color was rising. It looked like he might pop a vein in his neck. January tried once more. "Have you ever tried to imagine what one of your bombs would do to a city full of people?"

"I've had enough!" the man exploded. He turned to Dray. "I'm under no obligation to keep what I've heard here confidential. You can be sure it will be used as evidence in Captain January's court-martial." He turned and gave January a look of such blazing hatred that January understood it. For these men to admit he was right would mean admitting that they were wrong—that every one of them was responsible for his part in the construction of the weapon January had refused to use. Understanding that, January knew he was doomed.

The bang of Dr. Forest's departure still shook the little office. January sat on his cot, got out a smoke. Under Colonel Dray's cold gaze he lit one shakily, took a drag. He looked up at the colonel, shrugged. "It was my best chance," he explained. That did something—for the first and only time the cold disdain in the colonel's eyes shifted, to a little, hard, lawyerly gleam of respect.

The court-martial lasted two days. The verdict was guilty of disobeying orders in combat and of giving aid and comfort to the enemy. The sentence was death by firing squad.

For most of his remaining days January rarely spoke, drawing ever further behind the mask that had hidden him for so long. A clergyman came to see him, but it was the 509th's chaplain, the one who had said the prayer blessing the *Lucky Strike*'s mission before they took off. Angrily January sent him packing.

Later, however, a young Catholic priest dropped by. His name was Patrick Getty. He was a little pudgy man, bespectacled and, it seemed, somewhat afraid of January. January let the man talk to him. When he returned the next day January talked back a bit, and on the day after that he talked some more. It became a habit.

Usually January talked about his childhood. He talked of plowing mucky black bottomland behind a mule. Of running down the lane to the mailbox. Of reading books by the light of the moon after he had been ordered to sleep. And of being beaten by his mother for it with a high-heeled shoe. He told the priest the story of the time his arm had been burned, and about the car crash at the bottom of Fourth Street. "It's the truck driver's face I remember, do you see, Father?"

"Yes," the young priest said. "Yes."

And he told him about the game he had played in which every action he took tipped the balance of world affairs. "When I remembered that game I thought it was dumb. Step on a sidewalk crack and cause an earthquake—you know, it's stupid. Kids are like that." The priest nodded. "But now I've been thinking that if everybody were to live their whole lives like that, thinking that every move they made really was important, then . . . it might make a difference." He waved a hand vaguely, expelled cigarette smoke. "You're accountable for what you do."

"Yes," the priest said. "Yes, you are."

"And if you're given orders to do something wrong, you're still accountable, right? The orders don't change it."

"That's right."

"Hmph." January smoked a while. "So they say, anyway. But look what happens." He waved at the office. "I'm like the guy in a story I read—he thought everything in books was true, and after reading a bunch of westerns he tried to rob a train. They tossed him in jail." He laughed shortly. "Books are full of crap."

"Not all of them," the priest said. "Besides, you weren't trying to rob a train."

They laughed at the notion. "Did you read that story?"

"No."

"It was the strangest book—there were two stories in it, and they alternated chapter by chapter, but they didn't have a thing to do with each other! I didn't get it."

"Maybe the writer was trying to say that everything connects to everything else."

"Maybe. But it's a funny way to say it."

"I like it."

And so they passed the time, talking.

So it was the priest who was the one to come by and tell January that his request for a presidential pardon had been refused. Getty said awkwardly, "It seems the President approves the sentence."

"That bastard," January said weakly. He sat on his cot.

Time passed. It was another hot, humid day.

"Well," the priest said. "Let me give you some better news. Given your situation I don't think telling you matters, though I've been told not to. The second mission—you know there was a second strike?"

"Yes."

"Well, they missed too."

"What?" January cried, and bounced to his feet. "You're kidding!"

"No. They flew to Kokura but found it covered by clouds. It was the same over Nagasaki and Hiroshima, so they flew back to Kokura and tried to drop the bomb using radar to guide it, but apparently there was a . . . a genuine equipment failure this time, and the bomb fell on an island."

January was hopping up and down, mouth hanging open, "So we n-never—"

"We never dropped an atom bomb on a Japanese city. That's right." Getty grinned. "And get this—I heard this from my superior—they sent a message to the Japanese Government telling them that the two explosions were warnings, and that if they didn't surrender by September 1 we would drop bombs on Kyoto and Tokyo, and then wherever else we had to. Word is that the Emperor went to Hiroshima to survey the damage, and when he saw it he ordered the Cabinet to surrender. So . . ."

"So it worked," January said. He hopped around, "It worked, it worked!"

"Yes."

"Just like I said it would!" he cried, and hopping in front of the priest he laughed.

Getty was jumping around a little too, and the sight of the priest bouncing was too much for January. He sat on his cot and laughed till the tears ran down his cheeks.

"So—" He sobered quickly. "So Truman's going to shoot me anyway, eh?"

"Yes," the priest said unhappily. "I guess that's right."

This time January's laugh was bitter. "He's a bastard, all right. And proud of being a bastard, which makes it worse." He shook his head. "If Roosevelt had lived . . ."

"It would have been different," Getty finished. "Yes. Maybe so. But he didn't." He sat beside January. "Cigarette?" He held out a pack, and January noticed the green wrapper, the round bull's-eye. He frowned. "You haven't got a Camel?"

"Oh. Sorry."

"Oh well. That's all right." January took one of the Lucky Strikes, lit up. "That's awfully good news." He breathed out. "I never believed Truman would pardon me anyway, so mostly you've brought good news. Ha. They *missed*. You have no idea how much better that makes me feel."

"I think I do."

January smoked the cigarette.

"So I'm a good American after all. I *am* a good American," he insisted, "no matter what Truman says."

"Yes," Getty replied, and coughed. "You're better than Truman any day."

"Better watch what you say, Father." He looked into the eyes behind the glasses, and the expression he saw there gave him pause. Since the drop every look directed at him had been filled with contempt. He'd seen it so often during the court-martial that he'd learned to stop looking; and now he had to teach himself to see again. The priest looked at him as if he were . . . as if he were some kind of hero. That wasn't exactly right. But seeing it . . .

January would not live to see the years that followed, so he would never know what came of his action. He had given up casting his mind forward and imagining possibilities, because there was no point to it. His planning was ended. In any case he would not have been able to imagine the course of the postwar years. That the world would quickly become an armed camp pitched on the edge of atomic war, he might have predicted. But he never would have guessed that so many people would join a January Society. He would never know of the effect the Society had on Dewey during the Korean crisis, never know of the Society's successful campaign for the test-ban treaty, and never learn that, thanks in part to the Society and its allies, a treaty would be signed by the great powers that would reduce the number of atomic bombs year by year, until there were none left.

Frank January would never know any of that. But in that moment on his cot looking into the eyes of young Patrick Getty, he guessed an inkling of it—he felt, just for an instant, the impact on history.

And with that he relaxed. In his last week everyone who met him carried away the same impression—that of a calm, quiet man, angry at Truman and others, but in a withdrawn, matter-of-fact way. Patrick Getty, a strong force in the January Society ever after, said January was talkative for some time after he learned of the missed attack on Kokura. Then he got quieter, as the day approached. On the morning that they woke him at dawn to march him out to a hastily constructed execution shed, his MPs shook his hand. The priest was with him as he smoked a final cigarette, and they prepared to put the hood over his head. January looked at him calmly. "They load one of the guns with a blank cartridge, right?"

"Yes," Getty said.

"So each man in the squad can imagine he may not have shot me?"

"Yes. That's right."

A tight, unhumorous smile was January's last expression. He threw down the cigarette, ground it out, poked the priest in the arm. "But I *know.*" Then the mask slipped back into place for good, making the hood redundant, and with a firm step January went to the wall. One might have said he was at peace.

Afterword: Allohistory in Science Fiction

Gordon B. Chamberlain

UCHRONIE, *n.f.* . . . *Utopie appliquée à l'histoire; l'histoire refaite logiquement telle qu'elle aurait pu être.*

Nouveau Larousse Illustré (1913)

"Mistory refashioned logically as it could/might have been." In English *uchronia* and *uchronian* will do for the thing described, by analogy with *utopia;* but for the theoretical discipline and the literary genre *uchronics* seems uncouth, *uchronian romance* wordy, *metahistory* and *parahistory* ambiguous. Even *alternative history* has been used to mean something else (a sort of social-commentary sf).[1] *Allohistory* is short, unambiguous, and used here.

A uchronia is not the same thing as an alternative or parallel universe. Earths where the human species, if it exists at all, coexists with dinosaurs, walking trees, or Norse gods do not branch from our historical tree. Also excluded are alternative or modified histories of the *Dear Brutus* type affecting only fictional individuals, from O. Henry's "Roads of Destiny" (1903) to Steven Spielberg's recent *Back to the Future*. And so are disguised surrogates of the world we know: historical burlesque on the lines of Baring's *Unreliable History* and *Monty Python's History of the World*, contemporary history in mufti from Disraeli to Allen Drury, and the imaginary principalities and powers—Ruritanias and Dukes of

Holdernesse—that provide settings and spear-carriers for thrillers. And obviously allohistory excludes change in any history that is still future to the writer—whether hopes and fears expressed in the past tense for verisimilitude, in the mode established by *The Battle of Dorking,* or struggles for existence between potential futures in "cause-'em-up" time opera.[2]

Allohistory (what might have been) must also be distinguished from secret history (what may have been, if only we knew).[3] This applies both to ancient "secrets," such as Atlantis and the world of Conan, and to modern escape yarns starring Napoleon or Hitler—unless, of course, the secret as such makes a known difference in the writer's past. (Revisionist history is not alternative history; "what if Jesus had escaped" is a different question from "what if some future person discovered proof that He did.")[4] Attempts to change the past, inside sf and out, often resolve into secret history. Outside, after sufficient suspense, the attempt simply fails: in the old original, Thackeray's *Henry Esmond,* the feckless James Stuart loses his chance pursuing a petticoat rather than a crown; in Kipling's "The Eye of Allah" invention of the microscope encounters *il gran rifiuto* from a prescient medieval abbot; in swastsell thrillers Nazi attempts to kidnap Churchill or Fermi are foiled by Our Side. In sf changing history is often attempted by a time-traveler and, if not rejected by ancestral wisdom or burked by native inertia, may be repressed by some sort of time police;[5] alternatively the supposed change may turn out to have been part of history all along, as the would-be remolder of this scheme of things keeps a history-making appointment in Samarra.[6] This Ouroboros paradox, in which time doubles back and the future causally affects the past, may end with a time-traveler actually taking on the identity of a historical individual—Cyrus or Leonardo or Hitler, Thor or Quetzalcoatl or Christ, the boy who saved Leyden, or the gander that saved the Capitol.[7]

Ideally history "as it could have been" should also exclude changes that could not have been—at any rate, not at the time and place proposed. Like Detection Club members under the rule of Father Knox allohistorical purists eschew unexplained weapons, mysterious aliens, Jiggery-Pokery, and Acts of God.[8] If the War of Secession is fought with airplanes, they want to know how an America so advanced industrially could generate such a war at such a time; and the same goes for providing Columbus with radio, Wellington with tanks, or the last Romanovs with a cure for hemophilia.[9] "If your grandmother had wheels, she'd be an omnibus"; in allohistory *tout pur* Granny may die in infancy, duplicate herself through time travel, or merely fail to produce your mother, but growing wheels on her is *infra dig.* But for a field as wide as sf such definitions serve only as blinders; and exactly where do we cut the view off? What about theoretically possible changes effected by aliens? Differences in Tellurian geography or even physics? Past scientific validation of magic? The eclectic approach advocated by Barton Hacker is the only one practicable. If the story changes the past we know, it goes in, whether the change makes sense as history or not. No doubt the quantum-physics theorists of alternative worlds can justify it on the grounds that reality is unknowable anyway.[10]

Writers of sf, of course, are not the only ones who change the past. Adepts of the "new economic history," with its statistically based thought-experiments, have counterfactualized out of existence—not without controversy—such historical "givens" as the Navigation Acts, the US railroad net, and the steamship;[11] other academicians have written allohistory with less explicit hypotheses, and a few have even dared to use it in teaching.[12] Thematically the utopia of the French definition, an imaginary world contrasted with ours for didactic effect, appears positively in Wells's *A Modern Utopia* and similar nontriumphs of barbarism and religion over classical civilization, negatively in nightmares of victorious popery or Nazism. Subtypes may erewhon our world, as by enthroning lesser breeds over white Anglo-Saxons,[13] or burlesque it, as by subjecting the greats of the past to today's bureaucracy;[14] the tone can range from contemporary social concern or political polemic to the whimsy of Joan Aiken and R.A. Lafferty or the burlesque of the *Journal of Irreproducible Results* and *National Lampoon.* Sometimes "the main situation of the story could never have arisen in the world we know," and hence an allohistorical England where young boys are still recruited as papal *castrati* or interesting things happen to the Royal Family.[15] Contrariwise, at the space-opera level, imagined times, like imagined planets, serve primarily to backdrop quasihistorical romance without demanding historical accuracy; and some writers have wasted such machinery on what are essentially near-future thrillers or even boy-meets-girl fairy tales not quite slick enough for the *Saturday Evening Post.*[16]

Allohistory, then, deals with the known past as it might have been—not as it may have happened behind the scenes, or to unknown individuals, but as we here and now are sure that it did not. This collection, moreover, concentrates on allohistory in English-language sf, operationally defined as what sf editors buy for sf readers. (For our purposes "sf" includes fantasy; the distinction, as a general rule, is useful only polemically.) This specialization is justified by the cult or ghetto nature of speculative fiction. Its writers read each other, but most are probably no more familiar with Napoleon's victory at Waterloo according to Trevelyan or American economic development without railroads according to Fogel than such academic types are familiar with sf.[17] (At least one sf reviewer has publicly resented allohistory by outsiders as an invasion of his turf.[18]) Outside sf, moreover, allohistory—unlike the conventional utopia—seems not to exist as a recognized form. Contributors to the classic British essay collection of 1931, Squire's *If,* show no familiarity with their nineteenth-century French precursors or with such English-language "scientific romancers" as Wells and Edward Everett Hale. Within sf the subgenre develops like the quasi-incestuous bloodlines of European royalty; its outcroppings in mainstream literature suggest incompletely articulated fossils of possibly unrelated hominids. Indeed so deep is the chasm between sf and the rest that a more telling metaphor might set bats against pterodactyls.

Like other sf themes allohistory can lay claim to respectable antiquity. About the time of Christ, well before Lucian reached the moon though long after Plato drowned Atlantis, the historian Titus Livy was inquiring "how the Roman State would have fared in a war with Alexander"; and Livy's conclusion that the legions would have shown him, all right, follows a familiar pattern of patriotic invasion yarns. But this "seed of allohistory," as Versins dubs it, was late in germinating. The first critical discussion of the form, published by Isaac D'Israeli under George IV, mentions only two then-recent speculations on the survival of Lorenzo de' Medici—a common theme for historians since Guicciardini.[19] The first separately published uchronia in English, discovered by Charles G. Waugh, may be Nathaniel Hawthorne's fantasy afterlives of Byron and others in "P.'s Correspondence" (1843); the first to be worked out from a single specific turning point, the kakotopic "Hands Off" (1881), by Edward Everett Hale, who had earlier launched the first artificial satellite;[20] the first in novel form, Edward Lawrence's *It May Happen Yet* (1899), which complicates a Victorian lost-will intrigue with a Napoleonic landing in East Anglia; the first utopia in our everyday sense, H.G. Wells's *A Modern Utopia* (1905). (Twain's Connecticut Yankee of 1889, despite his literary influence, visits only the past of dream—or nineteenth-century reformist nightmare—and ultimately fails to change even that.) But pending systematic scanning of *fin de siecle* scientific romance by computer or

Sam Moskowitz, it seems that none of this added up to a literary tradition. The uchronias of scholars and belletrists have typically drawn on contemporary politics, scholarship, and the arts, but not on the literary past or each other.

And the same may be true of uchronias in French. The very first book-length uchronia is L.-N. Geoffroy-Château's chauvinist pipe dream of Napoleon as world-conqueror (1836), which works the great-man theory beyond even Bonapartist credulity; second place and credit for the word go to the philosopher-reformist Charles Renouvier, whose *Uchronie* (1857) keeps the Roman Empire alive by properly subordinating Christianity. And in 1871 the aging revolutionary Louis-Auguste Blanqui beguiled his last imprisonment writing *Eternity Through the Stars*, the first known literary argument for duplicate Earths bearing duplicate individuals in countless variations. Rome preserved and Napoleon victorious have been routine in allohistory since, and the *tour de force* of Blanqui, despite its nineteenth-century cosmos, antici-pates by a century Larry Niven's "All the Myriad Ways." But did other French writers actually learn from these examples?[21] Did Anglo-phones even know of them? What bibliographers can find is not necessarily what contemporaries noticed; writers and critics of sf today are sometimes unfamiliar even with H.G. Wells.[22]

Once the modern sf genre is born with Hugo Gernsback's *Amazing* in 1926, influences within it can be assumed. Its first uchronias were by-products of time travel—not the mental contacts of earlier romance, observing or experiencing without change,[23] but the physical intervention of Wells; its chronic argonauts were constantly "popping back to the days of Nero and fixing things up there, or visiting the Vikings and setting them right, or changing the French Revolution."[24] First place among these movers and shakers apparently belongs to Nat Schachner's "Ancestral Voices" (1933), in which killing a fifth-century Hun dehistoricizes, among others, his descendant Hitler. The idea of alternatives—though not yet historical ones—took sf form in the August 1935 *Wonder Stories* with David Daniels's "The Branches of Time" and Stanley Weinbaum's "The Worlds of If." The first time-travelers to learn that their very existence in the past must *ipso facto* return them to an altered present (a conclusion too logical to be widely adopted in sf) appeared in William Sell's "Other Tracks" (1938). Barring Wells's extraterrestrial *Modern Utopia* and unhistorical *Men Like Gods*, the first sf writer to postulate alternative time tracks as in some sense coexistent was Murray Leinster with "Sidewise in Time"

(1934)—although none of the worlds opened by his catastrophic time-quake is treated at length, and a good many (such as his Roman villa and Carboniferous jungle) seem to have evolved not only unlike ours but slower. And by dispatching his hero across the time faults, in Macaulayan cadence, "through unguessable landscapes, to unimaginable adventures, with revolvers and textbooks as [his] armament for the conquest of a world," Leinster first acclimatized to the parallel-world subgenre, from its native Camelot, Zu-Vendis, and Barsoom, the familiar nineteenth-century superman-figure of the White Rajah.[25]

The most productive single originator of allohistorical themes is apparently L. Sprague de Camp. His *Lest Darkness Fall* (1939) first set a time-traveler to changing known history not only deliberately but realistically; as late as 1984 a clone of his mild-mannered archaeologist who brought Gothic Rome out of the Dark Ages was busy saving Aztec Mexico from Spanish darkness in Mack Reynolds's posthumous *The Other Time.* The following year De Camp's "The Wheels of If" first treated crosstime travel as theoretically routine rather than catastrophic, developed a single alternative timeline at length, and even worked out its own version of English.[26] Though Blanqui and Wells had postulated parallel identities on other Earths,[27] and other sf writers had duplicated individuals through time travel,[28] De Camp first extended this ancient myth of the *Doppelgänger* to alternative identities on coexistent timelines. Finally these two may be the only science-fictional alternative histories to boast sources in historical scholarship. "Wheels" originates in Toynbee's speculations on "lost opportunities" in *A Study of History,* which De Camp had just been reviewing for *Astounding.* *Darkness* also suggests academic reading: although the tavern brawl over the nature of Christ and the joke about Theodora's sex problems may come straight from Gregory of Nyssa and Procopius, a more probable proximate source is Gibbon's *Decline and Fall.*[29]

All these Wheels of If obviously needed government to keep them on track. In 1948 H. Beam Piper mobilized the Paratime Police, transtemporal Watergate plumbers patrolling other timelines to cover up economic exploitation by their own; but where De Camp had imagined crosstime travel as purely mental Piper emulated Wells by providing machines, whose fields of force occasionally picked up such victims of story requirements as the missing diplomat Benjamin Bathurst. Axis of operation shifting ninety degrees, in 1955 the Para-cops changed hats to become Poul Anderson's Time Patrol, preserving the past in the self-interest of the future. Police action in and across time has since provided plot motifs for such purveyors of adventure sf as Keith Laumer, Andre Norton, and Richard Meredith, and remunerative employment for such guardians of chronology as we know it as the Service Temporel, the Cosmos Corps, NBC's Voyagers, the Vatican's Congregatio Secreta ad Purificandos Fontes, the Temporal Entropy Restructure and Repair Agency (T.E.R.R.A.), and the TIA. Legitimate peaceful trade across the timelines is significantly scarcer.[30]

De Camp and Piper, however, still reached their alternative worlds by travel from our own. Outside sf Churchill in 1931 had imagined a uchronia from within with "If Lee Had Not Won the Battle of Gettysburg," and in 1945 "Randolph Robban" had done the same for Nazified Europe in *Si L'Allemagne avait vaincu.*[31] Not until 1952 did American sf break with the fantastic-voyage tradition to set stories allohistorically from the outset: Philip Jose Farmer's neglected fantasy "Sail On! Sail On!," with Columbus using radio on a nonspherical Earth, and Ward Moore's classic *Bring the Jubilee,* reminiscences of "life in the twenty-six states" two generations after Lee's victory at Gettysburg. For another first, old Hodgins Backmaker (born in 1921 on one timeline, writing in 1877 on another) could bequeath his story to the Union we know because it, not the defeated backwater of his birth, was the result of change. With his depressed North, hierarchic South, and generally backward planet Moore also adapted the utopian-didactic tradition to make implicit statements about the role of the War of Secession in American history and of America in the world. And though neglected by critics (perhaps for its *Bildungsroman* plot), in density of detail, precision in working out consequences, and general allohistorical verisimilitude *Bring the Jubilee* remains unsurpassed in sf.

"In parallel-worlds stories," remarks David Ketterer, "the opening pages typically present the reader with an incomprehensible jumble that begins to make sense only when he has established the point at which the 'fictional' reality shears off from the accepted 'historical' reality."[32] Though his description does apply to Farmer's "Sail On," its inspiration is the story that established this *in medias res* technique in sf, Philip K. Dick's Hugo-winner as best sf novel of 1962, *The Man in the High Castle.* Unaided by blurbs or reviews, readers need some time to discover that Dick's America is partitioned between Germany and Japan, and considerable alertness to figure out how and why. Axis-victory yarns, of course, had begun appearing twenty years before as awful warnings and had already produced such narrow-escape uchronias as Sarban's *The Sound of His Horn*

(1952) and Kornbluth's "Two Dooms" (1958); but *High Castle* was the first to begin with the victory taken for granted. It also doubled the ration of utopian commentary, implicitly contrasting the world of the reader both with the Oriental-Californian kalotopia of Mr. Tagomi, serenely devoted to art and the *I Ching,* and with the mad Nazi kakotopia beyond the Rockies.[33] Literary critics seem to agree that Dick's essentially projective and mythical image of Japan does not injure the work as sf.[34]

With *The Man in the High Castle* the main lines of allohistory were set. Whatever vehicle writers employed—document collection, biography, novel, thriller, slice-of-life—their use of it was logically limited. A uchronia might be presented as intrinsic (due to some such recognized historical chance as a reversed Gettysburg or Waterloo) or extrinsic (due to deliberate change by time-travelers or aliens); its existence might parallel that of our world (perhaps as one of many) or preclude it. The takeoff point of the story might be our own timeline (most crosstime and time-changing adventures), common history before the break (pseudo-journalistic alternative wars and battles), or uchronia as assumed independent reality (such post-Dick writers as Keith Roberts); roughly speaking, the first choice generates time-operatic adventure, the second political awful-warning or narrow-escape yarns, the third utopias.

Though allohistorical turning points in sf range from protohistoric Aryan migrations to Three Mile Island,[35] a few are consistent favorites. For the winner's plate it is Hitler's war first, the rest nowhere; for place money, surviving Roman Empires apparently nose out victorious Napoleons, Lees, and Montezumas and defeated Revolutions and Reformations.[36] Barring the weak showing of World War I and the near-absence of classical Greece and Israel (no doubt relegated by sf buffs to parents and schoolmarms),[37] the finish reflects the sort of Sellers-and-Yeatman history that Anglo-Americans remember from school, limited thematically to dates of wars and deaths of kings and geographically to the approximate great-circle route from Jerusalem to Foggy Bottom via Athens, Rome, Westminster, and Plymouth Rock. The ratio in this volume, one socioeconomic change to nine politico-military, is typical. And even for great-man history, the selection is limited. "If Napoleon had not divorced Josephine," people used to blather to Flaubert, "he would still be on the throne";[38] so far sf has preferred Waterloo to both that and Trafalgar, Gettysburg to Bull Run or Antietam or anything in the West, and officially recognized turning points to unknowns generally.

Admittedly sf writers must consider their public; it is hard enough to background the reader on an invented past without making it an obscure one. Taking off from our own time, of course, makes overt investigation natural; Philip Jose Farmer's bomber pilot Two Hawks, grounded in a very different World War II, hunts up reference texts just like Allister Park;[39] for Anderson's time patrollers the encyclopedia proves to be a walking one. Similarly the autobiographer of *Bring the Jubilee* starts explaining his world to ours with his second paragraph. But what if the story begins in *media uchronia*? The *Henry V* recap, or omniscient-narrator prologue, exemplified here by de Camp and Roberts, does seem a bit archaic. Authors more conscious of subtlety leave the job to their characters, commissioning several to tell each other what they already know (*Hamlet* recap), one to lecture on it to others (*Tempest* recap), or one to reminisce on it to himself (*Richard III* recap).[40] A more advanced technique, recalling Orwell's use of "the book" in *1984*, employs supposed documents: in Kingsley Amis's *The Alteration*, how England remained Roman Catholic is first shown through its arts (requiems by Mozart, stained glass by Gainsborough) and then explained through its equivalent of uchronian sf. Sometimes the subtlety is excessive: Dick's pitch for FDR's assassination in *High Castle,* discussed below, broke right past the critic Ketterer,[41] and Chelsea Quinn Yarbro's *Ariosto* employs stilted narrative for an unnecessary alternative fate of Richard III while tucking away the *sine qua non* of her Medici uchronia in a conversational throwaway line, apparent only to specialists, on page 79. Her "On St. Hubert's Thing" is perhaps unique, and certainly good training, in providing no explanation at all.[42]

The recap may even require characters to tell each other what they cannot possibly know, but the reader needs to. "My mother and dad used to say that we wouldn't have lost the war if [FDR] had lived," says a character in *High Castle* (Berkley ed., p. 66). But had President-Elect Roosevelt instead of Mayor Cermak bled to death in Miami before inauguration day of 1933, nobody in the defeated America of 1962 would have possessed the least image of him as President, particularly not as leader against Nazism; the lost opportunities to which they would advert would be tied to the war directly. "He must have had some kind of time sense," remarks Dick in another story. "Awareness of other possible futures."[43] Such a "third sight," focusing not on the faraway or the not-yet but on the might-have-been, is employed for effect by many allohistorians, and not only in sf. The Napoleon of Geoffroy-Château, sailing home victorious from China, blanches at the sight of St. Helena; in Mackinlay Kantor's *If the South Had Won the Civil War* Confederate rulers of Cuba are aware that without them it would have gone Communist.[44]

"Changing history is not a simple process. Some changes seem to damp out, while others oscillate in ever-widening arcs."[45] But which is which? Writers divide between "domino theory" emphasis and "nondomino"—one extreme exemplified by the world-historical Cretaceous butterfly in Ray Bradbury's "The Sound of Thunder" (*Collier's,* June 1952), whose death reverses a US election; the other, by Kantor's successful Secession, which leaves not only World Wars I and II unaffected but the entire North American economy. (The years 1914 and 1939, indeed, tend to stand whatever other dominoes tumble; in most Confederate-victory scenarios—though not Churchill's and Moore's—World War I at least comes off on schedule, and alternatively our side may be confronted with Franco-German wars, Emperors' wars, recrudescent Kaiserism, or expansionist Poles, Lithuanians, or Saracens.[46]) Contingent change makes especially vivid reading when it involves historical Great Men. Two styles can be distinguished: the commedia dell'arte, in which certain roles must be played whoever the actors, and the repertory theater, in which certain actors must have roles whatever the play. On the former theory, for instance, aggressive German dictatorship comes along even without Hitler,[47] and, failing Judea, alternative timelines kneel to a Savior from Egypt or Ireland.[48] On the latter theory Woodrow Wilson and other Southern-born politicians become presidents of the Confederacy, pagan Florentines enjoy a *Human Comedy* by Dante and a Pantheon by Brunelleschi, and in a Europe barely scarred by the Reformation the Holy Office is adorned by monsignors Henricius and Laurentius—Himmler and Beria.[49] That favorite historical character of sf and popular culture generally, Adolf Hitler, turns up as artist (failed or successful), sentimental German bourgeois, purveyor of cryptosodomitical heroic fantasy à la John Norman, dictator in other modes, and trusted feudatory of the Devil.[50] But outside the literary world who has done more to promote sf?

Compared with other settings for sf uchronias run to the socially and technologically backward: steamcars, superstition, even slavery. In Barton Hacker's view the explanation is literary technique: prophets of progress will logically stage their utopias not in a past or present that might have been but in a future that may be yet. Similarly the uchronian emphasis on physical symbols of archaism—kilts and horned helmets, dirigibles and steam—may serve to dramatize change visually to a reader age-group concerned with cars and clothes.[51] But sf is also notoriously given to "whig history," i.e., the tendency "to write on the side of Protestants and whigs, to praise revolutions provided they have been successful, to emphasize certain principles of progress in the past, and to produce a story which is the ratification of the present."[52] Marathon and Tours, Renaissance and Reformation, victories over kings and slavers and Reichs: any switch in this triumphal procession down the ringing grooves of change could only leave Progress itself derailed.

For instance: barring such magic-wand inventions as a spacewarp drive based on a sewing machine,[53] what sort of uchronia typically surpasses our world in technology? Almost always, one that has aborted the fall of Rome and the rise of that bugbear of whig history, the medieval Roman Catholic Church. (Aborting Rome itself may prove even more progressive; "if the Ionians had won," mused Carl Sagan on his *Cosmos* ego trip, "we might by now be going to the stars."[54]) What type most consistently lags behind? One like Roberts's in this volume, throttled back to steamcars and semaphores by the failure of the Reformation. Here political whiggery is reinforced by the socioeconomics of Max Weber, whose monograph of 1904–05 tentatively associating one selectively defined ideal type of Protestantism with one selectively defined ideal type of capitalism, controversial though it remains among scholars, undoubtedly underlies today's popular identification of the Protestant Ethic with the American Dream.[55] An unusually simplistic example is Phyllis Eisenstein's *Shadow of Earth* (1979), which reflects not only the "popery and wooden shoes" propaganda of whiggery and the antimedievalism of *Connecticut Yankee* but the "black legend" of a peculiarly brutal and decadent Spain.[56] In this science-fictional drugstore Gothic a blonde ingenue from the suburbs of Chicago finds herself sold into concubinage to the Spanish governor of a preindustrial upper Mississippi Valley on a timeline where an Armada victory brought cultural and economic stasis. In our world, Eisenstein explains (p. 32), "the failure of the Armada left the Protestants free to flourish. . . . Their worldly philosophy fostered the Industrial Revolution, which began in England and spread to other Protestant countries long before it touched the Catholic world. The steam engine, invented in Scotland by a Protestant, became the key to the Industrial Age. . . ." This "foolish and doctrinaire thesis," as a prescient Weber termed it, is implicit in nearly all uchronias dominated by the papacy.[57]

Yet unconvincing though such static and monolithic pseudopasts may be,[58] they evidently fill a need; some even have special charms. "Much of the ambience" of Michael Moorcock's "Jerry Cornelius" cycle, Hacker points out, "derives from persistent archaic technology." And not only physical technology; the lovingly detailed airships, steamcars, and superliners are matched by classes and values equally archaic. In allohistory's elaboration of costumes and courtesies, as in the tournaments of the Society for Creative Anachronism, the role-playing of *Dungeons & Dragons,* and the costume contests and even Regency dance sessions at sf conventions, we sense the antiquarian nostalgia of Miniver Cheevy. The most enthusiastic encores are awarded to the dear dead days beyond recall about the turn of the century, with their gaslight and gold coinage, horse-drawn cabs and handlebar moustaches, fog in Baker Street and phosphates on Broadway, garden parties and Gibson girls. Many an allohistorian seems to be reliving the escape technique of Ray Bradbury's "A Scent of Sarsaparilla."[59]

One field in which progressivism and archaism give way to serious extrapolation is that of language—specifically the allohistorical development of English, itself a subtype of the recurrent sf use of language differences for alien effect. Simple shifts in vocabulary are represented by Moore's chapter title "Of Decisions, Minibiles, and Tinugraphs" (steamcars and movies to us) and Amis's derivation of the contemporary catchwords of a Roman Catholic England from papal Italian instead of diplomatic French: *pacific concomitance* for "peaceful coexistence," *detensione* for "detente." Relying on the Anglophone reader's preference for pidgin German over pidgin French, several authors have followed De Camp in imagining English or its Teutonic fellows uninfluenced by Romance. Thus Poul Anderson's Cimbric (assumed to be Teutonic rather than Celtic), the Anglisch of a "Saxon-British Line" (presumably dating to 1066) in Richard Meredith's *No Brother, No Friend* (1979), and the Ingwinetalu or Blodland Spraech of Farmer's *Two Hawks from Earth:* "a creolized English with an enormous stock of Norse loan-words and a lesser amount of Semitic Cretan, Etruscan Rasna, and Greek-derived words. . . . The French and Latin words were missing, and oh, what a difference!"[60] The difference would be greater had Farmer not rendered "lady" as the obviously Romance *faemme.*

One general judgment to conclude. "Uchronia is less the refusal of real history than the recognition of its ineluctable laws; by altering the course of events the author gives birth to a new history, but one that still contains the same rational determinism and contingency as empirical history."[61] As an exercise in such historical alternatives which of the stories collected here is best? The answer is none of them; the short-story form is not ideally designed for allohistory, because the plot needs too much room. Logical development, though necessary, is not sufficient; "the value of history [and successful allohistorical fiction] lies in the richness of its recovery of the concrete life of the past."[62] At short-fiction length, with a story to tell, settings are limited to slice-of-life presentation without background or to bare-bones lecturing touched with the odd amusing sidelight. At book length, on the other hand, "nonfictional" allohistory in essay or textbook form suggests (as Van Herp remarks of *Uchronie*, p. 71) the sort of required reading one assigns one's enemies; it takes a fictional plot to maintain interest, holding the background together without hiding it. Here the uchronian novel comes into its own. For the verisimilitude derived from concrete richness of detail no allohistorical short story matches any of half-a-dozen essays in Squire's *If;* but no pseudofactual book-length uchronia matches *Bring the Jubilee* or *The Alteration.*

NOTES

Short source-listings in these notes refer to items in the bibliography, which also includes a list of abbreviations for journals. I take this opportunity of thanking my collaborator in the bibliography, Barton C. Hacker, Jr., for valuable advice; Charles Waugh and Frank McSherry, Jr., for additional source materials; E. Doris Tilles and her staff at Kerr Library, Oregon State University, for help with interlibrary loans; and Professor Margaret Meehan of the OSU Honors Program, for getting me to teach the course that started it all.

[1] "Alternative History can be identified as that form of SF in which an alternative locus (in space, time, etc.) that shares the material and causal verisimilitude of the writer's world is used to articulate different possible solutions of societal problems, these problems being of sufficient importance to require an alteration in the overall history of the narrated world"—Darko Suvin, "Victorian Science Fiction, 1871–85: The Rise of the Alternative History Sub-Genre," *SFS,* 10 (1983): 149. Suvin's examples include Butler, Verne, and Trollope; his colloquy with Marc Angenot and Jean-Marc Gouanvic, "L'uchronie, histoire alternative et science-fiction," adds Stapledon.

[2] For exclusions generally see Barton C. Hacker and Gordon B. Chamberlain, "Pasts That Might Have Been," *Extrapolation,* 22 (Winter 1981): 335. Allusions here include Josephine Young Case, *At Midnight on the 31st of March* (Houghton Mifflin, 1938); Clifford Simak, *City* (Gnome, 1952); and Mark Clifton, "A Woman's Place"

(*Gal.,* May 1955)—Earths without humans; Brian Aldiss, *The Malacia Tapestry* (Ace, 1978), and Harry Harrison, *West of Eden* (Bantam, 1984, 1985)—dinosaurs; J.R.R. Tolkien's *Lord of the Rings* (Allen and Unwin, 1954–55)—walking trees (Huorns and Ents); L. Sprague de Camp and Fletcher Pratt, *The Compleat Enchanter* (Ballantine, 1975; components c1940–41)—Norse and other myths. *Dear Brutus* yarns include Isaac Asimov, "What If . . ." (*Fantastic,* Summer 1952); Jorge Luis Borges, "The Other Death" (original title "La redención," 1949), in his *The Aleph and Other Stories,* ed. and trans. Norman Thomas Giovanni (Dutton, 1970); Ralph L. Finn, *Time Marches Sideways* (Hutchinson, 1949); O. Henry, "Roads of Destiny" (*Ainslie's Magazine,* April 1903), rpt. in his *Roads of Destiny* (Doubleday, Page, 1909); Damon Knight, "Time Enough" (*Amz.,* July 1960); J.T. McIntosh, "Tenth Time Around" (*FSF,* May 1959); Robert Sheckley, "World of Heart's Desire," alias "The Store of the Worlds" (*Playboy,* September 1959); Stanley G. Weinbaum, "The Worlds of If" (*Wonder Stories,* July 1935). *Future-as-past* stories include such political polemic as Ernest Bramah, *What Might Have Been* (John Murray, 1907); Upton Sinclair, *I, Governor of California, and How I Ended Poverty* (End Poverty League, 1932); and Philip Roth, "The President Addresses the Nation" (*New York Review of Books,* 14 June 1973, p. 11); also such invasion yarns as Douglas Brown and Christopher Serpell, *Loss of Eden: A Cautionary Tale* (Faber, 1940), and Martin Hawkin, *When Adolf Came* (Jarrold's, 1943), both inaccurately described as allohistory by Brian Stableford in Nicholls's *Encyclopedia* (p. 26). Time-traveling *struggles for the future:* Alfred Bester, "The Probable Man" (*ASF,* July 1941); Anthony Boucher, "The Other Inauguration" (*FSF,* March 1953); Barrington Bayley, *The Fall of Chronopolis* (DAW, 1974); E.M. Hull, "The Flight That Failed" (*ASF,* December 1942); John Jakes, *Time Gate* (Westminster, 1972; New American Library, 1978); C.L. Moore, "Greater than Gods" (*ASF,* July 1939); H. Beam Piper, "Time and Time Again" (*ASF,* April 1947); Ross Rocklynne, "The Diversifal" (*Planet Stories,* March 1951); Rog Phillips, *World of If* (Century, 1951); Jack Williamson, "The Legion of Time" (*ASF,* May–July 1938; book version Fantasy Press, 1952; Pyramid, 1967); Thomas Wilson, "The Entrepreneur" (*ASF,* September 1952).

[3]Some early allohistories appeared in disguise as secret history. Rolfe's *Hubert's Arthur* represents the Arthurian succession as the forgotten true line of England, grafting it back into known history with Edward I; Lawrence's *It May Happen Yet* documents Napoleon's invasion of 1805 from supposed family traditions and lost books. Poyer's *Tunnel War* (1979) similarly claims to be based on declassified intelligence files.

[4]Van Rjndt's *The Trial of Adolf Hitler* (1978) qualifies here because set in the writer's past (1970). Normally such fictional trials are left to an unspecified future: George Sylvester Viereck, *The Kaiser on Trial* (n.p., Greystone, 1937); Alfred Fabre-Luce, *The Trial of Charles de Gaulle,* trans. Antonia White (Praeger, 1963). "What if the Resurrection were proved false" has been a fruitful takeoff point for didactic thriller-writers since Guy Thorne's *When It Was Dark* (Greening, 1903). John Whitaker's *Mary Queen of Scots Vindicated* (John Murray; J. Creech, 1788, 2nd ed. 1789), listed in our *Extrapolation* bibliography, has been dropped as mere revisionism; its 1789 supplementary

volume of "additions and corrections," pp. 136–37n., discusses how historians today would treat Mary had she come to the throne, not what she would have done there.

[5]Among "failed" allohistories, besides those listed by Shippey in "SF and the Idea of History": *Prescient rejection*—Ray Bradbury, "The Flying Machine," in his *The Golden Apples of the Sun* (Doubleday, 1953); Ronald Clark, *Queen Victoria's Bomb* (Cape, 1967). *Saving Christ*—Arthur Porges, "The Rescuer" (*ASF*, July 1962); Maurice Vaisberg, "The Sun Stood Still" (*Science Fiction Stories*, November 1958). *Saving Lincoln*—Robert Silverberg, "The Assassin" (*Imaginative Tales*, July 1957). *Lost A-bombs*—Clark, *Queen Victoria's Bomb;* Frederik Pohl and C.M. Kornbluth, "Nightmare with Zeppelins" (*Gal.*, December 1958). *Miscellaneous*—John Buchan, "The Company of the Marjolaine" (*Blackwood's*, February 1909); Jean Giraudoux, *La guerre de Troie n'aura pas lieu* [The Trojan War will not take place], in his *Théâtre*, Vol. 2 (Grasset, 1949); William Golding, *Control* (Delacorte, 1982); Harry Harrison, *A Rebel in Time* (Tor, 1983).

[6]E.g., Isaac Asimov, "The Red Queen's Race" (*ASF*, January 1949); George Byram, "The Chronicle of the 656th" (*Playboy*, March 1968); Arthur C. Clarke, "Time's Arrow" (*Science Fantasy*, Summer 1950); Dudley Dell [Horace L. Gold], "The Biography Project" (*Gal.*, September 1951); Lester Del Rey, "Fool's Errand" (*Science Fiction Quarterly*, November 1951); Mack Reynolds, "Compound Interest" (*FSF*, August 1956).

[7]In order: Anderson, "To Be a King," in his Time Patrol series; Manly Wade Wellman, *Twice in Time* (Avalon, 1957); Ralph Milne Farley, "I Killed Hitler" (*Weird Tales*, July 1941), and Eric Norden, "The Primal Solution" (*FSF*, July 1977); Randall Garrett, "Frost and Thunder" (*Asimov's SF Adventure Magazine*, Summer 1979); Evan Hunter, *Find the Feathered Serpent* (Winston, 1952); Michael Moorcock, "Behold the Man" (*NW*, September 1966; book version c 1968, Avon, 1970); Edward Page Mitchell, "The Clock That Went Backward" (New York *Sun*, 18 September 1881); Robert Arthur, "The Hero Equation" (*FSF*, June 1959). In Octave Beliard's *Aventures d'un voyageur qui explora le temps* [Adventures of a traveler who explored time] (1909), according to Versins, *Encyclopédie*, p. 867, children accidentally carried back by a time machine grow up into Romulus and Remus.

[8]Ronald A. Knox, "A Detective Story Decalogue," in *The Best Detective Stories of 1928* (Faber; Liveright, 1929), rpt. in Howard Haycraft, ed., *The Art of the Mystery Story* (Simon & Schuster, 1946), pp. 194–96. "The Detection Club Oath" in Haycraft, pp. 197–99.

[9]Radio, etc., for Columbus: Charmatz, Farmer, Iverson. Modern weapons for Napoleon et al.: Thorne, Thrupp, White. Miracle cures: Bensen. Cf. also Chandler, *Kelly Country* (war balloons and tanks in Victorian Australia); Piper, "Crossroads of Destiny," followed by Meredith, *At the Narrow Passage* (breechloaders in the eighteenth century); Simulations Publications, *Space 1889* (ether-flyers); and Sucharitkul, *The Aquiliad* (bicycles in ancient Rome).

[10]For alternative worlds in physics see DeWitt, Everett, and Gribbin.

[11]McCloskey (navigation acts), Fogel (railways), and Gunderson (steamships); other econometric entries include Andreano, Bayard, Chambers, Conrad, Davis

(Lance L.), Elster, Gerschenkron, Green (George), Jacoby, Kelley, Lee (C.H.), Lee (Susan), McClelland, Meyer, Murphy, Neuberger, Parker (William N.), Pollard, Redlich, Thomas (Robert Paul), and Williamson. For the rebuttal see Fischer.

[12]Trevelyan's "If Napoleon," for example, implies certain preconditions for successful whig reformism; Sobel's *For Want of a Nail* tries separating politics from economics and liberalism from nationalism. See also remarks below on Moore, Dick, and whig history in sf. Allohistory in the classroom is recommended by Cooper, Dumas, Hollister, and Kneeshaw; my own experience is that the students most interested in what might have been usually know least about what was.

[13]Blacks, reds, and yellows over whites: Jakes; Cox; Hersey and Gillies. French over English in North America: Percy. Arabs over French: Boireau.

[14]Bureaucracies: Anon., "God . . ."; Anvil, Armor, Augeas, Bing, Charmatz, Goldiamond, Hall, Iverson, Mignard, Miller, Parkinson, Phelps, Phillips (Henry Irving), Rickey.

[15]Amis, *The Alteration,* author's note; Dickinson, *King and Joker.*

[16]Thrillers: Byrne, *The Tunnel;* Van Rjndt, *Trial of Adolf Hitler.* Romances: Butler, "What Number Are You Calling?"; Carter, "Case of the Duplicate Diamonds."

[17]Exceptionally, one popularizer of quantum mechanics, John Gribbin, is given to examples from sf.

[18]J.B. Post in *Luna,* 53 (1974): 21, citing Gygax, Kantor, and Sobel.

[19]Lorenzo lived 1449–92; "after his death . . . it seemed that the concord and felicity of Italy had disappeared with him"—Francesco Guicciardini (1483–1540), *The History of Italy* (1561), trans. and ed. Sidney Alexander (Macmillan, 1969), p. 60; cf. pp. 4, 10.

[20]Edward Everett Hale, "The Brick Moon" (*Atlantic,* October–December 1869); rpt. in his *The Brick Moon and Other Stories* (Little, Brown, 1899) and *Works,* Vol. 2 (Little, Brown, 1898–1900). Plodding, diffuse, and intolerably arch, this typical effusion of a third-rate Gilded Age hack is well worth avoiding by any but a dedicated completist.

[21]Blanqui's countless Earths are mentioned in Anatole France, "Sur la Pierre Blanche," serialized in *L'humanité* 1904 (book version Calmann-Lévy, 1905), in his *Oeuvres complètes,* Vol. 13 (Calmann-Lévy, 1927), p. 469; but the story focuses on a utopian future instead. In alternative history "there is no continuous, self-conscious tradition comparable with the major traditions of SF, those of Verne and Wells"—Darko Suvin, in Angenot, "L'uchronie, histoire alternative et science-fiction," p. 29.

[22]"You will find no parallel worlds in the pages of Wells," says Harry Harrison in his afterword to "Run from the Fire." In fact, *A Modern Utopia* (1905) takes place on a parallel Earth in distant space, identical with ours except in its history; *Men Like Gods* (1923), on a parallel world not historically connected with ours, reached through another dimension. Stableford, writing on "alternate worlds" in Nicholls's *Science Fiction Encyclopedia,* lists as "first major work to develop the idea" Guy Dent's *Emperor of the If* (1926). On the other hand, Heinlein's narrator in *Job* (p. 15) "goes out of his way" to credit the idea of travel between universes to *Men Like Gods;* cf. Geoff Ryman review in *Foundation,* 33 (Spring 1985): 81.

²³E.g., Poe's "A Tale of the Ragged Mountains" (1845) and H. Rider Haggard's jataka-yarns *The Ancient Allan* (Cassell, 1920) and *Allan and the Ice Gods* (Doubleday, 1927). Even *Connecticut Yankee* turns out to be a dream.

²⁴Groff Conklin, ed., *Science-Fiction Adventures in Dimension* (Vanguard, 1953), p. 69.

²⁵Leinster, "Sidewise in Time," *ad fin.* Cf. Hank Morgan, boss of Camelot, in Twain's *Connecticut Yankee* (1889); Sir Henry Curtis, king-consort of Zu-Vendis, in Haggard's *Allan Quatermain* (1887); and John Carter, Warlord of Barsoom, in Edgar Rice Burrough's Mars series. White Rajahs also turn up in Piper, *Lord Kalvan;* Reynolds, *The Other Time;* and Pierre Barbet, *The Napoleons of Eridanus* (DAW, 1976). In fantasy the type dates at least to Ludvig Holberg's *Journey of Niels Klim* (1741), trans. James I. McNelis, Jr. (University of Nebraska Press, 1960); its folklore analogue must be the poor woodcutter's son who wins the princess.

²⁶The English of *Wheels of If* is discussed in Myra Edwards Barnes, *Linguistics and Languages in Science Fiction-Fantasy* (Diss., East Texas State, 1971; Arno, 1974); but her treatment of C.S. Lewis's Malacandrian or Old Solar (pp. 98–101) is so slipshod that I cannot trust her on De Camp. Cf. judgments in *SFS*, 2 (1975): 291; 3 (1976): 96.

²⁷According to Blanqui an infinite universe must include countless identical individuals in countless variations; "everything you could have been here, you are somewhere else." Wells's *A Modern Utopia* (1905) allots Chapters 8 and 9 to conversations with the narrator's other-earth counterpart. George Griffith's "The Conversion of the Professor" (*Pearson's*, May 1899), involves a visit from an "other self, inhabiting the fourth dimension"—George Locke, bibliography in Griffith, *The Voyage of "le Vengeur"* (Ferret Fantasy, 1974), p. 57. In modern sf crosstimers assume other-track identities in Norton's *Wraiths of Time*, Parker's *Time to Choose*, and Wyndham's *Random Quest*, and make contact with alternative selves in Farber's "Trans Dimensional Imports," Laumer's *Worlds of the Imperium*, Russ's *Female Man*, and Smith's *Probability Broach*.

²⁸The best-known story of self-duplication in time is Robert A. Heinlein's "By His Bootstraps" (*ASF*, October, 1941); the first, perhaps Murray Leinster's "The Fourth-Dimensional Demonstrator" (*ASF*, December 1935), or Ralph Milne Farley's "The Man Who Met Himself," listed as "copyright 1935, by Street & Smith Publications, Inc."—presumably *ASF* or *Unknown*—in his *The Omnibus of Time* (Fantasy Publishing, 1950); the most elaborate, Gerrold's *The Man Who Folded Himself.*

²⁹De Camp, *Lest Darkness Fall* (Ballantine ed.), pp. 29–30, 39–40; cf. Gibbon, *Decline and Fall*, ed. J.B. Bury (7 vols., Methuen, 1909), Chapter 27, quoting Gregory of Nyssa, Vol. 3, p. 150; Chapter 40 quoting Procopius's *Anecdota*, Vol. 4, pp. 226–28. Gregory's description of the Christological polemics of Constantinople reappears in recognizably Gibbonian phrase in Iverson, "Unholy Trinity," p. 148; for exact translation see Timothy Ware, *The Orthodox Church* (Penguin, 1963), p. 381. De Camp's introduction to the magazine version of *Lest Darkness Fall* lists as sources "ancient: Cassiodorus, Jordanes, Procopius, and Sidonius; modern: Bury, Gibbon, Hodgkin, McGovern, and Moss," plus Robert Graves's *Count Belisarius.*

³⁰Service Temporel: Barbet, *Carthage*. Cosmos Corps: Haiblum, *Tsaddik*. Voyagers: Parriott. Vatican congregation: Amery, *Königsprojekt*. T.E.R.R.A.: Larry Mad-

dock, "Agent of T.E.R.R.A." series (4 vols., Ace, 1967–69). TIA: Simon Hawke, *The Timekeeper Conspiracy* (Timewars, 2; Ace, 1984). Legitimate crosstime traders include Crosstime, Inc. (Niven, "All the Myriad Ways"), Alternities Corp. (Ford, "Slowly by, Lorena"), and Trans Dimensional Imports (Farber).

[31]Though several essays in Squire's *If* take an alternative world's existence for granted, Churchill's is the only one to begin treating ours as imaginary with his title.

[32]David Ketterer, *New Worlds for Old: The Apocalyptic Imagination, Science Fiction, and American Literature* (Indiana University Press; Doubleday Anchor, 1974), p. 242.

[33]Warrick (s.v. "Dick" in bibliography) characterizes this pair as "Taoism and fascism"; unluckily she does not know the former well and does not define the latter at all.

[34]"[Dick's] Japanese are not historical Japanese, or are so only in part, to be exact the spiritual part. As in Spinrad's 'A Thing of Beauty' [*ASF,* January 1973], they are the Japanese of myth"—Boireau, "La machine à ralentir le temps," p. 37. See Chamberlain, "Ming Meets Yoda: The Oriental Stereotype in SF," unpublished talk presented at academic session of LACON II, 3 September 1985.

[35]Bronze Age Aryan migrations: Piper, *Lord Kalvan;* Three Mile Island meltdown (1979): Swanwick, *In the Drift.* Coverage can be extended to 1980 with Steve Jackson's war game, *Raid on Iran,* and into the prehuman past with Chandler's "The Hairy Parents," Dent's *Emperor of the If,* and Farmer's *Two Hawks from Earth.*

[36]My count of turning points in Anglo-American sf (and elsewhere): Hitler, WWII, and the Bomb, 30 (31); surviving Romes and Byzantiums, 10 (4); Wars of Secession and surviving Lincolns, 7 (15); Armadas and Reformations, 7 (6); Aztecs and other Amerinds, 7 (0); Napoleons at Waterloo and elsewhere, 6 (15); US Revolutions, 6 (7). Which turning points to count and which books to dub sf are sometimes judgment calls.

[37] Bensen's *And Having Writ* and Moorcock's *Warlord of the Air* avoid WWI, Silverberg's "Translation Error" ends it early, and Busby's "Play It Again, Sam" keeps us out of it by eliminating Wilson; none is distinguished for historical analysis. I count ten alternative WWIs outside sf.

[38]Gustave Flaubert, *Dictionary of Accepted Ideas,* trans. Jacques Barzun (New Directions, 1954), p. 29.

[39]Farmer, *Gate of Time,* pp. 36–40, 50–52; *Two Hawks from Earth,* pp. 60–72, 88–95. Farmer's alternative Earth changed its own past between editions, perhaps in response to criticism of its climate patterns.

[40] In Linaweaver's "Moon of Ice" the aging Doctor Goebbels plays Richard III by explaining to his own diary how Germany won the war.

[41]Ketterer, p. 243, twice refers to FDR's assassination as if it were an event of Dick's alternative WWII instead of a precondition for it.

[42]Yarbro's "On St. Hubert's Thing" features Churches of Alexandria and Lodz, the latter apparently Slavo-Celtic, but never explains why.

[43]Philip K. Dick, "Jon's World," in August Derleth, ed., *Time to Come* (Farrar, Straus & Giroux, 1954; Pyramid, 1969), p. 144. Dick's argument from FDR's assassination reappears in Norden, *The Ultimate Solution.*

[44]Geoffroy-Château, Book 5, Chapter 3; Kantor, p. 111. Similarly Confederates in Poyer's *Shiloh Project,* p. 23, know what horrors WWI would have brought had it lasted past 1916, and virtuous unaggressive Americans in Deloria's "Why the U.S. Never Fought the Indians" third-sight in on Vietnam.

[45]Ford, *The Dragon Waiting* (Simon & Schuster), p. 378; (Avon), pp. 383–84.

[46]WWI on schedule despite Confederate victory in Poyer, Stapp, and Nesbitt; Franco-German war of 1914 instead in Aldiss, "Matrix," and Emperors' War in Moore, *Bring the Jubilee;* Kaiserism again in Farmer, *Two Hawks;* Poles in Garrett, "Lord Darcy" series, especially "The Spell of War"; Lithuanians (Littorn and Perkunisha) in Anderson, "Delenda Est," and Farmer, *Two Hawks;* Saracens in Anderson's "Operation Afreet" in *Operation Chaos.*

[47]Yulsman, *Elleander Morning;* Farmer, *Two Hawks.*

[48]De Camp, "Aristotle"; Farmer, *Two Hawks.*

[49]Wilson as Confederate president in Churchill, Kantor, and Poyer (*Shiloh Project*); McAdoo in Poyer, Underwood in Stapp, Huey Long in Dabney. Dante and Brunelleschi in Ford, *The Dragon Waiting* (Simon & Schuster), pp. 96, 106; Himmler and Beria in Amis, *The Alteration,* p. 2.

[50]Hitler as artist in Bensen, *And Having Writ,* and Poyer, *Shiloh Project;* bourgeois in Leiber, *Catch That Zeppelin!;* heroic fantasist in Spinrad, *The Iron Dream;* dictator of Germany without a Bolshevist threat in Chalker, without American intervention in WWI in Effinger, "Red Skins," and without a Polish partition in Foster, "Polonaise"; renegade boss of Amerinds and blacks in Van Herck, *Caroline;* henchman of Satan in Anderson's "Operation Incubus," in *Operation Chaos.* Cf. Carter, "The Phantom Dictator: Science Fiction Discovers Hitler," Chapter 5 of his *Creation of Tomorrow.*

[51]The "golden age of sf" has been authoritatively estimated as twelve: Terry Carr, introduction to *Universe 3* (Random House, 1973).

[52]Herbert Butterfield, *The Whig Interpretation of History* (G. Bell, 1931), p. v. Cf. Tom Shippey, "SF and the Idea of History," and his "History of SF" in Nicholls.

[53]Brown, *What Mad Universe.* Other magic-wand uchronias include Leiber, *Catch That Zeppelin!* (Edison-Sklodowska marriage of intellects); Moorcock, *The Land Leviathan* (unexplained cheap power from 1899); Bensen, *And Having Writ* (shock of extraterrestrial contact); Silverberg, "Translation Error" (telepathy); Barrett, *Leaves of Time* (Amerind-Viking philosophy of personal honor); Smith, *Probability Broach* (libertarianism).

[54]Renouvier's *Uchronie* saves Rome from barbarism and religion to give Western civilization about an eight-hundred-year head start. Toynbee, "If Alexander," and Meredith, *Vestiges of Time,* skip not only the Dark Ages but the Roman Empire. Boyd's *Last Starship from Earth* uniquely presents a spacefaring twentieth century originating in a Christian takeover of the Roman Empire about A.D. 700.

[55]Specifically Weber causally related the "ascetic Protestantism" of late Calvinism, in which work in one's calling was reputed labor for God and success a sign of grace, with the waste-not-want-not practicality symbolized by the otherwise none-too-puritan Ben Franklin: Max Weber, *The Protestant Ethic and the Spirit of Capitalism,* trans. Talcott Parsons (Scribner's, 1958). Cf. Robert W. Green, ed., *Protestantism and*

Capitalism: The Weber Thesis and Its Critics (Heath, 1959) and works excerpted; S.N. Eisenstadt, ed., *The Protestant Ethic and Modernization: A Comparative View* (Basic, 1968); Jacob Viner, *Religious Thought and Economic Society* (Duke University Press, 1978); Gianfranco Poggi, *Capitalism and the Capitalist Spirit* (University of Massachusetts Press, 1983). Not seen: Gordon Marshall, *In Search of the Spirit of Capitalism* (Berkeley and Los Angeles: University of California Press).

[56]The "black legend" of uniquely Spanish cruelty, treachery, bigotry, etc., apparently was born among Jewish refugees, Dutch rebels, and British pamphleteers, and is not yet dead in American history texts. See Philip Wayne Powell, *Tree of Hate: Propaganda and Prejudices Affecting United States Relations with the Hispanic World* (Basic, 1971).

[57]"We have no intention whatever of maintaining such a foolish and doctrinaire thesis as that the spirit of capitalism . . . could only have arisen as the result of certain effects of the Reformation, or even that capitalism as an economic system is a creation of the Reformation"—Weber, p. 91. The thesis is also implicit in Amis's *The Alteration,* Brunner's *Times Without Number,* Garrett's "Lord Darcy" series, and Roberts's *Pavane* (the apparent disclaimer at the end of which does not weaken its total effect). Harrison's "Run from the Fire," probably the most balanced view of a Roman Catholic timeline, also shows whig-Weberian influence.

[58]"Thus in *Pavane,* thanks to the death of Elizabeth, Catholicism wins. What happens? Nothing at all! The dialectic of history stops, which is totally absurd"—Carl Amery, interviewed in *Heyne Science Fiction Magazin,* 10 (1983): 125.

[59]Ray Bradbury, "A Scent of Sarsaparilla," in Frederik Pohl, ed., *Star Science Fiction Stories No. 1* (Ballantine, 1952). The spell of the past is evident in Brunner, Chandler (*Kelly Country*), Farmer (*Two Hawks*), Finney, Garrett ("Lord Darcy"), Harrison (*Transatlantic Tunnel*), Laumer, Moorcock (especially *Warlord of the Air*), Piper (especially *Lord Kalvan*), and Poyer (*Shiloh Project*).

[60]Farmer, *The Gate of Time,* pp. 51–54; *Two Hawks from Earth,* pp. 94–99.

[61]Marc Angenot, "Science Fiction in France Before Verne," trans. Jean-Marc Gouanvic and Darko Suvin, *SFS,* 5 (1978): 62.

[62]Butterfield, p. 68.

Pasts That Might Have Been, II: A Revised Bibliography of Alternative History

Barton C. Hacker and
Gordon B. Chamberlain

Criteria for inclusion here are stated in the Afterword to this volume. To limit quantity, as in the first published version (*Extrapolation,* Winter 1981), "we have also excluded works in which the effects of change are merely alluded to, mentioned in passing, or otherwise left largely undeveloped. Without this limit, most time-travel stories and a fair share of all the history ever written would have to be listed." How much development is enough? Not just a sentence, certainly; perhaps a paragraph, if sufficiently detailed; almost certainly a page. We have tried to err toward inclusiveness.

The list can claim a reasonable degree of completeness only for book-length sf published as such in the US. Separate British, Canadian, and Australasian sources are all but ignored; American sf magazines have not been checked systematically, and despite invaluable suggestions, photocopies, and even loans of rare old issues from Charles G. Waugh and Frank D. McSherry, Jr. (involving many more entries than carry their names as sources), there is probably more to be found, especially from the twenties and thirties. The same goes *a fortiori* for the "scientific romances" published in general-readership pulps earlier in the century and for belletristic essays of any period. (A look at the names we do include suggests that without at least one effort at allohistory periodical essayists of the older generation had hardly paid their dues.) And we have made no real effort to keep up with counterfactual literature in econometrics or with speculations on alternative universes in theoretical physics. War games, although they commonly create alternatives in play, are included only if their data are allohistorical from the start (e.g., an independent Confederacy).

Coverage of other languages also remains spotty. For Japanese we depend on one secondary source, for Polish on two; treatment of Italian, Spanish, and Dutch is haphazard. Soviet sf, if we interpret Jacqueline Lahana's work correctly, seems to produce every type of alternative universe but that which denies historical inevitability. Most of our new entries from German—another oddly unproductive language, considering that nation's interest in sf and reasons for wanting history changed— are due to the publications, personal letters, and bookfinding efforts of Dr. Franz Rottensteiner. French-language coverage, though fullest of all, suffers from lack of adequate libraries and bibliographies here, plus the difficulty of tracking down out-of-print sf paperbacks during one free afternoon on the Left Bank.

Since this is a bibliography for readers, not for completist collectors, we have not tried to list every edition; for sf stories, in particular, we give only first publication, leaving anthology reprints to the invaluable computerized indexes of William Contento.

Abbreviations: *Amz.* = *Amazing*, *ASF* = *Astounding* or *Analog*, *Extrap.* = *Extrapolation*, *EEH* = *Explorations in Entrepreneurial History*, *EcHR* = *Economic History Review*, *FSF* = *Fantasy and Science Fiction*, *FR* = *Fantasy Review*, *Gal.* = *Galaxy*, *IASFM* = *Isaac Asimov's Science Fiction Magazine*, *JEcH* = *Journal of Economic History*, *JIR* = *Journal of Irreproducible Results*, *JPE* = *Journal of Political Economy*, *NW* = *New Worlds*, *SFFBR* = *Science Fiction & Fantasy Book Review*, *SFS* = *Science-Fiction Studies*, *S&T* = *Strategy & Tactics*. Unless otherwise stated, place of publication for English-language entries is New York, for French Paris, for Japanese Tokyo. "D'day" abbreviates the commonest bibliographic listing for hardback sf, "Garden City, N.Y.: Doubleday."

ABC NEWS. "Invasion." *Nightline*, 5 August 1985. Executive producer Richard Kaplan, editorial manager Ted Koppel.
First half-hour of this Hiroshima commemorative special dramatized contemporary reportage of US invasion of Kyushu, 1 November 1945.

ABERNATHY, Robert. "Hostage of Tomorrow." *Planet Stories,* Spring 1949.
US soldiers in Germany go from March 1945 to a 2051 dominated by Nazism.
Since date of Nazi resurgence is same as year of publication (1949), this is not
an alternative WWII and should perhaps be regarded as a near-future
awful-warning yarn.

ADAMS, Robert. *Castaways in Time.* Virginia Beach: Donning, 1979; Signet,
1982.
Crosstime derring-do in a theocratic seventeenth-century Europe stemming
from Nestorian victory at the Council of Ephesus (A.D. 431).

———. *The Seven Magical Jewels of Ireland.* Signet, 1985.
"Castaways in Time No. 2"—i.e., more of the same.

AIKEN, Joan. *Black Hearts in Battersea.* D'day, 1964; London: Cape, 1965; Dell,
1969.
Hanoverian malcontents scheme against reigning Stuarts during "the reign
of James III, near the beginning of the nineteenth century, when England was
still sadly plagued by wolves." Second in juvenile series.

———. *The Cuckoo Tree.* London: Cape; D'day, 1971.
Sixth in same series (fifth published) features Hanoverian plot to spoil
Coronation by rolling St. Paul's into Thames.

———. *Nightbirds on Nantucket.* D'day, 1966; Dell, 1969.
Third in series; mad scientist attempts to zap St. James's Palace at transatlantic range with infernal machine.

———. *The Stolen Lake.* London: Cape; Delacorte, 1981.
Fourth in series (sixth published); adventure in Romano-British kingdoms
established in Andes by refugees from Saxon victory at Dyrham (A.D. 577).

———. *The Whispering Mountain.* London: Cape; D'day, 1969.
Fifth in series (fourth published); Welsh adventures involve Little People
with the Stuart Prince of Wales, the future Richard IV.

———. *The Wolves of Willoughby Chase.* London: Cape, 1962; London: Hutchinson, 1975; D'day, 1963; Dell, 1981.
First in series; nothing obviously allohistorical but the wolves.

ALDISS, Brian W. "Matrix." *Science Fantasy,* October 1962; rpt. as "Danger:
Religion!"
Crosstime adventure set mainly in a present where medieval papacy has
maintained hegemony over individual nations; besides briefer allusions characters include legionary from Mithraist Roman Empire stemming from
assassination of Constantine.

ALLEN, Louis. "If I Had Been . . . Hideki Tojo in 1941: How I Would Have
Avoided Bombing Pearl Harbor." In SNOWMAN, ed., *If I Had Been.*

AMERY, Carl [Christian Mayer]. *An der Feuern der Leyermark* [By Leyermark
campfires]. Munich: Nymphenburger, 1979; Munich: Heyne, 1981.
Aided by freelance riflemen from the late Confederacy, Bavaria ("the
Leyermark") replaces Prussia in 1866 as "the dominant power in Germany
and Europe": jacket blurb, letter from Dr. Franz Rottensteiner, and his

"Amery, Carl" in Hans Joachim Albers and Werner Fuchs, eds., *Reclams Science Fiction Führer* [Reclam's guide to science fiction] (Stuttgart: Philipp Reclam, Jr., 1982), p. 13.

————. *Das Königsprojekt* [Project Royalty]. Munich: Piper, 1974; Munich: Deutscher Taschenbuchverlag, 1978; Bibliothek der Science Fiction Litteratur, 35, Munich: Heyne, 1983.

Using time machine left by Leonardo, Vatican agents support a Bavarian-Stuart attempt to undo the Reformation (jacket blurb plus information from Dr. Rottensteiner, above).

AMIS, Kingsley. *The Alteration.* London: Cape, 1976; Viking, 1977; Frogmore: Panther, 1978.

Boy struggles to escape castration for papal choir in twentieth-century England deprived of Protestantism.

ANDERSON, Poul. "Delenda Est." *FSF,* December 1955; rpt. in his *Guardians of Time* (Ballantine, 1960; enl. ed. Pinnacle, 1981).

Finding backward Celto-Punic city on site of twentieth-century New York, Time Patrol traces change to liquidation of both Scipios by time-traveling filibusters in 218 B.C., giving Carthage victory over Rome and aborting entire Greco-Roman-Judeo-Christian tradition. In other Time Patrol stories, all in *FSF,* change is ultimately averted: "Time Patrol" (May 1955), "Brave to Be a King" (August 1959), "The Only Game in Town" (January 1960), and "Gibraltar Falls" (August 1975); first three rpt. in *Guardians of Time,* last in enl. ed. only. The Science Fiction Book Club twofer *Annals of the Time Patrol* (D'day, n.d.) teams *Guardians of Time* with *Time Patrolman* (Tom Doherty Associates, 1983), in which history isn't changed either.

————. *A Midsummer Tempest.* D'day, 1974; Ballantine, 1975.

Adventures of Prince Rupert in an English Civil War fought on a line where Shakespeare's plays are all real history and the Industrial Revolution has arrived two centuries early.

————. *Operation Chaos.* D'day, 1971: Lancer, n.d.; Berkley, 1978.

Adventure, social commentary, and an alternative World War II on a line where magic apparently gained scientific sanction about 1900. Fix-up of four stories from *FSF:* "Operation Afreet" (September 1956), "Operation Salamander" (January 1957), "Operation Incubus" (October 1959), "Operation Changeling" (May–June 1969).

ANDREANO, Ralph L., ed. *The New Economic History: Recent Papers on Methodology.* Wiley, 1970.

Cf. papers by DAVIS, GREEN, and REDLICH.

ANDREVON, Jean-Pierre, "L'Anniversaire du Reich de mille ans" [The anniversary of the Thousand-Year Reich]. In his *C'est arrivé mais on n'en a rien su* [It happened, but nobody knew about it] (Présence du Futur, 383, Denoël, 1984).

Like the deacon's shay, Nazi power lasts a thousand years, exactly.

————. "Qu'est-ce qu'il faisait, le jeune docteur Frankenstein, en mai 81? et en mai 68?" [What was he doing, young Dr. Frankenstein, in May 1981? and in May 1968?]. *Ibid.*

Late-twentieth-century descendant of original doctor extends lives of Albert Camus, Gérard Philipe, and Boris Vian (died 1959–60) to learn their might-have-been roles in the election of Mitterrand and the leftist riots against DeGaulle.

ANGENOT, Marc, Darko Suvin, and Jean-Marc Gouanvic. "L'uchronie, histoire alternative et science-fiction" [Uchronia, alternative history, and science fiction]. *Imagine,* 14 (Autumn 1982): 28–34.
Critical discussion.

ANON. "God Goes to Court." *American Lithographer,* date unknown; *Congressional Record,* ditto; *JIR,* 22 (1976): 6–7.
Environmental restrictions abort the Creation.

ANON. "If the Queen Had Abdicated." *Harper's,* August 1898, 454–63.
Across-the-board laudation of future Edward VII.

ANON. *The Last Inca.* 3 vols., London: Tinsley, 1874.
History of Tupac Amaru revolt in Peru (1780–82) concludes with speculations on its possible success (Charles Waugh, citing George Locke, *A Spectrum of Fantasy* [London: Ferret Fantasy, 1980]).

ANON. "Scene and Not Herd: Failure of a Revolution." *Harper's Bazaar,* November 1967, 128ff.
After bloody defeat of Russian Revolution, Tsarist performance pastiches that of Communists.

ANSEL, Walter. *Hitler Confronts England.* Durham: Duke University Press, 1960.
Study of why Operation Sea Lion didn't go includes detailed word-picture (pp. 306–16) of how it would have looked if it had.

ANVIL, Christopher. "Apron Chains." *ASF,* December 1970.
Premature development of wireless delays discovery of America.

APRIL, Jean-Pierre. "Canadian Dream." *Imagine,* 14 (Autumn 1982): 8–25.
Witch-doctor sees to it that Jacques Cartier discovers not Canada but Cameroun.

ARMOR, John C. "Bureaucrats and Quiche-Eaters on the Chisholm Trail." *JIR,* 30 (April–May, 1985): 30–32.
President Jefferson and his cabinet plan to promote western immigration via enterprise zones.

ARMSTRONG, Anthony, and Bruce Graeme [George A.A. Willis and Graham M. Jeffries]. *When the Bells Rang.* London: Harrap, 1943.
How the Nazi invasion of England in 1940 was defeated, according to NICHOLLS, ed., *Science Fiction Encyclopedia,* pp. 26, 41.

ARNOUX, Alexandre. *Faut-il brûler Jeanne?* [Must Joan burn?]. Gallimard, 1954.
Importuned by His saints, the Almighty allows Joan's supporters to rescue her—much to her own ultimate disillusionment.

ARON, Robert, *Victoire à Waterloo* [Victory at Waterloo]. André Sabatier, 1937; Plon, 1964.

Though victorious, Napoleon suffers an identity crisis on the field and abdicates anyway. See also MAUROIS, "Prefacio."

ASH, Brian, ed. *The Visual Encyclopedia of Science Fiction.* Harmony, 1977; London: Pan, 1978.
Includes sections, all with bibliographies, on alternative history (pp. 116, 121–23), parallel worlds (142–44), and time travel (145–54).

ASIMOV, Isaac. "Fair Exchange?" *Asimov's SF Adventure Magazine,* Fall 1978.
Time trip by Gilbert and Sullivan buff to recover lost score of *Thespis* produces public consequences but personal tragedy.

AUGEAS (D. Zuck). "On Shoe Buckles, Pulley Blocks, and Things." *JIR,* 30:2 (February–March 1985).
What nationalization of shoe buckle production in the 1790s did to the British economy.

AUTHORSHIP UNKNOWN. *An Englishman's Castle.*
TV drama set in "an England that exists as a slave state to the Third Reich," emphasizing "role television plays in controlling the masses" (ad for premiere that night, *Los Angeles Times,* 16 September 1979, sec. 1, p. 35).

AVALON HILL GAME CO. *Invasion of Malta—1942.* Baltimore, 1978.
War simulation game for German invasion that never happened, packaged with *Air Assault on Crete,* which did; for description see Editors of *Consumer Guide,* with Jon Freeman, *The Complete Book of Wargames* (Simon & Schuster, 1980), p. 168.

BAILEY, Hilary. "The Fall of Frenchy Steiner." *NW,* July–August 1964.
Life in 1954 Nazi-occupied London on a line where Hitler was smart enough to stay out of Russia.

BALTHASAR [pseud.]. "As-tu vu Montezuma?" [Did you see Montezuma?].
Serial, *Le Monde,* June–September 1980; book pub. Le Monde, 1980.
Listed without details by LECCIA.

BARBET, Pierre. *Carthage sera détruite: Setni enquêteur temporel, 2* [Carthage will be destroyed: time investigator Setni, 2]. Collection "Anticipation," 1298; Fleuve Noir, 1984.
Time opera; after helping Hannibal capture Rome, renegade Polluxian agent Setni schemes to found his own Carthaginian colony in Quebec. Preceding volume not seen: *Rome doit être détruite* [Rome must be destroyed], same coll. No. 1254, same pub.

———. *L'empire du Baphomet* [Baphomet's empire]. Fleuve Noir, 1972; trans. Bernard Kay as *Baphomet's Meteor,* DAW, 1972.
Advised and armed by alien castaway in France since 1118, Knights Templar set out in 1275 to conquer Eurasia. A sequel takes them into space: *Croisade stellaire,* Fleuve Noir, 1974, trans. C.J. Cherryh as *Stellar Crusade* in combined volume with preceding, *Cosmic Crusaders,* DAW, 1980.

———. *Liane de Noldaz* [Liane of Noldaz]. Fleuve Noir, 1973; trans. Stanley Hochman as *The Joan-of-Arc Replay,* DAW, 1978.

On Earth-equivalent Noldaz, experimental alien historians not only save mauve-skinned surrogate Joan from stake but arm her to conquer England.

BARBIER, J.-B. *Si Napoléon avait pris Londres* [If Napoleon had taken London]. Libraire Français, 1970.

Despite title, deals mainly with what he was trying to do, not with what might have happened had he done it.

BARING, Maurice. "The Alternative." *London Mercury,* 7 (November 1922): 26–35; rpt. in his *Half a Minute's Silence* (London: Heinemann; D'day, 1925; Freeport: Books for Libraries, 1970) and *Maurice Baring Restored,* ed. Paul Horgan (Farrar, Straus & Giroux, 1970); also in Philip Van Doren Stern, ed., *Travelers in Time* (D'day, 1947).

Some political and more literary results of young Napoleon's being sent into the British navy instead of the French army.

BARKER, Felix, and Ralph Hyde. *London As It Might Have Been.* London: John Murray, 1982.

Architecture and engineering planned but never realized, according to excerpt, "Crossing the Thames: London Bridges That Might Have Been," *History Today,* 32 (June 1982): 22–28.

BARRETT, Neal, Jr. *The Leaves of Time.* Lancer, 1971.

Alien-invasion yarn, much of it set in a modern "Vinaskaland" stemming from Leif Ericsson's success in colonizing Vinland.

BARTON, S.W. See KURLAND, Michael.

BASIL, Otto. *Wenn das der Führer wüsste* [If the *Führer* knew]. Vienna: Fritz Molden, 1966; trans. and slightly abr. by Thomas Weyr as *The Twilight Men,* Meredith, 1968.

Twenty years after a nuclear bomb on London wins World War II for Germany, Hitler's death leads to a struggle for succession.

BAYARD, Thomas, James Orr, Joseph Pelman, and Jorge Perez-Lopez. "MFN Treatment of Imports from China: Effects on U.S. Employment." *Journal of Policy Modeling,* 3 (October 1981): 361–73.

Economic counterfactual: what if China had received most-favored-nation treatment in US trade since 1978?

BEAR, Greg. "Scattershot." In Terry Carr, ed., *Universe 8* (D'day; Popular Library, 1978).

Disabled space battleship harbors beings from several alternative Earths, including one whose North American culture is macho Amerind-French.

BECK, Joan. "What If There Had Been No Atom Bomb?" *Chicago Tribune* column, syndicated in *Tulsa World,* 3 August 1985, p. A-9 (clipping from Frank McSherry, Jr.).

Scenario based on ideas of R.E. Lindgren: lengthened war lets Russian troops into Japan; lack of atomic deterrent lets Communism subvert Europe and Middle East.

BEERBOHM, Max. "Mr. Morley of Blackburn, on an Afternoon in the Spring of '69, Introduces Mr. John Stuart Mill." Uncollected drawing, Tate Gallery; reprod. in J.G. Riewald, ed., *Beerbohm's Literary Caricatures* (Hamden: Archon, 1977), pp. 176–79.

Young John Morley aims at pepping up Mill's *Subjection of Women* with illustrations by Dante Gabriel Rossetti.

———. "A Panacea." *Saturday Review* (London), 23 July 1904; rpt. in his *Around Theaters* (Knopf, 1930).

Satirical fantasy: how King Edward VII, on 1 April 1904, did the best thing possible for British drama by closing all theaters for ten years.

BELLOC, Hilaire. "If Drouet's Cart Had Stuck." In SQUIRE, ed., *If,* all eds.

With the road clear at Varennes, Louis XVI escapes to his foreign friends, returning to crush the French Revolution and with it European progress.

BENÉT, Stephen Vincent. "The Curfew Tolls." *Saturday Evening Post,* 5 October 1935; rpt. in his *Thirteen O'Clock* (Farrar & Rinehart, 1971; Freeport: Books for Libraries, 1971); *Selected Works, II: Prose* (Farrar & Rinehart, 1942); *25 Short Stories* (Garden City: Sun Dial, 1943), and *The Stephen Vincent Benét Pocket Book,* ed. Robert Van Gelder (Pocket Books, 1946); also in Philip Van Doren Stern, ed., *The Moonlight Traveler* (D'day, 1942), rpt. as *Great Tales of Fantasy and Imagination* (Pocket Books, 1954).

Home view of a Napoleon born before his time, in 1737 instead of 1769.

BENSEN, Donald R. *And Having Writ. . . .* Indianapolis: Bobbs-Merrill, 1978; Ace, 1979.

Aliens shipwrecked on Earth in 1908 first engineer Edison's election as President, then go to work on European rulers to avert World War I.

BESTER, Alfred. "The Men Who Murdered Mohammed." *FSF,* October 1958.

Since "time is a private matter," "when a man changes the past he only affects his own past—no one else's."

BIER, Jesse. "Father and Son." In his *A Hole in the Lead Apron* (Harcourt, 1964).

Post-Nazi government in 1945 Germany imposes literal decimation on its citizens to atone for the Holocaust.

BING, Richard J. "Withering and the Quarterly Journal of Negative Results." *Archives of Internal Medicine,* 3 (1963): 61–62; *JIR,* date unknown; George H. Scherr, ed., *Journal of Irreproducible Results: Selected Papers* (Chicago Heights: JIR, 1976), pp. 151–52.

How Dr. William Withering's pioneering digitalis study of 1765 would have fared under 1970s-style peer review.

BIRD, Maj. Gen. Sir W[ilkinson] D. "A Might-Have-Been of the Great War in 1914." *Army Quarterly,* 31 (October 1935): 30–35.

Had the Germans, in August 1914, not weakened their westbound invasion force to provide troops for East Prussia they might have gone on to besiege Paris; but would that have won them the war?

BIXBY, Jerome. "One Way Street." *Amz.,* January 1954.

Inadvertent crosstime traveler finds history altered but cannot explain why.

BLAKEMORE, Harold. "If I Had Been . . . Salvador Allende in 1972–3: How I Would Have Stayed in Power in Chile." In SNOWMAN, ed., *If I Had Been.*

BLANQUI, Louis-Auguste. *L'Éternité par les astres: hypothèse astronomique* [Eternity through the stars: an astronomical hypothesis]. G. Baillière, 1872.

Perhaps earliest statement of multiple-Earths theory: infinite universe of finite elements must necessarily produce parallel Earths with infinite variations, from the strictly personal ("Everything you could have been here, you are somewhere else") to different outcomes of Waterloo or Marengo.

BLISH, James. For *Star Trek* book versions see ELLISON, Harlan, and ROD-DENBERRY, Gene.

BLOCH, Robert. "The World-Timer." *Fantastic,* August 1960.

Glimpses of several possible timelines, as seen from a utopian alternative present in which human society is properly geared to human sexuality.

BOEHEIM, Carl von [Emil Frankel]. *Die Kaisersaga: Utopia Austriaca* [Imperial saga: an Austrian utopia]. Augsburg: A. Kraft, 1960.

Prince Franz Stephan, allohistorical second son of Emperor Franz Joseph, preserves Habsburg Empire via a "revolution from above" (blurb plus personal communication from Dr. Franz Rottensteiner).

BÖHME, Gernot, Wolfgang van den Daele, and Wolfgang Krohn. "Alternativen in der Wissenschaft" [Alternatives in science]. *Zeitschrift für Soziologie,* 1 (1972): 302–16; trans. E.G.H. Joffe, *International Journal of Sociology,* 8 (1978): 70–94.

Discussing contingent factors in the historical development of science, authors briefly wonder what might have happened had a chemical rather than a mechanical worldview prevailed at the outset of the scientific revolution.

BOIREAU, Jacques. "Les enfants d'Ibn Khaldoun" [Children of Ibn Khaldun]. In Jacques Sadoul, ed., *Univers 07* (J'ai Lu, 1976).

Thanks to Arab victory at Tours in 732, progressive Muslim Occitania (our southern France) confronts irredentism and emigration from the backward Christian north.

———. "L'été" [Summer]. In *Fiction,* 348 (Opta, 1984).

Listed as allohistory in LECCIA bibliography.

———. "La machine à ralentir le temps" [The time-slowdown machine]. *Imagine,* 14 (Autumn 1982): 35–43.

Contrasts "optimistic" nineteenth-century French uchronias (GEOFFROY, RENOUVIER) with "pessimistic" twentieth-century Anglo-American ones (DICK; MOORE, *Bring the Jubilee;* ROBERTS, *Pavane;* SILVERBERG, *Gate of Worlds*).

———. Title unknown. In Jean-Marc Gouanvic and Stephanie Nicot, eds., *Espaces imaginaires 1* (Montreal: "Les Imaginoides," 1983).

"A nostalgic slice-of-life story set in the universe of his justly famous story, 'Les Enfants d'Ibn Khaldoun'"—Jean-Daniel Breque in *FR,* 75 (January 1985): 52.

BON, Frédéric, and Michel-Antoine Burnier. *Si mai avait gagné: facétie politique* [It May had succeeded: a political pleasantry]. Pauvert, 1968.

Riots against DeGaulle produce socialist revolution instead of conservative backlash.

BOPP, Léon. *Liaisons du monde* [Life's conjunctions]. Vol. 1, Gallimard, 1938; Vols. 2–4, Geneva: Éditions du Dialogue, 1941–44; new ed., 2 vols., Gallimard, 1949.

Detailed sociopolitical history of France after the 1936 Popular Front government produced a leftist revolution.

BORDEN, Morton. "1759: What If Canada Had Remained French?" In BORDEN and GRAHAM, *Speculations.*

Consequences of Montcalm's triumph over Wolfe at Quebec.

————. "1784: What If Slavery Had Been Geographically Confined?" *Ibid.*

Had Jefferson succeeded in banning slavery beyond the original thirteen states.

————. "1789: Could the Articles of Confederation Have Worked?" *Ibid.*

If the states had rejected the Constitution.

————. "1801: Would Aaron Burr Have Been a Great President?" *Ibid.*

Had the House broken the electoral tie with Jefferson in favor of Burr.

————. "1832: What If the Second Bank Had Been Rechartered?" *Ibid.*

If Nicholas Biddle had not sought charter renewal prematurely.

————. "1850: What If the Compromise of 1850 Had Been Defeated?" *Ibid.*

Without President Taylor's untimely death the Civil War might have been fought a decade earlier at far less cost.

————, and Otis L. Graham, Jr. *Speculations on American History.* Lexington: Heath, 1977.

Six essays each by BORDEN and GRAHAM, listed separately.

BORGES, Jorge Luis. "El jardín de senderos que se bifurcan" [The garden of forking paths]. In his *El jardín de senderos que se bifurcan* (Buenos Aires: Sur, 1941). Rpt. in his *Ficciones (1935–44)* (Buenos Aires: Emece, 1944; rpt. by same pub. as Vol. 5 of his *Obras completas*, 1946). Trans. Helen Temple and Ruthven Todd in Borges, *Ficciones,* ed. Anthony Kerrigan (Grove, 1962; London: Weidenfeld & Nicolson, 1962; London: John Calder, 1965); rpt. in Michael Moorcock, ed., *The Traps of Time* (London: Rapp & Whiting, 1968).

A speculation on the philosophy of alternative history as alternative routes to the same end; the same theme is touched in several other pieces in *Ficciones,* e.g., "The Library of Babel."

BOYD, John. *The Last Starship from Earth.* Weybright & Talley, 1968; Berkley Medallion, 1969; Penguin, 1978.

Because Jesus lived to lead the storming of Rome at age seventy, the twentieth century boasts among other complexities a computer Pope.

BRENNERT, Alan. "Nostalgia Tripping." In Robert Hoskins, ed., *Infinity Five* (Lancer, 1973).

However good or bad alternative 1949s may be, they all look better than any 2003.

BRETNOR, R[eginald]. "Old Uncle Tom Cobleigh and All." *FSF*, October 1973.

Indian student's reinvention of Roger Bacon's speculum lets him alter history to perpetuate the British Raj.

BRIE, Marc-André. "Quelques repères pour une bibliographie de l'uchronie" [Some benchmarks for a bibliography of allohistory]. *Imagine*, 14 (Autumn 1982): 55–67.

Short list in order of publication, heavily reliant on secondary sources and not entirely accurate.

BROSNAN, John. See NICHOLLS, Peter.

BROWN, Fredric. *What Mad Universe*. Dutton, 1949; Bantam, 1950.

Mid-twentieth-century world of teenage sf fan's dreams differs from ours in many ways, one of them historical: the invention in 1903 of a spacewarp drive based on a sewing machine.

BROWNLOW, Kevin, and Andre Mollo (authors, producers, and directors). *It Happened Here*. Rath Films/Long Distance Films (distrib. United Artists), 1966.

Despite successful Nazi invasion of July 1940, British resistance continues in 1944; discussed with stills in Brownlow, *How It Happened Here* (D'day, 1968).

BRUNNER, John. *Times Without Number*. Ace Double, 1962, as fix-up of three stories first pub. in *Science Fiction Adventures* (London) in 1962: "Spoil of Yesterday" (March), "The Word Not Written" (June), and "The Fullness of Time" (July); exp. ed. Ace, 1969.

Twentieth century generated by Spanish Armada victory features time travel without Industrial Revolution.

BUCHAN, John. *The Causal and the Casual in History*. The Rede Lecture, Cambridge University Press, 1929; rpt. in his *Men and Deeds* (London: Davis, 1935; Freeport: Books for Libraries, 1969), pp. 1–20.

Allohistory as intellectual parlor game, with five brief studies of small turning points: Prince Henry lives to become king of Great Britain instead of Charles I, Marlborough captures Paris, Napoleon's Brumaire coup fails, Stonewall Jackson survives Chancellorsville to help Lee win at Gettysburg, and the Gallipoli operation succeeds.

BUCHWALD, Art. "Let's See Who Salutes." New York *Herald Tribune* syndicated column, Philadelphia *Evening Bulletin*, 10 December 1959; rpt. in Arthur Power Dudden, ed., *Pardon Us, Mr. President! American Humor on Politics* (South Brunswick: A.S. Barnes; London: Yoseloff, 1975), pp. 156–59.

How honchos of WJULY–TV, Philadelphia, reacted to Jefferson's proposed broadcast of the Declaration of Independence.

BUDDEN, Gilbert. "The Use of Imaginary Forces: The 80,000 Russians." *Army Quarterly*, 35 (October 1937): 104–16.

How the rumor of Russian troops in Belgium, in August 1914, might have been exploited by Britain to spook the German High Command.

BURNIER, Michel-Antoine. See BON, Frédéric.

BURROUGHS, William S. *Cities of the Red Night*. Holt, Rinehart & Winston, 1981.

Starting in the eighteenth century, anarchistic pirate communes raise the Third World against its oppressors.

BURY, J.B. "Cleopatra's Nose." *R.P.A. Annual*, 1916, 16–23; rpt. in his *Selected Essays*, ed. Harold Temperley (Cambridge: Cambridge University Press, 1930), pp. 60–69.

On historical causation and contingency, and why some things might well have happened differently.

BUSBY, F.M. "Play It Again, Sam." In Robin Scott Wilson, ed., *Clarion III* (Signet, 1973).

Speculations on how best to edit the past.

———. "Wrong Number." *IASFM*, 21 December 1981.

Having taken care of World Wars II and III, Sam works to sidetrack the expansionist tendencies of Russia. A third "Sam" story in *IASFM*, "Balancing Act" (16 February 1981), involves the sort of unhistorical change we bar.

BUTLER, Ron. "What Number Are You Calling?" *Fantastic*, October 1955.

Crosstime romance visits a New York that is still named New Amsterdam.

BUTTERFIELD, Herbert. "The Role of the Individual in History." *History*, 40 (1955): 1–17.

How great events may hinge on small causes, and might have turned out otherwise.

BYRNE, Robert. *The Tunnel*. Harcourt Brace Jovanovich; Dell, 1977.

Work on Channel tunnel authorized by 1973 Franco-British treaty is almost complete when terrorists strike.

CAILLOIS, Roger. *Ponce Pilate: récit* [Pontius Pilate: a story]. Gallimard, 1961.

Finding Jesus innocent, Pontius Pilate releases Him, thus aborting Christianity.

CALVERT, Peter. "If I Had Been . . . Benito Juarez in 1867: How I Would Have Pardoned the Emperor Maximilian—And, Perhaps, Have Saved Mexico from Decades of Political and Social Turmoil." In SNOWMAN, ed., *If I Had Been.*

ČAPEK, Karel. "Pseudo-Lot čili o vlastenectví" ["Pseudo Lot, or Concerning Patriotism"] (1923). In his *Kniha apokryfů* (Prague: Borový, 1945), trans. Dora Round as *Apocryphal Stories* (London: Allen & Unwin; Macmillan, 1949).

Why Lot rejected the angels' warning to leave Sodom (but story stops there).

CARON, Carlos María. "La Victoria de Napoleón" [Napoleon's victory]. In Eduardo Goligorsky, ed., *Los Argentinos en la luna* (Buenos Aires: Flor, 1968).

Landing on a distant planet, astronauts utilize alien science to observe Earth's past; but what they see includes Napoleon's entry into London, a Chinese invasion of Europe, and worse.

CARR, John F. See GREEN, Roland.

CARROLL, Tod. See O'ROURKE, P.J.

CARTER, Paul A. "The Constitutional Origins of *Westly v. Simmons.*" *ASF,* October 1985.

How "the absence of a Manhattan Project" could have reacted on US politics to bring about the obscurantist 1973 of Isaac Asimov's "Trends" (*ASF,* July 1939).

————. *The Creation of Tomorrow: Fifty Years of Magazine Science Fiction.* Columbia University Press, 1977.

See especially discussion of alternative histories (pp. 109–13) and Nazi victories (pp. 132–38).

————. "The Mystery of the Duplicate Diamonds." In Judy-Lynn Del Rey, ed., *Stellar No. 7* (Ballantine, 1981).

Contact between alternative Americas stemming from the 1968 Presidential election and Watergate.

CHADBOURNE, Billie Niles. See JOHNSON, Robert B.

CHALKER, Jack L. "Dance Band on the Titanic." *IASFM,* July–August 1978.

A Maine ferry plies between several North Americas, including Portuguese and Norse.

————. *Downtiming the Night Side.* Tom Doherty Associates, 1985.

Future time-manipulators aim at assassinating Karl Marx (summary of results, pp. 139–40).

CHAMBERS, Edward J., and Donald F. Gordon. "Primary Products and Economic Growth: An Empirical Measurement." *JPE,* 74 (August 1966): 315–32.

Canadian development without the 1901–11 boom in wheat exports.

CHANDLER, A. Bertram. "The Hairy Parents." *Void* (Australia), 2 (1975); rpt. *Fantastic,* October 1978.

Neanderthal throwback influences paleohistory to help his race survive (Charles Waugh).

————. *Kelly Country.* DAW, 1985 (Australian ed. 1983).

Thanks to mental time-traveler's interference, Australian bushranger Ned Kelly escapes police capture at Glenrowan in 1880 to spark anti-British proletarian revolution and become president of an Irish-dominated Australian republic. The novel is foreshadowed in Chandler's "Grimes at Glenrowan," *IASFM,* March–April 1978; background on weaponry is provided in "The Way It Was," *Omega Science Fiction,* March–April 1981, rpt. as "A New Dimension" in *Up to the Sky in Ships* (Chicon IV volume, Cambridge: NESFA, 1982). Not seen: "Kelly Country," Van Ikine, ed., *Australian Science Fiction* (St. Lucia: University of Queensland Press, 1982), noted in *SFFBR,* 15 (June 1983): 29.

CHARMATZ, A. "Sailing Through Program Management." *ASF,* 5 January 1981.

Columbus returns from his first voyage to find further exploration stifled by bureaucracy.

————. "A Second Chance." *ASF,* 9 November 1981.

Columbus's next voyage has no better luck.

CHESNOFF, Richard Z., Edward Klein, and Robert Littell. *If Israel Lost the War.* Coward McCann, 1969.

Three *Newsweek* reporters describe the Six-Day War of 1967 that began with a preemptive air strike by the Arabs.

CHESTERTON, G.K. "If Don John of Austria Had Married Mary Queen of Scots." In SQUIRE, ed., *If,* all eds.; also in *London Mercury,* 23 (January 1931): 328–42, and Chesterton, *The Common Man* (Sheed & Ward, 1950).

The *Lepanto* theme in allohistory: how romance might have lived on as a Catholic England battled not Spain but the Turk.

CHILSON, Robert. "The Devil and the Deep Blue Sky." In LEY, ed., *Beyond Time.*

Kerosene crisis due to fuel demands of steamcars elicits Congressional investigation of the more efficient internal-combustion engine.

————. *The Shores of Kansas.* Popular Library, 1976.

Future time-traveler to Mesozoic apparently (pp. 19–20) inhabits world where Theodore Roosevelt was assassinated; but no further development is given.

CHRISTOPHER, John. *Fireball.* Dutton, 1981; Tempo, 1984.

Derring-do for boys on crosstime line where survival of Julian the Apostate kept the Roman Empire alive but culturally stagnant.

————. *New Found Land.* Dutton, 1983.

The boys sail west to discover Vikings on Nantucket, Aztecs in South Carolina, and a Chinese pagoda in Southern California.

CHURCHILL, Winston S. "If Lee Had Not Won the Battle of Gettysburg." In SQUIRE, ed., *If,* all eds.; also *Scribner's,* 88 (December 1930): 587–97.

Northern victory might have prevented both reunion of the English-speaking peoples and peaceful resolution of the European crisis of 1914.

CLAGETT, John. *A World Unknown.* Popular Library, 1975.

Classical Latin civilization in the Southern California of a timeline where Jesus never existed and the Roman Empire was first reorganized and then peacefully dissolved under Constantine.

CLARK, Ronald W. *The Bomb That Failed.* Morrow, 1969; as *The Last Day of the Old World,* London: Cape, 1969.

Thanks to sabotage by Klaus Fuchs, the Trinity bomb test fails, sharply altering the course of World War II.

CLARO, Joe. See PARRIOTT.

CLIMO, T.A., and P.G.A. Howells. "Possible Worlds in Historical Explanation." *History and Theory,* 15 (1976): 1–20.

A philosophical analysis of the logic of counterfactuals in history. Cf. B.C.

Hurst, "A Comment on the Possible Worlds of Climo and Howells," *ibid.*, 18 (1979): 52–60.

COCKBURN, Alexander. "The Tedium Twins." *Harper's*, August 1982, 24–27.
How the *MacNeil/Lehrer Report* would have covered cannibalism, the slave trade, and the Crucifixion.

COLLYN, George. "Unification Day." *NW*, May 1966.
England on the 150th anniversary of its incorporation into the French Empire after Napoleon's victory at Waterloo.

COMPTON, Karl T. "If the Atomic Bomb Had Not Been Used." *Atlantic*, December 1946, 54–56.
A mover of the Manhattan Project defends using the bomb on Japan by weighing alternative costs of invasion.

CONSUMER GUIDE, Editors of. *Cars That Never Were.* Beekman House, 1981.
Specifications and photos of such aborted offerings as 1943–45 Fords, premature Detroit compacts, revived LaSalles, and gas-turbine Chryslers.

COON, Gene L. See RODDENBERRY, Gene.

COOPER, B. Lee. "Beyond Flash Gordon and 'Star Wars': Science Fiction and History Instruction." *Social Education*, 42 (1978): 392–97.
Includes discussion of alternative history, with references. Much the same material is dealt with in two other papers by Cooper: "Folk History, Alternative History, and Future History," *Teaching History*, 2 (1977): 58–62; and "Science Fiction: A New Frontier for History Teachers," paper presented at the annual meeting of the American Historical Association, San Francisco, 27–30 December 1978.

COOPER, Edmund. "Jupiter Laughs." In LEY, ed., *Beyond Time.*
The slaying of Jesus by Herod's troops, with an epilogue on Queen Victoria as Roman satrap.

COPPEL, Alfred. *The Burning Mountain: A Novel of the Invasion of Japan.* Harcourt Brace Jovanovich, 1983.
Japanese and American experiences during Operations Olympic and Coronet, 1945–46, after lightning aborts the first bomb test at Trinity.

CORES, Lucy. "Hail to the Chief." In LEY, ed., *Beyond Time.*
Manipulating the 1996 election in an America where the Watergate break-in went unreported.

CORLEY, Edwin. *The Jesus Factor.* Paperback Library, 1970.
Borderline allohistory/secret history; if nuclear weapons would explode when fixed in place but not when dropped, the Hiroshima-Nagasaki bombs and the arms race since might all prove a gigantic hoax.

CORVO, Baron. See ROLFE, Frederick William.

COSTA, A. *L'appel du 17 juin* [The appeal of June 17]. Lattes, 1980.
Listed without details in LECCIA; an allusion to Pétain's appeal for peace in 1940 and/or to DeGaulle's *L'appel*?

COULSON, Juanita. "Unscheduled Flight." In LEY, ed., *Beyond Time.*
Bermuda Triangle proves a one-way gate to Americas colonized by Vikings and English buccaneers.

COULSON, Robert. "Soy la Libertad." *Ibid.*
Chicanos in a balkanized America originally discovered by Magellan react to terrorist assassination of Texas President Johnson.

COUPLING, J.J. "Mr. Kinkaid's Pasts." *FSF,* August 1953.
"Principle of historical indeterminacy" allows time-traveler an infinite number of alternative pasts consistent with the known present.

COX, Irving E. "In the Circle of Nowhere." *Universe Science Fiction,* July 1954; *Fantastic,* January 1960.
Amerind crosstime visitor to our world knows Caucasians only as conquered slaves.

COX, Richard, ed. *Operation Sea Lion.* London: Thornton Cox, 1975; San Rafael: Presidio, 1977.
The 1940 Nazi invasion of England as dramatized in a 1974 war game between British and German officers.

CRONIN, Philip M. "If Britain Had Suppressed America's War for Independence." *Harvard Magazine,* July–August 1976, 44–47.
Suggestions for subsequent American history from three Cambridge historians, with map.

CROSBY, Ernest. "If the South Had Been Allowed to Go." *North American Review,* 177 (December 1903): 867–71.
Slavery would have died naturally, the nation would have reunited, and much evil would have been avoided.

DABNEY, Virginius. "If the South Had Won the War." *American Mercury,* October 1936, 199–205.
Menckenish look at Huey Long's CSA as woolhat utopia, thanks to Pickett's charge and Vicksburg's tenacity.

DANIELS, David A. "The Branches of Time." *Wonder Stories,* August 1935.
Early statement of alternative-timeline theme: "It has all been—this world, your world, . . . my world. They all exist in the absolute time of the cosmos, and the possibilities of what has been or what may be are manifold, like tree branches." Actual changes depicted involve only the remote future (Yellows vs. Whites) and remote past (reptiles vs. mammals). Same issue as WEINBAUM.

DAUTZENBERG, J.A. See MULISCH.

DAVID, P.A. See FOGEL, Robert W., *Railways.*

DAVIDSON, Avram. "O Brave Old World." In LEY, ed., *Beyond Time.*
How the eighteenth-century British came to declare independence from American tyranny. See also GOLDSTONE, Cynthia.

DAVIN, Eric L. "Avenging Angel." In Jerry Pournelle and Jim Baen, eds., *Far Frontiers II* (Baen Enterprises, Summer 1985).

With Judah P. Benjamin as first secretary of state, Confederacy gets European scientific aid to drop ballistic missile on Lincoln's second inaugural.

DAVIS, F.C. *Atlantica.* US war game distributed in UK by Albion.

"A 'Diplomacy' variant set in 1872, bringing in the Confederate States, the Union, and Canada," according to G.I. Gibbs, *Handbook of Games and Simulation Exercises,* 3rd ed. (Beverly Hills: Sage, 1974).

DAVIS, Lance L. "'And It Will Never Be Literature'—The New Economic History: A Critique." *EEH,* 2nd ser., 6 (1985): 75–92; rpt. in Robert P. Swierenga, ed., *Quantification in American History: Theory and Research* (Atheneum, 1970), and ANDREANO, ed., *New Economic History.* See especially Part 3, "The Counterfactual." Cf. GREEN, George.

DEAN, William. "A Passage in Italics." *FSF,* May 1972.

Occupied New York after Italy got the first atomic bomb and won the war.

DE CAMP, L. Sprague. "Aristotle and the Gun." *ASF,* February 1958.

After attempting to teach proper scientific method to Aristotle, a time-traveler returns to find the scientific revolution long delayed by Aristotle's authority.

————. "Lest Darkness Fall." *Unknown,* December 1939; book version, Holt, 1941; rev. ed., Ballantine, 1974.

Time-traveler's special historical knowledge plus modest technical innovations promise to push sixth-century Italy out of the Dark Ages.

————. "The Wheels of If." *Unknown,* December 1940.

The "forfeited birthrights" of Far Western Christian and Scandinavian civilizations, as described by TOYNBEE, come to fruition in a contemporary America colonized by Celts and Norsefolk after Celtic Christianity broke with Rome in 664 and was kept apart from it by Arab victory at Tours in 732. Cf. De Camp's review of *A Study of History,* "The Science of Whithering," *ASF,* July–August 1940.

DEIGHTON, Len. *SS-GB: Nazi-Occupied Britain, 1941.* London: Cape, 1978; Knopf, 1979; Ballantine, 1980.

Scotland Yard inspector joins underground in raiding secret Nazi atomic research lab in Devon.

DELISLE DE SALES, Jean Claude Izouard. *Ma République* [My republic]. Paris, 1791.

According to VERSINS, *Encyclopedie,* p. 904, Chapter 21 of this multivolume work outlines an alternative course for the French Revolution had Louis XVI been firmer with the nobility.

DELORIA, Vine, Jr. "Why the U.S. Never Fought the Indians." *Christian Century,* 7–14 January 1976, 9–12.

Bicentennial commentary on US history since 1815, when Adams and Jefferson emerged from retirement to plead for a moral Indian policy, and Tecumseh founded a viable Indian Nation. With HILL and WENTZ, part of a series, "What If . . . ?—Rewriting U.S. History."

DEL REY, Lester. *The Infinite Worlds of Maybe.* Holt, Rinehart & Winston, 1966. "Winston SF Series" juvenile potboiler includes crosstime stopoff in US of "Second War Between the States."

DENT, Guy. *Emperor of the If.* London: Heinemann, 1926.

Rated by STABLEFORD (in NICHOLLS, p. 26) as "the first major work to develop the idea" of alternative worlds; according to BRIE, p. 56, presents a contemporary England never subjected to the glaciers.

DEVAUX, Pierre, and Henry-Gérard Viot. *La conquête d'Almériade* [The conquest of Almeriada]. Magnard, 1954.

Time travel, but not alternative history—because, as Devaux explains in a postface (citing MAUROIS), readers already know what happened from their textbooks.

DE WITT, Bryce S. "Quantum Mechanics and Reality: Could the Solution to the Dilemma of Indeterminism Be a Universe in Which All Possible Outcomes of an Experiment Actually Occur?" *Physics Today,* 23 (September 1970): 30–35.

Sums up, with bibliography, the "Everett-Wheeler-Graham interpretation of quantum mechanics," according to which "this universe is constantly splitting into a stupendous number of branches"; cf. EVERETT.

——, and Neill Graham. *The Many-Worlds Interpretation of Quantum Mechanics: A Fundamental Exposition.* Princeton University Press, 1973.

Reprints DeWITT and EVERETT articles with others on same theme and illustrative citations from BORGES's "Garden of Forking Paths" and William James on indeterminism.

DICK, Philip K. *The Man in the High Castle.* Putnam's, 1962; Berkley Medallion, 1974.

Life in Japanese-occupied California and elsewhere in the partitioned US due ultimately to FDR's assassination in 1933. See Patricia Warrick, "The Encounter of Taoism and Fascism in Philip K. Dick's *The Man in the High Castle,*" *SFS,* 7 (1980): 174-90, rpt. in Martin Harry Greenberg and Joseph D. Olander, eds., *Philip K. Dick* (Taplinger, 1983); and KETTERER.

DICKINSON, Peter. *King and Joker.* London: Hodder & Stoughton; Pantheon, 1976; London: Magnum; New York: Avon, 1977.

Murder in a British Royal Family descended from George V's elder brother Albert Victor.

D'ISRAELI, Isaac. "Of a History of Events Which Have Not Happened." In his *Curiosities of Literature,* ed. Benjamin D'Israeli, 3 vols., 14th ed. (London: Moxon, 1849), Vol. 2, pp. 474–85.

First known essay on allohistory as a genre, with references to LIVY, PIGNOTTI, and ROSCOE, and comments on possible consequences of Charles Martel's defeat at Tours, better treatment for Luther at the Diet of Worms, Henry VIII's reconciliation with Rome, an Armada victory, and a longer life for Lorenzo de' Medici. According to STABLEFORD, this must first have seen print in the second series of the *Curiosities* (1823–34).

DONALD, David Herbert. "The Limits of Innovation, 1865–1869." In Bernard Bailyn et al., *The Great Republic: A History of the American People* (Lexington: Heath, 1977), Chapter 21; rpt. in Donald, *Liberty and Union* (Lexington and Toronto: Heath, 1978), Chapter 6.

Opening section, "Paths Not Taken," suggests plausible alternative courses for Reconstruction.

D'ORMESSON, Jean. *La gloire de l'empire* [The glory of the empire]. Gallimard, 1971.

Recounts in the grand historical manner the life of Alexis, nineteenth-century emperor of all Eurasia; a French Academy prizewinner (BRIE).

DOUAY, D. *Le principe de l'oeuf* [The egg principle]. Calmann-Lévy, 1980.

Cited without details in LECCIA.

DOWNING, David. *The Moscow Option: An Alternative Second World War*. St. Martin's, 1980.

Hitler's crucial disability lets the Wehrmacht go on to Moscow, but even Japanese victory at Midway as well leaves the Axis faced with hard geographical and economic reality.

DOZOIS, Gardner, and Jack Dann. "Playing the Game." *Twilight Zone*, February 1982.

Young boy wanders across timelines, looking for home; perhaps personal rather than allohistorical (Charles Waugh).

DROIT, Jacques. *Malheureux Ulysse* [Unhappy Ulysses]. N.p., 1956.

Louis XVI escapes arrest, so that France in 1870 is ruled by Louis XIX, according to VAN HERP, p. 66; author's theme is apparently akin to that of COUPLING.

DUITS, Charles. *Ptah Hotep*. Denoël, 1971; 2 vols. pb. ed. 1981.

Romance and court intrigue in far-future syncretic Egyptian-Roman-Arab civilization stemming ultimately from Constantine's repression of Christianity.

DUMAS, Wayne. "Speculative Reconstruction of History: A New Perspective on an Old Idea." *Social Education*, 33 (1969): 54–55.

A plea for alternative history in the classroom.

DUPUY, Trevor N. *Options of Command*. Hippocrene, 1984.

Military historian describes how different command decisions might have altered ten crucial moments of World War II: the Maginot Line strategy of May 1940, the Battle of Britain and Sea Lion, Barbarossa, Moscow, Pearl Harbor, Midway, Stalingrad, Rome, Overlord, and the Bulge.

DYER, Gwynne. "Even Without the Revolution, America Would Be on Top Today." Portland *Oregonian*, 23 June 1976, p. C-7.

America as democratic world leader, independent or not.

EDMONDSON, G.C. *To Sail the Century Sea*. Ace, 1981.

Murder at the Council of Nicaea (A.D. 325) alters US politics in the 1980s. Preceding volume, *The Ship That Sailed the Time Stream* (Ace, 1965, enl. ed. 1981) involves time paradoxes but not changes in history.

EDWARDS, Malcolm J. See NICHOLLS, Peter.

EDWARDS, Owen Dudley. "If I Had Been . . . William Ewart Gladstone in 1880: How I Would Have Solved the Irish Problem." In SNOWMAN, ed., *If I Had Been.*

EFFINGER, George Alec. *Relatives.* Harper & Row, 1973; Dell, 1976; portions pub. separately as "The City on the Sand," *FSF,* April 1973, and "Relatives," in Thomas M. Disch, ed., *Bad Moon Rising* (Harper & Row, 1973).
Experiences of analogous characters on our timeline, another where Germany won WWI because Russia stayed out, and a third in which America was discovered but ignored.

———. "Target: Berlin! The Role of the Air Force Four-Door Hardtop." In Robert Silverberg, ed., *New Dimensions Science Fiction No. 6* (Harper & Row, 1976).
WWII is delayed by mutual agreement to 1974–80, with bizarre results.

EISENSTEIN, Phyllis. *Shadow of Earth.* Dell, 1979.
American student trapped in still-frontier Midwest of world in which the Armada triumphed.

EKLUND, Gordon. *All Times Possible.* DAW, 1974.
Democratic failure to nominate FDR in 1932 engenders two alternative totalitarian Americas, Right and Left.

———. "Red Skins." *FSF,* January 1981.
On timeline where Americas were discovered in 1219 and liberated by their natives in 1846, confederated Amerinds confront Nazi demand for return of refugee nuclear scientists.

———. "The Rising of the Sun." In LEY, ed., *Beyond Time.*
Brief history of Western civilization since the eighth-century Arab conquest, interwoven with account of nineteenth-century Inca development of nuclear energy for sun worship.

———. *Serving in Time.* Don Mills: Laser, 1975.
Boys' adventure on multiple-change timeline beginning with delay of US independence to 1800 by Washington's defeat and capture on Long Island.

ELLIOTT, George P. "Sandra." *FSF,* October 1957.
More political fantasy than allohistory: power and sex roles in a contemporary US where slavery is legal but not based on race.

ELLIS, Charles D. *The Second Crash.* Simon & Schuster, 1973.
Critique of Wall Street practices in form of speculation on what might have happened in September 1970 if one key creditor had failed to help out a failing broker.

ELLISON, Harlan. "The City on the Edge of Forever: An Original Teleplay." In Roger Elwood, ed., *Six Science Fiction Plays* (Pocket Books, 1976).
If a Depression-era social worker is not accidentally killed, she fosters a pacifist movement strong enough to delay US entry into World War II, letting Germany develop the first atomic bomb and win. This alternative

remained intact despite substantial changes in the televised version, for which see Bjo Trimble, *The Star Trek Concordance* (Ballantine, 1976), p. 50, and Mandala Productions, *Star Trek: The City on the Edge of Forever* (Bantam, 1977), a "fotonovel" version. James Blish, "The City on the Edge of Forever," in his *Star Trek 2* (Bantam, 1968), is an adaptation based on Ellison's script and the televised version.

ELSTER, Jon. *Logic and Society: Contradictions and Possible Worlds.* Chichester: Wiley, 1978.

See especially Chapter 6, "Counterfactuals and the New Economic History."

ERIKSSON, James S. [pseud.]. *America Vicchinga* [Viking America]. Milan: Frasinelli, 1984.

"America as colonized by the Vikings on the east coast, and by the Mongols, led by Marco Polo, on the west coast"—not to mention the Welsh and the Irish; in series "Se E" (What if) or "Il naso di Cleopatra" (Cleopatra's nose)—Bill Collins, review in *FR*, 81 (July 1985): 26 Cf. MENARD.

ÉTIENNE, Gérard. *Un ambassadeur-macoute à Montréal* [An ambassador from Baby Doc at Montreal]. Montreal: Nouvelle Optique, 1979.

Involves the Duvalier dictatorship of Haiti with the Quebecois separatist upheaval of October 1970; "allohistory stops at nothing"—GOUANVIC, "Québec uchronique"; also reviewed in *Imagine*, 4, 41–43.

EVERETT, Hugh, III. "'Relative State' Formulations of Quantum Mechanics." *Review of Modern Physics*, 29 (July 1957): 454–62.

On Heisenberg's uncertainty principle the author theorizes that each possible outcome of an experiment corresponds to a possible observer, implying infinite parallel worlds. Cf. John A. Wheeler's "Assessment," *ibid.*, pp. 463–65, and DE WITT.

FARBER, Sharon N. "Trans Dimensional Imports." *IASFM*, August 1980.

Different fates of literary works support an active trade between alternative timelines.

FARMER, Philip José. "Sail On! Sail On!" *Startling Stories*, December 1952.

Columbus sails with radio-equipped ships on a physically different Earth.

———, *The Gate of Time.* Belmont, 1970; enl. and debowdlerized ed. as *Two Hawks from Earth*, Ace, 1979.

On an Earth whose Americas exist only as a chain of mountainous islands an Amerind bomber pilot whose World War II was fought against the Kaiser tangles with a Nazi fighter pilot from our own timeline.

FEHRENBACH, T.R. "Remember the Alamo!" *ASF*, December 1961.

When his time machine jumps the tracks, a historian finds himself in the beleaguered Alamo of a "screaming alternate" where the US never broke an Indian treaty, Napoleon sacked London in 1806, and pioneer Texans behave like twentieth-century knee-jerk liberals.

FINNEY, Jack. "The Other Wife." *Saturday Evening Post,* 30 (January 1960); as "The Coin Collector" in his *I Love Galesburg in the Springtime* (Simon & Schuster, 1963; London: Eyre & Spottiswoode, 1975); book-length work-up as *The Woodrow Wilson Dime* (Simon & Schuster, 1968).

Hero shuttles between our New York and another full of minor variants due to past choices—other Presidents on coins, updated Stutz Bearcats on the streets, another Huckleberry Finn novel by Twain.

FISCHER, David Hackett. *Historians' Fallacies: Toward a Logic of Historical Thought.* Harper & Row, 1970; London: Routledge & Kegan Paul, 1971.

Includes a forceful case (pp. 15–21) against counterfactual history as fundamentally flawed.

FISHER, H.A.L. "If Napoleon Had Escaped to America." In SQUIRE, ed., *If,* all eds.; also in *Scribner's,* 89 (January 1931): 35–48, and his *Pages from the Past* (Oxford: Clarendon, 1939; Freeport: Books for Libraries, 1969).

A triumphal tour of the US, a new empire in South America, a fatal voyage to India.

FLEMING, Peter. *Operation Sea Lion: The Projected Invasion of England in 1940—An Account of the German Preparations and the British Countermeasures.* Simon & Schuster, 1957; Ace, n.d.; Westport: Greenwood, 1977. As *Invasion 1940: An Account of the German Preparations and the British Countermeasures,* London: Hart-Davis, 1957; London: Pan, 1975.

Final chapter explicates conditions and consequences of successful invasion, plus Hitler's alternative of ignoring Britain entirely.

FOGEL, Robert W. "The New Economic History: Its Findings and Methods." *EcHR,* 19 (1966): 642–56; rpt. in Don Karl Rowney and James Q. Graham, Jr., eds., *Quantitative History: Selected Readings on the Quantitative Analysis of Historical Data* (Homewood: Dorsey, 1969), pp. 320–35.

Includes discussion and justification of counterfactual history.

————. *Railways and American Economic Growth: Essays in Econometric History.* Baltimore: Johns Hopkins University Press, 1964.

An effort to assess the economic significance of railways in nineteenth-century America by hypothesizing an alternative system based on canals and roads. The heart of the argument was first published as "A Quantitative Approach to the Study of Railroads in Economic Growth: A Report of Some Preliminary Findings," *JEcH,* 22 (1962): 163–97; rpt. in Robert P. Swierenga, ed., *Quantification in American History: Theory and Research* (Atheneum, 1970), pp. 288–316. Another version, perhaps more accessible to the nonspecialist, appeared as "Railroads as an Analogy to the Space Effort: Some Economic Aspects," in Bruce Mazlish, ed., *The Railroad and the Space Program: An Exploration in Historical Analogy* (Cambridge: M.I.T. Press, 1965), pp. 74–106. Both these papers were reprinted in Peter Temin, ed., *New Economic History: Selected Readings* (Baltimore: Penguin, 1963), pp. 183–260, along with a commentary by P.A. David, "Transport Innovation and Economic Growth:

Professor Fogel On and Off the Rails," orig. pub. in *EcHR*, 22 (1969): 506–25.
See also Patrick O'Brien, *The New Economic History of the Railways* (London:
Croom Helm; St. Martin's, 1977); LEE and PASSELL, *New Economic History*,
Chapter 13, and POLLARD.

FORD, John M. *The Dragon Waiting: A Masque of History.* Simon & Schuster for
Timescape, 1983; Avon, 1985.

Intrigues surround Lorenzo de' Medici and Richard III on a timeline where
Byzantium remained strong thanks to Julian's enforcement of religious
tolerance and Justinian's longer reign to solidify his conquests.

————. "Slowly by, Lorena." *IASFM*, November 1980.

Customer of intertime Alternities Corp. is trapped in an 1867 where the War
of Secession drags bloodily on with British help. Other Alternities stories in
IASFM, not allohistorical, include "Mandalay" (October 1979) and "Out of
Service" (July 1980).

FORESTER, C.S. "If Hitler Had Invaded England." *Saturday Evening Post*,
16-23-30 April 1960; rpt. in his *Gold from Crete* (Boston: Little, Brown, 1970;
Pinnacle, 1976).

Hitler's snap decision after Dunkirk produces a landing on 30 June 1940,
measurably shortening the war.

FOSTER, Alan Dean. "Polonaise." In LEY, ed., *Beyond Time.*

Peacekeeping in a modern world whose strongest and stablest power is
Poland.

FRY, Brian R., and John S. Stolarek. "The Nixon Impeachment Vote: A
Speculative Analysis." *Presidential Studies Quarterly*, 11 (1981): 387–94.

Based on House and Senate attitudes, "our evidence indicates that the
President would have been impeached and convicted even if the 'smoking
gun' had not appeared."

GARDNER, Martin. "Mathematical Games: On the Contradictions of Time
Travel." *Scientific American*, 230 (May 1974): 120–23.

Changing the past, self-duplication, and parallel worlds, with references.

GARRETT, Randall. "Gentlemen: Please Note." *ASF*, October 1955.

How Newton came to write the *Principia Theologica* instead of the *Principia
Mathematica.*

————. *Lord Darcy.* D'day, n.d.

Science Fiction Book Club 3-in-1 volume comprising detective stories set in
the world where Richard Lion-Heart survived his wound at Chaluz in 1199
to found an Angevin Empire that today unites England and France, dominates Western Europe, and controls the Americas—and where magic rather
than science forms a systematized body of law. Component volumes: (1)
Murder and Magic, comprising "The Eyes Have It," *ASF*, January 1964; "A
Case of Identity," *ASF*, September 1964; "The Muddle of the Woad," *ASF*,
June 1965; and "A Stretch of the Imagination," in Dean Dickensheet, ed.,
Men and Malice (D'day, 1973). (2) "Too Many Magicians," serial, *ASF*,

August–November 1966, book pub. D'day and Modern Library, 1967; Ace, 1979; and with intro. by Sandra Miesel, Boston: Gregg, 1978. (3) *Lord Darcy Investigates*, comprising "A Matter of Gravity," *ASF*, October 1974; "The Ipswich Phial," *ASF*, December 1976; "The Sixteen Keys," *Fantastic Stories*, May 1976; and "The Napoli Express," *IASFM*, April 1979. "The Bitter End," *IASFM*, September–October 1978, appears in *The Best of Randall Garrett*, ed. Robert Silverberg (Pocket Books, 1982), together with a glimpse of Lord Darcy's World War II equivalent, "The Spell of War," orig. pub. in Reginald Bretnor, ed., *The Future at War, I: Thor's Hammer* (Ace, 1979). See also KURLAND, *Unicorn Girl*.

GAT, Dmitri. "U-Genie SX-1—Human Entrepreneur: Naturally Rapacious Yankee." In LEY, ed., *Beyond Time.*

Commercial venture in time travel drastically changes an unpolluted future by retroactively creating Henry Ford.

GATCH, Tom, Jr. *King Julian: A Novel.* Vantage, 1954.

Contemporary US ruled by descendants of a Washington who accepted a crown.

GEOFFROY-CHÂTEAU, Louis-Napoléon. *Napoléon et la conquête du monde, 1812–1823: histoire de la monarchie universelle* [Napoleon and the conquest of the world, 1812–1823: history of the universal monarchy]. Dellaye, 1836; J. Bry, 1851; Tallandier, 1983 As *Napoleon apocryphe* [The apocryphal Napoleon], by Louis Geoffroy, Paulin, 1841; Librairie Illustrée, 1896.

The first separately published allohistory; instead of lingering fatally in Moscow, Napoleon marches on to seek out and destroy the Russian army and ultimately everyone else's, too.

GERROLD, David. *The Man Who Folded Himself.* Random House, 1973; Popular Library, 1974.

Striving for a perfect lifestyle for himself and his alternative-timeline duplicates and lovers, a time-traveler edits into and out of history such figures as Jesus, Lincoln, and the Kennedys.

GERSCHENKRON, Alexander. "The Discipline and I." *JEcH*, 27 (1967): 443–49.

Presidential address discusses the new economic history with specific reference to counterfactuals; this section with some additional comments is reprinted as a postscript to his "Continuity in History," in *Continuity in History and Other Essays* (Cambridge: Belknap Press of Harvard University Press, 1968). Cf. also the rather abstruse comment by David J. Loschky, "Are Counterfactuals Necessary to 'The Discipline and They?'" *JEcH*, 4 (1975): 481–85.

GIBSON, William. "The Gernsback Continuum." In Terry Carr, ed., *Universe 11* (D'day, 1981).

Glimpses of an existent "tomorrow that never was" as imagined in sf pulps of the 1930s, complete with soaring neon spires and gyrocopters.

GILBERT, Mike. See PIPER, *Lord Kalvan.*

GILLIES, John. "A Sending Parable: What Might Have Been the Result Had St. Paul Traveled East to the Orient Instead of West?" *Christian Century,* 24 February 1971, 253–56.

Missionaries from advanced Japan undergo culture shock in third-worldish North America.

GOLDIAMOND, Israel. "A Crucial Experiment Resubmitted." *American Psychologist,* 32 (1977): 669–71; abr. in *JIR,* 28, 1 (1982).

Academic peer review deals with Elijah's test match against the prophets of Baal (1 Kings 18:17–40).

GOLDMAN, Eliot. "Justice William O. Douglas: The 1944 Vice-Presidential Nomination and His Relationship with Roosevelt—An Historical Perspective." *Presidential Studies Quarterly,* 12 (Summer 1982): 377–85.

If Douglas instead of Truman had run with FDR in 1944, how would he have acted in the White House—and off the Supreme Court?

GOLDRING. *La République populaire de France* [The French People's Republic]. Belfond, 1984.

Listed as allohistory in LECCIA bibliography.

GOLDSTONE, Cynthia, and Avram Davidson. "Pebble in Time." *FSF,* August 1970.

Time-traveler inadvertently diverts Brigham Young's Mormons past Salt Lake ("This is not the place!") to San Francisco.

GOODMAN, Arthur. *If Booth Had Missed: A Drama of the Reconstruction Period.* New York: Samuel French, 1932.

Lincoln survives to have much the same troubles over Reconstruction as Johnson. Contest-winner, Morningside Players, Columbia University, 13 May 1932; opened on Broadway, 4 February 1932, running twenty-one performances. Reviewed by Joseph Wood Krutch, "Cleopatra's Nose," *The Nation,* 14 February 1932, 238; details in Burns Mantle, ed., *The Best Plays of 1930–31* (Dodd, Mead, 1932), pp. 524–25, and *The Best Plays of 1931–32* (1933), pp. 11–12, 473–74.

GORDON, Donald F. See CHAMBERS, Edward J.

GOTSCHALK, Felix C. "The Napoleonic Wars." In LEY, ed., *Beyond Time.* New Orleans in 1958 under a degenerate Napoleonic dynasty.

GOUANVIC, Jean-Marc. "Pourquoi un 'Spécial Uchronie'" [Why an "allohistory special"]. *Imagine,* 14 (Autumn 1982): 6–7.

Editorial justification of the genre. See also ANGENOT.

———. "Québec uchronique" [Allohistorical Quebec]. *Ibid.,* pp. 26–27.

Review article on HERTEL (primarily) and ÉTIENNE.

GOULD, J.D. "Hypothetical History." *EcHR,* 2nd ser., 22 (1969): 195–207.

Perhaps the most accessible discussion of counterfactual history for the nonexpert.

GRAEME, Bruce. See ARMSTRONG, Anthony.

GRAHAM, Neill. See DeWITT, Bryce S.

GRAHAM, Otis L., Jr. "1887: Whites and Indians—Was There a Better Way?" In BORDEN and GRAHAM, *Speculations*.

For all its shortcomings the Dawes Act may have been the only feasible approach at the time.

———. "1917: What If the United States Had Remained Neutral." *Ibid.*

Neutrality was a real option, whose result would probably have been German victory.

———. "1933: What Would the 1930s Have Been Like Without Franklin Roosevelt?" *Ibid.*

Had FDR lost the nomination or died by Giuseppe Zangara's bullet, reform would have suffered, radicalism gained, and the US possibly stayed out of WWII.

———. "1945: The United States, Russia, and the Cold War—What If Franklin Roosevelt Had Lived?" *Ibid.*

The Cold War might simply have been delayed to his leaving office.

———. "1974: What If There Had Been No Watergate?" *Ibid.*

The growth of presidential power would not have abated, even temporarily.

GREEN, George. "Comment" (on papers by DAVIS and REDLICH). *EEH,* 2nd ser., 6 (1968): 109–15; rpt. in ANDREANO, ed., *New Economic History.*

Adds some ground rules for counterfactual history, aimed at forestalling pure speculation.

GREEN, Martin. *The Earth Again Redeemed: May 26 to July 1, 1984, on This Earth of Ours and Its Alter Ego.* Basic, 1977; London: Sphere, 1979.

Victory of King Antonio I of the Kongo over Portuguese invaders in 1665 ultimately leads Western Christendom to reject science for religious mysticism.

GREEN, Roland, and John F. Carr. *Great Kings' War.* Ace, 1985.

Authorized sequel to PIPER, *Lord Kalvan,* but double its length thanks to plethora of military detail; includes maps and summary history (pp. 86–89) of Aryan-settled North America.

GRIBBIN, John. *Timewarps.* London: Dent, 1979; Delacorte/Eleanor Frede, 1979; Delta, 1980.

Includes reasoned discussion of possible scientific basis for alternative or parallel worlds, part pub. as "Sideways in Time," *New Scientist,* 26 April 1979, 284–86.

———. *In Search of Schrödinger's Cat: Quantum Physics and Reality.* Bantam, 1985.

See Chapter 11, "Many Worlds," and sf citations in bibliography. Argument summarized as "Right-Angle Realities," in Jerry Pournelle and Jim Baen, eds., *Far Frontiers III* (Baen Enterprises, Fall 1985).

GRIGG, John. *1943: The Victory That Never Was.* Hill & Wang, 1980.

Concludes with chapter on "The Victory That Might Have Been" if the Allies had mounted a cross-Channel invasion in 1943.

GROUSSET, René. *Figures de proue* [Figureheads]. Plon, 1949.

Series of untitled speculations extrapolates peace between Athens and Sparta, a Roman Empire ruled by Antony, medieval unification of Holy Roman Empire, stronger French efforts at overseas expansion, Napoleon's victory over the Turks at Acre in 1799, European peace unmarred by the Alsace-Lorraine issue, continuance of Eurasian unity under the Mongols, and survival of the Indian spiritual unity promoted by Akbar.

GUEDALLA, Philip. "If the Moors in Spain Had Won. . . ." In SQUIRE, ed., *If,* all eds.

Victory over Ferdinand and Isabella at Lanjaron in 1491 keeps a well-documented Muslim Granada alive to our own day.

GUNDERSON, G.A. "The Social Saving of Steamships." Diss., University of Washington, 1967.

Counterfactualizes "the pattern of world trade in 1900 . . . in the absence of the steamship"—*Dissertation Abstracts,* 28 (1968): 4806A.

GYGAX, E. Gary, and Terry Stafford. *Victorious German Arms: An Alternate Military History of World War II.* Baltimore: T-K Graphics, 1973.

What happened after intelligent planning and strategy produced a quick German victory at Stalingrad.

HAIBLUM, Isidore. *Transfer to Yesterday.* Ballantine, 1973; D'day, 1981.

Repressive future traces itself to elimination of key Allied leaders in 1936–41.

————. *The Tsaddik of the Seven Wonders.* Ballantine, 1971; D'day, 1981.

Glimpses of alternative Judaic history feature Herzl laughing off the idea of a Jewish state, defenders of Masada counterattacking, Maccabees tolerating pagan sacrifice, Ezra and Nehemiah staying in Persia, Esther refusing to marry "that drip King Ahasuerus," Solomon refusing to answer questions, David giving up music, and Hebrews in Egypt rejecting "Moses the turncoat."

HALE, Edward Everett. "Hands Off." *Harper's,* March 1881; rpt. in his *Our Christmas in a Palace* (Funk & Wagnalls, 1883); *Hands Off* (Boston: J. Stillman Smith, 1895); and *Works* (Boston: Little, Brown, 1898–1900), Vol. 2.

On an experimental Earth created by the Almighty as a teaching aid Joseph's escape from the slavers deprives Pharaoh of crucial advice. See Jan Pinkerton, "Backward Time Travel, Alternate Universes, and Edward Everett Hale," *Extrap.,* 20 (1979): 168–75, which also includes a short bibliography of allohistory.

HALL, Brig. Gen. William C. "A Medal for Horatius." *Army Magazine,* January 1955; rpt. in Leon E. Stover and Harry Harrison, eds., *Apeman, Spaceman* (D'day, 1968).

How Pentagon bureaucracy would have rewarded Horatius's defense of the bridge.

HAMMEL, E.A. "Experimental History." *Journal of Anthropological Research,* 35 (1979): 274–91.

How experiments concerning alternative outcomes of past situations may expand our understanding of reality.

HANMURA Ryō. *Sengoku jieitai* [The Self-Defense Force in the Age of the Nation at War]. Hayakawa Shobō, 1971.

According to David LEWIS, "Japanese SF," "time slip" drops SDF unit into a sixteenth century where the great unifier Oda Nobunaga is a minor figure. "The basis of the 1980 Kadokawa movie *Time Slip.*"

HARNESS, Charles L. "O Lyric Love." *Amz.,* May 1985.

Time-machine inventor from timeline where Robert Browning is known mainly as Elizabeth Barrett's husband decides to help him out by sending back sources for *The Ring and the Book.*

———. "Quarks at Appomattox." *ASF,* October 1983.

Neo-Nazi from 2065 offers disintegrator weapons to Robert E. Lee, computing that American partition will let Germany win WWI.

HARRIS, Henry. "1066 As It Might Have Been." *Cosantoir* (Irish defense journal), October 1966; cited without details in "Recent Writings in Military History," *Military Affairs,* 30 (1966–67): 231.

HARRISON, Harry. "Run from the Fire." In Robert Silverberg and Roger Elwood, eds., *Epoch* (Berkley/Putnam's, 1975).

Crosstime adventure, partly set on a line where Europe remains medieval and the Iroquois dominate North America; a brief afterword offers some thoughtful remarks on writing alternative history.

———. "A Transatlantic Tunnel, Hurrah!" Serial, *ASF,* April–June 1972; book version London: Faber, 1972; London: New English Library, 1976; as *Tunnel Through the Deeps,* Putnam's, 1972; Berkley Medallion, 1974.

On a line where Spain remained Muslim after Christian defeat at Las Navas de Tolosa in 1212 a descendant of executed rebel George Washington supervises construction of a new link in the British Empire. Cf. Harrison, "Worlds Beside Worlds," and Fletcher Pratt, "Las Navas de Tolosa and Why the Americas Were Conquered," in his *The Battles That Changed History* (D'day, 1956), pp. 92–110.

———. "The Wicked Flee." In Robert Silverberg, ed., *New Dimensions I* (D'day, 1971).

Contemporary results of a Reformation aborted by the premature deaths of Henry VIII and Luther.

———. "Worlds Beside Worlds." In Peter Nicholls, ed., *Science Fiction at Large* (London: Gollancz; Harper & Row, 1976).

On writing alternative history, with special reference to his *Transatlantic Tunnel.*

HAWTHORNE, Nathaniel. "P.'s Correspondence." *United States Magazine and Democratic Review,* April 1845; rpt. in his *Mosses from an Old Manse* (Wiley & Putnam, 1846; *Complete Works,* Riverside Edition, Vol. 2, Boston: Houghton-Mifflin, 1882).

Poësque madman fantasizes afterlives of such Romantic poets as Byron and Shelley, plus early deaths of Dickens, Whittier, and Longfellow.

HEARNSHAW, F.J.C. *The "Ifs" of History.* London: George Newnes, 1929.

Nineteen brief essays, ten first published in *John o'London's Weekly* (1929): if Alexander the Great had not died prematurely; if Varus had not lost his legions; if Constantinople had fallen [to the Arabs] in A.D. 718; if William the Conqueror had not conquered; if King John had been good; if Genghis Khan had never lived; if Joan of Arc had stayed home; if Columbus had not discovered America; if Henry VIII had not met Anne Boleyn; if Henry of Navarre had not been assassinated; if Charles I had been quicker [in dealing with Parliament]; if the Spanish garrison of Gibraltar had not been pious [when the British attacked in 1704]; if Queen Anne had been longer in dying; if the [Young] Pretender had not turned back [in 1745]; if Clive's pistols had gone off; if Nelson had caught Napoleon in 1798; if Napoleon had not gone to Moscow; if there had been no electric telegraph in the 1850s [to affect handling of the Crimean War and Indian Mutiny]; if the Ems telegram had not been sent. Introduction suggests other possibilities for Socrates, Rousseau, and Cleopatra.

HEINLEIN, Robert A. *Job: A Comedy of Justice.* Ballantine, 1984.

Adventures of involuntary multiple crosstime transferee from forty-six-state North American Union where Bryan beat McKinley.

HERSEY, John. *White Lotus.* Knopf, 1965; Bantam, 1966.

Life of American slaves in China after US defeat in the Yellow War of the early twentieth century.

HERTEL, François. "Lepic et l'histoire hypothétique" [Lepic and hypothetical history]. In his *Jérémie et Barabbas* [Jeremiah and Barabbas], Collection "Romanciers du Jour," Montreal: Le Jour, 1966.

Written in 1940s; the prosperous yet devout super-Canada that would have developed from Montcalm's victory over Wolfe (GOUANVIC).

HILL, Samuel S., Jr. "Could the Civil War Have Been Prevented?" *Christian Century,* 31 March 1976, 304–08.

Though published in the same series, "What If . . . ? Rewriting U.S. History," with DELORIA and WENTZ, this essay in fact insists that nothing could possibly have been different.

HIPOLITO, Jane. See BOYD, John.

HIROSE Tadashi. *Erosu* [Eros]. Hayakawa Shobō, 1971.

"A young girl . . . changes world history as she works her will through the career of a young electrical engineer"—LEWIS, David, "Japanese SF."

HOGAN, James P. *The Proteus Operation.* Bantam, 1985.

Time-travelers from world of Nazi victory return to alert Winston Churchill.

HOLLISTER, Bernard C. "Teaching American History with Science Fiction." *Social Education,* 39 (1975): 81–86.

Includes brief discussion of alternative history.

329

HOOD, Gwenyth. *The Coming of the Demons.* Morrow, 1982.

Spacetime exiles accidentally halt execution of Conradin, last of the Hohen-staufen, in 1268; rest of novel is preachy-teachy space opera a la *Battlestar Galactica.*

HOWELLS, P.G.A. See CLIMO, T.A.

HOYLE, Trevor. *The Gods Look Down.* Frogmore: Panther, 1978; Ace, 1982.

Distant future worries about alternative past in which Jesus never existed; Vol. 3 of the "Q Series."

———. *Seeking the Mythical Future.* Frogmore: Panther, 1977; Ace, 1982.

Vol. 1 of "Q" series, partly set in repressive twentieth-century "New Amerika" that exiles nonconformists to Australia.

———. *Through the Eye of Time.* Frogmore: Panther, 1977; Ace, 1982.

Vol. 2 of series; one subplot stars Hitler's doctor Theodor Morell in a world where a fascist Britain fought WWII as Germany's ally.

HURST, B.C. See CLIMO, T.A.

HUXLEY, Aldous. *Antic Hay.* London: Chatto & Windus; Doran, 1923; numerous later eds.

In vignette at end of Chapter 11 aging architect displays model of London as it might have been had rebuilding after Great Fire been entrusted to Sir Christopher Wren. For Wren's original plan, which Huxley baroquely embroiders, see *Parentalia, or Memoirs of the Family of the Wrens* (London, 1721), pp. 267–69.

HYDE, Ralph. See BARKER, Felix.

IMAGINE, Editors of. "Spécial Uchronie" [Allohistory special]. *Imagine* (Mont-real), 14 (Autumn 1982): 1–67.

Unique critical assemblage; see ANGENOT, APRIL, BOIREAU, BRIE, GOUANVIC, LE BRUN, PELCHAT.

ING, Dean. See REYNOLDS, Mack.

IVERSON, Eric G. (Harry Turtledove). "Archetypes." *Amz.,* November 1985.

Thanks to Muhammad's conversion to Christianity, fourteenth-century Byzantium still rules the Mediterranean world—but now it must confront technologically sophisticated religious subversion from Persia.

———. "Report of the Special Committee on the Quality of Life." In Terry Carr, ed., *Universe 10* (D'day, 1980).

Environmental-impact report rejects proposed voyage of Columbus.

———. "Unholy Trinity." *Amz.,* July 1985.

In Byzantine world of "Archetypes" (above), imperial agent Basil Argyros checks out secret weapons from Franco-Saxon north.

———. "Vilest Beast." *ASF,* September 1985.

Jamestown colonists confront not Powhatan's Indians but hairy, beetle-browed paleolithic "sims."

JACKSON, Steve, designer. *Raid on Iran.* Austin: Steve Jackson Games, 1980.

Simulation game set at the US embassy in Tehran, assuming the April 1980 rescue mission had gone in; an alternative scenario diverts the raid to Qom to seize the Ayatollah.

JACOBS, Will, and Gerard Jones. *The Beaver Papers: The Story of the Lost Season.* Crown, 1983.

Literary parody: last-ditch attempt to keep *Leave It to Beaver* alive in 1963 elicits support from President and Pope alike, plus scripts from such as John Steinbeck, Tennessee Williams, Ray Bradbury, and Philip Jose Farmer.

JACOBY, Neil H. *U.S. Aid to Taiwan.* Praeger, 1966.

Appendices E–K, pp. 310–58, present counterfactual models of Taiwan's economic growth from 1952, assuming little or no US aid and/or no military costs; the worst-case model has actual 1965 GNP achieved only in 2020.

JAKES, John. *Black in Time.* Paperback Library, 1970.

Black extremist assassinates Muhammad to save African civilization from Muslim conquest; elsewhere in time he witnesses race war in New York after the assassination of Booker T. Washington.

JAKIEL, S. James, and Rosandra E. Levinthal. "The Laws of Time Travel." *Extrap.,* 21 (1980): 130–38.

First of twelve "laws" (whether natural or moral is never clarified) bars time-travelers from altering history; a few relevant stories are cited. For criticism see "There Are Laws and Then There Are Laws," *ibid.,* 23 (1982): 290–303.

JAMMER, Max, and John Stachel. "If Maxwell Had Worked Between Ampère and Faraday: An Historical Fable with a Methodological Moral." *American Journal of Physics,* 48 (1980): 5–7.

Physics need not have developed exactly as it did during the nineteenth century.

JAMROZIAK, Wojciech. "The Historical SF of Teodor Parnicki." *SFS,* 5 (1978): 130–33.

On untranslated novels by a contemporary Pole; for titles explicitly cast as alternative history see PARNICKI.

JAUCHIUS, Dean. See RHODES, James A.

JEANNE, René. See LAUMANN, E.M.

JEFFRIES, Graham M. See ARMSTRONG, Anthony.

JENKINS, Will F. See LEINSTER, Murray.

JOHNSON, Alvin S. "Cleopatra and the Roman Chamber of Commerce." *American Scholar,* 18 (1949): 417–24.

Dissertation on real-estate values in history, à la Henry George, also includes speculation on world empire that might have followed Cleopatra's partnership with a surviving Julius Caesar.

JOHNSON, Robert B., and Billie Niles Chadbourne. *Times-Square Samurai; or, The Improbable Japanese Occupation of New York.* Rutland, Vt., and Tokyo: Tuttle, 1966.

Cartoons erewhonning American behavior in occupied Tokyo.

331

JOHNSTON, Moira. "How the West Was Dressed: A Fable." *S.F. Sunday Examiner & Chronicle*, 30 July 1972, *California Living*, 20–23.
Today's California clothing styles if Spanish explorers had been anticipated by colonists from Ming China.

JONES, Diana Wynne. *Witch Week*. Greenwillow, 1982.
Guy Fawkes's premature explosion generates timeline where witchcraft is real.

JONES, Douglas C. *The Court-Martial of George Armstrong Custer*. Scribner's; Warner, 1977.
Custer survives the Little Big Horn to stand trial the following year for his part in it. In 1978 Warner Bros. produced a 100-minute TV-movie version with the same title, with Brian Keith, Ken Howard, and Stephen Elliott. Distinguish from Lawrence A. Frost, *The Court Martial of General George Armstrong Custer* (Norman: University of Oklahoma Press, 1968), the account of a real court-martial in 1867.

JONES, Langdon. See MOORCOCK, Michael.

KAGLE, Steven. "Science Fiction as Simulation Game." In Thomas D. Clareson, ed., *Many Futures, Many Worlds: Theme and Form in Science Fiction* (Kent: Kent State University Press, 1977), pp. 224–36.
Includes discussion of alternative history.

KANTOR, MacKinlay. "If the South Had Won the Civil War." *Look*, 22 November 1960; book version, Bantam, 1961.
Grant dies accidentally en route to Vicksburg, Lee wins at Gettysburg, and in 1960 three American nations (including Texas) are considering reunion. Cf. letters by Harry S. Truman et al., *Look*, 3 January 1961.

KAZANTZAKIS, Nikos. *The Last Temptation of Christ*, trans. P.A. Bien from *Ho teleutaios peirasmos* (1955). Simon & Schuster, 1960.
In Chapters 30–33 Jesus imagines the fates of himself and his followers if he simply escaped and went home.

KELLEY, Allen C., and Jeffrey G. Williamson. *Lessons from Japanese Development: An Analytical Economic History*. Chicago and London: University of Chicago Press, 1974.
"New economic history" of Japan, 1887–1915, first proposes a model of Japanese development, then (Chapters 6–12) explores several explicit counterfactuals: e.g., if Japan had experienced the same population growth as today's UDCs, or had invested more in industry and less in war.

KETTERER, David. *New Worlds for Old: The Apocalyptic Imagination, Science Fiction, and American Literature*. Bloomington: Indiana University Press; Garden City: Anchor, 1974.
Includes comments on alternative history and analyses of BOYD and DICK.

KILIAN, Crawford. *The Empire of Time*. Ballantine, 1978.
"Temporal incongruity" allows our "chronoplane" to influence others at different temporal stages in our interest—e.g., by arranging unification of Europe by Napoleon.

KLEIN, Edward. See CHESNOFF, Richard Z.

KLEIN, Judith L. See PARKER, William N.

KNEESHAW, Stephen John. "'Alternativing' the American Past: Teaching What Might Have Been."
Paper presented at annual meeting of American Historical Association, Dallas, 28 December 1977; includes references.

KNIGHT, Damon. "What Rough Beast." *FSF,* February 1959.
Wanderer between timelines ends on one where Jesus never existed.

KNOX, Ronald. "If the General Strike Had Succeeded." In SQUIRE, ed., *If,* all but 1931 US ed.
Social results of the 1926 strike as reported in a socialized *Times.*

KOMATSU Sakyō. "Chi ni wa heiwa o" [Peace on earth]. *SF Magajin* (Tokyo), ca. 1961; rpt. in his *Chi ni wa heiwa o* (Hayakawa Shobō, 1963).
"Mad scientist" attempts to change a past in which the US invaded Japan to end WWII—LEWIS, David, "Japanese SF," p. 483.

KORNBLUTH, C.M. "Two Dooms." *Venture Science Fiction,* July 1958.
Transported to a future US partitioned between Japan and Germany for failing to develop the bomb, a Los Alamos physicist returns to his job in 1945 with no further qualms.

KROHN, Wolfgang. See BÖHME, Gernot.

KRUTCH, Joseph Wood. See GOODMANN, Arthur.

KURLAND, Michael. *The Unicorn Girl.* Pyramid, 1969.
Picaresque junket through alternative worlds includes stopover in North America of GARRETT's "Lord Darcy" series.

————. *The Whenabouts of Burr.* DAW, 1975.
Crosstime adventure, largely staged on timeline where Alexander Hamilton survived his 1804 duel with Burr to create a more authoritarian US.

————, and S.W. Barton [Barton Whaley]. *The Last President.* Morrow, 1980.
Successful Watergate coverup brings US to brink of civil war.

KUTTNER, Henry. "The Portal in the Picture." *Startling Stories,* September 1949; book version as *Beyond Heaven's Gates,* by Lewis Padgett and C.L. Moore, Ace Double D-69 (with Andre Norton's *Daybreak—2250 A.D.*), 1954.
In advanced present derived from unchristened Roman Empire, "alchemy" (science) is preserve of Egyptian-type priests.

———— [Lewis Padgett, pseud.]. "Tomorrow and Tomorrow." *ASF* serial, January–February 1947; in his *Tomorrow and Tomorrow and The Fairy Chessmen,* Gnome, 1951.
A century after the Japanese kamikaze raid on Washington, researchers discover numerous "Earths that might have been," one of which may be ours.

LAFFERTY, R.A. "Assault on Fat Mountain." In LEY, ed., *Beyond Time.*
Late-eighteenth-century "State of Franklin" survives to generate a very different US.

333

———. "Entire and Perfect Chrysolite." In Damon Knight, ed., *Orbit 6* (Putnam's; Berkley Medallion, 1970).
Hinterland Africa on our earth interfaces with the Cinnamon Coast of Libya (lat. 15°N.) on one whose three continents are limited to the area known to Eratosthenes.

———. "Interurban Queen." In Damon Knight, ed., *Orbit 8* (Putnam's; Berkley, 1970).
The modern America in which cars lost out to trolleys.

———. "Rainbird." *Gal.,* December 1961.
How Yankee inventor Higginston Rainbird (1759?–1844?) "destroyed southern slavery with a steam-powered cotton picker" and went on to try to improve on his inventions via time machine.

———. "Selenium Ghosts of the Eighteen Seventies." In Terry Carr, ed., *Universe 8* (D'day; Popular Library, 1978).
First dramas created for the newly invented television based on photoelectric effect in selenium.

———. "The Three Armageddons of Enniscorthy Sweeny." In his *Apocalypses* (Los Angeles: Pinnacle, 1977).
Title character (1894–1984) shapes up twentieth-century history by sublimating its horrors as theater.

———. "Thus We Frustrate Charlemagne." *Gal.,* February 1967.
Future experimenters mess about with Charlemagne's rearguard stand at Roncesvalles, changing their own history without being aware of it.

LAHANA, Jacqueline. *Les mondes parallèles de la science-fiction soviétique* [The parallel worlds of Soviet science fiction]. Collection "Outrepart," Lausanne: L'Âge d'Homme, 1979.
Included on dog-in-the-nighttime principle: detailed, thoroughgoing monograph never mentions alternative history.

LAMBELET, John C. "The Anglo-German Dreadnought Race, 1905–1914." *Papers of the Peace Science Society,* 22 (1974): 1–45; "A Numerical Model of the Anglo-German Dreadnought Race," *ibid.,* 24 (1975): 29–48; "A Complementary Analysis of the Anglo-German Dreadnought Race, 1905–1916," *ibid.,* 26 (1976): 49–66.
Computer simulation of rival policies and results touches hypothetical building programs (24:46–47) and German naval victory in WWI (22:34–35) and aims at computerized battle alternatives.

LASKI, Harold J. "If Roosevelt Had Lived." *The Nation,* 13 April 1946, 419–21.
Labor Party chairman ponders effects of another year of FDR on Cold War, control of the bomb, and America's world role.

LASKI, Marghanita. *Tory Heaven; or, Thunder on the Right.* London: Cresset, 1948.
Voters turn Labor out, restoring the class-conscious "England of all decent Conservatives' dreams" à la early Waugh or perhaps P.G. Wodehouse.

LAUMANN, E.M., and René Jeanne. *Si, le 9 thermidor . . .: hypothèse historique* [If, on 27 July, 1794 . . .: an historical hypothesis]. Tallandier, 1929.

Avoiding the guillotine, the radical Robespierre continues his intrigues.

LAUMER, Keith. *Assignment in Nowhere*. Berkley Medallion, 1968; published with *The Other Side of Time* (below) as *Beyond the Imperium*, Pinnacle, 1981.

Third in "Imperium" crosstime adventure series includes action on timeline where Richard Lion-Heart refused battle at Chaluz in 1199 to enjoy a decadent old age.

———. "The Other Side of Time." Serial, *Fantastic Stories*, April–June, 1965; book version, Berkley Medallion, 1965; Walker, 1971; Signet, 1972; with *Assignment in Nowhere* (above) as *Beyond the Imperium*, Pinnacle, 1981.

Second in "Imperium" series, set largely on Napoleonic timeline stemming from "glorious victory at Brussels" in 1814.

———. "Worlds of the Imperium." Serial, *Fantastic Stories*, February–April 1961; book version, Ace Double, 1962; Berkley Medallion, 1977; with two added short stories, Tor, 1983.

First in series features "zero-zero" timeline dominated by Imperium centered on London, plus another where divergent events from 1911 let Germany win WWI and later conquer America.

LAWRENCE, Edmund. *It May Happen Yet: A Tale of Bonaparte's Invasion of England*. London: The Author, 1899.

Once ashore in February 1805, Napoleon has trouble deciding what to do next.

LEACOCK, Stephen. "The Hohenzollerns in America." In his *The Hohenzollerns in America, With the Bolsheviks in Berlin, and Other Impossibilities* (John Lane; London: John Lane, The Bodley Head; Toronto: S.B. Gundy, 1919), pp. 9–72.

Earning a living in America instead of cutting trees at Doorn, Wilhelm II remains a megalomaniacal ignoramus.

———. "If Germany Had Won." *Ibid.,* pp. 137–42.

Horrors of Prussianism revealed in "the *New York Imperial Gazette* of 1925."

LE BRUN, Claire. "Les chansons de geste: la tentation de l'uchronie au moyen âge" [The *chansons de geste:* the temptation of allohistory in the Middle Ages]. *Imagine*, 14 (Autumn 1982): 44–49.

Chivalric romance as a sort of allohistory; refers to author's "La science-fiction au moyen âge" [Medieval sf], *ibid.,* Nos. 8–9 (Summer 1981):

LECCIA, Pierre. "Uchronie: l'histoire detournée" [Allohistory: history side-tracked]. In Daniel Riche, ed., *Politique/Fiction* (exhibit catalog, Centre Georges Pompidou, 1984), p. 7.

Brief discussion of uchronias in sf; bibliography, pp. 29–31.

LEE, C.H. *The Quantitative Approach to Economic History*. St. Martin's, 1977.

See especially Chapter 4, "Counterfactual Models and Social Savings."

LEE, Susan Previant, and Peter Passell. *A New Economic View of American History*. Norton, 1979.

Comprehensive view of the new American economic history, with due attention to counterfactual hypotheses and extensive annotated bibliographies.

LEGUIN, Ursula K. See SPINRAD, Norman.

LEHRER, Jim. "If TV Had Covered World War II." *TV Guide*, 7 September 1985.

Dan Rather, Peter Jennings, and Roger Mudd bring the boys home before Christmas 1941.

LEIBER, Fritz. "The Big Time." Serial, *Gal.*, March–April 1958; book version, Ace, 1961; with intro. by Robert Thurston, Boston: Gregg, 1978.

Chief volume of the "Change War" series; possibility of changing history is ever-present, although individual changes (such as a victorious Confederacy and "a Nazi empire . . . stretching from Nizhni Novgorod to Kansas City") are no more than mentioned in passing. For others in the series see the two listed below and two short-story collections with overlapping contents, *The Change War* (Boston: Gregg, 1978) and *Changewar* (Ace, 1983).

———. "Catch That Zeppelin!" *FSF*, March 1975.

The peaceful, airship-linked world of 1937 that might have resulted from (among other changes) the marriage, intellectual as well as physical, of Marie Sklodowska and Thomas A. Edison.

———. "No Great Magic." *Gal.*, December 1963.

Only story in Leiber's "Change War" series with allohistory central: if Queen Elizabeth fails to execute Mary Queen of Scots and the Armada triumphs, then England declines and Spanish colonies share North America with New Scandinavia.

———. "Try and Change the Past." *ASF*, March 1958.

Though not strictly speaking allohistory, this story vividly dramatizes science fiction's belief in a "law of conservation of reality" that makes history almost *want* to go a certain way.

LEINSTER, Murray [Will F. Jenkins]. "Sideways in Time." *ASF*, June 1934.

First sf story of crosstime travel; time disruption juxtaposes our world with others derived from Southern victory at Gettysburg, American colonization by Russians, Vikings, Romans, or Chinese, or slower patterns of prehuman evolution.

———. *Time Tunnel.* Pyramid, 1964.

A Napoleonic dynasty and four nineteenth-century emperors of Mexico flicker across the scene as time-travelers try to avert nuclear war by eliminating its ultimate cause, a scientist in 1804 Paris. Leinster's similarly titled *The Time Tunnel* and *Timeslip! A Time Tunnel Adventure* (both Pyramid, 1967) are novelizations of TV shows involving time travel and Ouroboros effects but not allohistory.

LEM, Stanislaw. "The Time-Travel Story and Related Matters of SF Structuring." *SFS*, 1 (1974): 143–54.

Discusses allohistory, pp. 146–47.

LESAGE, Alain-René. *Les Aventures de Monsieur Robert Chevalier, dit de Beauchêne* [The adventures of M. Robert Chevalier, a.k.a. de Beauchêne]. Ganeau,

1732; Maestricht: Jean-Edmé Dufour & Philippe Roux, 1780.
Early borderline allohistory: Book 4 of this adventure-biography by the
author if *Gil Blas* (Maestricht ed., 2:54 – 55) imagines how Amerinds might
have viewed Europeans had they done the discovering.
LEVINTHAL, Rosandra E. See JAKIEL, S. James.
LEWIS, David. "Japanese SF." In Neil Barron, ed., *Anatomy of Wonder,* 2nd ed.
(Bowker, 1982).
Includes summaries of HANMURA, HIROSE, KOMATSU, MITSUSE,
and TOYOTA.
LEWIS, David K. *Counterfactuals.* Cambridge: Harvard University Press, 1973.
Justifies existence of "possible worlds," pp. 84–91.
LEWIS, Oscar. *The Lost Years.* Knopf, 1951; rpt. in Anthony Boucher, ed., *A
Treasury of Great Science Fiction,* Vol. 2 (D'day, 1959).
Lincoln's declining years after recovery from Booth's bullet.
LEY, Olga. "Checkmate in Six Moves." In LEY, ed., *Beyond Time.*
How Kerensky managed to exile Lenin and Trotsky.
LEY, Sandra, ed. *Beyond Time.* Pocket Books, 1976.
Original collection of allohistorical short stories; see author listings for
CHILSON, COOPER (Edmund), CORES, COULSON (Juanita), COUL-
SON (Robert), DAVIDSON, EKLUND, FOSTER, GAT, GOTSCHALK,
LAFFERTY, LEY (Olga), MOORE, ORGILL, PERCY, THOMPSON
(Don), and ZEBROWSKI.
LINAWEAVER, Brad. "Moon of Ice." *Amz.,* March 1982.
Twenty years later Dr. Goebbels's last diaries reexamine implications of
Hitler's atomic victory of 1945; cf. letters from Andre Norton et al.,
"Intercom," *ibid.,* September 1982.
LINDGREN, R.E. See BECK, Joan.
LIONEL, Robert. *Time Echo.* Arcadia House, 1964; Modern Promotions, n.d.
Derivative—not to say plagiarized—time opera unaccountably includes
lengthy Chapter 6 on theory of time travel and alternative history.
LITTELL, Robert. See CHESNOFF, Richard Z.
LIVY (Titus Livius). *Ab urbe condita* [Rome since its founding], 9.17–19; trans.
E.O. Foster in Loeb Classical Library (Cambridge: Harvard University
Press, London: Heinemann, 14 vols., 1917–59), 4:225–41.
In this "seed of allohistory" (Versins, 775, s.v. "Rome") Livy digresses from
his narrative to suggest how Alexander the Great might have fared had he
lived to try the mettle of Rome.
LOCKE, Robert Donald. "Demotion." *ASF,* September 1952.
Increasingly complex manipulation of its own past by future based on
Hitler's death by Allied bombs in 1943.
LONGMATE, Norman. *If Britain Had Fallen.* Stein & Day, 1974; London: BBC
Publications; Arrow, 1975.
Based on a BBC-TV production of the same title, premiering 12 September

1972, suggests how Nazis might have mounted invasion and what life would have been like in occupied Britain.

LONGYEAR, Barry N. "Collector's Item." *ASF,* 27 April 1981.
Silver 1978 quarter reveals how our world has been reshaped since the 1950s through intervention by an alternative individual destroyed in the world war of ca. 1980.

LOSCHKY, David J. See GERSCHENKRON, Alexander.

LUDWIG, Emil. "If the Emperor Frederick Had Not Had Cancer." In SQUIRE, ed., *If,* all eds.
Instead of dying in 1888 the liberal Kaiser survives until August 1914, leaving William II the throne of a pacific near-republic.

LUPOFF, Richard A. *Into the Aether.* Dell, 1970.
Unexplained features of this pastiche Gilded Age scientific romance include the spacegoing galleon of a Spain that was liberated from Islam by the Muscovites in A.D. 1000.

MACKESY, Piers. *Could the British Have Won the War of Independence?* Chester Bland-Dwight E. Lee Lectures in History. Worcester: Clark University Press, 1976.
Though dwelling more on British problems than on alternative courses of action, Mackesy does suggest how, even after Yorktown, the British might have quelled the rebellion with counterinsurgency tactics just then being developed, while simultaneously dealing with the threat to their seaborne empire from France.

MACKESY, Kenneth. *Invasion: The German Invasion of England, July 1940.* Macmillan, 1980.
Simulated campaign history; invasion planning starts even before Dunkirk (cf. FORESTER).

MADARIAGA [y Roja], Salvador de. *Christopher Columbus.* Macmillan, 1940.
Brief vignettes in this biography (pp. 14–15) suggest how without Columbus, and with fewer royal deaths, a united Iberia might have worked off its crusading urges in the Mediterranean.

MALZBERG, Barry Z. *Chorale.* D'day, 1978.
Department of Reconstruction looks back from twenty-third century to ensure the existence, in a past continually in flux, of such figures as Thomas Alva Guinzanburg and Lord Holmes.

―――― . "January 1975." *ASF,* January 1975.
If JFK had been elected President in 1960, as seen from a timeline where Nixon was.

―――― . *The Remaking of Sigmund Freud.* Ballantine/Del Rey, 1985.
As sensual, extroverted laureate of the Gilded Age, Emily Dickinson changes lives of both Freud and Mark Twain: Lynn F. Williams review, *FR,* 82 (August 1985): 23. Part published as "Emily Dickinson―Saved from Drowning," in Roy Torgeson, ed., *Chrysalis 8* (D'day, 1980; Zebra, 1982).

MANDALA PRODUCTIONS. See ELLISON, Harlan.

MANNING, Patrick. "Analyzing the Costs and Benefits of Colonialism." *African Economic History Review*, 1 (1974): 15–22.

Suggests hypothetical alternatives to European colonialism in Africa; cf. SIMENSEN.

MARRIOTT, J.A.R. "If Queen Victoria—? An Historical Phantasy." *Fortnightly*, n.s., 149 (April 1941): 392–98.

Had William IV's heir in 1837 been male, Hanover would have remained under the British crown, with far-reaching effects on German reunification and two world wars.

MARTINE-BARNES, Adrienne. *Fire Sword*. Avon, 1985.

Woman from our age copes with magic-ridden thirteenth-century England where marriage of "Henry the Young King," son of Henry II, produced a different bad king John.

MASON, David. *The Shores of Tomorrow*. Lancer, 1971.

Crosstime adventure involves exiles from two 1965 North Americas, both devastated by civil war.

MAUROIS, André. "If Louis XVI Had Had an Atom of Firmness." In SQUIRE, ed., *If*, all eds.

Reform from above after 1774 saves France from revolution; alternatively, unreformed monarchy in 1789 rallies royal troops to maintain power. Cf. DEVAUX.

————. "Prefacio" [Preface] to *Napoléon venció en Waterloo*, trans. of ARON by Eduardo Blanco (Buenos Aires: Sur, 1939).

Defends allohistory against imputations of frivolity by likening it to nonmilitary war-gaming.

MAX, Nicholas. *President McGovern's First Term*. D'day, 1973.

Out of Vietnam but into difficulties with Congress and party.

MAYER, Christian. See AMERY, Carl.

MAYFAIR GAMES. *Red Star Falling: Patton Attacks the Russians, March 1945*. Chicago: Mayfair Games, 1981.

According to blurb of this war game, "the Western Allies and the defeated German Wehrmacht challenge the Russians for control of Central and Eastern Europe."

MAZARIN, Jean. *L'histoire detournée* [History sidetracked]. Collection "Anticipation," 1270, Fleuve Noir, 1984.

Nazi victory with nuclear bombs leads in 1989 to WWIII against Japan.

McCLELLAND, Peter D. *Causal Explanation and Model Building in History, Economics, and the New Economic History*. Ithaca: Cornell University Press, 1975.

See especially Chapter 4, "Counterfactual Speculation . . .," and the extensive bibliography.

McCLOSKEY, Donald N. "The Achievements of the Cliometric School." *JEcH*, 38 (1978): 13–28.

Cliometrics is synonymous with new economic history; this paper offers a good survey of the field.

_____. "Britain's Loss from Foreign Industrialization: A Provisional Estimate." *EEH*, 2nd ser., 8 (1970–71): 141–52.

Foreign industrialization meant not only competition but markets; in a nonindustrialized world of 1913 British exports might have been only slightly greater than in our own.

MENARD, Pierre [pseud. taken from a story by BORGES]. *1938: La distruzione di Parigi* [1938: The Destruction of Paris]. Milan: Frasinelli, 1984.

Same series as ERIKSSON. After Pétain's 1934 coup in France "feisty right-wing government calls Hitler's bluff on the Rhineland" only to wage a colonial war against Britain and Italy—Bill Collins review in *FR*, 81 (July 1985): 26.

MEREDITH, Richard C. *At the Narrow Passage*. Putnam's, 1973; Berkley Medallion, 1975; rev. ed. (The Timeliner Trilogy, Book I). Chicago: Playboy, 1979.

Crosstime mercenary from surviving Macedonian empire encounters one timeline where British suppressed American and French Revolutions with breechloaders, another where orthodox crusaders failed to suppress Albigensians.

_____. *No Brother, No Friend* (The Timeliner Trilogy, Book II). D'day, 1976; rev. ed. Chicago: Playboy, 1979.

From an America that avoided WWII but went fascist to another colonized by an England that escaped Norman conquest.

_____. *Run, Come See Jerusalem!* Ballantine, 1976.

Time-traveler from a world where Nazi Germany nuked Chicago in 1947 before losing WWII flees to Chicago in 1871, where his pursuers set the Chicago Fire to smoke him out.

_____. *Vestiges of Time* (The Timeliner Trilogy, Book III). D'day, 1978; rev. ed. Chicago: Playboy, 1979.

Van-Vogtish series finale takes place largely on "Neo-Carthaginian" timeline dating to Punic victory over Rome.

MERWIN, Sam, Jr. "The House of Many Worlds." *Startling Stories*, September 1951; book-length version, D'day, 1951; Galaxy Science Fiction Novel, 12, 1952: Modern Literary Editions, n.d.

Crosstime adventure set mostly in Columbian Republic founded at New Orleans by Aaron Burr after War of 1812.

_____. "Journey to Misenum." *Startling Stories*, August 1953; as *Three Faces of Time*, Ace Double, 1955.

Combined crosstime and in-time travel to alternative ancient Rome, differing from ours only in minor points (e.g., more active trade with China).

MEYER, John R. "An Input-Output Approach to Evaluating the Influence of Exports on British Industrial Production in the Late Nineteenth Century." *EEH*, 8 (1955): 12–34.

If British exports during 1875–1900 had maintained earlier levels, British industrial production might have held up likewise. This, the first published article to base itself explicitly on a counterfactual hypothesis, was actually written in collaboration with Alfred H. Conrad. Together with two other papers of theirs—"Economic History, Statistical Inference, and Economic History," *JEcH*, 17 (1957): 524–44, and "The Economics of Slavery in the Ante Bellum South," *JPE*, 66 (1958): 95–130—it kicked off the "new economic history," though the term itself was coined later. All three papers are reprinted in Conrad and Meyer, *The Economics of Slavery, and Other Studies in Econometric History* (Chicago: Aldine, 1964).

MIGNARD, James E. "Memo to Moses from HEW." *JIR*, 28, 2 (1982): 11.
Bureaucratic guidelines rewrite the Ten Commandments.

MILLER, James E. "How Newton Discovered the Law of Gravitation." *American Scientist*, 39 (1951): 134–40; *NYU Engineering Research Review*, date unknown; *Worm Runner's Digest*, 3 (1961): 157–64; Robert A. Baker, ed., *A Stress Analysis of a Strapless Evening Gown and Other Essays for a Scientific Age* (Englewood Cliffs: Prentice-Hall, 1963; pb. 1982); James V. McConnell, ed., *The Worm Re-Turns: The Best from the Worm Runner's Digest* (Englewood Cliffs: Prentice-Hall, 1965); R.L. Weber, comp., *A Random Walk in Science* (London: Institute of Physics; Crane, Russak, 1973).
Government grants for apple research long delay Newton's discovery.

MITCHELL, Kirk. *Procurator.* Ace, 1984.
Defending the twentieth-century Roman Empire derived from Pilate's sparing of Jesus.

MITSUSE Ryū. *Seitō totokufu* [Colonial HQ for the East]. Hayakawa Shobō, 1975.
"Members of the Time Bureau . . . find a past in which Japan has lost the Sino-Japanese War [of 1894–95] and is controlled by China"—LEWIS, David, "Japanese SF," p. 487.

MOLLO, Andrew. See BROWNLOW, Kevin.

MONTANA, Ron. *The Sign of the Thunderbird.* Manor, 1977.
Soldiers from postholocaust US, thrown back to 1860, help create a United Indian Nation and Free State of New Mexico.

MOORCOCK, Michael. *Gloriana; or, The Unfulfill'd Queen. Being a Romance.* London: Allison & Busby; London: Fontana, 1978; Avon, 1979.
Explicitly framed as allohistory (Chapter 4), this romance is set in an Elizabethanish modern London ruling the world-circling Empire of Albion founded by refugees from the fall of Troy.

——— . (Jerry Cornelius cycle.)
One common setting for this cycle is an alternative history centered on worldwide war and revolution, 1900–75; allusions usually involve specific events rather than a general pattern (e.g., an early Cossack invasion of Canada, a German Civil War in 1933) and much of the ambience derives

from persistent archaic technology. See *The Adventures of Una Persson and Catherine Cornelius in the Twentieth Century: A Romance* (London: Quartet, 1976); *The English Assassin* (London: Allison & Busby; Harper & Row, 1972); *The Condition of Muzak* (London: Allison & Busby, 1977; Boston: Gregg, 1978). The last two are reprinted in his *The Cornelius Chronicles* (Avon, 1977). Cf.. MOORCOCK and JONES, RABKIN, and SALLIS.

———. *The Nomad of Time*. D'day, n.d.
Science Fiction Book Club selection anthologizing three in-time and cross-time adventures of Edwardian ingenu Oswald Bastable (named for one of E. Nesbit's "treasure seekers"): (1) *The Warlord of the Air* (London: New English Library; Ace, 1971; rev. ed. London: Quartet; DAW, 1978; London: Granada, 1981) takes Captain Bastable from 1902 to a 1973 where continued European peace has kept the world imperialist. (2) *The Land Leviathan* (D'day; London: Quartet, 1974; DAW, 1976) involves him in the devastating race wars of a much more advanced 1904; (3) *The Steel Tsar* (DAW, 1982) focuses on the revolt of ex-priest Josef Djugashvili against a Russian republican regime established in 1905. Such characters as Una Persson tie in with Jerry Cornelius cycle (above) and its League of Temporal Adventurers.

———, and Langdon Jones, eds. *The Nature of the Catastrophe*. London: Hutchinson, 1971.
Includes "Jerry Cornelius" contributions by other writers, according to NICHOLLS, p. 407.

MOORE, C.L. See KUTTNER.

MOORE, Ward. "Bring the Jubilee." *FSF,* November 1952; book-length version, Farrar, Straus & Young; Ballantine, 1953; Avon, 1972.
Growing up in the twentieth-century US generated by Lee's victory at Gettysburg; first English-language sf to begin on another timeline, treating ours as the derivative alternative.

———. "A Class with Dr. Chang." In LEY, ed., *Beyond Time.*
Student revolt in the America that stayed out of WWII because Nazi Germany allied with China rather than Japan.

MORGAN, Roger. "If I Had Been . . . Konrad Adenauer in 1952: How I Would Have Accepted Stalin's Proposal for a United Neutralized Germany." In SNOWMAN, ed., *If I Had Been.*

MORIN, Edgar. "Le Camarade-Dieu: un conte de Noël" [The comrade-god: a Christmas story]. *France Observateur,* 28 December 1961, 24.
After only brushing death in 1953, Stalin is proclaimed a living god by the Soviet Presidium in 1961, with mixed reactions from French intellectuals and politicians.

MORRIS, Howard L. "Not by Sea." *If,* February 1966.
Foiling a Napoleonic balloon invasion of England in a style out of Georgette Heyer by C.S. Forester.

MOTTA, Luigi. *Il tonnel sottomarino* [The undersea tunnel]. Milan, 1927.

Adventures constructing a tunnel from Manhattan to Brittany, 1924–27, nguel and Gianni Guadalupi, *The Dictionary of Imaginary Places* (Macmillan, 1980), pp. 23–24.

MULISCH, Harry. *De toekomst van gisteren: protokol van een schrijverij* [Yesterday's future: outline of a work]. Literaire Reuzenpocket, 409; Amsterdam: De Bezige Bij, 1972.

Reflections on a potential novel based on Hitler's assassination in 1944, an SS countercoup, and German victory. Cf. summary in J.A. Dautzenberg, "A Survey of Dutch and Flemish Science Fiction," *SFS,* 8 (1981): 181.

MULLALLY, Frederic. *Hitler Has Won.* Simon & Schuster, 1975.

Or so his earlier start on invading Russia makes it seem.

MURPHY, George G.S. "On Counterfactual Propositions." *History and Theory,* Beiheft 9: *Studies in Quantitative History and the Logic of the Social Sciences* (1969): 14–38.

Defends use of counterfactuals as required for "asking some of the really important questions in economic history."

NABOKOV, Vladimir. *Ada, or Ardor: A Family Chronicle.* McGraw-Hill, 1969.

On Antiterra, "a distortive glass of our distorted globe," among other Nabokovian historical and linguistic complications, Russia has colonized North America and through trains run from London to Sydney.

NATIONAL LAMPOON. "Grand Fifth Term Inaugural Issue: JFK's First 6,000 Days." *National Lampoon,* February 1977, 27–101.

Jackie, not Jack, died in Dallas. Cf. O'ROURKE.

NEAL, Donn C. "'What If Al Smith Had Been Elected?'" *Presidential Studies Quarterly,* 14 (Spring 1984): 242–48.

On his administrative record and public statements, "Smith would have regarded the depression more as Roosevelt did than as Hoover did."

NELSON, R.F. *Blake's Progress.* Toronto: Laser, 1975.

Chapter 5 of this time-travel extravaganza is set in the eighteenth-century London resulting from the victory of Antony and Cleopatra at Actium (31 B.C.).

NESBITT, Mark. *If the South Won Gettysburg.* Gettysburg: Reliance, 1980.

Mainly a detailed account, backed by a substantial bibliography, of how tactics of mobility could have won for Lee; a final chapter speculates on American and world history afterward.

NEUBERGER, Hugh, and Houston H. Stokes. "The Anglo-German Trade Rivalry, 1887–1913: A Counterfactual Outcome and Its Implications." *Social Science History,* 3 (1979): 187–201.

Had World War I been avoided, Germany might have outstripped both the US and Britain in exports by 1926, with revived protectionism the likely result.

NICHOLLS, Peter, ed. *The Science Fiction Encyclopedia.* Garden City: Dolphin, 1979.

Includes articles on alternative worlds (Brian Stableford), history in science fiction (Tom Shippey), parallel worlds (Stableford), time paradoxes (Malcolm J. Edwards), and time travel (John Brosnan).

NICOLSON, Harold. "If Byron Had Become King of Greece: 'The Gamba Papers.'" In SQUIRE, ed., *If*, all eds.

From heroic young poet to doddering old figurehead.

NIVEN, Larry. "All the Myriad Ways." *Gal.,* October 1968.

In the world where the Cuban missile crisis led to war, crosstime commerce produces economic benefits but social costs.

———. "Bird in the Hand." *FSF,* October 1970.

Time-traveling souvenir hunters accidentally destroy Ford's first auto, with drastic results for their future.

———. "Death in a Cage." In his *The Flight of the Horse* (Ballantine, 1973).

Postholocaust time-traveler generates world we know by defusing Cuban missile crisis.

———. "The Theory and Practice of Time Travel." In his *All the Myriad Ways* (Ballantine, 1971).

Includes discussion of alternative history, a form that Niven dismisses as too easy to write, requiring only a good history text.

NOCK, Albert Jay. "If Only—." *Atlantic,* August 1937, 228–35.

Jocose speculation on the possible careers of Henry George and both Napoleons had their early lives not been blighted by poverty, and on what might have happened had Jeanne Poisson not henpecked Louis XV into the Seven Years War.

NOËL-NOËL [Lucien Noël]. *Voyageur des siècles* [Traveler through the centuries]. Cited with VAN HERCK by VAN HERP, p. 64, without details but in context suggesting alternative history of Napoleon.

NOLAN, William F. "The Worlds of Monty Wilson." *Amz.,* July 1971.

A glimpse into the world where Sirhan missed Bobby Kennedy, who went on to become President and get the US out of Vietnam.

NORDEN, Eric. *The Ultimate Solution.* Warner Paperback Library, 1973.

Police work in Nazi-occupied New York, because FDR's 1933 assassination delayed US entry into WWII.

NORTON, Andre. *The Crossroads of Time.* Ace, 1956; Boston: Gregg, 1978.

Crosstime adventure, much of it in the ruined anarchic New York produced by Nazi air raids from conquered England.

———. *Quest Crosstime.* Viking; Ace, 1965; as *Crosstime Agent,* London: Gollancz, 1975.

Sequel to the above, partly set on timeline where Richard III won at Bosworth in 1485 and the death of Cortez aborted Spanish conquest of Mexico.

———. *Wraiths of Time.* Atheneum, 1976; Fawcett Crest, n.d.

Intrigue and magic in modern African empire descended from ancient Egypt without interference from nonexistent Islam. Cf. Brian M. Fraser, "Interview with Andre Norton," *Fantastic Science Fiction,* October 1980, 6–7.

NOURSE, Alan E. "Symptomaticus Medicus." *Universe Science Fiction,* September 1954.

A seventeenth-century pact with Satan puts Western medicine on a basis of magic, but scientific development remains otherwise unchanged.

O'BRIEN, Patrick. See FOGEL, *Railways.*

ORGILL, Michael. "Many Rubicons." In LEY, ed., *Beyond Time.*

Possible outcomes of MacArthur's options at the Yalu, 1950.

O'ROURKE, P.J., and Tod Carroll. "If World War II Had Been Fought Like the War in Vietnam." *National Lampoon,* October 1980, 54–57.

Cartoon history.

————. "The Seventies That Never Happened." *Ibid.,* February 1980, 97–101.

How the decade might have looked with the counterculture in control.

ORR, James. See BAYARD, Thomas.

OVERGARD, William. *The Divide.* Jove, 1980.

In 1976, thirty years after America's defeat and partition by Axis powers armed with jets and nonnuclear V-4s, resistance blossoms.

PADGETT, Lewis. See KUTTNER, Henry.

PARKER, Geoffrey. "If the Armada Had Landed." *History,* 61 (1976): 358–68.

Scholarly discussion of plans and possibilities.

PARKER, Richard. *A Time to Choose: A Story of Suspense.* Harper & Row, 1973.

Juvenile fantasy puts modern teenagers into alternative roles in an England that has gone ecological; setting may be future rather than allohistorical.

PARKER, William N., and Judith L.V. Klein. "Productivity Growth in Grain Production in the United States, 1840–1860 and 1900–1910." Conference on Research in Income and Wealth, *Output, Employment, and Productivity in the United States After 1800* (National Bureau of Economic Research, 1966), pp. 523–82.

US agricultural progress with a closed frontier or without technical improvements.

PARKINSON, C. Northcote. *The Law and the Profits.* Boston: Houghton Mifflin, 1960.

Includes speculative reconstruction (pp. 155–57) of how government aid might have hamstrung Sir Isaac Newton.

PARNICKI, Teodor. *Czas siania i czas zbierania* [A time to sow and a time to reap]. Joan of Arc does not burn but does go to America. Second in the cycle *Nowa Basri* [The new fable], 1962–70; this and other uchronias by Parnicki are listed following JAMROZIAK.

————. *I u możnych dziwny* [Strange even among the mighty]. 1965.

Introduction discusses and defines author's idea of allohistory.

————. *Muza dalekich podróży* [The muse of distant journeys]. 1970.

Success of 1793 uprising establishes Fourth Polish Kingdom.

————. *Sam wydę bezbronny* [I shall leave defenseless]. 1977.
Had Julian the Apostate survived his Persian campaign of A.D. 363 to reign twenty years longer.

————. *Srebrne orly* [The silver eagles]. Jerusalem, 1943.
Rise of Polish state in tenth-century Europe divided between Germanic and Greco-Roman civilizations.

PARRIOTT, James, "created by." *Voyagers!*
NBC-TV series, 1982–83, with handsome hunk Phineas Bogg (Jon-Erik Hexum) and cute sidekick Jeffrey Jones (Meeno Peluce) seeing to it that key historical events come off as scheduled. Though some episodes threatened change but never showed it, overtly allohistorical ones apparently by Parriott himself include "Voyagers!" (October 3; World War I without the Wright Brothers); "Cleo and the Babe" (November 14; Babe Ruth's early retirement aborts Yankee Stadium); "The Day the Rebs Took Lincoln" (November 21; rescuing kidnapped President from Confederate prison to give Gettysburg Address); "Old Hickory and the Pirate" (November 28; without Jean Lafitte, the British take New Orleans in 1815); "Pursuit" (March 6; Russian capture of Von Braun in 1945 ruins US space program); "Buffalo Bill and Annie Play the Palace" (British intervene actively against Bolshevik Revolution); and episodes in which Harriet Tubman is kept off the Underground Railroad (October 10) and Teddy Roosevelt is gunned down before entering politics by Billy the Kid (October 24). The Wright Brothers episode was novelized by Joe Claro as *Voyagers!* (Scholastic Book Services, 1982). See also SHERMAN, Jill.

PASSELL, Peter. See LEE, Susan Previant.

PEARTON, Maurice. "If I Had Been . . . Adolphe Thiers in 1870: How I Would Have Prevented the Franco-Prussian War." In SNOWMAN, ed., *If I Had Been.*

PEETERS. See SCHUITEN.

PELCHAT, Jean. See YARBRO, Chelsea Quinn, *Ariosto.*

PELMAN, Joseph. See BAYARD, Thomas.

PERCY, H.R. "Letter from America." In LEY, ed., *Beyond Time.*
Plight of Anglophone Americans in the Republic of New France, thanks to French victory in the French and Indian War.

PEREZ-LOPEZ, Jorge. See BAYARD, Thomas.

PETRIE, Charles. "If: A Jacobite Fantasy." *Weekly Westminster*, 30 January 1926; rpt. in his *The Jacobite Movement: The Last Phase, 1716 - 1897* (London: Eyre & Spottiswoode, 1950) and SQUIRE, ed., *If*, 1972 eds. only.
Looking back on Bonnie Prince Charlie's restoration of the Stuarts in 1745.

PHILLIPS, Henry Irving. "Everything Under Control: Suppose the New Deal Had Hit Plymouth, Mass., in 1620, and the Puritans Had Got All Tangled Up in the Alphabet." *Collier's*, 12 January 1935, 21.
Earliest example discovered so far of allohistory's use to satirize bureaucracy.

PHILLIPS, W.A.P. "Chance in History: Nelson's Pursuit of Bonaparte, May–June 1798." *History Today,* 15 (1965): 176–82.
Napoleon might well have been captured or killed, and without him there would have been no Consulate or Empire.

PHILMUS, Robert M. See BORGES, Jorge Luis.

PIGNOTTI, Lorenzo. *Storia della Toscana.* Pisa: Didot, 1813–14; Florence: Marchini, 1821, &c.; trans. John Browning as *The History of Tuscany* (London: Black, Young, & Young, 1823, &c.).
Had Lorenzo de' Medici (1448–92) lived longer, he might have saved Italy from foreign invasion and Europe from Protestantism. Cf. D'ISRAELI.

PINKERTON, Jan. See HALE, Edward Everett.

PIPER, H. Beam. "Crossroads of Destiny." *Fantastic Universe,* July 1959.
In an America where George Washington's death at Germantown in 1777 made Benedict Arnold the first President, apparent misfit discussing alternative timelines in a club car turns out to hail from such an alternative.

———. "He Walked Around the Horses." *ASF,* April 1948.
Diplomat Benjamin Bathurst, who went missing in 1809, turns up on a Napoleonless timeline where Arnold's death at Quebec in 1776 let the British win at Saratoga, quashing the American and precluding the French Revolution. Bathurst's mishap was explained as a side-effect of Paratime Police activity (see below) via a mention in Piper's "Police Operation," *ASF,* July 1948.

———. *Lord Kalvan of Otherwhen.* Ace, 1965; Garland, 1975; as *Gunpowder God,* London: Sphere, 1978. Fix-up of "Gunpowder God," *ASF,* November 1964, and "Down Styphon," *ASF,* November 1965, with previously unpub. conclusion; earlier draft as romantic space opera, "When in the Course—," first pub. in his posthumous *Federation,* ed. John F. Carr (Ace, 1981).
Accidentally dumped by Paratimers in a North America colonized by protohistoric Aryans, Cpl. Calvin Morrison plays white-rajah role to hilt. Cf. authorized sequel by GREEN (Roland); also GILBERT, Mike, *Down Styphon! A Musket and Pike War Game Based on Lord Kalvan of Otherwhen* (Fantasy Games Unlimited, 1977). Other Paracop stories, all first published in *ASF,* are essentially exotic adventures in settings far removed from known history: "Police Operation" (July 1948), "Last Enemy" (August 1950), "Temple Trouble" (April 1951) and "Time Crime" (serial, February–March 1955); these four were collected with "He Walked Around the Horses" (above) as *Paratime* (Ace, 1981).

PIRIE-GORDON, C.H.C. See ROLFE, Frederick William.

POHL, Frederik. "The Deadly Mission of Phineas Snodgrass." *Gal.,* June 1962.
Short-short sendup of DeCAMP, *Lest Darkness Fall:* time-traveler brings Augustan Rome modern medicine but also a population explosion.

———. "Target One." *Gal.,* April 1955.
Victims of blasted future devise machine to assassinate Einstein, but the altered world has its own problems.

POLLARD, Sidney. "The New Economic History Re-Assessed: Railroads and Slavery." *Interdisciplinary Science Review,* 6 (September 1981): 229–38.
Includes discussion of counterfactuals; cf. FOGEL.

PONTEN, Josef. *Architektur, die nicht gebaut wurde* [Architecture that was not built]. Stuttgart: Deutsche Verlags-Anstalt, 2 vols., 1925.
"Period piece and collector's item" cited in SKY and STONE, p. 7.

POYER, David C. *The Shiloh Project.* Avon, 1981.
In modern world fathered by Pickett's successful charge at Gettysburg, Confederate planners try to hold their own in the Almost War by hijacking a Union secret weapon.

POYER, Joe. *Tunnel War.* Atheneum, 1979.
Work on a Channel tunnel in 1911 faces attempted German sabotage.

———. *Vengeance 10.* Atheneum, 1980.
If Wernher Von Braun and his cohorts had wangled enough Nazi loot and slave labor to make Germany first on the moon. (Borderline secret history; moonshot exerts no influence on events until discovered in 2009.)

PRATT, Fletcher. "The Blue Star." In his *Witches Three* (edited anonymously, Twayne, 1952); book-length version Ballantine, 1969.
Magic rather than science rules "a world like this one [i.e., ours] in which gunpowder has never been invented."

QUILLIET, B. *La véritable histoire de France* [The true history of France]. Presses de la Renaissance, 1983.
Listed without details by LECCIA.

RABKIN, Eric S. *The Fantastic in Literature.* Princeton: Princeton University Press, 1976; pb. rpt. 1977.
Includes rationale for classifying allohistory as sf (pp. 121–22) and discusses BORGES, "Garden of Forking Paths," and MOORCOCK, *Warlord of the Air.*

RAWLEY, James A. *Turning Points of the Civil War.* Lincoln: University of Nebraska Press, 1966.
Though none is much sustained, speculative alternatives abound, perhaps because turning points as such imply them.

REDLICH, Fritz. "'New' and Traditional Approaches to Economic History and Their Interdependence." *JEcH,* 25 (1965): 480–95.
Vigorous attack on concept of counterfactuals, later somewhat modified in his "Potentialities and Pitfalls in Economic History," *EEH,* 2nd ser., 6 (1968): 93–108; rpt. in ANDREANO, ed., *New Economic History.* Cf. GREEN (George).

RENOUVIER, Charles. *Uchronie.* Bureau de la Critique Philosophique, 1876; Alcan, 1901.
Marcus Aurelius joins forces with a dissident general to reform the Roman Army, free the slaves, and repress Christianity, thus averting the Dark Ages. An earlier version, according to VERSINS (pp. 736–37, 904), appeared anonymously in *Revue philosophique et religieuse,* 1857; the title, according to LECCIA, gave French the word *uchronie* (cited to *La grande encyclopédie,* 1892).

REYNOLDS, Mack, with Dean Ing. *The Other Time.* Simon & Schuster for Baen Enterprises, 1984.
Posthumously completed white-rajah yarn with Marxist touches; modern archaeologist in Aztec Mexico repulses Cortez by taking on role of Quetzalcoatl.

REYNOLDS, Pamela. *Earth Times Two.* Lothrop, Lee, & Shepherd, 1970.
Juvenile crosstime adventure to timeline where development of telepathy since eighteenth century has ended wars but stunted technology.

RHODES, James A., and Dean Jauchius. *The Trial of Mary Todd Lincoln.* Indianapolis: Bobbs-Merrill, 1959.
How Mrs. Lincoln's defense in her 1875 insanity trial might have been handled by better lawyers.

RICHARD-BESSIÈRE, F. *Croisière dans le temps* [Cruise in time]. Collection "Anticipation," Fleuve Noir, 1951.
Because time-travelers save Henri IV from assassination in 1610, France unifies Europe, world wars break out a century early, and in the twentieth century civilization collapses. "We were wrong to go against the laws of nature"—VERSINS, *Encyclopédie,* 412.

RICHARDS, John Thomas. "Minor Alteration." *FSF,* December 1965.
Mental time-traveler in Booth's identity lets Lincoln live, but the results are worse even than Reconstruction.

RICHARDSON, Hal. "The Time of Fear." Serial, Melbourne *Argus,* 28 July–6 September 1956.
Occupied Australia after Japan's victory in the Coral Sea. Donald H. Tuck, *The Encyclopedia of Science Fiction and Fantasy* (3 vols., Chicago: Advent, 1974–84), Vol. 2, s.v. "Richardson," erroneously identifies this serial with a true war story, *One-Man War* (Sydney: Robertson; Toronto: Ryerson, 1957). With Mr. Tuck's help, we obtained a microfilm of the serial from Graham Stone of Sydney.

RICKEY, John. "The Free Enterprise Patriot." *Research/Development Magazine,* 14–15 (September 1963–October 1964).
Arms procurement for the American Revolution founders on bureaucracy.

RIGAUT, Jacques. "Un brillant sujet" [A brilliant subject]. *Littérature,* 18 (March 1921); rpt. in his *Papiers posthumes* (Sans Pareil, 1934), pp. 109–13.
Time-traveling picaroon, among other alterations, poisons Jesus, rhinotomizes Cleopatra, and corrupts Homer.

ROBBAN, Randolph [pseud.]. *Si l'Allemagne avait vaincu* [If Germany had won]. "Translated [from alleged 'Sycambrian' original] by Henriette Duplex." Editions de la Tour du Guët, 1950.
After volleys of Nazi A-bombs win the war, a neutral diplomat imagines a world—not ours—in which they lost. First book-length uchronia to treat its timeline as real and ours as potential; cf. CHURCHILL.

ROBERTS, John Maddox. *King of the Wood.* D'day, 1983.
Adventure in fifteenth-century America with Christian Viking kingdom in

New England, pagan Vikings in Maryland, Moors in Florida, and Mongols conquering Mexico.

ROBERTS, Keith. *Pavane.* D'day, 1968; Ace, n.d.; Berkley Medallion, 1976. Collection of six stories set in modern England resulting from Queen Elizabeth's assassination, which produced civil war, victory for the Armada, and suppression of Protestantism. Five stories were originally published in *Impulse* (1966): "The Signaller" (March), "The Lady Anne" (April; retitled "The Lady Margaret" in *Pavane*), "Brother John" (May), "Lords and Ladies" (June), and "Corfe Gate" (July); the sixth, "The White Boat," in *New Worlds,* December 1966.

————. "Weihnacht[s]abend." In Michael Moorcock, ed., *New Worlds Quarterly No. 4* (Berkley Medallion, 1972). Freedom fighters in the Nazi-occupied Britain that surrendered after a 1940 putsch.

ROBINETT, Stephen. "Helbent 4." *Gal.,* October 1975. Product of a timeline where the US was founded in 1521, a sentient battleship dispatched against a menace in space returns to find our modern America.

ROBINSON, Kim Stanley. "The Lucky Strike." In Terry Carr, ed., *Universe 14* (D'day, 1984). When Col. Paul Tibbets crashes the *Enola Gay,* a different bomber crew has to make the first nuclear drop on Japan.

ROCHE, John P. "And That's the Way It Was, July 4, 1776." *TV Guide,* 28 June 1975. TV interview with defector Benedict Arnold in 1780 (despite title) helps keep America part of British Empire.

RODDENBERRY, Gene, and Gene L. Coon. "Bread and Circuses." *Star Trek* episode; in distant star system "Hodgkins' Law of Parallel Planetary Development" produces a 1960s Earth where a surviving Roman Empire still enjoys gladiatorial combat and slavery. Book version by James Blish in his *Star Trek 11* (Bantam, 1975).

[ROLFE, Frederick William (self-styled Baron Corvo), and C.H.C. Pirie-Gordon.] *Hubert's Arthur: Being Certain Curious Documents Found Among the Literary Remains of Mr. N.C.* London: Cassell, 1935; Arno, 1978. Prince Arthur of Brittany, nephew of Richard Lion-Heart, escapes wicked uncle John, turns crusader, and finally returns to claim his throne.

ROMANO, Deane. *Flight from Time One.* Walker; Toronto: Fitzhenry & Whiteside, 1972. In 1988 astral-body exploration along Ouspensky's "sixth dimension" reaches Times Two and Three: the former a Muslim-dominated world utilizing pyramid power, the latter a "Reichworld" stemming from peaceful British capitulation in 1940 and interfacing with our Time One via the Bermuda Triangle.

ROSCOE, William. *Illustrations, Historical and Critical, of the Life of Lorenzo de' Medici.* London: Cadell, 1822.

Speculates, according to D'ISRAELI, on how a surviving Lorenzo might have prevented the invasion of Italy by Charles VIII of France; cf. PIG-NOTTI. STABLEFORD, "A Note on Alternate History," incorrectly attributes this passage to Roscoe's earlier *Life of Lorenzo* (1796), which D'Israeli could hardly have described as "lately" published. In fact, its judgment on Lorenzo's premature death is perfunctory: new ed. (London: George Bell & Sons, 1891), p. 332.

ROSEBERY, Archibald Philip Primrose, fifth earl of. *Napoleon: The Last Phase.* New ed., London: Arthur L. Humphreys, 1909.

Introduction to this ed. speculates on Napoleon's style had he gone on to rule in peace.

ROSEN, Elliot A. "Baker on the Fifth Ballot? The Democratic Alternative, 1932." *Ohio History,* 75 (1966): 226–46, 273–77.

How Wilson's Secretary of War, Newton D. Baker (1871–1937), might have won the nomination and why he did not, with remarks on the probable foreign and domestic stances of a Baker presidency.

ROSINSKY, Natalie M. See RUSS, Joanna.

RUSS, Joanna. *The Female Man.* Bantam, 1975; Boston: Gregg, 1977.

Analogous characters in several alternative worlds, one allohistorical: Hitler's natural death in 1937 prevents World War II and lets the Depression continue to the present. Cf. Natalie M. ROSINSKY, "A Female Man? The 'Medusan' Humor of Joanna Russ," *Extrap.,* 23 (1982): 31–36.

RUSSETT, Bruce M. *No Clear and Present Danger: A Skeptical View of the U.S. Entry into World War II.* Harper Torchbooks, 1972.

Isolationist revisionism in the light of Vietnam: what if the US had provided only economic aid to Britain and Russia while maintaining technical neutrality toward Germany and reaching compromise with Japan?

RYAN, J.B. "The Mosaic." *ASF,* July 1940.

Time-traveling emir from modern Far Damascus (Manhattan) saves Charles Martel from assassination on the eve of Tours, aborting the Arab victory, his own world, and himself.

SABERHAGEN, Fred. *A Century of Progress.* Tom Doherty Associates, 1983.

Combating Hitler on a timeline where he visited the US in 1934.

———. *The Mask of the Sun.* Ace, 1979.

History turns on an Incan struggle to overthrow Spanish rule in sixteenth-century Peru.

SALLIS, James. "The Anxiety in the Eye of the Cricket." In Langdon Jones, ed., *The New S.F.* (London: Hutchinson, 1969).

Contribution to MOORCOCK's "Jerry Cornelius" cycle, set in warlike mid-twentieth century where Czechs have apparently outclassed both Germany and Russia.

———. "Jeremiad." *NW,* February 1969.

Same setting as above.

351

SARBAN [John W. Wall]. *The Sound of His Horn*. London: Davies, 1952; Ballantine, 1960.
Nightmare vision of the 102nd year of the First German Millennium, made possible by Hitler's decision to finish off Russia before invading England in 1945.

SAUNDERS, Jake. "Back to the Stone Age." In George W. Proctor and Steven Utley, eds., *Lone Star Universe* (Austin: Heidelberg, 1976).
Failure of American A-bomb development lets the war against Japan go on interminably.

SCHACHNER, Nat. "Ancestral Voices." *ASF,* December 1933.
When he accidentally kills a fifth-century Hun who was his ancestor, a time-traveler ceases to exist; so do thousands of contemporary Jews and Germans, including a thinly disguised Hitler (CARTER, *Creation of Tomorrow,* p. 123).

SCHOLZ, Carter. "The Ninth Symphony of Ludwig van Beethoven and Other Lost Songs." Terry Carr, ed., *Universe* 7 (D'day, 1977).
Time-traveler eavesdropping on Beethoven's mind drives him mad in 1823, leaving Ninth Symphony fragmentary.

SCHUITEN and PEETERS. *Les murailles de Samaris* [The walls of Samaris]. Casterman, 1984.
Listed as utopian allohistory in LECCIA bibliography.

_____. *La fièvre d'Urbicande* [The fever of Urbicande]. Casterman, 1984.
Ditto.

SCHUYLER, Robert Livingston. "Contingency in History." *Political Science Quarterly,* 74 (1959): 321–33.
On the value of historical speculation as seen, e.g., in BUCHAN and RENOUVIER, with 9): 321–33. a sample: what if Mary Tudor had borne Philip of Spain a Roman Catholic Habsburg heir to the throne of England?

SCHWARTZ, Edward. (Untitled.) *Social Policy,* 5 (July–August 1974): 10–11.
What federal grant-proposal requirements might have made out of the Declaration of Independence.

SCORTIA, Thomas N. "Artery of Fire." *Science Fiction Stories,* March 1960; book-length version, D'day, 1972; Popular Library, n.d.
On a timeline where the A-bombs on Japan were failures, energy-transmission problems create openings to alternative worlds.

SEABURY, Paul. "The Histronaut." *FSF,* April 1963.
US revisionary retaliation agent destroys Lenin's sealed train from Switzerland, but returns to a present-day Washington occupied by Germany.

SELL, William. "Other Tracks." *ASF,* October 1938.
Probably first sf argument that travelers into past must inevitably return to an altered present.

SHECKLEY, Robert. "The Deaths of Ben Baxter." *Gal.,* July 1957.
Altering past events on our timeline and two alternatives: one stemming

from Hamilton's 1804 dueling victory over Burr, the other from the peaceful conquest of America by a form of Buddhism.

SHERMAN, Jill. "Destiny's Choice." *Voyagers!,* NBC-TV, 13 March 1983.
Finding FDR in 1928 Hollywood as "Wild Frank . . . top director in town," the Voyager team returns to 1924 to redirect him into politics. Cf. PARRIOTT.

SHINER, Lewis. See STERLING, Bruce.

SHIPPEY, Tom. "Science Fiction and the Idea of History." *Foundation,* 4 (July 1973): 4–19.
Contrast between "whig" and "Malthusian" approaches in sf and between "possibility" and "desirability" of changing history, as exemplified in DeCAMP's *Lest Darkness Fall* and "Aristotle and the Gun," as well as such "failed" allohistories as Twain's *Connecticut Yankee,* Kipling's "Eye of Allah," and William Golding's "Envoy Extraordinary." See also NICHOLLS, *Encyclopedia.*

SHIRER, William L. "If Hitler Had Won World War II." *Look,* 19 December 1961.
Invading Russia in May instead of June brings victory by Christmas, conquest of England in 1942, Axis partition of the US by 1945. Cf. letters in response, *Look,* 30 January 1962.

SHUKMAN, Harold. "If I Had Been . . . Alexander Kerensky in 1917: How I Would Have Prevented the Bolshevik Revolution." In SNOWMAN, ed., *If I Had Been.*

SILVERBERG, Robert. *The Gate of Worlds.* Holt, Rinehart & Winston, 1967.
Boy's adventures on timeline where Black Death killed so many Europeans that Ottoman Turks conquered the rest and New World developed independently.

———. "Translation Error." *ASF,* March 1959.
Alien arranges early end to WWI, hoping to slow technical progress and keep humanity out of space.

———. "Trips." In Edward L. Ferman and Barry N. Malzberg, eds., *Final Stage: The Ultimate Science Fiction Anthology* (Charterhouse, 1974; Penguin, 1975); rev. and enl. in Silverberg, *The Feast of St. Dionysus* (Scribner's; Berkley, 1975).
Travel across a series of alternative timelines, in the most detailed of which FDR's retirement in 1940 left the US to neutrality and the Eastern Hemisphere to Axis conquest; includes afterword on alternative history.

———, ed. *Worlds of Maybe: Seven Stories of Science Fiction.* Thomas Nelson, 1970; Dell, 1974.
Includes introduction on alternative history, his own "Translation Error," short stories by ANDERSON, FARMER, and LEINSTER, and NIVEN, "All the Myriad Ways."

SIMAK, Clifford D. *Enchanted Pilgrimage.* Putnam's for Berkley, 1975.
Part unexplained allohistory, part something else: in our Upper Midwest, Inquisition survives, but so do goblins and Neanderthalers.

———. *The Fellowship of the Talisman.* Ballantine, 1978, 1979.
Sword-and-sorcery explicitly framed as alternative history: modern world remains medieval because aliens aborted the Crusades in the eleventh century and Portuguese expansion in the fifteenth.

———. *Special Deliverance.* Ballantine, 1982.
Timelines of six quest participants include one where American Revolution failed and both Britain and Spain still possess empires; others relate to our history only vaguely.

SIMENSEN, Jarle. "Counterfactual Arguments in Historical Analysis: From the Debate on the Partition of Africa and the Effect of Colonial Rule." *History in Africa,* 5 (1978): 169–86.
Implications of counterfactuals for studying history, as exemplified by possible courses for African development without colonialism. Cf. MANNING.

SIMULATIONS PUBLICATIONS. *Dixie: The Second War Between the States.* War game, *S&T,* 54 (January–February 1976).
A South independent since 1863 squares up to the North in three scenarios set in the 1930s.

———. *Operation Olympic: The Invasion of Japan, 1 November 1945.* War game, *S&T,* 45 (July–August 1974).
Accompanying article by Frank Davis simply describes situation and plans of both sides.

———. *Seelöwe: The German Invasion of Britain, 1940.* New York: SPI, 1974.
Game background is described in Frank Davis, "Seelöwe: The German Plan to Invade England, 1940," *S&T,* 40 (September–October 1973), including section on "The German Victory Scenario (Hypothetical)." For more on the game itself see *S&T,* 43 (March–April 1974): 3, and 45 (July–August 1974): 38–40.

———. "Space: 1889." *S&T,* 60 (1977): 43.
Description of proposed game based on US invention of ether-flyer in 1889 followed by spaceforce use in WWI.

———. "What If . . . ? Time Capsules." *S&T,* 75 (July–August 1979): 43.
Proposed games of hypothetical battles: Bonaparte lands in England, Austria resists the *Anschluss,* Japan invades Hawaii after Pearl Harbor, England allies with the Confederacy, and Soviets collide with Western allies over Germany in 1945.

SKY, Alison, and Michelle Stone. *Unbuilt America: Forgotten Architecture in the United States from Thomas Jefferson to the Space Age.* McGraw-Hill, 1976.
Rejected designs and unfeasible proposals, including a floating airport off Manhattan, an oriental-rococo Washington Monument, a Potala-like summer White House in the Rockies, and built-in apartments on the Bay Bridge.

SLADEK, John T. "1937 A.D.!" *NW*, July 1967.
Time-machine inventor leaves US of Columbia in 1878 to reach a 1937 alternative both to his world and ours.

SLONIMSKI, Antoni. *Torpeda czasu* [Time torpedo]. Warsaw, 1967.
Altering the past to obviate one war produces another (LEM, "The Time-Travel Story").

SMITH, L. Neil. *The Probability Broach*. Ballantine, 1980.
Where America might be today if only the Articles of Confederation had not been nefariously replaced with the Constitution. A sequel, *The Venus Belt* (Ballantine, 1981), carries the libertarian dream into space; in *The Gallatin Divergence* (Ballantine, 1985), scheming Hamiltonians attempt to undo history's verdict.

SMITH, Martin Cruz. *The Indians Won*. Belmont, 1970; rpt. with new intro., Leisure, 1981.
European arms shipments after the Little Big Horn help a Mormon-Amerind coalition dominate the Great Plains and Rockies.

SNOWMAN, Daniel, ed. *If I Had Been . . . Ten Historical Fantasies.* Totowa: Rowman & Littlefield, 1979.
An introductory discussion of the nature and philosophy of alternative history, followed by scholarly essays; see ALLEN, BLAKEMORE, CALVERT, EDWARDS (Owen), MORGAN, PEARTON, SHUKMAN, THOMPSON (Roger), WINDSOR, and WRIGHT.

SOBEL, Robert. *For Want of a Nail: If Burgoyne Had Won at Saratoga.* Macmillan, 1973.
Detailed textbooklike history of the Confederation of North America and the US of Mexico from the failed Revolution to the present.

SPINRAD, Norman. *The Iron Dream.* Avon, 1972; Boston: Gregg, 1977; Jove/HBJ, 1978; Pocket Books, 1982.
The prize-winning sword-and-sorcery novel Adolf Hitler might have written had he emigrated to the US in 1919 to work as an sf illustrator. Cf. Ursula K. LeGuin, "On Norman Spinrad's *The Iron Dream*," *SFS*, 1 (1973): 41–44.

SPRUILL, Steven G. *The Janus Equation.* In Joan D. Vinge and Spruill, eds., *Binary Star No. 4* (Dell, 1980).
Intrigue swirls around the invention of time travel in the twenty-second-century corporation-dominated world derived from JFK's reforms in his second term.

SQUIRE, J.C. "If It Had Been Discovered in 1930 That Bacon Really Did Write Shakespeare." *London Mercury*, 23 (January 1931): 244–56; rpt. in SQUIRE, ed., *If*, all eds., and as "Professor Gubbitt's Revolution" in his *Outside Eden* (London: Heinemann, 1933).
Mainly a satire on contemporary literary punditry.

———. "What Might Have Happened." In his *Outside Eden* (above), pp. 211–39.
If Britain had adopted Prohibition.

————, ed. *If It Had Happened Otherwise: Lapses into Imaginary History.* London: Longmans, Green, 1931; 2nd imp. 1932.

The classic essay collection, comprising BELLOC, CHESTERTON, CHURCHILL, FISHER, GUEDALLA, KNOX, LUDWIG, MAUROIS, NICOLSON, SQUIRE, and WALDMAN. US ed., titled *If; or, History Rewritten* (Viking, 1931; Port Washington: Kennikat, 1964), replaces KNOX with VAN LOON. New ed., *If It Had Happened Otherwise* (London: Sidgwick & Jackson; St. Martin's, 1972), supplements 1931 British ed. with PETRIE, TREVELYAN, and WHEELER-BENNETT.

STABLEFORD, Brian. "A Note on Alternate History." *Extrap.,* 21 (1980): 395–99.

Mainly discusses D'ISRAELI. See also NICHOLLS, *Encyclopedia.*

STACHEL, John. See JAMMER, Max.

STAFFORD, Terry. See GYGAX, E. Gary.

STALL, Michael. "Rice Brandy." In Kenneth Bulmer, ed., *New Writings in SF 25* (London: Sidgwick & Jackson, 1975; London: Corgi, 1976).

With help from our century Jayavarman VIII, King of the Khmers, turns back the fifteenth-century Thai invasion and presides over an industrializing world empire that has pleasant results for an alternative twentieth century.

STAPP, Robert. *A More Perfect Union.* Harper's Magazine Press, 1970; Berkley Medallion, 1971.

Nuclear confrontation between USA and CSA in the world where Lincoln let the wayward sisters depart in peace.

STAR TREK. See ELLISON, Harlan, and RODDENBERRY, Gene.

STEPHENSON, Andrew M. *The Wall of Years.* London: Futura, 1979; rev. ed., Dell, 1980.

Wordy time opera kicks off from future derived from Menshevik victory in 1917, but specific results are not developed.

STERLING, Bruce, and Lewis SHINER. "Mozart in Mirrorshades." *Omni,* September 1985.

Time-travelers exploiting eighteenth-century Austria tangle with Freemason Liberation Front.

STOKES, Houston H. See NEUBERGER, Hugh.

SUCHARITKUL, Somtow. *The Aquiliad.* Pocket Books for Timescape, 1983.

Burlesque adventure, thick with sf in-group jokes, in second-century Roman Empire that has colonized "Terranova" (North America). Fix-up of "Aquila," *IASFM,* 18 January 1982; "Aquila the God," *IASFM,* April 1982; "Aquila Meets Bigfoot," *Amz.,* January 1983; and "Aquila: The Final Conflict," *Amz.,* May 1983.

————. "Sunsteps." *Unearth,* 1977; rpt. in his *Fire from the Wine Dark Sea* (Norfolk and Virginia Beach: Donning Starblaze Edition, 1983).

Aztec world empire depopulates planet to provide divine Sun with human hearts.

SUVIN, Darko. See ANGENOT, Marc.

SWANWICK, Michael. *In the Drift.* Ace, 1985.

Struggling to cope in Pennsylvania, a century after the Three Mile Island meltdown of 1979 broke the US apart. Two chapters appeared elsewhere: a shorter "Mummer Kiss" in Terry Carr, ed., *Universe 11* (D'day, 1981), and "Marrow Death" in *IASFM,* mid-December 1984.

THIRY, Marcel. *Échec au temps* [Repulse in time]. Éditions de la Nouvelle France, 1945; new ed., Brussels: La Renaissance du Livre, 1962.

In world where Napoleon won at Waterloo, future observers inadvertently cause him to lose.

THOMAS, Donald. *Prince Charlie's Bluff.* Viking, 1974.

British failure to take Quebec in the French and Indian War sets the stage for Stuart restoration in the southern colonies.

THOMAS, Robert Paul. "The Automobile Industry and Its Tycoon." *EEH,* 2nd ser., 6 (1969): 139–57.

The vision of other automakers and the burgeoning used-car market would have put America on wheels, even if Henry Ford had never lived.

————. "A Quantitative Approach to the Study of the Effects of British Imperial Policy upon Colonial Welfare: Some Preliminary Findings." *JEcH,* 25 (1965): 615–38; rpt. in Don Karl Rowney and James Q. Graham, Jr., eds., *Quantitative History: Selected Readings in the Quantitative Analysis of Historical Data* (Homewood: Dorsey, 1969).

How the colonies might have prospered had independence in 1763 freed them from the burden of the Navigation Acts. Though Thomas was the first to tackle this problem counterfactually, it had been posed in quantitative terms a generation earlier by Lawrence A. Harper, "The Effect of the Navigation Acts on the Thirteen Colonies," in Richard B. Morris, ed., *The Era of the American Revolution* (Columbia University Press, 1939; Harper Torchbooks, 1965). For a review of further controversy over the Thomas thesis, with bibliography, see LEE and PASSELL, *New Economic View,* Chapter 2.

THOMPSON, Don. "Worlds Enough." In LEY, ed., *Beyond Time.*

Illegal crosstime-traveler touches several alternative worlds, finding differences sometimes very subtle.

THOMPSON, Robert E., teleplay by. *The Trial of Lee Harvey Oswald.* World-vision TV-movie directed by David Greene, starring John Pleshette, Ben Gazzara, Lorne Greene; premiered ABC-TV, 30 September 1977.

What really happened in Dallas, as revealed in the trial that would have been held had Oswald survived. Reviewed inter al. in the *New York Times,* same date, sec. 3, p. 26. Anon. novelization, same title, Ace, 1977 (Frank McSherry, Jr.).

THOMPSON, Roger. "If I Had Been . . . the Earl of Shelburne in 1762–5: How I Would Have Steered British Policy in Such a Way as to Have Prevented the American Colonies from Wanting to Rebel a Decade Later." In SNOW-MAN, ed., *If I Had Been.*

357

THORN, G.W.P. "The Salamanca Campaign, 1812: An Illustration of Modern Ideas." *Army Quarterly*, 29 (October 1934): 117–24.
Tactical study: had both Wellington and Marmont possessed radio, tanks, and air reconnaissance.
THRUPP, Major C.G.D. "If There Had Been A.F.V.'s [armored fighting vehicles] at Mons and Le Cateau in 1914." *Army Quarterly*, 32 (April 1936): 48–55.
How the British Expeditionary Force might have done with "the arms and equipment of 1935."
THURBER, James. "If Grant Had Been Drinking at Appomattox." *New Yorker*, 6 December 1930; rpt. in his *The Middle-Aged Man on the Flying Trapeze* (Harper, 1935), *The Thurber Carnival* (Harper & Row, 1945), and *Vintage Thurber* (London: Hamish Hamilton, 1963); also in *FSF*, February 1952.
Burlesque prompted by *Scribner's* publication of CHURCHILL, FISHER, and WALDMAN.
TOYNBEE, Arnold J. "The Forfeited Birthright of the Abortive Far Eastern Christian Civilization." In his *A Study of History*, Vol. 2 (2nd ed., London: Oxford University Press, 1935), pp. 446–52.
Had the Umayyad Caliphate lost its hold on Transcaspia, as it almost did in A.D. 731, Christianized Mongols might have destroyed Islam in the thirteenth century.
———. "The Forfeited Birthright of the Abortive Far Western Christian Civilization." *Ibid.*, pp. 427–33.
Celtic Christian options assuming different outcomes of the Synod of Whitby (A.D. 664) and Battle of Tours (A.D. 732). Cf. DE CAMP, "Science of Whithering" and "Wheels of If."
———. "The Forfeited Birthright of the Abortive Scandinavian Civilization." *Ibid.*, pp. 438–43.
With a little more push in the ninth and tenth centuries, Viking power might have straddled the globe.
———. "If Alexander the Great Had Lived On." In his *Some Problems of Greek History* (London: Oxford University Press, 1969), pp. 441–86; abr. rpt. in Eugene N. Borza, ed., *The Impact of Alexander the Great* (Hinsdale: Dryden, 1974), pp. 163–79.
He might have founded a genuine and permanent world empire.
———. "If Ochus and Philip Had Lived On." In *Some Problems of Greek History* (above), pp. 421–40.
Different leadership in Persia and Macedonia would have given Hellenic civilization another direction.
———. "The Lost Opportunities of the Scandinavians and the 'Osmanlis." In *A Study of History*, Vol. 2, pp. 444–45.
By seizing a series of just-missed chances in the late fifteenth and early sixteenth centuries, the Ottoman Empire could have achieved a greater destiny.

———. "The Role of Individuals in Human Affairs." In *Some Problems of Greek History*, pp. 418–20.

Introduction to above alternative biographies of Ochus and Philip, and of Alexander, discusses significance of individuals as against historical forces.

———. "Some Great 'Ifs' of History." *New York Times Magazine,* 5 March 1961, 32–33ff.

On the kinds of events that really change history, and what changes were possible.

TOYOTA Aritsune. *Mongoru no zankō* [Afterglow of the Mongols]. Kadokawa Shoten, 1967.

Time-changing in "a world controlled by the descendants of the Mongol Empire . . . the most complete of Toyota's many time-patrol stories"— LEWIS, David, "Japanese SF," p. 490.

———. *Taimu surippu daisensō* [The time slip war]. Kadokawa Shoten, 1967.

"Timequakes" send contemporary Japan back to the eve of Pearl Harbor (changing WWII), then to the arrival of Commodore Perry (LEWIS, *ibid.*).

TREVELYAN, G.M. "If Napoleon Had Won the Battle of Waterloo." *Westminster Gazette,* July 1907; rpt. in his *Clio: A Muse* (London: Longmans, Green, 1913; rev. ed. 1930), and in SQUIRE, ed., *If,* 1972 eds. only.

The repressive "Napoleon of Peace" and his effect on British and Continental reformism.

TREVOR-ROPER, H.R. *History and Imagination: A Valedictory Lecture, University of Oxford, 20 May 1980.* Oxford: Clarendon, 1980.

Why historians should pay attention not only to what happened, but also to what might have happened: specifically, "hypothetical accidents" by which Hitler might have won, and how historians would have explained them.

TRIMBLE, Bjo. See ELLISON, Harlan.

TUCHMAN, Barbara W. "If Mao Had Come to Washington: An Essay in Alternatives." *Foreign Affairs,* 51 (1972): 44–64; rpt. in her *Notes from China* (Collier, 1972), and *Practicing History* (Knopf, 1981).

If pro-Chiang Ambassador Hurley had not burked the request by Mao and Chou En-lai to meet with Roosevelt in 1945.

TUCHOLSKY, Kurt. "Was wäre, wenn . . . ?" [What if . . . ?]. Series of political comments, orig. pub. 1918–27, rpt. in his *Gesammelte Werke,* ed. Mary Gerold-Tucholsky and Fritz J. Raddatz (4 vols., Hamburg: Rowohlt, 1960–62), Vol. 1, pp. 283–84, 399–401, 560–61, 975–80; Vol. 2, pp. 212–14, 883–87; the second item also in his *What If—?,* trans. Harry Zohn and Karl F. Ross (Funk & Wagnalls, 1967), pp. 9–10.

Alternative history as vehicle for satire: e.g., what Germans would have learned about the true character of their Crown Prince had Germany won WWI.

TURTLEDOVE, Harry. See IVERSON, Eric G.

UTLEY, Steven, and Howard Waldrop. "Custer's Last Jump." In Terry Carr, ed., *Universe 6* (D'day, 1976; Popular Library, 1977).

The War of Secession and Indian Wars as waged with air power.

VAN ARNAM, Dave. See WHITE, Ted.

VAN DEN DAELE, Wolfgang. See BÖHME, Gernot.

VAN DOREN, Charles. "How the Second Punic War Could Have Put a Negro in the White House." *Monocle,* 6, 1 (Summer 1964): 74–79.

"Essential humanism of Carthage" could have brought racial equality and religious toleration.

VAN HERCK, Paul. *Opération Bonaparte.*

Cited as more adept than THIRY, but without details, in VAN HERP, *Panorama,* p. 64; context suggests alternative history of Napoleon. Cf. NOËL-NOËL.

————. *Caroline oh Caroline.* Champs-Elysées, 1976.

In the world where Napoleon won at Waterloo, the rengade Adolf Hitler leads an Amerind-Negro army against Europe (BRIE).

VAN HERP, Jacques. *Panorama de la science fiction* [Panorama of science fiction]. Verviers, Belgium: André Gérard, 1973.

Chapter 2, "Dans les corridors de l'espace-temps," includes references to alternative worlds.

VAN LOON, Hendrik Willem. "If the Dutch Had Kept New Amsterdam." In SQUIRE, ed., *If,* 1931 US ed. only.

The town remains a tolerant, profiteering enclave into the nineteenth century, and its laws persist into the twentieth with interesting consequences for Prohibition.

VAN RJNDT, Philippe. *The Trial of Adolf Hitler.* Summit Books, 1978.

Hitler survives in obscurity until 1970, when he seeks vindication before an international tribunal.

VERSINS, Pierre. *Encyclopédie de l'utopie, des voyages extraordinaires et de la science fiction* [Encyclopedia of utopia, extraordinary voyages, and science fiction]. Lausanne: L'Âge d'Homme, 1972; enl. rpt., 1984.

See esp. s.v. "Napoleon," "Temps," "Uchronie," and names of individual authors. The 1984 ed. includes a new intro. and a useful index, according to s and Pascal J. Thomas, *Fantasy Review,* 80 (June 1985): 36.

VILLARD, Oswald Garrison. "Issue and Men." *The Nation,* 22 October 1938, 411.

Why "the world would be a better place today [i.e., after Munich] if the Germans had won the Battle of the Marne."

VIOT, Henry-Gérard. See DEVAUX, Pierre.

VOYAGERS! See PARRIOTT, James D., and SHERMAN, Jill.

WALDMAN, Milton. "If Booth Had Missed Lincoln." In SQUIRE, ed., *If,* all eds.; also in *Scribner's,* 88 (November 1930): 473–84.

Unsympathetic book review of revisionist historian's attempt to clear name of a President whose ill-conceived postwar policies cost him whatever credit was due his wartime success.

WALDROP, Howard. "Ike at the Mike." *Omni,* June 1982.

Among other changes in celebrity roles, Eisenhower decides to play jazz clarinet instead of attending West Point. See also UTLEY, Steven.

_____ *Them Bones.* Ace, 1984.

Time-traveler out to undo WWIII lands near a twentieth-century Mississippi River where Arabs and Vikings trade from paddlesteamers.

WALL, John W. See SARBAN.

WARRICK, Patricia. See DICK, Philip K.

WEBB, Lucas. *The Attempted Assassination of John F. Kennedy: A Political Fantasy.* San Bernardino: Reginald/Borgo, 1976.

Interviewed on the eve of swearing in as James VII, 42nd Lord President of the US, James Lister reminisces on (among other anomalies) his boyhood reaction to Kennedy's brush with death in Dallas.

WEINBAUM, Stanley G. "The Worlds of If." *Wonder Stories,* August 1935.

Early sf restatement of *Dear Brutus* theme: "subjunctivisor" lets feckless narrator see what would have happened to him "if only." Same issue as DANIELS.

WEISSMAN, Barry Alan. "Past Touch-the-Sky Mountain." *If,* May 1968.

Merchant from Chinese section of an America discovered by Marco Polo gets into trouble on a timeline nearer ours.

WELLS, H.G. *A Modern Utopia.* London: Chapman & Hall, 1905; in his *Works,* Atlantic Edition, Vol. 9 (Scribner's, 1925), pp. 1–331.

On otherwise-identical twentieth-century Earth "out beyond Sirius," history has somehow skipped the Dark Ages. Wells continued this utopian theme in *Men Like Gods* (London: Cassell, 1923) and "The Dream" (serialized, *Nash's* and *Pall Mall Gazette,* October 1923–May 1924; book version, London: Cape, 1924)—the former taking a few caricatured contemporaries to a historically unrelated and geographically different earth in "the F dimension," the latter looking back from our own future; see his preface to rpts. of both, *Works,* Vol. 27 (1927), pp. 1–328, 329–654.

WENTZ, Richard E. "Reflections on a Rebellion Averted." *Christian Century,* 23–30 June 1976, 596–99.

Complacent nineteenth-century retrospect on America's peaceful development as a sort of confederal British dominion; same series as DELORIA and HILL.

WEST, Wallace. *River of Time.* Avalon (Thomas Bouregy & Co.), 1963; fix-up of unnamed stories, copyright 1950 and 1954.

Modern teenagers hope to avert WWIII by saving Julius Caesar and preventing Roman decline.

WESTHEIMER, David. *Lighter Than a Feather.* Boston: Little, Brown, 1971; as *Downfall,* Bantam, 1972.

Worm's-eye view of US landing on Kyushu, October 1945, after failure of atomic bomb.

WHEELER, John A. See EVERETT, Hugh.
WHEELER-BENNETT, John. "Introduction" to SQUIRE, ed., *If,* 1972 ed.
Comments on alternative history.
WHITE, Maj. O.W. "Past Events and Future Possibilities." *Journal of the Royal United Service Institution,* 67 (1922): 311–25.
How Russians and Japanese might have maneuvered in south Manchuria, May–June 1904, given 1922-level airpower, armor, and motor support.
WHITE, Ted. *The Jewels of Elsewhen.* Belmont, 1967; rev. ed. listed as planned, Norfolk and Virginia Beach: Donning.
Crosstime adventure with some action in world where Holy Roman Empire achieved European hegemony and dominates both hemispheres.
———, and Dave Van Arnam. *Sideslip.* Pyramid, 1968.
Intrigue among communists and Nazis in contemporary New York, after alien intervention obviated WWII.
WILLIAMS, Emlyn. *Headlong.* London: Heinemann, 1980; Viking, 1981; London: Magnum, 1982.
British throne seeks an heir after entire Royal Family is wiped out in a 1935 airship disaster.
WILLIAMSON, Jeffrey G. *Late Nineteenth-Century American Development: A General Equilibrium History.* Cambridge: Cambridge University Press, 1974.
Analyzes, individually or in combination, such counterfactuals as a closed frontier, static technology, nonrailway transport, and an end to European immigration. See also KELLEY, Allen C.
WILLIS, George A.A. See ARMSTRONG, Anthony.
WINDSOR, Philip. "If I Had Been . . . Alexander Dubček in 1968: How I Would Have Saved the 'Prague Spring' and Prevented the Warsaw Pact Invasion." In SNOWMAN, ed., *If I Had Been.*
WOLFE, Gene. "How I Lost the Second World War and Helped Turn Back the German Invasion." *ASF,* May 1973.
Trying to extend its economic suzerainty, Nazi Germany invades the British market with cheap VWs, while Lt. Col. Dwight D. Eisenhower war-games WWII before retiring to a Buick dealership in Kansas.
WRIGHT, Esmond. "If I Had Been . . . Benjamin Franklin in the Early 1770s: How I Would Have Prevented American Discontent from Becoming Revolution." In SNOWMAN, ed., *If I Had Been.*
WYNDHAM, John. "Random Quest." In his *Consider Her Ways* (London: Michael Joseph, 1961; Penguin, 1965) and *The Infinite Moment* (Ballantine, 1961).
Romance on a timeline where obscure events in the late 1920s strengthened the League of Nations and averted WWII. Basis for the British film *Quest for Love,* Peter Rogers Productions, 1971, produced by Peter Eton, directed by Ralph Thomas, screenplay by Bert Batt; see Walt Lee, comp., *Reference Guide to Fantastic Films: Science Fiction, Fantasy, & Horror* (Los Angeles: Chelsea-Lee, 1972–74), Vol. 3, p. 388.

YARBRO, Chelsea Quinn. *Ariosto: Ariosto Furioso, a Romance for an Alternative Renaissance.* Pocket Books, 1980.
Political machinations in sixteenth-century Italy federated under Medici leadership alternate with fantasy adventure in Italian-colonized New World. Cf. review by Jean Pelchat, "Pour une 'Renaissance alternative'" [Toward an "alternative Renaissance"], *Imagine,* 14 (Autumn 1982): 50–54.
_____. *On Saint Hubert's Thing.* New Castle: Cheap Street, 1982.
Intrigues of church and court in a feudal Europe where Christendom is divided North vs. South instead of East vs. West.

YEATES, Maj. E.P. "German Strategy in 1914 and in the Future." *Army Quarterly,* 33 (October 1936): 73–78.
Had Germany reversed its field, attacking Russia all-out while standing on the defensive against France.

YULSMAN, Jerry. *Elleander Morning.* St. Martin's/Marek, 1984.
In a world that knows neither Hitler nor WWII, a Time-Life *History of the Second World War* from our own timeline sparks political crisis in a surviving Weimar Republic.

ZEBROWSKI, George. "The Cliometricon." In LEY, ed., *Beyond Time.*
Titular machine (unrelated to cliometrics) lets historian study alternative outcomes of D-Day.

ZELAZNY, Roger. "The Game of Blood and Dust." *Gal.,* April 1975.
Aliens play life and death with history of Earth.
_____. *Roadmarks.* Ballantine, 1979.
A man drives the endless highway of time with a load of guns for the Greeks at Marathon, hoping to restore the Greek victory he remembers.

ZIEGLER, Thomas. "Stimmen der Nacht" [Voices of the night]. In Michael Görden, ed., *Phantastische Literatur 83* (Bergisch-Gladbach: Bastei-Lübbe, 1983).
In this first in a proposed four-part series of alternative modern Germanies, the Morgenthau Plan was put into effect after World War II; in the next, according to a blurb, the July 1944 attempt on Hitler succeeded. Book publication is promised.

ZUCK, D. See AUGEAS.